W9-DFV-772

"Bizarre, funny, and . . . downright creepy."
—*Booklist*

"A darkly comic, genuinely unnerving, incredibly well-executed horror novel."
—*B&N Sci-Fi and Fantasy Blog*

"If Hunter S. Thompson had written a *Blair Witch* tie-in, it might have looked a little something like this."
—*Tor.com*

"Wow. Seriously hard to put down."
—M. R. Carey, author of *The Girl with All the Gifts*

"Funny, creepy, and totally nuts."
—Paul Tremblay, author of *A Head Full of Ghosts*

THE
LAST
DAYS OF
JACK
SPARKS

JASON ARNOPP

orbit

www.orbitbooks.net

Orbit
Hachette Book Group
1290 Avenue of the Americas
New York, NY 10104
orbitbooks.net

Originally published in 2016 by Orbit in Great Britain
First U.S. Ebook Edition: March 2016
First U.S. Edition: September 2016
First U.S. Trade Paperback Edition: April 2017

Orbit is an imprint of Hachette Book Group.
The Orbit name and logo are trademarks of Little, Brown Book Group Limited.

The publisher is not responsible for websites (or their content)
that are not owned by the publisher.

The Hachette Speakers Bureau provides a wide range of authors for speaking events. To find out more, go to www.hachettespeakersbureau.com
or call (866) 376-6591.

Library of Congress Control Number: 2016942732

ISBNs: 978-0-316-36226-9 (hardcover), 978-0-316-43303-7 (paperback),
978-0-316-36225-2 (ebook)

Printed in the United States of America

LSC-C

10 9 8 7 6 5 4 3 2 1

For my mum and dad,
who never told me to get a proper job

"IF YOU THINK YOU KNOW WHAT THE HELL IS GOING ON, YOU'RE PROBABLY FULL OF SHIT."

Robert Anton Wilson

FOREWORD BY ALISTAIR SPARKS

At the centre of the house in which my late brother Jacob and I grew up, there was a black hole.

That's what we called it. In reality, it was a small room born of inexplicable architectural design. A roughly square space, right in the middle of a suburban Suffolk bungalow. No lights, windows or ventilation. No bigger than two department store changing rooms pushed together. Three doors led in and out.

Our mother made a virtue of this pointless junction box, as was her way, and hammered a coat rack to one of the walls in there. So it became the cloakroom.

Jacob, who would rise to fame and infamy as Jack Sparks, shared my instinctive fear of the word "cloak." Cloaks covered people, rendering them sinister, and so our dread of that room deepened. Calling it "the black hole" had actually made it less intimidating. Something science could explain.

The cloakroom was a place we took special measures to avoid. We would take the long route around every time—anything rather than having to enter that stale pocket of black.

As you hurried through, your pulse would gallop. You'd gasp or even cry out as you mistook a prickle on the nape of your neck for the cold breath of the dead and gone.

The incident happened one Saturday in the summer of 1983, when Jacob was aged five, four years my junior. As with all siblings, there was some rivalry between us, but brotherly harmony was the norm. We would climb trees, ride bikes, play football. Then we would lean against each other as we limped home, after accidents that tended to involve trees, bikes or football.

This incident was born of pure childish innocence, but feels unexpectedly relevant here, in a book to which I never dreamt I would contribute. I really feel it sheds light on my brother's nature and, I'm sorry to say, his severe downward spiral.

Most of the windows were open that day. Outside, hot air rippled. Our mother was in the garden, stretched out on a reclining lounger that occasionally broke and made her swear so loudly that our neighbours complained. She had one of her suspense novels, a pack of Silk Cut and her usual lack of suncream.

Jacob was absorbed with a toy car, whooshing it across the dining room floor, his face flushed. Seizing my chance for a bit of mutual fun, I stalked around the house and jammed all but one of the cloakroom's doors shut, dragging furniture to create blockades. The architect had at least thought to make these doors open outwards.

I peered out through the kitchen window and saw Mum dozing, the book splayed on her belly. Then I told Jacob we were going to play a game.

He, I explained, would be a ghost-hunter. And I would be

a ghost, chasing him. The rules of the game were simple. I would pursue him around the house. He had to try and pass through the black hole three times without being grabbed and turned into a ghost himself.

Jacob looked uncertain. "If I'm a ghost-hunter, why am I running?"

"'Cause you've met *me*," I told him. "I'm a ghost that's too big and evil to deal with."

He thought this over, then to my relief accepted it. The trap was set.

Jacob ran whooping ahead of me as I waved my arms about and made spooky noises, restricting my speed so as not to catch him. Making a beeline for the exact cloakroom door I'd planned, he raced across the length of the dining room and bolted into the black.

Sprinting to catch up, almost slipping over, I slammed the door shut on him. Then I gripped the handle tightly with both hands, the muscles in my arms taut with anticipation.

There was a muffled thump as Jacob tried to exit through one of the other doors, only to find it impossible. His voice was indistinct, as if piped down a bad phone line.

"Hey! It won't . . ."

His voice trailed away as he tried another door. Another thump, and this time just a bewildered cry.

The blood thundered in my head as I squeezed that door handle, ready for the assault, which began in seconds. When Jacob wrenched it, only to encounter the perceptibly imperfect force of human resistance, his voice became charged with fear.

"Ali, stop it! Ali!"

There was no chance of our mother hearing, and yet Jacob's pitch rose along with his volume. Sometimes he would abandon his vain attempts to open the door, only to suddenly try again in the hope of surprising me. Or I would hear the *whumphs* as he slammed himself against one of the other doors, yelling for Mum. Still I did not relent. Since he didn't sound terrified and was not crying, I felt confident he too would see the funny side when I released him.

Then those calls from inside the cloakroom stopped dead.

Biceps burning, I twisted around and leant heavily back against the door. While watching flies chase each other, I listened hard.

I listened for what felt like a long time.

Nothing.

The sense of fun began to fade.

"Don't worry," I called through the thick wood. "I'll let you out now, okay?" I laughed, lightly.

There was no reply.

Despite standing in a room flooded with sunlight, I began to feel uneasy.

A sly, arcane image snuck unbidden into my mind.

I pictured Jacob transformed, inside that room.

In my head, he now stood wearing a cloak, with hollow darkness where his face should be.

I became convinced that this spectral monk who was once my brother now stood silently waiting for me to see him. When I opened the door, I decided, he would lurch out of the room. He would tear off my limbs, one by one, laughing as he did so.

"Jakey?" I called out.

Still nothing.

"*Jacob?*"

My heart, which had thumped so excitedly only moments

beforehand, now felt like it was banging on a door, wanting out.

I felt sick with worry about what had happened to my brother. About what he had become in that unknowable space.

Seconds later, I saw it all coming out from under the door.

The purpose of my anecdote is certainly not to lend further ammunition to my online trolls, who nonsensically hold me responsible for the direction Jacob's life took. I merely seek to offer a glimpse of his formative years, as a child who reacted in an unusually extreme manner to an otherwise harmless prank. On that front, at least, my conscience is clear. I also felt it prudent to present my side of the story, given that my brother also includes it in this book. He will pick up the story later, but sadly tells an exaggerated version, employing far less honesty than I.

Despite the suffocating media coverage that followed my brother's untimely death at the age of thirty-six, the casual reader may be unaware of his achievements.

As a child, I had wanted to work in entertainment, but became a scientist. Conversely, Jacob had often spoken of ambitions within science, but of course became a writer and media personality. His first step along that road was a work experience placement at the *New Musical Express* in 1996. I still smile when I think of the phone call I received from this cocky eighteen-year-old upstart, telling me, "I'm in!" The *NME* had commissioned him to write his first published record review. Jack knew his music, even if it wasn't to my taste. Come our teens, it would be the Sex Pistols, Motörhead and The Sisters of Mercy blaring out of his den, while mine played host to a bit of Pet Shop Boys.

He quickly changed his name, thinking Jack Sparks cooler. I was snowed under with my degree in biochemistry, but was pleased that my brother was showing signs of fulfilling my own earlier dream.

From work experience onwards, Jack left Mum and myself in Suffolk to move to London's Camden Town, burrowing tenaciously into the business. During his twenties, he excelled himself, hopping back and forth across the Atlantic. While unable to catch many issues of the *NME* at the time—although I often asked Jack for copies—I gathered that his direct interviewing technique and unflinching opinions generated debate among readers. This polarising effect would continue when he sought horizons beyond the musical ghetto.

His first non-fiction book, *Jack Sparks on a Pogo Stick* (Erubis Books, 2010), seemed ostensibly light-hearted, as he travelled from Land's End to John O'Groats on the titular device. But since he was unable to use motorways during his journey, it was also a fascinating study of the bygone curiosities to be found on British roads less travelled.

Jack Sparks on Gangs (Erubis, 2012) saw him dive headlong into choppier waters, perhaps as a result of the first book's mixed reviews. I had my concerns about my brother mixing with violent gangs and documenting his discoveries, but of course there was no use in pressing such points with Jack.

Gangs won the Sara Thornwood Prize. It was undeniably insightful, and broadened my own views on gang culture, in both Britain and America. Around this time, Jack established himself as a prominent atheist and began to make guest appearances on UK TV panel shows like *Never Mind the Buzzcocks*, *Would I Lie To You?* and *Shooting Stars*.

His third book was his most divisive to date. The title

alone, *Jack Sparks on Drugs* (Erubis, 2014), ensured plenty of free publicity, but the concept was for my brother to try every drug under the sun and document his experiences. I was very much against him doing it, and our relationship fell on stony ground as a result of this and other matters at the time. It didn't help that drugs had made Jack more difficult and headstrong than ever. Our parting of ways—even after he entered rehab that summer—is something I shall always regret.

I am only too aware that Jack's final book, which he originally intended to be called *Jack Sparks on the Supernatural*, has been controversial from the moment its release was announced.

I have now experienced every conceivable online attack on me, including direct threats on my life and those of my family. One troll even turned up on our doorstep one night armed with a meat cleaver. She is now behind bars.

While there has been considerable support for this book, many have called for it to be banned. To some, it must feel like a cold, cynical and rather distasteful cash-in on my part, especially as Jack had no dependants. I've stated this on social media several times, but such words are easily lost amid the deafening hubbub—a portion of my fee will be divided between prominent motor neurone disease charities around the world. I have absolutely no desire to profit from my brother's death, which I am still coming to terms with. Working on this book has been deeply cathartic. Jack's editor of five years, Eleanor Rosen, has been nothing but accommodating throughout, while standing up to me where necessary.

We are fortunate indeed that my brother always wrote his books during the process of researching them. While others might squirrel away a horde of recorded interviews, thoughts and scribbled notes, electing to deal with them all together at the end, Jack wanted to get it *down*. He hated interview transcription and so dealt with that workload in chunks as he went.

While co-editing this book, Eleanor and I have corrected only small, inconsequential typos and errors, while vitally retaining the format and feel of Jack's writing, especially in the book's second half, when it becomes very different. Dividing the book into two sections was our decision. To her eternal credit, Eleanor supported my push to retain Jack's written notes directed at her, which are peppered throughout his text.

I extend my heartfelt gratitude and condolences to the families of the deceased, who mostly gave permission for their loved ones' true identities to be used. Other names have been changed. Believe me, the decision to publish *Jack Sparks on the Supernatural* in its entirely uncensored form was in no way taken lightly, and I know how very difficult it is for the bereaved to read accounts of such horrendous events. Yet I also hope this book may yield some form of closure and put an end to unhelpful internet speculation—not least concerning the nature of my brother's death.

I would like to thank my beautiful wife Chloe and our children Sophie and Xanna for their incredible support.

How I wish Jack had never attended that exorcism.

How I wish he had never laid eyes on that YouTube video.

Rest in peace, my brother, and please know that I forgive you.

Alistair Sparks: "Jack's former agent Murray Chambers has supplied me with this email exchange, which began the day after my brother attended the exorcism in Italy."

Date: 1 November 2014
From: Jack Sparks
Subject: RE: RE: My new book!
To: Murray Chambers (The Chambers Agency)

Murray. Why the fuck would Erubis need to see 30,000 words of this book "before going ahead"? We're still under contract with them—and eight weeks after it came out, *On Drugs* might as well be NAILED to the Top 10s!

Did they not actually read my proposal paragraph? An exorcist, a possessed girl, a scary YouTube video . . . a fuck-ing mystery. A mission!

Does *Bill Bryson* have to write 30,000 words before he can sell *his* latest book that he's written all about himself? Of course he doesn't, and neither should I. Sort it out.

J

Date: 1 November 2014
From: Murray Chambers (The Chambers Agency)
Subject: RE: RE: RE: My new book!
To: Jack Sparks

Jack, let me refresh your memory on a few points.

(1)   While writing *On Drugs*, you became a drug addict.
(2)   The book had to be hauled back from the brink of disaster with a ghost writer.
(3)   You phoned Erubis' MD at home at 3 a.m., while coked off your face, and repeatedly called him "a huge cunt."

That last point in particular means there are bridges to be rebuilt. *Jack Sparks on the Supernatural* might well be the fourth of the four books we signed for, but Erubis (a) didn't expect a book about ghosts; and (b) need to know you're back on the straight and narrow. They're jittery. I'm working on it, but sadly we can't rely on Eleanor sticking up for you after the way you've treated her. So you need to show willing here, mate. Write the 30K.

Mx

PS Bryson's books aren't strictly speaking all about himself. Yours pretty much are. (Not a criticism, just FYI.)

Date: 1 November 2014
From: Jack Sparks
Subject: RE: RE: RE: RE: My new book!
To: Murray Chambers (The Chambers Agency)

Fuck you, Murray.

Fuck. You.

This is insane! So I had a blip. I'm still JACK SPARKS, Murray. If anything, rehab raised my profile even more and you know it.

I won't write 30,000 sample words for Erubis. I won't even write 30. Apart from anything else, I can't do any more travelling without advance cash. Get them on the phone and straighten them out.

Date: 2 November 2014
From: Murray Chambers (The Chambers Agency)
Subject: RE: RE: RE: RE: RE: My new book!
To: Jack Sparks

Okay . . . I've managed to talk them into releasing the next part of the advance. I've promised them you're fine. I've personally put my neck on the block here and I hope you appreciate that.

Just make it a great and, above all, *smoothly delivered* book. Also: when can I get my £500 back? It's been six months.

Mx

Date: 2 November 2014
From: Jack Sparks
Subject: RE: RE: RE: RE: RE: RE: My new book!
To: Murray Chambers (The Chambers Agency)

Ha! Knew they'd see sense. Murray, this is gonna be one hell of a book.

Let's STORM THE HILL!

JACK SPARKS ON
THE SUPERNATURAL

Part
One

CHAPTER ONE

Before we vanish into Satan's gaping mouth, Bex wants to get something straight.

Sitting beside me in a very small car, she says, "So your new book's going to be about the supernatural. Which you don't believe in. At all."

"It's already riling people," I tell her. "Did you see the bust-up yesterday?"

She scrunches her face. "Why can't you accept that social media isn't a part of my life?"

"Because I don't believe you."

"Last time I looked, in about 2009, social media was one big room full of people not listening to each other, shouting, 'My life's great!' I doubt this has changed."

"So why are you still *on* there?"[1]

Bex makes her frustrated, dismissive noise: the sound of a

---

1 Jack very rarely named specific social media sites in his books. According to his agent, Murray Chambers, this policy was his "revenge" against sites who refused to pay him for name-checking them. —*Alistair*

brief, chaotic catfight. "I have *profiles*, Jack, so old friends can catch up, but I don't read anything. Social media makes me think less of people. I'd rather not know all the self-obsessed shit in their heads."

"How selfish of you."

"Won't this book be kind of *short*? Just a great big atheist travelling round the world saying 'Bullshit' a lot?"

I frown at her underestimation of the concept. "Obviously I'm going to keep it rational. But I'll also keep a completely open mind. Social media's full of people who think ghosts are real, so I'll give them a chance to guide me in the right direction. I've got this ongoing list of hypotheses for paranormal phenomena, which I'm calling SPOOKS. That's short for—"

"I think I can do without knowing."

"And when the book's done, I can at least tell all the mad believers, 'Look, you had your chance to convince me and you blew it.'"

"How very magnanimous of you."

My hopeless love for Bex intensifies when she employs long words and sarcasm together. Long-time readers will recall her as the late-twenties fitness instructor I've known and shared a flat with too long for anything to happen between us. They'll also know I've found it challenging to listen to her banging men in an adjacent bedroom. This may explain why my books tend to involve travel. (By the way, she doesn't bang loads of men. She's not like that. She's been seeing a guy called Lawrence for six months, even if he is a smarmy, chinless loser. And he is.)

I can openly discuss this love of mine because Bex doesn't actually read my books. "Jack, I *live* with you," she once said while we half watched *EastEnders* and fully ate Chinese food on our big fat yellow sofa. "I don't actually need to read these books. Why would I want to relive you overdosing on coke in our toilet?"

Apart from making the mistake of not reading my books, Bex is the most sensible person I know. In truth, I always seek her approval on my book ideas. Which makes me want to win her around on this one.

A burst of power makes our very small car rattle and hum. We roll forwards with a creak.

"So," she says. "How was Greece?"

"*Italy*," I say, forced to raise my voice as people start squealing behind us. "It caused the big bust-up. I did a bad thing and got yelled at by an exorcist."

"On Halloween. Perfect."

"Then I saw this weird YouTube video."

Bex processes all this information. As our car gains speed, she settles on a question: "What video?"

"I'll tell you after this."

And into the mouth we go.

So I'm deep in rural Italy, over twenty-four hours ago. The first stop on my epic journey into the supernatural world, which will see me visit a combat magician in Hong Kong, a ??? in ??? and a ??? in ???, not to mention a ??? in ??? *(Eleanor: I'll fill these in later, once I know who I'm actually meeting and where I'm going. If I forget, you can do the honours.)*

I am about to enter a church.

The ancient building sits isolated and forlorn on a hill that becomes a sheer cliff face on one side. Hurl a stone from up here and it vanishes halfway down, caught by the twisted, arthritic fingers of bare trees. This church, this stone sentinel, keeps watch over dense woodland and clustered hills that mark the horizon.

Inside, it is functional, relatively bare bones. There are still a few of the usual looming statues calculated to intimidate and belittle, plus a few glistening symbols of opulence and power. Yet the most elaborate feature is the stained-glass window in the back wall, shot through with winter sun.

I always think the beauty of stained-glass windows is wasted on a church.

Everything is so quiet and serene, you'd scarcely credit the fact that in ninety minutes we'll need an ambulance.

Arriving half an hour late at 1:30 p.m., I barrel in looking windswept and interesting. Eighty-year-old Father Primo Di Stefano greets me with a stiff smile and matching handshake. Sporting a large black frock, he is flanked by two frosty aides, who are both short and stocky, in black shirts and grey trousers. The only real visual difference between these two is that one has facial hair, so let's call them Beard and Beardless. I also have a handy Italian translator at my disposal, named Tony. So he'll be Translator Tony, obviously. Despite his werewolf-hairy hands, a monobrow crowning shifty brown eyes, and teeth you could ride a Kawasaki between, Tony's the only halfway personable guy here. We bond over a cigarette outside, when he admires my brass Zippo. A dull, tarnished old thing these days, but it does the job.

Di Stefano does not run this church. To all intents and purposes, the priest is a guest here, like me. One of the Pope's most trusted foot soldiers, he is based in Rome and has travelled many miles to commandeer the place on a mission of mercy. Specifically, he has come to drive the Devil out of a thirteen-year-old girl with the use of words, gestures and a great deal of biblical *Sturm und Drang*. This man claims to have carried out over two hundred exorcisms. As a purely incidental side effect, this has provided him with material for a lucrative string of books detailing his crusades. The titles include *At War with the Devil, My Lifelong Battle with the Antichrist* and of course *Satan & I*. That last title is my favourite, like a wacky sitcom. "In this week's episode of *Satan & I*, Father Di Stefano attempts to throw a house party for friends, only for his mischievous flatmate Satan to slay them all while denouncing God!"

Bitterly cold winds sail up and down the aisle as Father Di Stefano, Translator Tony and I literally pull up a pew for a chat. We have time to kill before the subject of the priest's latest ritual arrives.

Exorcism can be traced back through millennia to the dawn of civilisation. Right from the word go, man was all too keen to ascribe sickness, whether physical or psychological, to evil spirits. And of course people from the ancient Babylonian priests onwards were all too keen to present themselves as exorcists. As saviours. The most famous was allegedly Jesus Christ, who couldn't get enough of it.

Di Stefano considers exorcism more vital than ever in the online age. "The internet," he tells me via Tony, "has made it much easier to share information, but not always good information. People experiment with Ouija boards and get themselves in trouble. And then they call us, asking for help."

This man has the lived-in face and manner of a mastiff dog. There is not the faintest flicker of humour in his dark eyes. He is barely tolerating me. His aides hover within earshot, which always irritates me during interviews. I ask for them to move further away, but the request is rudely ignored. I soon discover that Di Stefano's hearing is poor when he wants it to be—when I ask a challenging question, for instance. At other times, when I say something he wants to pounce on, his ears sharpen the hell up.

Di Stefano has granted a fair few interviews over the years—most notably when he's had a new book out—but as far as I can tell, no journalist has been allowed to watch him perform an exorcism. Today feels like a concession to the modern media, a canny PR exercise: if the Church is seen to be helping people, it stays relevant in the eyes of the world. And if there's one thing religion should be worried about these days, it's relevance. There's no question that converting Jack Sparks would be quite the coup.

I can't help but picture Di Stefano conducting an exorcism with an entirely straight face, then bursting into uncontrollable fits later on, the moment he shuts his front door behind him. Just *hooting* at the nonsense he gets away with on a daily basis. But there's undoubtedly a very serious side to all this. After all, Di Stefano deals with often quite severely distressed people of all ages (except babies, seemingly. Babies are so consistently insane that it's hard to tell if they're possessed, unless they start floating about). The lion's share of these people arguably suffer from some form of mental illness, or have experienced abuse.

"That is true," allows Di Stefano, to my surprise. "Very often we realise, you know, that a person does have a mental illness or there is some other history there. In those cases, a demon is not to blame after all. When this happens, of course, the person will be sent for the correct treatment. The need for an exorcism is actually very rare."

"How can you tell when an exorcism is required?" I ask.

Di Stefano looks down his nose at me, regarding me like the rank amateur I am. His stare is unyielding, those eyes dead as a cod's. "You get to know the sign of a true demonic posses-sion," he says. "You can feel it. The feeling is completely different."

So far, so vague. "How *exactly* does it feel when it's a real demon?" I persist.

"The air feels . . . thick," he says, with distaste. "And black, like oil. It is . . ." He rubs his forefinger and thumb together as he searches for the word. Then he exchanges rapid-fire Italian with Tony, who provides the word on the tip of Di Stefano's tongue: "Oppressive."

"Also," the priest continues, "you can see it in the subject's eyes. The eyes, you know, are the windows to the soul. You can see who, or what, is living inside."

"How do you know it isn't all in *your* head?" I ask.

That mastiff face crumples. No mean feat when your face is already a sponsored crumple-thon. He doesn't enjoy this line of questioning, no doubt because it could just as easily be applied to religion as a whole. Still, he gamely indulges me. "As far as I know, I am perfectly sane. So are my exor-cist colleagues. The things we have seen . . . the way people have behaved with demons within them . . . this is no make-believe." He gestures around the church. "You will see today, I think."

"Have you seen *The Exorcist*?" I ask.

"The movie? A long time ago. I don't remember too much about—"

"Are exorcisms anything like that?"

"Sometimes they are," he says wearily. As if anticipating my next question, he adds, "But you know, exorcism existed for a long time before that movie. The movie took its cue from exorcisms before it. But I must say, I have seen things far more terrible in real life."

I lean forward, quote-hungry. "Could you give me an example?"

Di Stefano recalls a middle-aged single mother in Florence who would cry blood. Her skin turned sickly green and broke out in open sores. When he tried to expel her demons in an attic room, she whispered the Lord's Prayer backwards as she gouged out one of her own eyeballs with a rusty antique spoon. Di Stefano (then a mere assistant, in the late seventies) and his exorcism instructor restrained her, encased the eye in ice and rushed her to hospital. Despite a five-hour emergency operation, the eyeball could not be reinstated. Still, Di Stefano claims that they eventually exorcised the demon from this woman, who was reunited with her children.

When pushed for his very worst memory, he reluctantly dredges up the 2009 case of a ten-year-old boy in Milan. As he speaks of this boy, his full-bodied voice becomes little more than a murmur.

"The first time I tried to exorcise him, he laughed in my face, as he broke each of his fingers one by one."

"Just the fingers on one hand?" I ask, genuinely curious. "He couldn't do both, right?"

Di Stefano glares at me, as if I'm trying to be funny.

He bows his head. "I could not save him. The demons had such a firm hold. I think they wanted to make a point, to scare me away from my life's mission. During exorcism number three, the boy smashed his face against the corner of a glass table, blood everywhere. In number five, he threatened my nieces' lives. He said he would cut all the skin from their faces as I watched, then force me to eat it."

Translator Tony pops a square of nicotine gum into his mouth.

Di Stefano takes a moment to compose himself. "Two nights later, I had one of my visions."

Ah yes, Di Stefano's famous visions. His books are full of them. These visions physically root him to the spot and flood his mind with astonishing psychic sights. Interestingly, he rarely seems to tell anyone about them *before* their real-life counterparts occur. Why, it's almost as if he pretends to have had the vision in retrospect.

"In my mind, I saw the boy murder his sleeping stepfather with a hammer, then jump out of the window. And this actually happened, thirty minutes later. The boy, he jumped ten floors down to the busy road. Such a terrible, terrible . . . People said he screamed blasphemy as he fell."

Satisfied that I can't come back with a smart answer to such a grim story—or worried that I might ask for more information about that stepfather—he stands, ending our cosy chat. He needs, he says, to pray and mentally prepare.

As I leave him to kneel before the altar, I wonder how many exorcisms actually take place in churches. Aren't the possessed supposed to burn up when they walk through the door, or at least protest and writhe around? Have these people never seen *The Omen*?

I open my notepad and review the SPOOKS List I've created . . .

THE SPOOKS LIST (Sparks' Permanently Ongoing Overview of Kooky Shit) (Full disclosure: I had to ask social media's hive mind to help with the "K" word. Prior to that I only had "Kreepy," which simply wasn't good enough.)

People claim to have witnessed supernatural phenomena for the following reasons:

(1) They're trying to deceive others
(2) They've been deceived by others

Those, then, are the only two *viable* explanations as I see them, in top-down order from most to least likely. It won't surprise you to learn that I don't consider "Ghosts are real" to be a viable hypothesis. Neither can I entertain the notion that people can be deceived by their own minds to the extent that they "see" a ghost. Not without the use of LSD, anyway, and in such cases the drug is clearly the mother of total delusion. I should know this better than most, after the incident with the dive-bombing spider-geese.[2]

What I'll be looking to do, both here today and throughout this book, is to fit everything I see to one of the two explanations above. Should neither of them fit, I'll potentially add a third explanation to the list.

That's highly unlikely, I'm saying, but let's get stuck in.

Thirteen-year-old Maria Corvi arrives on foot, alongside her fifty-something mother Maddelena. The frigid Halloween air converts their breath to vapour. They live somewhere off in all those forbidding woods, which offer few helpful footpaths. During the last hour and a half of my drive out here, I saw neither towns nor villages—just the occasional run-down cottage or cabin set far back from recklessly winding dirt roads. If this little church ever served a bustling community, then such a thing has long since dissolved.

2 *Jack Sparks on Drugs* (Erubis Books, 2014), p.146. —*Alistair*

At first sight Maria doesn't strike me as demonic. Neither is she all cute-as-a-button smiley like Linda Blair's *Exorcist* character, Regan MacNeil, who was one year younger. Maria Corvi radiates the sullen nonchalance of your typical teenager who's doing her best to mask fear. Look closer and you see that, like her mother, Maria is quietly desperate. The pair are decked out in the same plain, practical blue smocks and boots they wear for their work as farm labourers. Maria is pretty and worryingly thin. Gaunt, too, and those dark-ringed eyes suggest sleepless nights. Her unwashed black hair hangs halfway down her back.

Apart from a splash of grey up top, Maddelena is so self-evidently Maria's mother that they could be nesting Russian dolls.

I watch Maria carefully as she crosses the threshold into the church. Her flesh does not burn and she does not shriek. She does, however, bring a hand up to her throat and swallow hard, as if resisting the urge to be sick. Catching my eye awkwardly, almost shyly, she looks away and continues with her mother towards Di Stefano as if nothing has happened.

The priest greets Maria and Maddelena by launching into a formal speech in Italian. It reminds me of company reps who read legal tedium over the phone, while you play Candy Crush and say "Yes" every thirty seconds. It very clearly reconfirms, no doubt partly for my information, that Maria and her mother have agreed to this rite. The Church, stresses Di Stefano, would only force such a thing on someone if they had harmed others or were deemed to be at risk of doing so.

"Please do not be afraid," he tells the women. "Today, Maria, you will be free of the negativity that has no business within you." I later learn that "negativity" is a euphemism the Church often employs. They claim it helps to avoid leading the subject through the power of suggestion. Which seems unusually sensible of them.

Maria nods, her expression neutral. I can't tell whether she believes in this stuff, or is going through the motions for her mother's sake. Did Maddelena find an Ozzy Osbourne album on Maria's iPod and hurriedly dial the Vatican's 1-800-DEVILCHILD hotline?

Di Stefano briefly explains why I'm present. Then he leads Maria to the strip of dusty floor that passes in front of the altar. Her mother signs legal papers handed to her by Beard (oh yes, legal papers—the Church likes being sued about as much as any other multinational corporation). Then he and Beardless usher her, along with me and Translator Tony, to our designated pew five rows back from the front.

Maddelena chews what's left of her fingernails while Tony translates her. "I know this has to be done. But . . . she is my baby, you know? I do not understand. Why has Satan chosen her?"

It doesn't seem the right time to tell her Satan doesn't exist. Or indeed to ask if, you know, Maria might just be your average teenager who seems a bit nuts—especially against the backdrop of a quiet rural expanse like this. Instead, I ask what led Maddelena to hire an exorcist.

"Maria started to sleepwalk," she says, never taking her eyes off her daughter as Di Stefano gives the girl a final briefing in hushed tones. "Or at least I thought she was sleepwalking. In the middle of the night I found her standing outside our home, at the edge of the clearing . . ."

Maddelena flicks her eyes around the church before continuing. "She was naked, in the freezing cold. I thought she was asleep, so I said to her, 'Maria, please wake up.' But she turned her head, with her eyes wide open. And she smiled. I'd never seen a crazy smile on her face like that. She said to me, 'I *am* awake.' And then . . ."

Maddelena looks set to cry, but steels herself. When she lowers her voice, Translator Tony follows suit. "*And then . . .* she slapped my face and said, '*You* wake up, you Christ-loving whore, before I rip out your fucking heart.'"

After that night, Maria's nocturnal wanderings escalated. Maddelena claims she tried locking both of the house's external doors and hiding the keys, but still her daughter managed to break out. One time, Maddelena and a search party of friends found Maria a mile away from home, in the dead of night. She was writhing around, naked again, covered in the blood of a deer that she'd slain with a butcher's knife taken from the kitchen.

"She was laughing when we found her," says Maddelena with a shudder. "After that, I felt so lost. I knew that only the Church could help with something like this. The old pastor who owns this church helped me make contact with Father Di Stefano in Rome. The good father sent an assistant to meet Maria, then it was decided that a blessing would be best."

Another euphemism, there. It's so much easier to agree to a blessing than an exorcism. When I ask if Maddelena ever considered medical help for her daughter, her face suggests that she trusts doctors and science about as much as I trust priests and religion.

"If this does not work, then *maybe* . . ." she says, as if that really would be the last resort.

★ ★ ★

I'm unprepared for the transformation of Maria Corvi. I just didn't expect this skinny kid to have it in her.

Sitting on a simple, creaky wooden chair in front of the altar, she appears withdrawn but compliant, her head bowed, hands clasped on her lap. The only small sign of any real emotion comes when she glances over at her mother. I would place good money on it being a look of resentment. A look that says, "Happy now? I'm doing it."

Maria's mother doesn't seem to interpret this look the same way. She smiles back encouragingly and wrings her bony hands in anticipation, as if her daughter is about to audition for *The X Factor*.

Father Di Stefano stands before Maria, an ancient leatherbound Bible spread across his palms. Beard and Beardless position themselves at either far side, hands behind their backs.

Di Stefano reads interminable passages from the book. His words echo darkly around the ceiling. Maria looks embarrassed, as if wondering what she's supposed to do. It's weirdly hypnotic. Thanks to a late night out in Rome, my eyes lose focus and I drift into a dreamlike state . . .

Maria's whole body goes electric-shock rigid. Her eyes bulge and her hands and feet shoot out in all directions. I can't see her toes from here, but her trembling fingers are spread wide. She holds this bizarre position for no more than a second before the chair beneath her gives way, breaking with a loud crack.

Maria falls to the ground, her back arching awkwardly over the pile of broken wood, her body limp. I shake my head, disappointed that the all-powerful Church has resorted to age-old slapstick ruses like sawing halfway through chair legs in order to jazz things up. Coming next: Maria and Di Stefano attempt to carry a piano up a tall flight of steps, with amusing consequences.

Beside me Maddelena gasps, a rosary gripped tight in one hand, the beads fit to burst. Beard and Beardless dash in and examine the lifeless girl, while carefully removing the pieces of chair from beneath her. They return to the sidelines: twin roadies who scurried on to fix a rogue microphone stand during a gig.

Di Stefano switches his attention from the Bible to the prone teenager. "I am addressing directly the spirit that dwells within Maria Corvi," he says. "Speak your name, before I have cause to do so myself."

On the word "myself," something dramatic happens. Something that, I'll admit, is harder to explain than the magical breaking chair.

As a kid, I owned what is generally referred to as a thumb puppet. A small wooden donkey standing on a cylindrical base, its tiny constituent parts joined by string. When you pushed your thumb up inside this base, it made the donkey collapse. On the withdrawal of your thumb, the donkey would spring back up into its former rigid state.

Maddelena cries out in shock as Maria Corvi springs up from the church floor like my donkey used to. Her heels remain on the ground, but the rest of her rises fast, as if hoisted by some invisible pulley system. Unlike my donkey, Maria remains loose. Her body appears boneless. Eyes shut, she drifts from side to side as if underwater. I stand and peer over the pews, spotting that she's now up on her tiptoes. It doesn't seem possible for a human being to achieve this stance, or at least to maintain it for so long. Her centre of gravity is not so much *off* as non-existent. The magician David Blaine would take notes.

Father Di Stefano, of course, is not fazed. He's seen all this stuff many times before. Truth be told, he invented it. Because as he repeats his exhortations for the evil within Maria to speak its name, the truth hits me. Remember Jim Carrey's character in *The Truman Show*—the guy who discovers that the world around him is artificial? All of this is one big set-up, for my benefit. It's a feeling journalists will know well on a smaller scale: the sense that you're no longer a non-influential observer of events, but instead the spark that brought them about.

If Maria Corvi isn't an actual actress, then she and her mother have surely agreed that she will become one, no doubt in exchange for a better life. *(Eleanor: please don't kick off about libel here. I really can't be dealing with another debate like the one about Katy Perry and the bag of . . . well, you know.)* The arrangement of the pews and the space before the altar resembles audience and stage, with stage managers Beard and Beardless lurking in the wings. After all, what has the Church always been about, if not an audience flocking to watch a performance? And of course here I am, hemmed in several rows back— all the better to stop me seeing this propaganda display from the wrong angles.

Maria's eyelids flick open, revealing that her eyes now swim with some cunningly applied yellow dye. Nice touch. She's still up on her tippy-toes, and I now suspect that her conveniently oversized smock harbours some kind of body harness. Her lips stretch back over her teeth to form a sickly grin. When she speaks, her voice is lilting and childlike, in direct contrast to her words. "You cock-sucking prick," she tells the priest, thereby fulfilling the minimum post-Friedkin quota of fellatio mentions during an exorcism. Translator Tony lowers his voice reverentially as he continues to whisper her words in English: "You fuck children and yet judge me?"

Maria's laugh is slithery. If a snake could laugh, it would sound like that.

This Maria, if that really is her name? She's good.

To a man like Father Primo Di Stefano, child abuse accusations, whether from entities alive or dead, are water off a duck's back. Delving into his robes, he produces a sturdy, old-school wooden cross with a Christ figurine on it.

When he presents this trump card to Maria, it's as if she's being made to look directly into the sun. She lashes out at the priest and the cross, her fingers cramped into claws. Di Stefano takes a step back, while Beard and Beardless hurry in to restrain Maria, each gripping an arm. She struggles against them with surprising force and sends Beard tumbling to the ground.

"Maria is ours," she says. Her voice is now deep and throaty, but punctuated by freakish high notes. "We are her blood. Her flesh, her bones, her guts. We have freed her soul. By hurting us with your trinkets, you only hurt her."

Di Stefano steps back into the fray, his cross to the fore, bellowing, "That is a sacrifice I'm prepared to make in order to secure her freedom."

I wonder how Maddelena feels about Di Stefano taking that decision into his own hands. To my consternation, she seems okay with it. Oh, hey, she's in on all of this anyway. Just playing along with the script.

And so it goes on. Yellow-eyed Maria verbally abuses Di Stefano, spits, shrieks and generally misbehaves. Di Stefano remains devout and steadfast. He brandishes his religious iconography as a pepper-spray threat and mentions Jesus Christ at least three times per minute. Translator Tony struggles to keep up with them.

Now. Here's the thing. It's a universal truth that laughter becomes more insanely delicious the more wrong it is.

Taboos are funny. They just are. When you're absolutely, definitely not supposed to laugh, that's when laughter is all the more potent and combustible. As scarily inevitable as a sneeze, or an itch you just *have* to scratch, no matter how demented you'll look.

You might be sitting among heartbroken folk at a funeral. You might be sitting behind a TV news desk, staring into a camera and telling the world about the latest genocide.

Or, as in my case, witnessing a faux exorcism.

Surely I can't be the only man on earth who considers *The Exorcist* a comedy. Even when I first saw it as a child, in the late eighties, the film provoked far more chuckles than shivers. Friedkin's po-faced seriousness really tickled my ribs. "The power of Christ compels you!" became something to yell at other kids in the playground with a big grin.

As the action escalates, so does my urge to laugh at it. This whole charade is so very deadpan that laughter is the only sane response. Part of me *needs* to laugh, in order to exorcise myself of these ridiculous characters. And while I'm genuinely overcome by mirth, there's no doubt that my laughter will also be a statement. Because people's enduring belief in conveniently invisible devils makes the work of science so much harder. It slaps a leash on progress and encourages backward thinking.

In 2012, while appearing on a TV show in the Dominican Republic, U.S. magician Wayne Houchin unexpectedly had his head set on fire by a man who reportedly believed him to be a voodoo practitioner. In 2013, a YouGov poll found that over fifty per cent of Americans believe in the Devil and exorcism. And earlier this year, in his documentary about "gay cures," British doctor and TV presenter Christian Jessen encountered American teenagers who genuinely thought homosexuality was caused by demonic infestations.

Belief in the concept of Satan possessing children has led to murders around the world. Sometimes these murders are deliberate: kids have been burned and buried alive. Such things are straight out of the Dark Ages. Other deaths have resulted from misguided attempts to get those imagined demons out, often by one of those maverick exorcists. In the Philippines as recently as 2011, an anorexic girl named Dorca Beltre starved to death during a botched five-day exorcism.

And so we must laugh at this medieval crap. It is our duty to do so.

My laugh explodes out of me in a great belly-pumping blast, amplified by its own inappropriate glory.

Bex is still shrieking as we bash our way out through Satan's mouth, which frames the entrance and exit.

A simple ghost train transforms her into a distressed damsel. Every single time, her frightened koala arms grasp me as nylon cobwebs brush our faces and gurning ghouls spring up left, right and centre.

The Hell Hotel sits in a tangled web of gaudy light bulbs, roller-coaster tracks and crazy crane-like rides at the far end of Brighton Pier. When we're both home and need a catch-up, this is our ritual: ghost train, then pints, then chips. I've checked into the Hell Hotel more times than I have into *actual* hotels. So has Bex, and yet it never seems to lose that primal power over her. I, on the other hand, simply appreciate the ancient gear-grinding mechanics that propel our car through darkness. This visit feels extra special, being our first since I got out of rehab a few weeks back.

We stroll back along the pier's charmingly uneven floorboards, heading for Victoria's Bar stationed halfway along it. To the west, the horizon is ablaze. Gulls soar overhead, seemingly carried against their will by freak winds—the kind that can jump down your throat and steal your breath. Bex takes her wild red corkscrew hair in both hands and reins it in with a scrunchie.

"I don't think I've ever asked you this," I say. "I know you're not exactly religious, but you *do* think there might be a God. So do you actually believe in ghosts?"

"If you accept the possibility of God, then you have to accept the possibility of ghosts. Because you just never know, do you?"

"Well, that's the thing. Thanks to science, we *do* know."

"How can we know what happens after death? It's death! The great unknown. But we can't imagine having no consciousness; feeling nothing forever."

"What do you feel while you're asleep, though?"

"I dream."

"Good for you." I'm about to explain the burden of proof and the truth about so-called near-death experiences on the operating table when a new urgent query consumes her: "Anyway, what happened in Italy?"

I tell her about the Laugh, on the way to the pub. Whenever Bex laughs, or even smiles, she holds one hand over her mouth because she wrongly thinks her teeth are too big. "You're a bad man. So where does the YouTube video come into it?"

"I'll get to that. Give me a chance!"

"Okay. So. You laughed during the exorcism . . ."

"Yes," I say, revving myself up into a clickbait headline. "And you'll *never believe what happened next.*"

Alistair Sparks: "There follows a series of text messages exchanged between Jack and myself during the week prior to his trip to Italy."

28 October 2014

> Hi, Jack. Long time, etc. Hope you're okay. Heard from Murray the Agent earlier—I'm pleased you're out and starting a new book. What's it about?

> Oh please, like you really care. Don't talk about me behind my back.

> Of course I care, Jack.

> Have you become a born-again Christian or something?

> Despite everything, there's no need for things to be unpleasant. What's the new book about?

> HA, "despite everything"—thanks for reminding me. It's about ghosts. Now fuck off.

> Really?! Why ghosts?

(Jack never replied.)

CHAPTER TWO

Father Primo Di Stefano straightens until he's the height of the silver cross on the altar behind him. His frock sweeps dramatically and his eyes are the size of eggs.

"*Signor!* Please, what are you doing? Show some *respect.*"

Di Stefano gives good rage. As an octogenarian, he has much to be furious about in life, ranging from the world's decaying moral core to having to push when he urinates. Throw in a Vatican-load of righteous zeal and you have a man capable of apoplexy.

Beard and Beardless grimace, fists clenched by their sides. Maddelena's gaze scorches the side of my face.

The church falls grimly silent.

Grinning broadly, I applaud the assembled players, hands above my head, each clap resounding in the rafters.

"Chill out," I tell them. "I'm just enjoying the show. Highly entertaining." Tony helpfully translates.

Maria's reaction is the most curious. Instead of raving about the crucified Nazarene, she looks straight at me. A glint of sun makes those yellow eyes burn as she cocks her head to one side, quizzical. And she *smiles* at me. Everyone else is scowling, but Maria smiles. Still playing the role, I suppose. Improvising. *Riffing.* What a trouper.

She turns to look back across the church at something. I follow her gaze over to that towering stained-glass window on the rear wall. Then her eyes are back on me and she's got a weird, knowing look on her face. For the life of me I can't work out what this odd little moment with the window is supposed to mean.

Evidently keen to re-establish the mood, Di Stefano intones what I later discover is an exorcism prayer. Maria ignores him. She's still looking right at me. Getting sick of her smile and B-movie eyes, I pull out my smartphone. The reception here is patchy, but I grab a scrap of signal.

Di Stefano's pronouncements and Tony's translations ("In the name of Jesus Christ, our God and Lord, strengthened by the intercession of the immaculate Virgin Mary, mother of God . . .") fade into the background as I check my updates. Social media is the usual heady potpourri of hearts and minds.

"How long were you in rehab for, dawg?" enquires *Jack Sparks on Drugs* fan Monky617 (two months is the answer, in case you're similarly curious—and the only drug I've done since leaving is alcohol, which was never my problem in the first place), while PaulTrema8 wants to know what my next book is going to be about (as if the exorcism isn't a pretty good clue). SpazzDick2, on the other hand, kindly offers, "I'll punch ur fucken head off u arogunt [*sic*] cock." I'm pretty sure I blocked him last week, but apparently not. Must have been his earlier incarnation, SpazzDick1.

". . . as wax melts before the fire, so the wicked perish at the presence of God . . ." drones Di Stefano, as Maria gnashes something feral back.

I might seem to shirk my journalistic duty by reading social media during an exorcism. But in the face of this amateur dramatics society play, social media provides a vital lifeline to the real world. Feeling a strong urge to connect, I fire a message into the ether:

"Probably bad to laugh during the exorcism of a thir-teen-year-old girl, right? Well, I just did. You should SEE this bullshit."

I consider attaching a photo of the exorcism in full swing, then ditch the idea. It might prompt Beard and Beardless to wrestle me to the floor while trying to confiscate my device. I could take them both on, no question, but just don't need the bother.

Di Stefano seems back on a roll, clutching a wooden rod with a perforated metal ball on the end. He emphasises certain bits of banter by using this device to fling droplets of some-thing at Maria.

"We *drive* you from us, whoever you may be . . ."

Maria shrieks every time this stuff hits her. Oh yes, he's bringing out the big guns now. Holy water! Another box ticked.

"Unclean spirits, all satanic *powers*, all infernal *invaders* . . ."

Maria shrieks again and bares her teeth. "Poor Maria," she growls. "In such pain, locked deep inside herself. She will die before we ever let her go."

"All wicked *legions*, *assemblies* and *sects* . . ."

Maria twists in agony as this last triple whammy of water gets her right in the face. Interestingly, her skin reddens, as if scalded. Wonder how they did that. I should pay more attention.

"Remember what a small boy once told you, about your nieces?" Maria says. "He meant what he said. Believe it."

Di Stefano shoots a swift, meaningful glance my way, weirdly vindicated.

It's a great moment. Very clever. I do love a bit of continuity.

Online, there are already over two hundred responses to my exorcism post. Most of these ask whether I'm really at an exorcism or where exactly it is taking place. Some say how scared they'd be to see an exorcism, while others laugh along with me. "Are they really still doing that stuff?" says Domina22 from Cape Town. "It's like science never happened."

Beard and Beardless hold Maria as firmly as they can, as the exorcism builds to a grand finale. Di Stefano dishes out his pious gems, louder and more forceful than ever. One thing's for sure: if Maria Corvi *isn't* giving the performance of her young life, she needs an MRI scanner right away. She froths at the mouth, her irises are nowhere to be seen and her neck appears to have stretched, which must be down to the angles again. Always working the angles, these guys.

Finally she convulses, breaks free of the aides and falls to her knees. Then she regurgitates something red and unexpectedly solid, which hits the ground with an even less expected clang.

Okay, they've upped their game. They've got me back. Yes, vomiting is yet another exorcism cliché, but I'm curious—why the clang? I crane my neck to see, but this brings no satisfaction, so I spring up, edge past Maddelena and head to the front. I am an audience member evading security and running to get a closer look during a Penn & Teller show.

Beardless gestures for me to stay back, offering a clear challenge. Ignoring him, I strain to see what Maria's thrown up.

There's blood, some kind of spongy matter . . . and pieces of metal that are hard to identify.

"You will leave this poor girl," commands Di Stefano, "this child of Christ!"

The teenager cackles, still on all fours. Strands of bloody drool connect her chin to the floor.

"You will return to the foul depths whence you came. The power of Jesus Christ compels you!"

The latter phrase may amuse me, but it rocks Maria. As if in response to this upping of the ante, she yells fiercely up at him: "Leave us be, Di Stefano! Or we will slaughter this bitch."

Her whole body spasms and her fingertips dig hard into the floorboards.

I wince as one of her fingernails bends back, strains, snaps.

Her head jerks back and a solid object explodes from her mouth in a torrent of red mist. This startling missile punches into Di Stefano's left upper thigh and stays there, the end quivering. When he cries out and grabs at it, his own blood spritzes his hand.

Mr. Beard steps in between Maria and Di Stefano, as if intending to block further projectiles. Beardless rushes to support Di Stefano, who nevertheless topples backwards and crashes to the floor, banging his head.

I've never seen anything with this kind of impact, even in the fiercely unpredictable world of gangs. It's all so convincingly chaotic that my *Truman Show* theory falters.

For now.

Since we're in the middle of nowhere, it takes half an hour for paramedics to arrive.

During the wait, Beard and Beardless tend to Di Stefano as

best they can. They lay him down along two pews pushed together to form an impromptu bed. He groans, rocks to and fro and mutters prayers in Italian. The aides rip and cut the robes around his wound to reveal a rusty six-inch nail jutting out of his pale, bony thigh. I examine it as closely as seems polite, but it certainly strikes me as real. No prosthetic special effects here.

Interesting. So Di Stefano will go to any lengths to convince an infidel like me that Satan is real—even if it means taking a nail to the leg. Either that, or he and the Corvis actually aren't in cahoots. If the latter is true, then Di Stefano was just doing his theatrical shtick with a disturbed teenager who swallows pieces of metal, and he has tumbled under the wheels of rough justice.

I inspect the vomit on the floor. Oh, the glamour. There's another nail there, like the one in Di Stefano's leg, plus a piece of jagged, indistinct metal. When I go to touch the nail, Beardless barks something that will turn out to mean "Leave it alone!" when I get the audio translated. Happily, Translator Tony is nowhere to be seen, so I feign ignorance while rolling the nail back and forth. It really is made of weighty metal.

"Do not touch that!" commands Beard. "This is now a police matter."

"No no no," says Di Stefano, through gritted teeth. "I will not press charges against a young girl who does not know what she is doing."

I suspect the old boy regrets having allowed a journalist to witness an exorcism. This one presumably hasn't gone as smoothly as he'd hoped. How fortunate, then, that I signed the wrong name on the papers which would have granted Di Stefano copy approval. In case you don't know, copy approval is when the interviewee gets to read the finished piece and object to certain bits and pieces, which are generally then pruned to suit them. This phenomenon happened to journalism a decade or two back, when some sackless editor caved in and agreed to give some big-shot celebrity that ridiculous power. It has been a blight on the profession ever since, along with other regular mandates such as PRs sitting in on interviews, and questions having to be approved in advance. And you wonder why I moved into books . . .

Now that the show's over, Maria has returned to her normal self. The whites of her eyes are white again and her neck appears the conventional length, although the redness on her face remains and that broken, bleeding fingernail looks painful. Sitting with her mother across the aisle, she looks frightened and bewildered, firing off questions in Italian. Maddelena fights back tears as she tries to answer those questions, while using a handkerchief to dab blood from around Maria's mouth.

Feeling the heat of Maddelena's long, hard stare, I try to explain how I was laughing at the situation, rather than at her daughter. Without Tony present to do his job, the distinction doesn't register. When I ask what her next move will be, she manages some English: "I don't know. *Maybe* doctor."

"That's good," I say. "It's good to try all options."

I want to add, "Especially as, you know, your daughter's just puked blood and metal," but surely that's self-evident.

"Signor," says Di Stefano from across the aisle. This sounds like a summoning, so I search for Tony. I find the work-shy bastard outside, standing on grass, gazing along the side of the church towards the cliff edge, with cigarette smoke billowing from his nostrils. I'm telling you this part for a reason: Tony actually *starts* at the sight of me, confused and shaken, instinctively touching the small cross hanging around his neck. It reminds me how very powerful things like exorcisms can be to believers. He pulls himself together and follows me back in, tossing his cigarette aside.

The Beard Brothers have staunched the priest's bleeding as best they can, but he's pallid. His aides whisper to him in Italian, presumably advising him to forget about the stupid journalist and conserve his strength. Yet the question on Di Stefano's mind is too pressing to wait.

"Why was the exorcism funny?"

Those dead eyes burrow right into me.

At this point, if I was a Louis Theroux or a Jon Ronson, I would nervously pop my spectacles back up onto the bridge of my nose and utter something evasive, most likely in the form of another question. (*Eleanor: I know you and Murray don't like me mentioning these guys in print, but I heard Ronson slagged me off on the radio last week. He didn't mention me by name, but blatantly cast aspersions in my direction. And in the Fitzroy Tavern, one of Theroux's flunkies couldn't resist telling me all about Louis' book sales and viewing figures and asking whether I'd landed myself a TV series yet. So as far as I'm concerned it's open fucking season.*) Instead, I tell Di Stefano I laughed because his exorcism struck me as a pantomime.

Di Stefano absorbs these body blows with dignity, for a man stretched awkwardly across a pew in a torn dress, with a filthy piece of metal sticking out of him.

"But I suppose that's the way I see all religion," I add. "I'm an—"

"Atheist," interrupts the priest. "Yes. I know about you. An atheist and a drug addict."

He groans and clutches his leg with one liver-spotted hand. I'm glad he's in pain. Because I'm not a drug addict, whatever they told me every day in rehab. Much like religion, drug addiction is for the weak. Right here, right now, on this bright, chilly afternoon, I feel in control. I feel good. Great, even. Haven't even thought about cocaine, my number one fix, in a long time.

Beardless intently reads the small print on the packaging of some painkillers. He and Beard debate whether they can give Di Stefano more before the ambulance gets here.

"At first," I tell Di Stefano, "I thought Maria was in on the deception." I glance at the nail and the wound. "But now, I don't think so."

"Well," says the priest, "then we have changed your mind in some way. But I assure you, there has been no deception here. The only deception is in your mind."

Sidestepping that odd, tit-for-tat playground comment, I say, "Seriously, mate, can't you see she's mentally ill?"

Di Stefano's selective deafness kicks in. "A word of warning," he says. His voice may be slighter now, having lost its boom, but nevertheless I wonder if he's about to threaten me. "You can laugh at the Church, no problem. We are laughed at every day. But when you laugh at . . ."

His eyes flit across the church.

"At the Devil?" I ask, raising my voice for Maria's benefit as much as anyone else's, hoping she and Maddelena will understand. "There's no such thing as the Devil!"

Di Stefano makes a kind of horse's whinny. I think it's supposed to mean I'm treading on thin ice with The Man Downstairs.

Across the church, Maddelena stands alone. She must have

been keenly eavesdropping on our conversation, because only now does she realise that Maria is no longer beside her. The woman's hair flails as she scans the church.

I frown my most irritating frown at Di Stefano. "Why would the Devil care? Isn't his greatest trick supposed to be convincing the world he doesn't exist?"

"Maria?" calls Maddelena. With one swipe of a curtain, she reveals an empty confession box.

Di Stefano opens his mouth so Beardless can insert pills, then gulps them down with water. He tells me, slowly and deliberately, as if instructing a child, "That was a *movie*."

The priest has underestimated me in assuming I was paraphrasing cinematic dialogue as opposed to the Charles Baudelaire quote, but I'm impressed that he's seen *The Usual Suspects*. It makes him seem more human when I imagine him lounging around in his underwear, throwing a DVD on the box. I resist the urge to ask which other cool nineties films he's seen, like *Reservoir Dogs*, or *Goodfellas* ("My exorcism is funny, huh? I amuse you, I make you laugh?")

Maddelena's voice is smaller and without echo, suggesting that she's outside. "Maria? Maria? *Dove sei, la mia bambina?*"

I nod over at the stained-glass window that Maria looked at so pointedly during the exorcism. Its coloured-glass panels collectively depict a glum Jesus Christ sitting on some rocks.

"What is the meaning of that?" I ask.

"No more, no more," says Beard, making the universal gesture for "No more" with his hands. "Move away."

Di Stefano glances irritably at the window.

"It is Christ during his forty days in the wilderness," he says, sagging with relief at the approaching wail of an ambulance siren.

★   ★   ★

You'd think the paramedics' arrival would end the madness here, but no. There will be one more burst, for my pleasure.

Mother and daughter have been reunited. Maria, it transpires, only wanted some fresh air. Besides attending to Di Stefano's obvious needs, the paramedics check the girl over and swab samples of that worryingly rust-infused blood from the church floor.

Basically, everyone's going to hospital except me and Translator Tony. I have to catch a flight back to London, which means Tony is no longer required. It's a shame the fun has to end: I might derive perverse pleasure from spending time in a crowded ambulance with a Catholic priest, a nail-spitting teen and two lunkheads. Great material for another episode of *Satan & I*.

While Di Stefano is being strapped on to a stretcher, I pull out my phone and walk around, fishing for reception.

My post about laughing during an exorcism has caused a furore. I honestly hadn't imagined that, in this day and age, chuckling in the Devil's face would be so controversial. Of course, plenty of people support me, but at least as many spiritually minded folk object to my "arrogance," "disrespect" and "rudeness." These are people with whom my good friend Richard Dawkins spars on a daily basis. The kind of people who believe the Earth is only six thousand years old. I feel like I'm getting a taste of Rich's online life. I've sampled it before while posting about atheism, but never to this extent.

"An exorcism can be a very dangerous thing, both for priest and exorcee!!! Shame on you!!!" writes GodsAmy12 from Tucson, Arizona. Loving the word "exorcee." Is that really a thing?

"Your [*sic*] gonna be laughing on the other side of you're [*sic*] face when you burn in hell!" suggests the incongruously named TickleTumTina from Ipswich, Suffolk. Sorry for reposting your post, Tina! Hope you didn't get *too* much grief from the rest of my 251,043 followers . . .

"You are SO self-obsessed," offers TheRossotron in Tampa, Florida. "Not just laughing during an exorcism, but telling everyone. Why do we need to know? Is it impressive?" I should point out that TheRossotron is following me. Presumably by choice.

I learned a while back that it's pointless to try and reason with individuals on the internet. Even if you do succeed in changing one person's mind, ten more will spring up asking the same questions and making the same stupid points. When you have as many followers as I do, the whole thing becomes untenable. You may as well try to scoop up the sea, one cup at a time. I soon realised that addressing everyone collectively was the best use of my time and energy. As was following no more than fifteen people.

It's famously unwise to feed the trolls, but on this occasion the stream of abuse riles me. As I watch Di Stefano gruffly berate the paramedics who are trying to make him more comfortable, I see a stupid old man with way too much power over the "little people." I see a man who, just like most people who promote the supernatural, is *trying to deceive others.*

I post a new missive: "Everyone, seriously. If the Devil, ghosts and ghouls existed, don't you think they'd be all over YouTube by now? Where's the EVIDENCE?" Then I return to the ambulance to try and prise some final words from exorcist and, ahem, exorcee.

It seems Father Primo Di Stefano, now in the back of the ambulance and impatient to be off, has nothing left to say.

When asked to sum up how the exorcism went, he bats off an imaginary fly with one hand.

"I did not expect it to be like this," is all a distressed Maddelena can manage, several times.

Maria winces as a paramedic carefully bandages her forefinger. "I can't remember anything that happened," she says, with more than a note of despair. "It is just like all the other things Mamma tells me I've done, at night. But this is the first time it's happened during the day."

A shadow crosses Maddelena's face—I think she just twigged that Di Stefano's rite has only made her daughter worse.

I'm concerned about Maria and can't help myself. Screw journalistic impartiality: I implore—no, *tell*—Maddelena to take proper medical advice at the hospital. Hopefully, this time, my words sink in. I wish them well and head for my Alfa Romeo rental, keys jangling in hand.

"Hey there," calls Maria, in English. "Hey, Jack Sparks."

Except her voice doesn't come from the ambulance. It comes from the opposite direction. It comes from Translator Tony, who is approaching his own car. As if on cue, he spins around to face me, a dazed puppet, his centre of gravity awry.

His mouth opens and continues to move as Maria's voice comes out of him.

"Enjoy your journey," he says. Or, rather, Maria says it. His mouth, but her voice. Tony looks as surprised as anyone else that a thirteen-year-old girl's words just sprang out of him. Then his jaw drops again and Maria's voice says: "I'll be back in a few hours, okay?" Whatever that's supposed to mean.

Back in the ambulance, Maria regains the power of speech and emits a childish giggle. She wears that same knowing smile she had during the exorcism, the one just after she looked at the window. The eyes are back jaundice-yellow.

Maddelena's face falls, as if this is the final straw. Father Di Stefano begins to pray out loud, on his stretcher.

The effect is disorientating and I don't know how to react. We're now all so accustomed to being able to replay moments over and over again that my first instinct is to reach for a non-existent rewind button.

I'd previously thought of Tony as a third party unconnected to the trickery here. So how did Maria's voice come out of him—and how did she know my name? Di Stefano never spoke it. When telling Maria and Maddelena why I was here, he only described me as "a journalist from England."

Salvation soon comes when I remember that Di Stefano's office recommended Tony in the first place—and Maria's knowledge of my name only hastens the return of that *Truman Show* feeling. She and her mother are Vatican glove puppets after all. This whole thing really was an elaborate set-up. What the hell was I thinking there, for a while? Given the Catholic Church's wealth, the ultra-convincing illusion of a nail spat into a leg is both achievable and relatively subtle. Making a young girl's voice come out of a man's mouth? Child's play.

This whole thing has been organised religion to a T: the use of man-made lies to try and make people feel small, protected and grateful.

I award everybody the slowest, most sarcastic handclap I can muster, before getting in my car.

This time, no amount of further dicking around will make me look back.

*   *   *

During the long, dull drive back to civilisation, I mentally run through the SPOOKS List. Today's experience clearly does not require any further possible explanations to be added. At some point during the exorcism I'd believed Father Di Stefano was "trying to deceive others" (Explanation #1) while Maria and Maddelena were in turn "being deceived by others" (Explanation #2.) By the end, it had become obvious that only Explanation #1 was required. Everyone, to their eternal shame, was acting. Lying their heads off.

A call comes in from an unknown number. The word "Unknown" doesn't pop up as usual: the screen is completely blank except for the options to answer or reject.

When I answer, a piercing electronic shriek crashes out of the speakers. Warped digital feedback: the kind of thing Aphex Twin used to put on his records *(Eleanor: I know you'll ask me to update this reference and make it a more current band. Sorry, but it sounded like Aphex Twin. Not my fault you're too young to remember him.)* And it's loud. So loud. I had no clue my phone was capable of such decibels.

The sheer physical shock makes me cover my ears with both hands. Which is bad, because I'm negotiating a tight bend.

The Romeo hammers along the middle of the dirt road. If something hurtles around that bend towards me, there'll be a head-on smash, no survivors.

Clutch. Brake. Steer. Terminate call with built-in steering wheel button. Pray.

I sail around the rest of the bend, sick with adrenalin, ears ringing. Edging the Romeo back to safety.

The noise sounded demonic. It was the natural, or unnatural, soundtrack to Edvard Munch's *Scream*. And afterwards, however fleetingly, I find myself pondering how this call might be connected to Maria Corvi and her internal lodger. Which is ridiculous. Completely batshit. But it gets me thinking about the supernatural and how damn seductive that world can be. Because such connections are insidious. Once you start making them, it must be so easy to become seduced. To get sucked right in. Connections would lead to endless others: a vast social media network of belief. Before you knew what was going on, you'd be dragging your daughter to meet one of the Pope's right-hand men at a knackered old church in the back of beyond.

By the time I'm propping up a brutally impersonal Rome airport bar, the outside world is studded with coloured runway lights. My ears still ring and my phone holds more surprises. When I'd asked, "Where's the EVIDENCE?," hordes of people took this to be a genuine request for EVIDENCE, or at least their interpretation of what constitutes EVIDENCE. So my feed is now jam-packed with helpful links to recommended ghost videos.

"Check this one out, Jacky boy! [Link]"

"Oh yeah? Try THIS video on for size! [Link]"

"Fuk u watch dis. [Link]"

At first it all looks overwhelming.

Then I decide I'm going to watch these videos. Every last one of them.

If all these followers truly believe that a YouTube video provides evidence of life after death, then the least I can do is humour them by taking a look.

I post as follows: "All right, all right, thank you, guys, for the spooky YT links. I will have a look at this vital EVIDENCE and get back to you. Cannot WAIT."

I slip my earphones' jack into my handset. The bar atones for its lack of character with good Wi-Fi. Watching a whole row of videos will help pass the two and a half hours before my delayed flight, as will a whole row of large Jack and Cokes.

For the sake of my sanity, I discount the clips that are patently rubbish. People giggling while filming their partners with white sheets over their heads going "Wooo!" You can see these clips coming a mile off, from titles like "What lurks within my shed? LOL!" or "Danny's ass is haunted—hear what it has to say!"

Frankly, I don't think the people who sent me those particular links were taking the whole thing seriously. Skipping these (all right, I *was* curious about the pronouncements of Danny's ass—and there's a sentence I never thought I'd write) removes half of the list.

The videos I do watch embroil me in a world that knows no boundaries when it comes to lame attempts at scaring the viewer. A world that never settles for just the one exclamation mark and knows nothing of the apostrophe's correct function. A world that owes Mark Snow, the composer of *The X-Files* theme tune, millions of royalty dollars.

I suffer through photo slideshows with voiceover narration, none of which convince. Photographs have, after all, been doctored since their early-nineteenth-century inception. Double-exposure shots may have retained their power to alarm the gullible, but only then at a pinch. Photoshop and similar programs have equipped fakers with more advanced tools, while simultaneously making their work all the more obvious. One video from user WooWooWooo, boldly entitled "Scariest Photographs of 2014—DO NOT Watch Alone!," does not make me glad to be surrounded by businessmen, depressed tourists and camp baristas. I'm bored stiff by the time the third old family photo appears with a "chilling" cymbal crash, a circle superimposed around the alleged spectre peeking from behind Aunt Maude's skirts. Over one million people have been suckered into watching this thing. A nice chunk of advertising revenue for the video's creator.

"Thanks for watching. Please comment and subscribe. ☺"

I endure videos that—gasp—actually *do* feature moving pictures. Most of these betray their lineage from Oren Peli's successful "found footage" movie franchise *Paranormal Activity*. The clue tends to be the word "Paranormal" in their titles. Shot in people's houses, generally in America, they show someone clowning around or presenting a video about some random topic, before a door slams shut in the background. Whereas *Paranormal Activity* did a good job of convincing the viewer that its stars might be real people, the protagonists here are less gifted in the fields of acting and improv.

"Thanks for watching. Please comment and subscribe. ☺"

I somehow sit through clips that push the boundaries of taste by exploiting celebrity death. You might glimpse the terrifying ghost of a film star who specialised in fast-car movies (*Eleanor: See? I can self-censor. I didn't use the guy's name. Anything to stop you and those lawyer guys quacking on about libel or whatever it is*) walking away from his real-life fatal wreck. The dumbest example I see is a video from user HiggsBassoon4 that claims to show Princess Diana's ghost on his own wedding day. We see the same few looped seconds of the happy couple cutting their cake, magnified closer and closer. We screw our eyes ever tighter in a vain attempt to see something in the window behind them that plainly isn't there.

"Thanks for watching. Please comment and subscribe. ☺"

I growl at videos that instruct you to keep a very close eye on static CCTV-style footage of a room or corridor. After thirty seconds, they attempt to jolt you with a sudden jump-cut to a close-up of a hideous face overlaid with a screech. The finest specimens manage to make you jump even when you're blithely expecting them, but of course as evidence of the supernatural they leave everything to be desired.

"Thanks for watching. Please comment and subscribe. ☺"

If you ever start to get suckered in by a video that claims to show a "super-white ghost" during a school nativity play, abandon it. After replaying user ScalpLaughs65's video several times, unable to see the ghost, I finally realised the whole thing was a joke at the expense of an unusually pale boy.

"Thanks for watching. Please comment and subscribe. ☺ ☺ ☺ ☺ ☺ Don't forget to collect your brain on your way out. ☺ ☺ ☺ ☺ ☺ LOL PMSL ROFLCOPTER" ☹ ☹ ☹ ☹ ☹

The further I trudge through this shit, the more I drink, the more I bemoan the lack of creativity. I swear I could do better myself. None of it is remotely unnerving, scary or—most importantly—convincing. My jeans remain unsoiled. My heebies are jeebie-less. There are no willies up me.

As I tried to explain to people in the first place, if a genuine ghost video came along, we'd know all about it. The damn thing would be on BBC News and bounced around the planet faster than a Barack Obama sex tape.

To couch this in SPOOKS List terms, all these people are filming fake ghosts, whether trying to deceive others or being deceived themselves. No third explanation is required.

Confident that the people of social media have wasted my time yet again, I do battle with my phone's autocorrect function, which seems so much less helpful when you're drunk: "Okay, guys! I've watched this ghost video 'EVIDENCE' of yours. These videos are all—and I mean ALL—idiotic fakes. NO MORE."

I'm satisfied this has put an end to the matter. I can give scary videos no further thought. And then I check my feed. Big mistake.

While I've been watching the last thirty videos, lots of people have messaged me with variations on "Did you make this one yourself, then?" or "This is actually pretty scary!" Others have posted to their own followers, saying things like "Creepy new video from TheJackSparks!" These posts have two things in common: they're all spreading fast and they all feature the same clickable YouTube link.

It confuses the balls off me.

I click on one of these identical links and am surprised to be taken to my own YouTube channel. This is where I post sporadic videos, talking to a whole ocean of fans about whichever burning issue springs to mind. Usually something about science, technology, music or my books. Since entering rehab, I've let it slide, and three whole months have passed since the last post.

Or at least that's how long it's been since the last post by *me*.

There's now a forty-second video on this page that I did not post.

It has no title or accompanying details, other than the date and time it was posted. Today, about half an hour ago. It appears that I posted it myself, although this patently isn't the case.

I stare at the page. At this video, waiting to be watched. I frown, hit the "Back" button, then reclick the link. Surely the presence of a completely alien video on my YouTube channel was a random glitch that is about to repair itself.

Except I know others have seen it too.

Yep. The video's still there.

All forty seconds of it.

My forefinger hovers over the "Play" button. My stomach clenches, mainly because I'm worried that a complete stranger has dumped something obscene and incriminating on my YouTube channel.

Several thudding heartbeats later, I press "Play."

Alistair Sparks: "The following are words written on a napkin with biro pen, found on 21 November 2014 in a compartment of a suit-case in a room booked under the name Jack Sparks at Los Angeles' Sunset Castle Hotel. The napkin has been verified as originating from the Rome airport bar that Jack claimed to have visited."

Notes on vid:

Feet/legs, black
Fade in, fade out. Weird
Dark space. Basement?
Something on ground. Human?
Slowly turns [unintelligible word on napkin].
Around corner—argh!
Three long words—mean same thing?

CHAPTER THREE

White fire scorches one side of Bex's face, making her look even more radiant. Behind her, a million dust motes hang in suspended animation, showcased by the broad rays of sun invading Victoria's Bar.

Blinking and pushing on her shades, she says, "So it wasn't paedo porn, I take it." As usual, she says this far too loudly. She's banned from every library in East Sussex. "Because if there was paedo porn in that video," she continues as I shush her, "I'd have heard about it by now. And you'd be chased off the pier by locals."

Many large, heavy random objects hang from the bar's ceiling, including a tuba, a pram, a model plane and a limbless dress-maker's dummy. I know that when I've finished telling Bex about the video, she and I will play our traditional cool game, whereby we nominate which of these objects we'd prefer to fall down and kill us. Best game ever, yes?

Fine, suit yourself.

Bex is especially lively today, a crack-addled Tigger, and we argue more than usual. We waste half a pint bickering about whether I pocket-dialled her yesterday from Italy. She insists I did, even after I scroll back through my outgoing calls and show evidence to the contrary. I can't decide whether such intensely petty squabbles indicate a brother-and-sister relationship or latent sexual tension.

"So what *was* in the video?" she finally says, agonised, torn between relishing the moment and really wanting to know. "Actually, no, don't tell me, show me."

She nods at my phone, but I sigh. "Wish I could."

"You dropped that thing in the toilet again, didn't you."

"No. It's just that . . ."

"What-what-what?"

And I tell her what I'm about to tell you.

So I'm in that Rome airport bar. Pissed. In both the sense of being drunk and the American sense of being angry. I've had a great deal of Jack Daniel's, and some weirdo has gained access to my YouTube channel.

I've watched the video two, three, four times. I've also posted this: "If anyone knows who posted this video on my YT channel, I'd REALLY like to hear about it. Because it wasn't me (no, seriously): [YouTube link]."

The damn video's hard to absorb, what with it having been shot in near darkness and my eyes often seeing two of it, until I concentrate and refocus. I order a quadruple espresso, then check my feed. There's lots of "WTF?!?!," ":-O," "O_o" and "OMG that's creepy!!!," as well as the inevitable variations on "Er, is that supposed to be creepy or something?!"

While I naturally belong to the latter camp, this video already has me fascinated.

My espresso is plonked down beside me, its bitterness stroking my taste buds via osmosis. I chug it down and hit "Replay," finding it easier to keep my eyes open. This time, I want to pay more attention to this freaky little clip. There's just something about it. Something so very different from all the rest. *Something*.

This time, a message pops up: "This video is no longer available. It has been deleted by user."

Now, in my *head*, I'm saying "No! Fuck you—*I'm* the user!" inwardly, to *myself*. Turns out I'm actually bellowing it while pointing at my phone and making everyone flinch. Lots of hard stares fly my way, but seeing as I've already incurred the wrath of Father Primo Di Stefano today, they may as well be fragrant rose blooms caressing my skin. These fuckers are amateurs, all of them. Still, I apologise, to buy myself some time. I need to stay here. Yes, I must stay here and change my YouTube account password. I must keep hitting refresh until that stupid message disappears and the video returns. Where the hell has it gone? Why has the "user" deleted it, so soon after posting it? Thousands of fans are asking the same thing. They're trying to work out what I'm playing at, and I'm trying to tell them I'm not playing at anything.

A bald and bespectacled barista lumbers over and gets right in my face, telling me to calm down and keep quiet. I tell *him* to calm down and keep quiet, which neither calms nor quietens him. So I tell him to get fucked, figuring that this reverse psychology might work instead.

I post this: "Nope, it REALLY wasn't me who made/posted that video. And neither was it me who remo—"

Before I can finish typing the word "removed," I'm bodily removed from my chair by Baldie and another barista. I accidentally hit "Send," which makes me look like the kind of plum who thinks nothing of ending sentences with "who remo," without so much as a full stop.

As the bastards kick me out, an agitated voice announces my name over the Tannoy. Apparently I'm the last passenger Flight 106 is waiting for. Everything becomes a blur as I run for my gate. Corridors, confusing signs, conveyor belts inconsiderately not designed for drunkards . . . and *people*, far too many people. Zombie sheep, milling around.

I'm blinded by it all, then dizzied by a massive head rush. Everything flashes green. I stop running, close my eyes and centre myself.

When I come back to reality, the first thing I see, clear as day, is the face of Father Primo Di Stefano. Several of him, in fact.

Even in my inebriated state, I soon register that it's his face on the cover of multiple copies of the same book, lining a promo rack at the front of a shop. I don't recognise the title: *The Devil's Victims*. Must be brand new. Without stopping to think how I've already bought three of this guy's books as research and probably don't need the latest collection of reheated dogma and anecdotes, I grab one from the English language row and ferry it to the cash desk. The Tannoy crackles into life again and demands that Jack Sparks come to the gate *immediately*.

Oh yeah, I'm a rock star, baby. Who doesn't love their name being spoken over PAs, for whatever reason? A killer mention from a user with thousands of followers. Right here, right now, everyone in Rome airport knows my name. This thought triggers another crazy head rush, flashing red this time for some reason, which almost makes me keel over.

As I saunter on to the plane, I'm far too busy thinking about that video, and its disappearance, to worry about the rows of narrowed eyes passing by. Once strapped into my window seat, I charm the cute Irish stewardess into sneaking me a large gin and tonic. Come the stroke of midnight, we taxi on to the runway. I rest back and gather my thoughts.

That video felt like something no one was ever supposed to see, as opposed to your average clip shouting, "Woot! Look at this!" No irritating captions squeaked, "Add me on FB!" or "See more on my other channel!" It had no accompanying details whatsoever, not even a title. That very fact reeled me in. This was a *found thing*. The digital equivalent of a video cassette tape bearing no label and placed on your doorstep . . . that is then stolen from your living room a short while later. Someone wants you to see it, but not keep it. A glimpse of spooky stocking.

YouTube videos are all about the attention. The hits, the numbers, the advertising. Monetise your content, it's the new way. The only way. So when an arresting YouTube video appears, then vanishes after just a few hundred hits, I want to know why. While I have no doubt that its makers are "trying to deceive others" (SPOOKS Explanation #1), the video's *raison d'être* is something other than the norm. For whatever reason, these people have targeted me and it would be churlish for me not to react and play along.

So then. Fair play to them. Game on.

As our many tons of aeroplane arc gracefully up into the night, all I know is, I must see that video again ASAP. My obsession also cements my resolve to finish writing this book—an idea that came to me one day as a mere whim.

Stretching my toes in 40A, I pledge to find the people

behind this video. Because when I prove the most convincing (not that this is saying much) ghost video to be a fake, then all the others must be fake too.

I gaze out of my small round window at puffball clouds, the light that pulses reassuringly on the wing and, thousands of miles below, the broad swathes of Italy on Halloween. The mighty forces of coffee and alcohol lock horns to make me feel distinctly alive, as I notice the tiny glow of a fire somewhere down in the hills. Someone's bumpkin barbecue, way out of control.

I feel even better when I remember that I have *The Devil's Victims* to enjoy. I tug it from my shoulder bag, relax, turn to page one and chuckle all the way home.

A huge devil-eyed gull bursts into flight, making a group of tourists duck in alarm beside the tarot wagon. Bex stares out of the bar window at this, her face bearing the healthy, happy flush of someone on their third pint.

"So, have you found out who made the video?" she wants to know.

"What I'm doing," I say, "is investigating upfront, to make sure I'm not about to make a fool of myself."

"God," she says with a smirk, auto-covering her mouth. "Imagine that. Impossible." Having enjoyed her own hilarious sarcasm, she becomes curious. "How d'you mean?"

"It did occur to me," I say, "that the video could be a viral advertising thing for some company. God knows how they'd do it, or whether it would be legal, but I thought they might have shoved it on to several journalists' YouTube channels, then withdrawn them to create interest. Leave 'em wanting more, all that stuff."

She thinks this over. "If that were true, what's it advertising? What's the brand—ectoplasm? And by the way: *when* are you going to tell me what's in the video?"

"What's ectoplasm?"

"You don't know what ectoplasm is. And you're writing a book about the supernatural . . ."

"Well, I propose to learn as I go along."

She affects a ludicrously pompous take on my voice, rolling her eyes up into her head: "*Well, one proposes to learn as one goes along.*"

"Hey," I say, jab-jab-jabbing her shoulder with an affectionate forefinger. "I don't talk like that! I'm not *Prince Charles*. You're posher than me. Anyway, I put the word out to the few journalists who actually still talk to me, and then they asked the ones who don't. None had received this video. Social media doesn't seem to have heard of it . . . apart from the people who saw it that evening, obviously."

The booze is making Bex increasingly enthralled and frustrated, like this video is the one thing left in the world. She shifts over to sit directly beside me, then grabs the front of my T-shirt. She twists it up into a ball, constricting my Adam's apple. At first, it feels like genuine retaliation for my forefinger poke. Maybe I jab-jab-jabbed her too hard.

"What. Was in. The fucking. Video?" she demands, her pouty lips worryingly, deliciously close to mine. Whatever would her boyfriend think if he walked in?

Go on, Lawrence, I dare you: walk in right now. Then run back out sobbing and jump in the sea, bashing your head on the way down.

"Have you considered anger management classes?" I say, my voice coming out as Donald Duck's. Bex's only reply is to tighten her grip on my shirt-ball. I hold my hands up in surrender, then smile when she releases me.

"As I said, I've only seen it a few times and I was really drunk. It's like trying to remember a dream. Basically, it's shot in what looks like a basement . . . and there's someone standing there on the other side of the room. You can only see their legs and feet and—"

"What, they don't have a top half?!"

"No, it's just that . . . Oh, you know what, I'm honestly not trying to wind you up, but it'll sound rubbish if I try to describe it like this. I'm a writer, not a talker."

Bex's expression is best described as tempestuous.

"You *need* to find this video."

"I'm bloody trying!"

"Yes," she says. "You really are."

It's dark by the time our backsides plunge back on to the big fat yellow sofa, even though it's only about half six. Bloody November. We're doing that thing where you can't stop the momentum of an afternoon's drinking, so just stumble blindly on. Hence the bottle of wine that I'm trying so hard to open, while Bex skins up. As much as I'm tempted to justify dope-smoking as research for communing with the spirit realm, I'm sticking to the booze.

On the TV we've selected a Channel 5 documentary about huge babies with syphilis or something. Behind us, an enclosed balcony offers panoramic views. The Palace Pier, a fuck-off Ferris wheel and a full moon highlighting the broad black sea, recalling the cover of The Sisters of Mercy's *Floodland* album. It's one hell of a flat: the reason I moved from London to Brighton five years ago. As faithful readers will recall, I then joined a gym where I met Bex and learned she urgently needed somewhere to stay. I wanted her to move in so badly that I sacrificed my study and hurriedly turned it back into a bedroom.

Get the fit girl to move in, even though you've only just met her? Yeah, that'll totally end in a fulfilling relationship. Loving your man-logic there, Sparks.

"Why didn't we get a screw top?" I grumble, neck arteries straining as I yank at the cork. "*Always* get a screw top."

"You big twat," she says, taking the bottle off me. As I watch her ease out the cork, it strikes me she's the only person on earth who I'd let speak to me that way.

By the end of the second bottle, things are hazy, and the room's pungency would rival an Amsterdam coffee shop. I have flashbulb memories of some freakishly large onscreen babies; of telling Bex about my myriad plans for this book; and of the room revolving in a good way: slow, manageable, chilled out.

There's only one part of the evening I remember vividly. Second by second, breath by breath, pore by pore.

I'm in the middle of proudly telling Bex what SPOOKS stands for when she leaps upon me, roaring as she pins me down on the sofa. This tigress straddles me, panting in my face, her hands tightly securing my wrists, her red ringlets dangling in random clumps. A breathtaking turn of events.

"Stop talking about *you*," she says, with comically exaggerated ferocity. "I've wanted to tell you something *huge* all day, but I haven't had a chance. You talk over me. You only ever talk about you and your work, which is also about you. Are you aware of that, you fucker? It's *really annoying* to live with someone who is either talking about themselves or waiting for their chance to talk about themselves. Do you know what I mean?"

I stare up at her, profoundly in love.

"Yes," I manage. "I'm really sorry, but you did keep asking about Italy. And I—"

She releases her grip on my right hand and clamps her palm over my mouth. "No, no, no, Scooby-Doo: I talk now, you listen."

I nod, conscious of how her denim-clad groin feels against my midriff. Also, how her smooth skin feels against my lips. I could so easily lick at the salt, but I don't.

Bex brings her face down closer. Only her hand separates her lips from mine. Then she uncovers my mouth and says, "Yeah. You listen closely."

Oh my God. I suddenly remember an app on my phone called Secret, which lets you read anonymous confessions from your contacts. Recently, one of them wrote, "I really want to sleep with my flatmate, but we've been friends too long."

That was Bex! She's going to tell me she likes me. Then she'll kiss me. And after the sex, in bed, or maybe still right here on the sofa, she'll tell me she's breaking up with Lawrence, that it's the right thing to do.

Bex's eyes are twin glowing lanterns. Her breath dances on my face as the words gush out. "Lawrence asked me to move in with him. And I said *yes.*"

The room starts to revolve in a bad way.

Matters only improve when, slumped beside our toilet, I check my email. Through bleary eyes, I see that someone has sent The Video whizzing right back to me.

Alistair Sparks: "Having felt somewhat stung by our exchange of texts on 28 October, I am sorry to say I never replied to the 3 a.m. email below."

Date: 2 November 2014
From: Jack Sparks
Subject: Huh?!?!
To: Alistair Sparks

While I was buying a book at Rome airport, I saw you on the shop's TV screen. You were talking to the camera, with the Hollywood Hills in the background. WTF? The sound was off so I couldn't hear what you were quacking about.

So what's the story?

You've always been gagging to follow in my footsteps, haven't you, eh? Must admit though, mate, I never expected to see you on the box. At a push, you've a good face for radio.

By the way: you know a guy at Scotland Yard, right? Tracks down child abuse videos and stuff? Do a passable impersonation of a brother and hand over his contact details, yeah?

Jack

Alistair Sparks: "Isla Duggan is a thirty-two-year-old air stewardess who lives in West Sussex and was born in Kinsale, Ireland. She was among the cabin crew on Flight 106 from Rome to London Gatwick, on which my brother claimed to be a passenger on 31 October 2014. The following is my interview with her . . ."

ALISTAIR SPARKS: Could you confirm which seat you believe Jack Sparks to have occupied that night?

ISLA DUGGAN: Yes, he was in 40A. A window seat.

ALISTAIR: Is there any doubt in your mind that this was Jack Sparks?

ISLA: None at all, now I've seen pictures and videos of him in the newspapers and on TV. He spoke the exact same way, you know, his mannerisms and stuff? And of course there's the fact that he had to show his passport at least twice, or he wouldn't have got on board. But he did act strangely on the plane, freaking out like that. I don't know how out of character that was.

ALISTAIR: Was he late for the flight?

ISLA: He delayed us by almost twenty minutes. People weren't happy, but it happens all the time. I keep saying we should have a zero tolerance policy like the budget airlines. Jack came on all casual, like, as if he hadn't done anything wrong. I could tell he'd been drinking heavily, and he wanted more before take-off. So I pulled the old stunt of handing him a glass of ice and tonic with a drop of gin rubbed around the rim.

ALISTAIR: So what then went wrong?

ISLA: Well, as we taxied along the runway, I moved up the aisle, doing the usual checks. I saw Mr. Sparks looking shocked and disturbed. He was all pale, like he'd just heard some really terrible news he couldn't take in.

ALISTAIR: Did you talk to him at that point?

ISLA: I asked if he was okay, and he flinched when I lightly touched his shoulder. I can't remember exactly what he said, but words to the effect of "I'm fine." But he didn't look it. He went back to reading a book, looking like he . . . I suppose . . . couldn't believe what he was reading.

ALISTAIR: The book seemed to be the cause of his disturbance?

ISLA: I guess I just assumed it was a Stephen King or something. Anyway, the real trouble started just as we were about to take off. Passengers are at their most tense, so the last thing you need is one of them becoming alarmed—especially as we crew members are all strapped into our own seats. We aren't even allowed to get up if the passengers start killing each other. The first thing I heard was a couple of passengers telling Mr. Sparks they couldn't "smell that" at all, like they were trying to reassure him. So as soon as our seat-belt lights went off, I made a beeline for Mr. Sparks. I wanted to get there before my number two, the guy I was working with, because he often got aggressive with problem passengers.

Mr. Sparks was basically having a panic attack. I gave him a sick bag to breathe into, but he just kept talking and insisted he could smell burning, when there was absolutely no burning smell. All around there were all these worried and irritated faces, expecting me to sort this. When I tried to reassure Mr. Sparks, he got angry: he told me I was "trying to cover it up" and called me "an effing liar." We're not supposed to take that kind of language, but there's no point escalating a situation if you've no need. At that point, our purser dimmed the overhead lights—purely, in my opinion, because she was still hungover from the previous night—and his eyes shot up to them, scared. I knew I had to act fast, before he really started yelling.

ALISTAIR: So how did you handle the situation?

ISLA: I could have given him Ativan, our on-board sedative, but it's not that easy: you have to radio America to get permission. Ativan plus alcohol isn't a great idea, either. Then the last resort would have been to restrain Mr. Sparks in his seat, which is no fun for anyone. If it turns nasty, a staff member can end up with a broken bone or worse. I really wanted to try a different approach. The people in 40B and 40C had already switched to other seats, so I sat next to Mr. Sparks and spoke to him very calmly, smiling.

I explained that if anything had been burning, our sensitive alarm system would have picked it up. That was a white lie, mind: there are smoke detectors in the toilets, and the flight crew might get an indication if something bad happens to the engine, but that's about it. I did also tell him a true fact. I said our plane had gone through freezing rain on its way to Rome, so needed to be sprayed with de-icing fluid on arrival. When a de-iced plane takes off, you get a smell coming through the air con. It's unusual and people don't know what it is. After I told him all this, he said, "Promise me you're telling me the effing truth." And I actually said back, without being at all aggressive, "Yes, I effing am." I've found that if you swear back at a sweary customer it kind of short-circuits their brain and bewilders them.

ALISTAIR: Did matters calm down from that point?

ISLA: Yes, he started breathing into the bag. He still seemed nervous of the book, though, because he asked if I could "wrap it in something safe till London." Which was a bit mad, but anything for a quiet flight. Once we'd done the food service, I wrapped the book in loads of tin-foil lids from hot meals. Mr. Sparks disembarked at Gatwick without saying sorry or thanks, and that was that. When I came to read about, you know, the terrible things that happened, it took me a while to put two and two together. I was shocked. He seemed like a good guy. Cocky and quite troubled, but basically good, you know?

ALISTAIR: Did you ever get a sense of why the book had scared him?

ISLA: No, but I remember the title: *The Devil's Victims*, written by the priest on the cover. Creepy subject matter, right enough. The Devil's always frightening, isn't he?

CHAPTER FOUR

"Oh my God," says Bex, with stoner slits for eyes. "We're actually going to watch it?"

It's somewhere north of midnight. She and I stare at the video file that sits on my PC's desktop, waiting to be double-clicked. I'm at my desk with vomit stains down my shirt, dispelling any final hint of sexual frisson that might have survived after Bex's Lawrence bombshell. She's perched on one corner of my bed. I don't particularly want to talk to her right now, but also couldn't resist telling her about the video's return. Paradox.

The video has found its way back to me courtesy of one of my fans, Calvin from Cardiff. A confirmed tech-head, Calvin ripped the video from my YouTube channel during the brief period it was online, intending to scrutinise it. Seeing my online appeal after the video disappeared, he dropped me a line via JackSparks.co.uk with the file attached. Love this guy.

Bex frowns at me. "You all right, Dolly? Thought you'd be more excited about the video."

"Still don't feel well," I lie, smothering fury that she's moving in with a total cockhead when she should clearly be with me.

She nods, then folds her arms and faces the screen, expectant, demanding.

By the time you lay your hands on this book, dear reader, you'll probably have already seen the video. If not, you can do so online at (*Eleanor: insert the URL here, cheers*).[1] But since that's not strictly in the spirit of reading books, and because you may be optically challenged, I shall now describe it for you in full.

All aboard the ghost train . . .

The video is technically in colour, but so much black, grey and white are involved that it's mostly monochrome. The quality seems to place it in the digital age, but it's difficult to be sure. That is one of the avenues I intend to pursue during my investigation, m'lud.

The scene is dark, but with just enough light for us to see the basis of what's going on. Even if we don't fully understand it.

We are in a corridor in some kind of basement, or boiler room area, or both. Throughout what follows, there's a low, droning hum. The aforementioned light seems to come from a single bare bulb hanging at the end of a cord, which we glimpse at around the seven-second mark. The bulb is caked in dust, which dulls the light it gives out.

We know it's cold, from the misted breath of whoever's filming. For ease of reference, we'll call this person Camera

---

1 When the true nature of the video came to light, YouTube and every other online video platform banned it. They continue to ban its every reappearance. The video, however, still spreads via torrent sites. —*Alistair*

Boy. There is no audio-visual evidence to suggest he's a guy, but let's face it, no girl's going to be stupid enough to go filming in a cold, dark, spooky basement.

The camera is only a foot or two above ground level. It moves forward slowly, bumping as it goes. Feels very much like Camera Boy is crawling forward on his knees. To the left, a couple of feet away, there's a plain brick wall, the stone chipped, faded, old. To our immediate right is a spaghetti junction of pipes on the other wall, each a couple of inches thick. They're different primary colours, although much of the paint has peeled away. These pipes feed in and out of old-fashioned dust-caked boxes with dials and gauges on them.

We see that this corridor will widen up ahead, into an area flooded with black. That's where the wall with the pipes turns off to the right, forming a sharp corner. As Camera Boy approaches that corner, he stays close to this wall but slows down, as if wary of the imminent turn. We now hear as well as see his breath, which is fast and spidery. He's really quite scared.

There's a pause. You can almost feel Camera Boy steeling himself. You can almost smell Camera Boy shitting himself. (*Eleanor: I'll probably choose just one of these two sentences later. I know which one Little Miss Prim will prefer . . .*)

Then he's crawling again, closing in on that corner.

Don't worry: the video doesn't end there. That would have been infuriating beyond belief, wouldn't it? No, there are still about thirty seconds left.

Apparently being vaguely sensible, Camera Boy doesn't go blundering around that corner. Instead, he peeps, millimetre by millimetre. Impossible to tell for sure, but maybe he even edges the camera around the corner first, while keeping his own head back with an eye on the viewfinder. That's what I'd do, whether I believed in ghosts or not.

It takes a while for the camera to focus on what it sees, because it's gloomy and abstract. Eventually, though, we lay our eyes on a little scene across the basement floor. Camera Boy does too, because there's a sharp intake of breath and the camera wobbles.

For the next few seconds, the only noise will be provided by that bass-heavy hum, which now sounds like it emanates from a generator.

In the centre of this space, one person is lying down and one person is standing.

At least, I *think* that's a person on the floor. It's almost completely obscured by thick shadow. We see an arm, maybe a hand, get the general sense of a humanoid shape, nothing more. It could be a shop window dummy, or a scarecrow, but it certainly looks like an actual human person on their front, completely still, with only their top half in shot.

Conversely, as I tried to explain to Bex before, the camera's framing only allows us to see the lower half of the person standing over them. We see this person's legs and feet, which face away from us. They seem to be bare and, in these poor lighting conditions, appear quite black. They also appear to be . . . well, transparent. You can see through them, in the classic ghost tradition. These legs come very slowly in and out of sight in the manner of Christmas tree lights in fade mode, while never vanishing entirely or appearing fully corporeal. The effect is subtle and admittedly disquieting.

Camera Boy seems inclined to agree, because he whispers five words.

"Oh God . . . this is it."

These are the only words he utters throughout the clip. Because it's such a thin reed of a whisper and can only be heard with the volume cranked right up, it's still impossible— for me, at least—to discern the gender.

The camera half ducks back around the corner, as if Camera Boy fears having been heard. The right-hand half of the screen is abruptly obscured by a vertical slice of wall.

Across the room, those legs and feet remain still. Their state of slow, steady flux continues, blending in and out of existence.

Perhaps confident that he wasn't heard after all, Camera Boy moves the camera back into position, away from the cover the wall affords him.

With timing worthy of cinematic horror icons like Bela Lugosi and Christopher Lee, the figure across the room begins to slowly, oh so painfully slowly, turn around.

It seems to take our hero a while to realise that those feet are shifting position, a few inches at a time, to face him. Maybe his own eyes have been distracted, lingering on that body on the floor.

When he registers what's going on, we soon know all about it. For three seconds the camera becomes a jerky blur of brick, pipe, misty breath and nothing, as he concentrates on getting the hell out of here.

The camera settles down, though it's still very bumpy, to show us that corner, from which we now scurry away, backwards, low, possibly on our arse.

Something comes around the corner, fast.

We see only the dangling feet of that pitch-black spectre as it floats right at us.

Camera Boy doesn't scream or yell. Instead, his dry vocal cords click and pop. It's as if they can't produce an adequate response and give up the ghost, so to speak. The camera spasms and shakes, jerks to the right, briefly captures that mess of metal pipes . . .

And that's where the video ends.

One thing I didn't mention: three other words besides "Oh God . . . this is it" are spoken during the video. In my opinion, these words have been overdubbed, rather than having been recorded live during filming. They are spoken neutrally by what sounds like a young girl with an accent from somewhere like Spain or Italy. The voice is not entirely dissimilar to Maria Corvi's. It can't be her, though, fright fans, so don't get excited.

One second into the video, the voice says, "Adramelech."

Exactly halfway through, at the twenty-second mark, the voice says, "Mephistopheles."

One second before the video ends, the voice says, "Baphomet."

Bex wriggles on the corner of my bed, rubbing bare arms. "Bloody hell. Goosey-bumps."

I'm gutted: this could have been a green light to hug the scared drunk girl. But no. Because Lawrence. Because vomit stains. Because life.

"Yeah," I say. "It's the best ghost video I've seen. They did a good job."

"What . . . so you don't think it's real?"

The scorn in my voice surprises even me. "Bex, who do you think you're talking to? I mean, I suppose it would convince some people."

"That fadey-legs thing . . . that's a *ghost*."

"Oh God, woman! Don't you think it's all a bit too neat?"

"Don't 'woman' me, you fucking tit."

"It's all too, y'know . . . *Blair Witch*. Something scary happens at the end, the camera goes berserk, then blackout."

"If a ghost flew round a corner at me, then that would, to be fair, signal the end of my interest in filming. My camera work would suffer."

She's so annoying and confusing. Funny and heart-pulping. As we debate the video, I reinstate it on my YouTube channel, then post as follows:

"It's back! Anyone know anything about the origin of this scary video? Email VidInfo@JackSparks.co.uk: [YouTube link]."

"Hey, hold on," says Bex. "You didn't film this yourself, did you?"

I glower over my shoulder at her.

"Just checking," she protests. "Can we watch it again?"

"I'm too tired," I say, fighting the strong urge to watch it with her till dawn. To do anything with her till dawn. Count the Artex bumps on the ceiling. Separate a vast mound of pins into categories by length.

She stands with reluctance, an unsteady sleepwalker. High-fives me on her way past, then melts out into the darkness. Heading for the room that will soon revert to being either my study or a home to some new dickhead tenant who'll leave snarky Post-it notes everywhere.

I'd meant to ask what she made of "Adramelech," "Mephistopheles" and "Baphomet," which Google swiftly confirms to be the names of demons and devils. Never mind, it'll be a good excuse to talk to her again tomorrow. But no, no, triple no, I should ignore that instinct. Distancing myself from Bex is the right thing to do. Nothing stays the same forever and, God knows, it's her loss.

I yank a bottle of Jack out from under the desk, fish an old

pack of cigarettes from a drawer and watch the video until I
fall asleep in my chair.

Come morning, I feel like I'm finally seeing the video properly
for the first time. On Halloween, I was drunk and careless,
watching it on that small phone screen. Last night, I was drunk
and preoccupied with Bex. In the cold light of day, when I'm
sober, if acutely dehydrated and sprinkled with toast crumbs,
the video is so much more vivid. I had wondered whether
clarity might sap its power, but this remains undiminished. I
also notice more detail. For instance, the outline of a door on
the boiler room's back wall: the entrance to an ancient lift shaft.
There are two small square windows in this door, and every
few seconds, we glimpse the silhouette of old-school mechan-
isms within. The apparent lack of button on the wall beside
the lift door suggests we're talking pre-automatic, pre-1950s.

My immediate plan of action is to scour the video for clues
to its origin, while hunting down an expert to analyse it.
Cardiff Calvin may be awesome, but as an IT manager he has
limited insight to offer in this respect. He notes that the video's
resolution is "hard to pin down, because YouTube re-encodes
everything you upload. But at a guess, it looks like it was shot
in recent years, perhaps with a phone rather than a camcorder?
Deffo too jumpy to be a GoPro."

My feet itch. My passport bounces on my desk, begging for
action. The urge to leave is partly down to Bex, who seems
intent on spending the day pouting around in her bra and
pants with her hair in a towel. But while I'm noodling this
video, I may as well travel and discover just how super the
supernatural world can be. So I decide to become a leaf on
the winds of social media:

"Guys! Tell me where the scariest, most SCIENTIFICALLY DEMONSTRABLE spooks hang out. Anywhere in the world. Go!"

Suggestions flood in for the rest of the day. I find myself invited all around the planet, and soon discover that there are an insane number of global paranormal-interest groups. One such group, Braşov Inc., based in Transylvania, claims to have found Count Dracula's actual skull buried near ancient ruins. Given that Count Dracula is a fictional character, I respectfully decline their suggestion that I come and hold the thing in my own two hands. They counter that they actually meant Vlad the Impaler, the real-life character upon whom Bram Stoker supposedly based Count Dracula, and who was apparently also known as Dracula. At this point, I ask why a real-life person's skull would be of any interest to a man searching for the supernatural. Comms go quiet after that. Some people really will do anything for a bit of attention: their desperation consumes all reason.

A motley stateside crew named the Hollywood Paranormals write to tell me they're preparing a modern-day version of something called the Harold Experiment from the seventies. I don't read too far into it, but basically they want to see whether the human mind can invent and produce a bespoke ghost. Naturally, they want Jack Sparks involved. Fairly interesting stuff, which certainly beats Dracula's skull, but ultimately too esoteric. As I said, I don't believe the human mind can actually hallucinate a ghost, *sans* LSD. I also want to at least give people a chance to prove that *real* ghosts of the dead exist, as opposed to ghosts of the mind, so I wish group leader Astral Way all the best with his experiment and open the next email . . .

. . . which is a hacking threat from some dildo called Oscar, who bravely uses an untraceable email account. His mustard gas vitriol wafts from the screen. "Only an idiot would write a book about something they don't believe in. You think the Devil's so funny? You should ask yourself, Mr. Jack Sparks, what the Devil thinks of *you.*" No doubt shortly before his mummy tells him it's time for bed, Oscar signs off with, "You have displeased many in the hacking community, Mr. Sparks. We will SHUT YOU DOWN."

Amusingly impotent rattle-throwing trolls aside, none of the other invitations entice. It's all blah, blah, blah. "Read my blog" this; "I have a doctorate in the paranormal" that. After hours of carpet-bombing from spiritual snake-oil salesmen and people with Kindle books to promote, indirect recommendations hold far more sway with me. So I start to pay more attention to those.

One name pops up in my feed more than any other.

Sherilyn Chastain's Hong Kong Island apartment is hard to find, even when you have her address and the use of Google Maps. This is no doubt deliberate, given that her profession must attract even more lunatics than Dawkins or myself. Twice, I'm forced to phone her for directions. Each time, she provides the information in a clipped, businesslike manner, uttering the bare minimum of words.

Just as the video impressed me by underselling itself, Sherilyn Chastain attracted me by letting others do all the shouting from rooftops. "You should totally talk to SChastainReal," advised MightieAtom6 from New Jersey, among so many others. "She'll point you in the right direction and make sure you don't screw this book up." Thanks for the advice, MightieAtom6, although

I'm not in the habit of making mistakes (give or take the odd ounce of pre-rehab cocaine).

Chastain's website is low-key. A brief bio describes her Perth upbringing as the daughter of a local lawyer and a French artist. The rest focuses on her various paid services as a combat magician. Yes, you read that right: combat magician. Combat magic is new to me, but it sounds so very dramatic that I must know more.

Hong Kong's summer heatwave has long gone, leaving the air relatively cool but still more humid than I'm used to. I'm soon cloaked in sweat from traipsing these hectic and riotously colourful streets, whose market stalls sell everything you can imagine. Each street has a theme: you turn from one selling goldfish into the next selling shoes, then into another selling electronic goods. I'm assailed by that wonderwall of unique aromas that only China and various global Chinatown outposts can build. It's hard to believe open-air food stalls (*dai pai dongs*) are on the decline locally, because they're glorious. Like most sky-scraping cities, Hong Kong transforms you into a mouse running around an unfathomably tall maze, but the sights, smells and tastes are worth it.

Every other minute, my phone vibrates in my hand, signifying a new email in my inbox dedicated to information on the video. So far, four in every ten messages has been from someone claiming to have filmed it themselves. Unless they were all on the same crew, this is patently impossible. Of these emails, I'm replying to the ones that sound fundamentally plausible and don't make their confession with fuckwit textspeak. I tread carefully and remain non-committal, asking them to tell me just a little more, a little more . . . and waiting for them to trip up or just not get back to me. There's no way I want to throw any babies out with the bathwater here, but I've also come to understand how frustrating it must be for murder detectives when fruit loops confess to homicides they didn't commit.

The video has captured people's imaginations, bagging me over twelve thousand new followers as a result. Those who have blogged and posted about it tend to either present it as the first genuine supernatural event ever captured on film, or rip it apart as nonsense. I see very little middle ground. Some lazily and stupidly imply I've engineered the whole thing. I suppose the video having appeared on my own YouTube channel has played a big part there, but there's no call for the likes of CrazyHotBuzz.com to write, "This dumb and clearly fabricated video surely has to be attention-starved junkie Sparks' last roll of the dice. We sure hope so." As if I care what a bunch of inconsequential hipsters think. Let them keep quacking into the void. (*Eleanor: I did email you and Murray about this but received no response—please have our legal guys remove their libel ASAP!*)

While becoming legally high simply by passing incense stalls, I skip an incoming call that ends up as a new voicemail message. It's the third I've received from Astral Way of the Hollywood Paranormals since I turned them down. The man does not comprehend the word "no." How did he even get my number? He non-stop invites me to hook up on social media, and his voicemails become more passive-aggressive each time. The first message introduced me to his soft Californian hippy accent: "I would advise you to take a little more time to think about this decision. Believe me, Jack, when I say that our experiment cannot be ignored." I smirk my way through his latest recording, as he asks, "Please do me the courtesy of calling me back, provided you're not too busy, of course. And since you're visiting Sherilyn Chastain, perhaps you might want to ask her about our group's highly respected status in the paranormal community. Thank you."

Is anything more cringe-worthy than someone being curtly formal?

When a text springs up from Bex ("Looks like I might be shacking up with lover boy sooner than expected—will next week be okay?"), I'm very relieved to turn a corner and finally clock Sherilyn Chastain's street sign.

I once again consider what I'm trying to achieve here. Given that Chastain is a noted and respected member of what Astral Way calls the paranormal community, I'd like her thoughts on the video's authenticity or otherwise. Can't hurt. I also want to see if speaking to her, and perhaps learning more about what she does, can add a new hypothesis to my SPOOKS List. After hanging out with one of the world's foremost combat magicians, will I decide there's actually a third explanation for people seeing ghosts, besides them lying or being lied to by others?

Sherilyn Chastain buzzes me up to the seventh floor. As she opens her apartment door, she wrinkles her nose and looks dubious. Understandably so, you might argue, given my reputation. Then she slowly thaws. Ironically, when it comes to sharing solid facts, she is virtually monosyllabic, but when discussing unprovable arcane babble, you can't shut her up.

Her accent is Western Australian with a soupçon of Paris every once in a blue syllable. In her early fifties (my guess), she's about five foot two in her bare feet. Messily spiked purple-dyed hair suggests she never shook a Siouxsie Sioux fixation. Since she's surrounded by items straight out of Tolkien's universe, it's hard not to think of her as hobbitesque. She wears blue jeans and a plain T-shirt that matches the colour of her barnet—a shame, as I had really hoped for some kind of cloak adorned with mystic symbols.

I couldn't begin to count the number of skulls on these shelves. Animal skulls mostly—a dog, a cat, what looks like an otter, many birds. No Count Dracula or Vlad the Impaler, disappointingly, although there is one human skull on display ("Don't worry," says Chastain, placing a cup of Chinese tea on a small table beside the sofa, which I'm daubing with back sweat. "I got her through totally legit means. The estate was fine with it").

There are books, so many books, with titles including *Higher Principles of the Seven Winds*, *Hell's Sweet Cauldron*, *Man's Eternal Downfall* and—yes!—the already legendary *Satan & I*, by Father Primo Di Stefano. That last one surprises me: aren't Catholics and combat magicians very different beasts? Di Stefano would probably want this apartment razed to the ground. Would Chastain, as a witch or whatever she is, feel the same about his places of worship? The short answer: no. The long answer will become implicit during our interview.

There are rows of jars and bowls and bottles and test tubes of murky liquid, some of which are colours I don't believe I've seen in reality before. Some contain (presumably) dead creatures suspended in weird juice. Textbook witchery-pokery. The flat's actual decor is unexpectedly neutral and non-goth, although Chastain admits this is because she might be looking to sell up at some point. "I like to move around."

It has been surprisingly easy to gain an audience with Sherilyn

Chastain: she replied to my email within a few hours. Of course, a spot in Jack Sparks' latest book certainly won't hurt her profile, and therefore her trade. Maybe the priorities of Catholics and combat magicians aren't so mutually exclusive after all.

We relocate to deckchairs on her small but pleasantly leafy balcony. It overlooks Harbour Grand Kowloon, which is lined with everything from rag-tag junks to rich men's playthings. A pale blue ribbon of sea lies beyond, tainted only by the darting shadow of a paraglider suspended beneath a wide yellow fabric wing. No, Chastain doesn't mind if I smoke out here, and even provides an oddly curved ashtray, although she lights an incense stick "to neutralise the air." She does exactly that kind of thing for a living, on a larger scale.

I wonder aloud whether female combat magicians are very common. "There's a few of us dotted about," she says, slouching in her chair and propping her feet up on the balcony rail. "And most of us kick arse more than the guys. We got the advantage of a menstrual current, see. If something has blood, we're even more able to fuck it up."

I suppose the aggression here shouldn't really surprise me, given that Chastain has "combat" in her job description. When I try to nail the distinction between combat magicians and exorcists, she presents me with a suitably fight-based metaphor: "If exorcism is judo, then combat magic is ju-jitsu." This doesn't help much, so Chastain spells it out: "Exorcism tends to be relatively formal and slow. Quite boring, if you wanna know the truth. And you already do know, because you posted about an exorcism, very disrespectfully."

She pauses to gauge my reaction. When I don't supply one, she persists: "How's that girl now? The Italian girl?"

I explain that the whole thing was a set-up. Maria and her mum are no doubt doing very well, thanks to a Catholic cash injection. Chastain looks dubious and I lead her back on-topic. "Combat magic is the equivalent of street fighting: dirtier, faster. If you're in a situation where you need combat magic, you need it fast. You need it strong and you need it crude."

Chastain claims that she and her female partner (in a business sense, although who knows?) Fang regularly deal with people all over the world who "might have had a curse thrown at them, which we can usually break. Or a customer might feel that they or their house are being haunted. We do a hell of a lot of house clearings—ridding places of negative energy. Hey, can you please use the ashtray?"

I've flicked my ash willy-nilly. My heart's been too busy sinking at words like "curse" and "haunted," then plummeting altogether on "negative energy."

"What do you mean," I say, sticking the ashtray on my lap, "when you say 'negative energy'?"

Chastain believes the term needs no further explanation. "Energy," she says condescendingly, "which is negative. People have any number of names for the stuff that surrounds us. I happen to call it chi. The negative stuff creates bad feeling, bad vibes. It can do anything from tweaking people's emotions to making them violently throw up."

"So what do you do to rid a house of . . . negative energy?"

She grabs the arms of her deckchair and pushes herself upright, making the wood creak. "How long you in town for? We've got a job on Friday, over on Lantau. I could see if the clients would let you tag along. Some stuff, you have to see for yourself. That's what this book's all about, right?"

I nod. "It's about approaching the supernatural with an open mind."

Her heavy-lidded eyes become pinprick squints, scanning me. "So why does your mind feel so very shut; such a bloody steel trap? You've already reached conclusions."

"If I were to see something . . . some kind of hard evidence—"

She cuts me off by holding up a flat palm. "It's written all over you. The folded arms, the tension . . . you just wanna write me off and move on to the next deluded dickhead."

"*Now* who's reached a conclusion?" I counter. "I'll write you off if you deserve it."

"Nah. This is the age of certainty, mate. Everything's screwed and unpredictable, so people cling to these . . . these *ice floes* of opinion, holding on for dear life. They're terrified to show any doubt, especially of themselves. It's dangerous."

I scoff at this. "*Dangerous?* People having opinions?"

"People only speak certainty, fast as they fuckin' can. When was the last time you saw someone online posting, 'I don't yet have an opinion on this subject, but I'll come back to you when I do'?"

She says this with passion, then softens. "I'm just glad you came to see me early in this little process of yours."

Sidestepping her literal belittling of my "process," I ask what she means.

"You've walked into this whole world with your eyes and mind shut. Sooner or later, something's going to scare the crap out of you, whether you believe in it or not. So I'd strongly advise you to learn how to deal with fear. I can put it to one side for the sake of the job, but that comes down to practice and technique."

I'm tempted to ask what I owe her for this amazing advice,

but her sarcasm detection skills seem high. Instead, I solicit her opinion on the video. Does it ring any, er, psychic bells with her? Does it feel real?

Admitting that she hasn't had time to view it, she dons shades to ward off the sun and cradles an iPad on her lap. She asks for the video's title on YouTube, which is "Where Has This Alleged Ghost Video Come From?" As she taps her way to the clip, I watch that paraglider zoom towards the shore, then land with an ungainly thump. Came down too fast. Way too cocksure.

By this point, I have absolutely no need to watch the video along with her. During the forty-eight hours since it returned to my life, it has burned itself on to my brain. I watched the thing countless times during my sixteen-hour flight to Hong Kong on Erubis Books' dollar. I know Camera Boy's every single move. Every breath he takes, every camera bump he makes, I've been watching him.

Even if I wasn't able to hear the opening "Adramelech," the "Mephistopheles" that marks the midway point or the closing "Baphomet"—not to mention Camera Boy's whispered "*Oh God . . . this is it,*" of course—I would still know exactly which part of the video Chastain is watching at any given time. I can picture those supposedly spectral feet slowly turning to face the camera and I know exactly how long they take to do so. One day, I'll interview whoever created that subtly clever special effect of the in-out-fading spook. Whether they want me to or not.

Sherilyn Chastain—is it too soon to call her Shezza? Probably—says nothing while watching the video. Her expression is unreadable, although a couple of those wrinkles on her forehead deepen once Camera Boy turns the corner and beholds the macabre tableau.

After the climactic "Baphomet" is spoken, she says nothing. Just inhales, as if she's forgotten to do so for, oh, forty seconds. Then, as I expected, she hits "Replay."

I chain-smoke while she chain-watches, saving Zippo fuel by igniting each new cigarette with the tip of the last. Why did I resume this filthy habit? Oh yeah: Bex.

Chastain finally puts the iPad aside. "Yeah," she says. "That video's bad news."

I cough, screw half a cigarette against the ashtray and arch an eyebrow. "So you think it's real." *What a surprise.*

"I can't be certain," she notes, "and it wouldn't be healthy for me to *be* certain, but at this moment in time . . . yeah, I do. Never saw anything quite like it."

"What makes you think it might be real?" Even as I ask, I know the answer: she believes in this shit and/or it's beneficial to her career for others to believe. Just like everyone else on this godless globe, she's either lying or being lied to.

Chastain soothingly rubs the spot where her collarbones meet. "I get a bad feeling off it, Jack," she says, using my name for the first time instead of "mate."

"Can you be any more specific?"

She glances at the iPad by her side, disturbed. "I'll need to study it some more."

"What about the three words spoken at the start, middle and end? Not the 'Oh God . . .' stuff, but the 'Adramelech,' the 'Mephistopheles' . . ."

She gazes at me, then through me, then beyond me at who knows what, her mind ticking over.

"What was that third one again?" I get the impression she's picking her words carefully.

"Baphomet. What do you think they're all about?"

Her focus returns to the balcony and she scribbles brief notes on a pad. "I'll come back to you. But right off the bat—I'm advising you not to track down the makers of that video. Forget all about it."

A mile away, the sea rolls in over the shore. Inevitable, unstoppable.

"That video is central to the book," I tell her. "It's the *spine*. Once I expose this one as a fake, everything less convincing collapses too."

"That's important to you," she says gently, studying me again. "Pulling the curtain across to reveal all. You want your big *Wizard of Oz* moment. Why's that, Toto? Why do you think that is?"

First Scooby-Doo, now Toto: what is it with women comparing me to fictional dogs? I actually laugh—no mean feat, given the extent of my jet lag. My brain drifts, then catches up on something she said earlier. "What's wrong with being certain about things anyway?"

She pulls her legs up and crosses them beneath herself on the chair. She's surprisingly limber, Ms. Chastain, and not without sex appeal. "Ah," she says with troubling enthusiasm, as if settling down to tell an epic tale. "Ever heard of Robert Anton Wilson?"

"Yeah. Big Satanist guy."

"No, Jack, he wasn't. You're thinking of Anton LaVey."

"And you're running away from my question."

She tuts. "That's where you're wrong. Or maybe you're right. Robert Anton Wilson, y'see, gifted multiple-model agnosticism to the world."

I don't know what multiple-model agnosticism is, but strongly suspect I'm not going to like it. Sure enough, Chastain outlines how Wilson proposed that it was unhealthy for anyone to cling to one belief system all their lives. According to him, we should be prepared to shift our beliefs and mindset at any time. Apparently, Wilson once described belief as "the death of intelligence." I admit to Chastain that this makes me warm to him just a little, as that certainly applies to religion.

"It applies to everything, including science," she says, enjoying my exasperation. "I'm paraphrasing Bob here: no model or map of the universe should be totally believed in or totally denied."

"Science," I tell her, "is rock solid, thanks. Flapping about, changing your belief system every five minutes? Wishy-washy. You have to believe in something, and it can only be science. Because science deals with tangible things that we can see and touch. As opposed to your . . ." When I gesture dismissively at the knick-knacks that dominate Chastain's apartment, I sense the birth of irritation in her.

"The Higgs boson particle," she offers. "Can we see or touch that?" When I'm forced to concede we can't, she goes on: "Invisible to the human eye, right? And yet long, expensive investigation showed it was present. Quantum physics, as you must know, has posed vast questions about the role of consciousness in the universe. If we devoted as much effort to investigating the dead as we do to building the weapons that *make* them dead, we'd know a lot more about life after death."

"Dead is dead, Ms. Chastain."

"You have no idea," she says, tugging off her shades. "And neither, as a multiple-model agnostic, do I." I light another cigarette; she lights more incense. "So that's *something* we have in common, eh, Jack? Drink your tea, it's getting cold."

"You do know science would dismiss your conception of 'positive' and 'negative' energy as utter bollocks, right?"

"Oh, I adore science," she says, as if discussing a lovely old aunt with dementia. "But it's just a generalisation of the laws of Greek grammar. The entire Enlightenment project was about rediscovering stuff the ancient Greeks knew. And because it's coded so heavily on that Graeco-Roman knowledge, there's whole gaps of things they didn't have words for."

"There are always gaps," I say, "but when those gaps are filled, they'll extend the pre-existing framework. They won't suddenly serve up, I don't know, ghouls and goblins from out of the clear blue sky."

"You have no way of knowing," she says, wrongly. "Science is science, philosophy is philosophy, and never the twain shall meet. Listen: science is really good at describing things in *pieces*."

"It's really good at describing and connecting *everything*."

"Science is reductionism. You're reducing things down. You can dissect a sheep all you fuckin' like—it won't let you make an actual sheep. You're really good at comprehending the pieces, but you can't see the whole picture."

"We have made an actual sheep," I say, wincing my way through a nicotine headache. "A clone of a sheep."

"Nah." A firm shake of her head. "Nah. That's not making a sheep from scratch. Not an actual sheep. That's literally replicating what was there, created by . . . whoever the creator was."

"There was no creator," I say, "besides a big bang and evolution."

"And yet *again*," she says, slapping both thighs simultaneously, a little red creeping up from her collar this time, "you have no way of knowing. There might be a God, there might not. Near-death experiences and end-of-life experiences point to some kind of afterlife. But you bloody atheists, you have to nail your colours to the mast . . . and we're back to the age of certainty. You decide there's no afterlife, because it doesn't fit your current model. And you don't realise you're as mentally stagnant as a Jehovah's Witness."

"We examine the evidence," I say, disliking the Jehovah's Witness comparison a great deal. "And based on that, we—"

"Just because it's unfalsifiable," she interrupts, her frustration jagged, "doesn't mean it's wrong. It just means science can't disprove it. It's so arrogant to say that something science can't disprove isn't real. You guys think you know it all . . ."

"No we don't," I say, my own gall rising. "But neither are we about to set centuries of progress back by entertaining bullshit straight out of the Dark Ages."

We spar this way until Chastain unleashes a wild shriek, throws her hands in the air and lets them flop limply by her sides. "Should be a hell of a book, this," she says, bringing Bex to mind. "You, flying around the planet, disbelieving everything. Still, I recently read a book about atheism written by a Christian. No reason why a non-believer shouldn't tackle belief."

"Well, thanks for permission," I say, unable to keep the edge off it.

She laughs faintly, before the balcony falls silent and still. All the words we catapulted at each other now dead leaves piled around our ankles. The sea just keeps on coming, constant and clear. It's fair to say Chastain isn't quite the archaic witchy type I'd anticipated. Neither do I dislike her, exactly. She's strong, no question, but flaky multiple models will never earn my respect.

"So," says Sherilyn Chastain, eyeing me with amused contempt. "*Toto.* You coming to this job on Friday or what?"

I tell her I am.

Friday, incidentally, will be the day I see my first ghost.

Alistair Sparks: "There follows a 4 November 2014 email from Sherilyn Chastain to her sister Elizabeth Buckstable, a forensic scientist in New York City . . ."

Hey Lizzy!

Hope all's cool with you, Don and the kiddywinks.

Also hope the attachment on this email doesn't end up in spam. It contains something I need you to look at urgently.

Jack Sparks, this notorious Brit journalist, visited today to interview me. Last thing I needed when I've been so burnt out and stressed after the whole London thing. But he kept asking and asking, and in the end I thought why the hell not.

It was a strange experience. But then, he's a very strange guy. For one thing, he was supposed to be showing me a YouTube video, but then he produced this crazy paperback book too and wanted my opinion on *that* . . .

He smelt of booze from the moment I opened the door. Having read up on him, I knew he was a bit of a druggie— wrote a whole book about doing them, in fact—and you can sure as shit tell there's emotional instability. We had a false start with the interview: just after we settled on the balcony, he said he'd lost something and started scrabbling around for it.

He wouldn't tell me what he'd lost, which was sus. Made me think it was a bag of drugs, which would piss me right off. So I asked him point blank, no shit, and he swore it was nothing to do with drugs.

He got all agitated and searched the balcony, then looked down over the side, thinking he'd dropped it into the garden seven floors down. I know the lady, so we went to search the area. Half an hour later, Jack hadn't found what he was after. He came out of my bathroom with red eyes. At first, I thought he'd got stoned, but there was no smell of weed in there. He'd been crying, for sure. Then he went all sheepish, saying he'd found it in a pocket he'd forgotten about. He blamed his jet lag and said it was just an embarrassing little thing with real sentimental value. I wasn't sure what to make of it and still ain't. Anyway, we finally got down to talking.

Lizzy, this guy *lives online*. First thing he did on the balcony was take a selfie with the sea in the background and stick it on social media. Even during the interview, he had the phone cradled next to the ashtray on his lap. You could see his eyes flicking down every thirty seconds. For a journalist, he's also a really bad listener. Too much diarrhoea of the mouth.

Something about this book he's writing doesn't add up, and it makes me afraid for him. Neg energy hangs around the guy in clouds, whether he believes that stuff or not. He fought his theological corner hard as a lion, but still wanted my opinion on this video he's investigating. If I'm such a crazy bitch, why would he even care?

I did keep quiet about one aspect of this video of his, partly because he'd never believe me. He'd think I was mind-gaming him. And he already seems freaked enough about this priest's book.

So, yeah, the book. Whereas he taped my opinion of the video on the record, he only produced that book when he'd stopped recording.

I'll never forget how he pulled this thing out of his bag.

This bundle of shiny silver foil that smelt like a dead bonfire. He was talking about it all casually, while holding it by one corner like it was bloody radioactive. He smiled and said it was "just this stupid joke" and "probably nothing," but his eyes told a different story. He was scared of how I'd react.

Needless to say, I yelled at him. Told him to stuff it right back in his bag. He was shocked, so I explained that he couldn't just produce random objects in my home. I had no idea what he had there and it might have been cursed as fuck. I told him, "You've gotta be really careful with cursed objects: they leak. That shit's like *tar* and it *wants* to hurt people." He carried on pretending to be all casual, while blatantly soiling his pants. So we left the building and I took him to my lock-up around the corner, explaining that I needed to protect myself under secure lab conditions.

On the way, he told me what was so weird about the book. I won't tell you this info in case it prejudices your own thoughts, but it made me even more pissed off that he'd brought it to my apartment without permission.

When we got inside the lock-up, he looked around and reverted to journo mode, firing more questions. I told him how all the copper mesh on the walls basically turned the place into a huge Faraday cage, but the concept whooshed over his head. Funny, seeing as he's s'posed to be such a science fanboy, and Michael Faraday was even a bloody Pom!

The book, as you'll see in the attached PDF, was *The Devil's Victims* by Father Primo Di Stefano. I didn't so much as touch the thing until Jack had put it in my psychically sealed and cleansed examination box—and even then I used special gloves. My lock-up might already be a sacred space, but there's no harm in added precautions. If this thing is legit, then it's something *new* to me. So I treated it as carefully as I'd treated anything before in my life.

Before leaving the UK, Jack had set fire to the book, burning almost half of the pages before changing his mind and deciding to seek my opinion. I pushed my gloved hands into the box and picked up what remained. Jack watched me like a hawk. Thank God I'm an expert at appearing calm for the sake of clients. Yeah, clients might as well be your kids—you become their barometer of how scared they should be.

Jack got all jittery and was really distracting me, so I ordered him to rack off. Said I'd see him on Friday.

As I write this, I'm back home after a heavy shower combined with a ritual cleansing. I've reached no firm conclusions on the book. I'll examine it again tonight, but in the meantime, *purlease* take a look at the PDF, which contains photographs of the singed front and back covers, plus many surviving pages from inside. I'd really value your thoughts.

I'd like to think someone's playing a trick on the guy with the book, maybe to try and teach him a lesson, but my gut says the thing shouldn't exist. Combined with that video, it all spells bad ju-ju.

I hope there's something I can do to help Jack. At first my current clients, the Lengs, refused to let him tag along on Friday's job, but thankfully they changed their minds when he offered them a bunch of cash.

Perhaps if he sees Fang and me at work, it might broaden his mind. He might realise that the path he walks is narrow and self-destructive. It might not be too late for him to get off it.

Otherwise, if I'm honest? That guy has no fuckin' idea how screwed he is.

Love to everyone,

Sx

CHAPTER FIVE

Sherilyn Chastain and I run side by side along a corridor, limbs pumping.

"The entity knows we've got it," she says. "It'll avoid us for as long as it can, but it can't hide forever."

To our left, through a series of stylised rectangular portholes, the shores of Lantau Island and the other boats in the marina go sadly unadmired. We're far more interested in capturing and dealing with this ghost.

Or at least Chastain is interested in that. I'm interested in watching her and sidekick Fang pretend to catch a pretend thing for their clients' benefit. These fascinating specimens are the very definition of people making a fuss over nothing.

I always knew I'd have to visit a haunted house during the making of this book. That much was a given. I just never expected that house to be on water. And in fairness, neither did I expect this Hong Kong trip to permanently alter my thoughts on the supernatural.

Chastain jabs a finger at the floor. "Last level. Fang: seal up behind us." She darts through a side door, which reveals stairs going down. As I follow, two steps at a time for the hell of it, Fang hangs back to perform the door-sealing ritual, her face set in grim concentration. A Chinese girl barely out of her teens, acting like she's been doing this for a century.

"Jack!" Chastain's urgent alarm rebounds off the walls as I blunder in through the next door down, confused. I arrive in a long corridor that runs the length of the boat's underbelly. Chastain's head moves as if following something along the corridor towards me.

A sudden wind lashes my face and blows my hair up.

Chastain barks out a military order. "Get back!"

What do you do? When you're an atheist, and a mad combat magician tells you to take immediate action to avoid an incoming paranormal entity on a Hong Kong houseboat, what exactly do you do about that?

So it's two hours ago, and the Lengs are not happy with Sherilyn Chastain, not happy at all. They bristle with resentment and mistrust, which is interesting. It also makes having lunch with them an uncomfortable experience.

The Lengs, Chastain, Fang and I are dining al fresco at a Thai restaurant on Lantau Island's Discovery Bay Plaza. It's a gorgeous day, but windy. Every few minutes, a muscular gust forces us all to hold down the tablecloth and our wine glasses. This shared experience may not exactly break the ice, but there's at least a hairline crack. Fang doesn't help one bit. No charm offensive here. She just sits in her black hoodie and her metal-plated New Rock boots, which weigh more than she does. Straight-backed and austere, she spoons soup from bowl to mouth, tracking birds as they fly, moving her eyes not her head. I'm convinced she's one of those creepy new human-replacement droids.

The largest of Hong Kong's outlying islands, Lantau boasts scenery that does its damnedest to distract me from both the conversation and my rancid hangover. It's so much greener than the city. Buildings jut sparsely up from mountains. A quarter-moon sliver of beach provides a focal point for sunbathers, while the vast choppy sea carries a billion bobbing diamonds. You'd never know that in a nearby bay sits a boat that has reportedly put Guiren and Jiao Leng's family through a living hell.

My fresh green curry looks exquisite when I photograph it for my followers, but I'm finding it hard to eat. In my defence, the last three nights have been big. I've barely slept. Last night alone, I ventured off the beaten track in the party district of Wan Chai. On those narrower, darker and more intriguing streets, where market stalls were locked up for the night, I found bars and people dedicated to the pursuit of oblivion. I dimly recall onlookers wolf-whistling as tequila and triple sec were poured straight from the bottles into my mouth, all to a "Gangnam Style" soundtrack. Hence the cold-sweat horrors that cling to me today.

I've also made headway in my video investigation. This week, it became clear that my social media sniffer dogs—the great unwashed Sparks-following public—have no idea where the video came from and are unlikely to find out. It also became clear that the only websites sufficiently enthused to mount an in-depth analysis believe in the supernatural and are therefore not to be trusted. So in the early hours of Wednesday morning, while loaded, I took matters into my own hands. I watched the video again and again, obsessing over each and every pixel.

And on the fifty-sixth viewing, I finally saw something no one else had noticed. Something that only appears when Camera Boy dips his frame to very briefly capture the lower part of a wall.

You never quite see the *whole* thing, but you see enough to determine what it is: a two-pin plug socket embedded in that wall. Two vertical slits with an arch-shaped hole beneath them, the whole thing resembling a tiny shocked face. This means the video was shot in North America. Or Canada. Oh, or Mexico. Which admittedly doesn't narrow things down as much as I'd prefer, but hey, we now have the correct *continent*, ladies and gents.

The net closes in . . .

The Lengs are a naturally attractive couple, upon whom trauma has taken its toll.

The flesh around their eyes is baggier and darker than it should be on people in their mid-thirties, even given the ferocious work ethic of China's professionals, and they're prone to lapse into ten-mile stares. Guiren's left arm rests in a sling and he pops painkillers between his starter and main. Thanks to those charlatans Maddelena and Maria Corvi, I'm vigilant for signs that the Lengs are stooges hired to make Chastain look good. Thus far, the fact that they're disgruntled customers is achieving quite the opposite. So will this afternoon's findings correspond to my existing SPOOKS List? Are the Lengs either lying or being lied to?

They initially refused to have a journalist involved today. Only when they were told my name and realised they'd read and adored all my books did they acquiesce. I'm not allowed to actually quiz them myself, but it's agreed that they will relate their story, to serve the dual purpose of informing me while allowing everybody to agree on the events so far.

Chastain is modelling an unshowy business suit with her hair no less purple but slicked back. Even your modern combat magician has to ape corporate standards to reassure their clients. She speaks Cantonese fluently back at the Lengs, while Fang translates for my benefit, ignoring all requests for repetition or clarification. Truth be told, Fang doesn't like me. I've tried bonding with her over rock music, but she only likes Scandinavian black metal nonsense. Bands with spiky, incomprehensible logos.

In September, Guiren and Jiao "got tired of paying rent" (oh, the poor lambs) and decided to have their own houseboat built. Despite high operating costs and the occasional typhoon, houseboat-living is perfectly viable and popular in Hong Kong, with many communities clustered in bays around the region. Of course, it's especially viable when you're minted.

The couple moved in on 30 September, which they claim was an auspicious date for a big move. If you didn't know better, you'd swear all that astrology talk was meaningless twaddle. The Lengs' dream of "calm and centred living," to ease the stress of their work as finance directors for one of Hong Kong's biggest media companies, quickly became a nightmare once they took residence.

On the third night, Guiren awoke to hear distant footsteps. "It was like someone pacing about, endlessly," he says. "I didn't wake Jiao or the children: I just got up, grabbed a torch as a weapon and crept in the direction of the sound. I followed the footsteps up a level to the captain's bridge, which we use as a living space, because the boat is only ever moved when something needs to be repaired.

"The footsteps stopped when I entered. There were no other sounds, apart from the wind and water outside. The first things I noticed were my and Jiao's computer screens, which sit side by side at the front. They were both on, even though we'd turned them off. The browsers were open and each showed full-screen videos of blazing fire."

Gripping his torch so tight that he cracked the casing, Guiren searched the boat from bow to stern, finding nothing and no one. Assuming some freak had broken in, he had the locks changed, telling Jiao they were faulty. I've no idea why he lied to his wife. The woman is so clearly ruthless that I'd set her on an intruder in a heartbeat.

Yet Guiren couldn't keep his secret for long. The night after he switched those locks, the footsteps returned, closer to the bedroom. This time, they woke Jiao and five-year-old Bo, the youngest of their three daughters. Guiren locked his family in one bedroom, then mounted another search.

"That night," he says, "I saw a face in the fire on the monitor screens. A silhouetted face twisted into a silent scream. It kept moving from one monitor to the other, as if tormented."

That's when the kids started screaming. According to Jiao, they were being attacked by an invisible force. She claims she tried to protect them, "but how do you fight thin air?"

"The kids all ended up with bruises and scrapes," says Guiren. "At the time, I stupidly thought my family had suffered hysteria in that locked room, scaring themselves, bumping into each other. Still, I moved them to an apartment in the city and stayed on the boat by myself. I was determined to find out what was going on."

Guiren became fixated on the idea of the intruder's behaviour escalating to kidnappings and ransom demands. He even assigned a bodyguard to live in his family's apartment. Then, one night, on the boat, something happened that led him to call Sherilyn Chastain.

"The footsteps came back, but now they were harder, faster. Whoever this was, they were running around the boat. Running like crazy. The boat even shook, like they were careering into the walls. I heard things fall and break."

That night, Guiren was armed with more than a torch. He declines to specify the exact nature of the weapon due to restrictive national laws, but you can imagine. "I edged along a corridor on the starboard side. The floor was covered in broken glass, because our family portrait had been ripped from the wall and hurled to the ground. Further along the corridor, the monitors were glowing again on the bridge. Something came along that corridor at me fast, with footsteps to match. The best way I can describe it is a cloud of smoke in mid-air. A fat smoke cloud, thrashing about. I knew then that we were dealing with something . . . elemental. Suddenly it was all around me. This whirlwind: screaming, spinning me, hurling me against walls. I was so scared. I managed to get away, then ran and jumped over the side of the boat into the marina. The shock of the cold water at four a.m. almost killed me. I don't know whether it was the spirit's attack or the fall, but I ended up with this arm broken in three places."

It's a compelling story, but what's the reality here? If you're anything like me, you may sense a different and disturbing tale bubbling beneath. But when one of Guiren's work colleagues discreetly pointed him in Sherilyn Chastain's direction, the Aussie formed her own narrative.

Two weeks back, Chastain and Fang visited to assess the boat. Chastain did indeed detect a presence on board, then tried to deal with it the following day. They left satisfied their work was done, but this was seemingly not the case.

Five nights ago, those restless nocturnal feet made a big comeback. The Lengs' kids had already fallen ill with some grim vomiting bug, and Jiao suffered splitting headaches. When a dismayed Guiren investigated new footsteps, once again in the middle of the night, those bridge monitors again showed the screaming face in fire, jerking from one to the other. And once again while he wasn't present, the spirit attacked the kids, this time throwing Bo against a wall and giving her concussion. As the family fled the boat, middle daughter Mei-Hua fell screaming into the water, narrowly missing one of the poles supporting the jetty. Guiren jumped in and managed to save her, but the experience left everyone "very badly shaken" and living back at the apartment.

"It's not unusual," says Chastain of the ghost's return, as we all walk from the plaza, following the curve of the beach towards the marina. As much as she feigns nonchalance, this affair has left its mark on her too. By the end of lunch, she had succeeded in convincing the Lengs (a) not to sue her; and (b) that she fully intended to finish the job she'd begun, at no extra cost to them, but it was a close call.

"Nine times out of ten, the first thing I try and do is reason with the spirit," she explains. "And nine times out of ten that works. But sometimes you think you've reached an under-standing, when you actually haven't."

The misunderstanding, as Chastain sees it, was that she thought the entity had agreed to move on to the afterlife, when actually it had other ideas. Of course, my own view of the main misunderstanding here is that the entity never existed in the first place.

With typically wishy-washy vagueness, Chastain sees the entity as "possibly trapped here on earth, for some reason. I haven't been able to confirm, in my mind, whether it's a human spirit or a demon."

"Well, how could you," I jibe, "with all these multiple models flying about?"

She's clearly stressed out of her mind, because my comment earns me a glare instead of a snappy comeback. "Perhaps it only thinks it's trapped here. Either way, it has some kind of emotional attachment to this life. Our goal is to move it on."

Her face tightens when I ask what she'll do if it refuses to play ball this time. "Let's cross that bridge . . ." she says, trailing off and changing the subject. Chastain really is splendidly melodramatic good value.

The wind whips at Sherilyn Chastain as she stands on the front deck of the Lengs' boat. She's deep in concentration, arms stretched out as though practising t'ai chi.

This vessel, whose name translates as *The Good Life*, is a jaw-dropper. One hundred and twenty sleek feet of fibreglass. The most beautiful white bullet you ever saw. I can barely bring myself to glance at the hundreds of inferior vessels lined up all around—it would be too much of an anticlimax.

Fang tells the Lengs what Chastain's doing (they're blasé, having seen it all before), then explains for my benefit that the magician is "psychically sealing the whole boat's exterior." I nod with all the respect I can muster.

My phone vibrates. I hit "Reject" on the latest call from Astral Way, then ask Fang if she's actually magical herself. "I have certain abilities that some might describe as magical. These include remote viewing, which allows me to see a place from far away. After our first visit, I used this power to scan the boat and check we had done everything we needed to do."

"So you were wrong, eh?" I say, with a winning smile.

Fang does not smile back.

Inside the boat, it's time to bust some serious ghost. Fang stays on the bridge with the Lengs, to keep them appraised of developments (she and Chastain wear Bluetooth headsets) and protect them should the ghost turn nasty again. I jog off along that corridor with Chastain, noting that the family portrait has been reframed and rehung. Beside me, the magician brandishes an aerosol can, which she briskly describes as containing "High John the Conqueror Root. Perfect for casting fast barrier spells."

"Where'd you get that stuff?"

"Over the counter."

As we prowl the boat, I'll admit to feeling a buzz, if only because it reminds me of when my brother and I would hunt for ghosts in the woods behind our Suffolk home, back when we liked each other. We'd do it in daylight, because we weren't allowed out at night. Even as a kid, though, I thought of ghosts as a fun idea rather than something to be afraid of. One day, Alistair locked me in a pitch-black room in the middle of the house. I just stood silently in the darkness, laughing to myself, until he let me out looking disappointed.[1] Nowadays, my brother won't even return my emails. I've been trying to get hold of him all week, to ask if I can speak to a friend of his about analysing the video, but no response. Sad, very sad.

Holding her aerosol above her head, Chastain announces that we're getting close. She claims to hear footsteps, but I

---

1 This last sentence is untrue, as will become apparent later. —*Alistair*

only hear our own. I'm reminded of those interactive scary theatre productions, installed in empty multi-storey car parks or warehouses. You're led around at high speed by a bad actor pretending to be a marine sergeant or something, only to run into a gang of unconvincing aliens or zombies. It's a heady brew of artifice and embarrassment.

This place resembles a spotless show home—or show boat, if you will. We pass through a dining area and a richly equipped galley-style kitchen. I glimpse lavish bedrooms and a small home cinema. This boat is surely the least scary place on earth, although Chastain admirably attacks it with the same vigour she might devote to a moonlit gothic mansion on a hill.

"There's no way out," she tells the air. "I'm sorry, but it's time to go. Let's not make this harder than it needs to be, eh?"

She reminds me of a police negotiator trying to talk a pissed-up teen down from a supermarket roof. And I really feel that, as she speaks, she imagines every single word being typed straight into the pages of my book. Sherilyn Chastain, the caring combat mage. Of course, she only accepts those many thousands of Hong Kong dollars to cover her *expenses*, cobber.

Chastain halts in one of the boat's many leisure rooms. Sofa, two beanbag chairs, nothing else. Clean white walls. Great feng shui. She points at one high corner. "Feel that?"

I make a show of trying to decide, then wonder what the hell I'm doing.

"A fuck-load of neg energy," she explains. "Feel the temperature drop?"

Glancing over my shoulder, I spy a wide-open oblong porthole, which ushers in a briny breeze. "Yep," I say, with a sigh.

"Did you hear what I said?" she tells the corner ghost. "You've run out of time. There's no need to stay in this world."

As she awaits a response, there's no sound besides water lapping and glopping against the boat's hull. Here's how this works: Chastain gets to hear this ghost's reply but I don't. Because she has The Gift and I don't. That is the founding principle upon which an entire parasitic empire of faith healers, mediums and mages has been built. *We are special, you can't do this by yourself, you need us.*

"I do want to help you," Chastain declares. "But you can't stay here."

I'm basically listening to one side of a phone conversation. Another pause for the response.

"Of course you have a choice," she protests. "Why wouldn't you have a—No, wait!" She jerks into action as the spook seemingly makes a break. "Come back."

And we're running again, back the way we came. Blurred doorways and portholes flash by. Chastain yells for Fang to leave the Lengs and cut off the ghost as it tries to return to the bridge.

Further high-octane hysterics ensue from people who, whether by accident or design, never matured beyond my and Alistair's hijinks in the Suffolk woods. Chastain corners the ghost and demands that it see reason; the ghost refuses and flees again. Much time and aerosol spray is wasted, leaving the ozone layer in shreds.

Chastain and Fang cast their "barrier spells" on every doorway we pass through. The entity starts to run out of options, a badger in a collapsing sett, until we pursue it down to the ship's lowest level.

That's where Chastain calls out, "Jack!" as I blunder into that long corridor, confused. She stares at something that appears to head right for me, and a sudden gust of wind messes me about.

"Get back!" she orders.

So what *do* you do?

As you might have guessed, I have no intention of following her order.

Something severs the breath in my windpipe and makes me stagger backwards.

My vision blurs.

I feel squirming, bony flesh on the back of my neck.

These are Fang's fingers. She's grabbed the back of my shirt collar and heaved me towards her. To my mind, she did this harder than necessary. She doesn't even deign to make eye contact as we prise ourselves from each other, while the alleged ghost sails by.

"Phew!" I rasp, straightening my collar. "*Close call*. How can I ever repay—"

But Fang and Chastain are off on their heels again, disappearing around a corner. I hang back and lean against a wall, slick with sweat from all the running.

I sidle into a wide, sparkling bathroom and slam two big handfuls of cold water into my face, then use a luxuriously fluffy towel to dry off. In a spotlit mirror, I meet the gaze of a sleep-deprived, vitamin-poor and yet devilishly handsome rogue.

But wait. There's something else.

Something in the background, behind me, *moving*.

My own face blurs in the glass as I shift focus to see what it is.

Ball of smoke. It's Guiren's big ball of smoke. Those are my very first, wholly irrational thoughts.

The thing hangs in mid-air on the other side of this window-less space, beside the bathtub. No bigger than a helium fairground balloon, it resembles a pregnant grey ball (*smoke cloud, smoke cloud*, whispers the stupid voice in my head), curly around the edges. Its density prevents you from seeing through it to the tiled wall beyond. Most disquietingly of all, the thing pulses and quivers. A cartoon pressure cooker.

Let me tell you: Theroux would shit himself.

I blink, rather a lot.

The cloud darkens as if injected with ink and floats towards me. In my head, Guiren Leng jabbers crap: "Suddenly it was all around me. This whirlwind: screaming, spinning me, hurling me against walls . . ."

Gripped by the urge to see this thing directly, I tear my eyes from the mirror and spin around.

I'm alone in the bathroom.

I laugh to myself and realise there must have been something stuck on the mirror—perhaps some bloody shaving foam. Yet this is not the case. I scan the room's reflection carefully, as if expecting the cloud to reappear. But there's nothing.

Outside in the corridor, feeling silly, I hear Chastain's harsh tones before I see her.

"Jack? Jack? Where are ya?"

She skids around the corner, beetroot-purple face matching the hair, and sees me standing with my back to the bathroom door. She picks up on my body language, as Fang appears beside her. "Everything all right?"

A simple yes isn't good enough for her, so she lays the squint scan on me. "Did you see something in there?"

I'm still processing the answer to that. The last person I

want to discuss it with is a loon with a spray can full of herbs.

"Is it in there?" barks Fang. Before I can answer, she tells Chastain, "It's in there," and they bustle me aside to gain entry.

"In or out, Jack?" says Chastain, pausing in the open doorway. "Decide!"

And I'm back in the bathroom. Fang spray-seals the door (how does that work, anyway, seeing as spooks can move through walls?) before she and Chastain study the room, hunched, a pair of tag-team wrestlers waiting for the bell. The doofus in me can't help glancing inquisitively in the mirror, where I see only the three of us.

"So have you actually heard words from this thing?" I ask.

"You get . . . a strong sense of . . . emotion, intent, need," says Chastain distractedly. "It's like . . . someone speaking to you . . . through double-glazed windows."

"You actually hear it, with your ears?"

"You hear it with your *mind*, Toto, provided you're open to it." She signals to Fang and gestures solemnly towards the bath.

"Got you," Chastain tells a patch of air over the tub. "Sorry, mate." Fang produces a bright-red glass bottle. With a bulbous test-tube-style cork for a stopper, it looks like it was plucked straight from Shezza's shelves at home. I learn afterwards that the bottle contains two small chips of Scottish obsidian, some salt and various herbs and spices. Chastain's staunch secrecy regarding the exact nature of these latter items would do Colonel Sanders proud.

Fang hands the bottle to Chastain, who uncorks it and presents it to the bathtub. "In you go," she commands, "till we work out what to do with you."

We all stare over the tub.

A groan from the boat. A gentle lurch.

"Come on," says Chastain. "Don't make me break out the imprisonment ritual. *You could have killed a child.*" She thrusts the bottle again. "In."

"Is it saying anything back?" I whisper. "Are you sensing its emotion, intent and stuff?"

She glances my way and darkens. "Give it a rest, Jack. Won't work down here anyway."

I try to refresh social media one more time, then shove the phone back in my pocket. Chastain begins the ritual, intoning dark and portentous words in Latin. After just a few verses, she nods triumphantly, again seeming to track some invisible entity on the move. I hear a couple of footsteps, then realise it must have been Fang. I catch myself picturing that amorphous cloud being vacuumed inside the bottle. *Connections, connections, oh so seductive.*

Chastain squashes the cork back into the glass neck. "Job done," she says quietly. She and Fang don't exchange high-fives. I very much doubt Fang's much of a high-fiver. Instead, an ominous gloom descends.

"So, this is a good result, isn't it?" I offer, brightly.

Chastain speaks as though addressing a funeral crowd. "There's always mixed feelings, Jack, when an entity has to be captured like this. We can talk more up top." She nods at Fang, then gazes up through the ceiling. "Let's give 'em the good news."

Sherilyn Chastain slams her red spirit bottle on the table in front of me, with a face full of thunder. "All right, you arrogant prick, I've had enough. Let's see how certain you really are."

It's fair to say our wrap-up interview hasn't gone well.

So, a brief rewind. After the Lengs have been assured their ghost is finally leaving in a bottle with the old witch, they call off the lawyers and head off to live happily ever after on the marina. Shezza and I agree to conduct a final interview to discuss all that's happened. Fang peels away into the bustling marina crowds without so much as a goodbye, although I didn't offer one either.

We select a beach bar for the interview: the delightful Ooh La La. This time, she insists on placing her own digital recorder alongside mine. Such paranoia is fine by me: I've nothing to hide. Our first drinks go down quickly—too quickly. We're steeling ourselves for an ideological antler clash.

I tell Chastain about my SPOOKS List. I tell her she has done nothing to persuade me to add a third hypothesis. Her interactions with ghosts are all too convenient. Only she can hear the dead, sense where they are . . . Either the Lengs are lying and she's naïve, or she's a glorified confidence trickster, lying to the Lengs. Or both sides are lying to each other in an unspoken, mutually beneficial orgy of mistruth. For what it's worth, at least I haven't had that *Truman Show* feeling of watching a co-ordinated theatrical performance.

Chastain stops listening on "confidence trickster." Little muscles pulse on either side of her jaw.

"Your mind's been shut all along," she spits, tapping one side of her head hard for emphasis. "You're such an egotist and you don't even know it."

"I get that a lot," I tell her. "Usually from Brits, who tend to hate confidence. I would've thought better of an Aussie. Especially a French one."

"Oh, you think you're just confident?" she fires back. "Nah. Nah, mate. I've read your so-called journalism. Do you have any idea how many times you use 'me,' 'myself' and 'I'? Not just in your writing either."

I try and steer her back to the subject of her work as opposed to mine, to no avail.

"Heard of Aleister Crowley?" she demands. As I nod vaguely, she barges on: "Now *there* was a guy who knew the power of ego. He ran an experiment where he and others cut themselves with straight razors every time they said 'I.'"

She beckons a waiter, orders a drink for herself only, then screws her gaze back into me. "Why don't you give Crowley's idea a go, Jack?"

"What's so wrong with 'I'? What's wrong with having a personality and being opinionated? And by the way: wasn't Crowley all *about* ego and indulgence? He was the Great Beast, right? Why would he even do an experiment like that?"

"Crowley," she says, "was intelligent enough to try and hack his own monstrous ego. He was all about balance. The most *sensible people*," she adds pointedly, "are all about balance."

Growing bored, I ask her, "Have you ever actually seen a ghost?"

"Have *you*, Jack?"

I consider pointing out that I asked first. Instead, being an adult, I say, "Look, I did *think* I glimpsed something in that bathroom mirror on the boat, but I'm very tired."

She glows with vindication. "Anything like a ball of smoke, was it?"

"Your turn to answer the question."

Behind Chastain, the sun is setting on both Lantau Island and our tattered relationship. "It's all about the *seeing* with you, Jack. The scientist demands evidence, or it can't possibly exist.

And even if evidence *does* pop up? Hey, let's bury it. Doesn't fit what we wanted."

"That'll be a no, then. You've never seen an actual ghost."

"Oh, get a dog up ya."

The word "dog" comes out as "dawg." Charming. "I've been thinking about something you said yesterday," I tell her. "All that Robert Anton Watkins stuff . . ."

Her nostrils flare. "*Wilson.* Robert Anton *Wilson.*"

"So you're into this flim-flam about concepts being temporary models, and yet you present yourself as a combat magician. The Lengs, and anyone else with more money than sense, pay you to be that person. And yet you don't even fully believe in ghosts yourself."

"All that matters is my client being content with my work," she says defensively. "If I banish or even destroy a negative presence in their home, am I really dealing with a dead person? Gotta tell you, I have no idea. A ghost is a useful model, which *fits* sometimes. And when you meet that model, you treat it with the respect it deserves."

I sigh. "As if it really is a dead person? Just in case?"

"Exactly that. And the same should go for this video of yours. Your head is way too black and white. Start thinking in greys, Jack. Trust me, you're gonna need 'em. And read my lips: I *do* believe in hauntings. But the *cause* of a haunting? That's a different matter. Most of 'em feel like emotional events imprinted on the energy of certain spaces."

"Then why was this ghost on a new-build boat? Makes no sense."

"Like I said, I felt it was stuck there for some reason. Maybe my psychic seal wasn't even needed."

"How can you say 'psychic seal' with a straight face?"

"How can you keep a straight face while saying science knows everything? You're not even a normal atheist, mate, you're a weirdo."

Oh Christ, not the gaps in science's knowledge again. The prospect of us spiralling back into that debate propels me in for the kill. "Does no part of you feel bad that, by working for the Lengs, you may have helped one or both of them cover up child abuse?"

Chastain may have just swallowed a wasp. "*What?*"

"Oh come on," I say. "The story's ridiculous: a ball of smoke that makes footsteps? Did it not strike you as strange that the Leng kids only got knocked about when they were with Jiao?"

She tries to speak, but can't stop me. I am Hercule Poirot with my fingers linked behind my back, circling a room full of suspects. "Guiren couldn't face reality. His conscious mind thought he was hiring a live-in bodyguard for that temp apartment in case someone tried to kidnap his family, but *really* it was to keep an eye on his stressed-out, slap-happy wife. Then he became so set on a supernatural explanation that he mistook a bit of shore mist for a violent ghost, or just made up this story about the spook attacking him. He even broke his own arm—anything rather than contemplate his wife abusing their daughters. And then he hired *you*, the cherry on the cake. The mother of delusion, who happily went along with it. Sucking all that hideous, unpalatable truth into your world of fairy-tale fluff."

Chastain stares at me in disbelief. "So tell me, Sherilyn," I conclude. "What do you really care about: those kids, or cold, hard cash? Because it can't be both."

Wham, bam, fuck you ma'am.

She bares her teeth. "How fuckin' dare you. I would *never*

leave kids high and dry, if I thought . . ." Her eyes glisten and she firmly reins herself in, voice brittle. "You're unbelievable, y'know that? Do you realise you didn't say 'maybe' once during that whole bullshit version of events? Just said it like it was fact. Certainty. Stupid, blind *certainty*."

She pulls her so-called spirit bottle from her bag and slams it down on the table between us.

"All right, you arrogant prick, I've had enough. Let's see how certain you really are. This is by far my least favourite part of my job. Because I now have the burden of deciding whether to keep this thing imprisoned or to destroy it."

"Eh?" I say. "How can you destroy a spirit, or a demon, or whichever model it fits today? It's already dead, right?"

"Anything that's made from energy can be torn apart. So, Big Man. Here's my challenge to you. You get to choose its fate. If you're so very *certain* I'm full of shit, then just say the word." She nods at the sea. "I'll wash the bottle's contents in salt water and destroy the spirit. On the other hand, if you're not a hundred per cent sure, then spare its life and I'll try to help it move on."

She leans back in her chair, arms folded, awaiting my reaction.

I look at the bottle.

At its asymmetrical hand-made curves.

At the rough texture of the red glass. The assorted bits and bobs inside.

I see a face: just my own reflection distorted by the glass. No sign of any smoke cloud.

"Last chance," I say, holding steady eye contact with Chastain. "Have you ever *seen an actual ghost*?"

"I can't *answer* that. The things I've seen could be *labelled*—"

I point at the bottle. "Kill it."

She's astonished as I stand to leave. This woman truly expected me to give credence to her make-believe world.

"Jack, I'm sorry I lost my temper, okay?" she blurts, suddenly desperate now that her precious allotted time in my book has come to an end. "Listen, there's something you should know about that video. Something about the words." But there's nothing I need to know about that video—at least not from Sherilyn Chastain.

Trudging off along the sand, I steal one last look back. There's Chastain in the water, head bowed, soaking those suit trousers up to the knees. She dunks her uncorked spirit bottle under the surface. A burdened mother drowning kittens.

A pathetic sight.

I've done as social media suggested. Toto visited the Wicked Witch of the East. But it's time to move on.

I don't know if you've ever woken up and felt watched.

It's not an experience I can recommend.

After a day of tearing around a houseboat with two madheads, followed by a boozy beach barney, even a hardened party warrior needs a nap. As the afternoon sky begins to bruise, I take the metro system back to Hong Kong Island, wanting my hotel bed. To keep myself awake, I figure out this afternoon's bathroom cloud incident to my satisfaction. It was purely and simply the last hurrah of Tuesday night's mushrooms. Yes, yes, I had a Hong Kong drug blip, for one night only. No big deal.

Guiren's story seeded the smoke cloud image in my head, which my body's final vestiges of psychotropic juice distorted reality in order to create. For a second or two. In a mirror.

Crucially, a *mirror* as opposed to reality. The SPOOKS List need not even be troubled by this ripple in the Matrix.

When I finally reach the fortieth floor of the Jade Star Hotel, I'm fit to drop. Wandering through the suite, I shrug off my jacket and stumble out of my jeans, chuckling at the memory of Sherilyn Chastain weeping over a bottle of seawater. Since the whole suite measures 850 square feet and I've barely been here during my stay, I hit a couple of dead ends before finally locating the bedroom. Golden twilight paints the walls as I crash face first on to the plush king-size bed, conscious-ness flooding happily out of me.

I don't usually remember dreams. So who can say whether some nightmare, sunk forever in the mind's murky waters, informs my mood when I'm woken by someone clearing their throat.

My fogbound brain tries to make sense of that noise. Did I make it myself, or was it someone in the dream?

I only consider a third possibility when the feeling of being watched beds itself in.

As much as I don't believe in some cat-like sixth sense of feeling someone's eyes on you, that's the sensation I get. Strong enough to make me roll on to my back, pull myself up to lean against the headboard, then scan my surroundings.

No one's in this bedroom but me. Those wardrobe doors are shut tight. The twilight is long dead, the walls slathered with blacks, dull greys, electric yellows and an isolated patch of rainbow light cast by a neighbouring tower.

If I really did have a nightmare, it left an unusually strong impression on me. I feel nervous, which I could well ascribe to that terrible moment of the day when last night's alcohol wheedles its way out of your system. Silly as it sounds, the rainbow light comforts me as I run a hand over my face and knuckle the sand from the corners of my eyes. I try to get my head together but find only fuzz. The bedside clock's big red retro LED numbers testify that it's two minutes to midnight.

Here comes that sound again. And this time, I know it's not me.

Someone clears their throat, as if I've somehow fallen asleep in *their* suite.

When I jerk my head in the direction of the sound, it leads my focus out through the open bedroom door, along a short corridor and into the lounge.

Through there, in that big room—maybe twenty strides away—there are no rainbows. All is black. Those heavy curtains must be fully drawn.

I sit up, adrenalin dripping into my system, and gaze along that corridor into the lounge. I consider that, in my exhausted state, I may have left the suite's door open. Could a maid have come in? Did I miss her knock? And is midnight any kind of time for housekeeping?

"Hello?" I say, managing to slur even this word.

My suite has a European-style energy-saving system. These overhead lights won't work until I stick my room's keycard into a slot. As you'd expect, the slot is on the far side of the suite by the entrance door, and the keycard's in my jeans, also somewhere over there. Useless.

As my eyes adjust, the darkness of the living room resolves itself into recognisable shapes.

The shape of a dining table.

The shape of a chair at that table.

The shape of a wide sofa.

The shape of someone sitting on that sofa.

Yeah, someone's there all right. I can see their head, their shoulders. Long hair?

As I push myself up off the bed, the silhouette on the sofa becomes an animated ink swirl, also rising to its feet. For one fleeting moment, I wonder if I'm gazing dumbly into a full-length mirror.

My mind's eye replays the moment when Maria Corvi sprang unnaturally up from the church floor. But this can't possibly be Maria Corvi. Nonetheless, this is either a youth or a short adult.

I grab my battered Zippo from the bedside table, flip the cap and spark the wheel. The flame casts light over my end of the connecting corridor, but can't even scratch the living room.

Whoever's through there, they're not moving a muscle. They're taut as a spider, waiting for my next move. Not wishing to disappoint them, I stride towards the living room. The Olympic flame of my Zippo rides high, shooting light up the walls. My own shadow makes me jump when it appears beside me, bearing testimony to just how tired and bewildered I am.

I'm halfway along the corridor when my Zippo light penetrates the lounge.

I glimpse a familiar teenage face, framed with long dark hair.

No way. No fucking way . . .

Before you ask: at no point do I consider that I might be dreaming. Only simpletons actually need to pinch themselves in real life.

Every step brings me closer, my halo of light and truth revealing more and more. The intruder's face, still cloaked in black.

I whip my head to and fro: a dog coming in from the rain.

Determined to finally shake off sleep's residual crap. That's when I fumble the Zippo. It falls to the ground and snaps shut, plunging everything into impenetrable gloom.

I drop to my haunches and feel quickly around over likely areas. My fingers plough deep furrows in the carpet, finding nothing.

"Maria?" I say, despite myself.

No reply.

Cold air licks the back of my neck.

I think of *The Good Life*, with its open porthole. A maid must've left a window open in here.

My left hand brushes cool, smooth metal. I seize the Zippo and flip it back open.

Ignition. Flame. Light.

The intruder is now standing so close to me that I almost set fire to her smock.

Her blue smock. The one she wears for work on the farm.

I scramble back a couple of feet, then the ligaments crackle in my legs as I rise.

The Zippo light flickers its way up the intruder's body.

I recoil and cry out. Can't be helped: it's an animal reflex.

Maria Corvi's grin is ugly, her face red and inflamed. Those feverishly yellow eyes burn into me, the pupils silver stars, carrying the same shine they had in the church. *I know something you don't know.*

I stare at her, throat dry. The air feels thick, like oil . . . or am I imagining that?

Maria raises her arms and assumes a Jesus Christ pose.

"Enjoy," she whispers, her breath rancid.

Then she topples backwards, down, out of the light, her body rigid as wood.

I don't hear her strike the carpet. When I jerk the Zippo down to illuminate the spot where she would've-should've landed, I see nothing and no one.

I move the Zippo all around, exposing the whole carpet. Nothing and no one.

I'm shaking. With anger. Rage, even.

How dare the Catholic Church try to terrorise me?

My blood boils as I snatch a phone from a wall cradle. I tell some front-desk goon that an intruder's been in my room. No, I don't need anyone sent up from security, but I do need them to keep an eye open downstairs for a thirteen-year-old Italian girl dressed as a farm labourer trying to sneak out. Yes, keep me informed, cheers, bye.

I run through the dark suite, Zippo flame dancing, until I reach the entrance door.

It's not only shut, but locked and latched on the inside.

No way could the actress Maria Corvi have got out.

I fish the keycard out of my discarded jeans and jam it down into the wall box. The whole suite floods with light, glorious light.

"Let's see how fucking scary you are now," I babble. The plan must have been for me to run petrified from the room, allowing Corvi to make her escape. Well, that ain't going to happen.

I search all 850 square feet in a methodical frenzy. Every inch of every cupboard, every walk-in wardrobe, both bathrooms. Every plush curtain gets yanked up to reveal the wall behind.

No sign of Maria Corvi anywhere.

As I check to see if there's a connecting door between my suite and an adjoining one—which there is not—the word "connecting" jams inside my mental filters.

I sink into a chair that overlooks the yawning nightscape. I empty two small whisky bottles into a glass. This crazy rush badly needs dampening.

Connections, connections. How seductive they can be.

The scenario of a targeted Catholic Church set-up slowly loses viability. Talk about extreme measures. Shipping an actress to Hong Kong? Breaking into my suite to stage this weird little scene? What would be the goal? Me stating in these pages that I'd been a fool to disbelieve what I saw in the wilds of Italy? Besides: Maria Corvi seemed to vanish as a ghost would, as opposed to a possessed teenager. Unless I've missed breaking news, the girl's still alive. So tonight's scene doesn't even match the Italian scenario.

I revisit the idea that Maria Corvi is genuinely disturbed and not part of the Catholic propaganda show. Maybe she came out here of her own free will. This is *vaguely* possible. In a public post two nights ago, I mentioned the hotel's name while photographing my dinner in its revolving top-floor restaurant.

But how did she get out of this locked suite? Perhaps Hercule Poirot might have an answer, but I don't, so this Mad Maria theory crumbles too.

My head spins. I've actually become one of *those* people who's seen something that on the face of it seems supernatural.

I need to analyse myself. I need to throw SPOOKS at this situation. So I grab my laptop and edit the list.

THE SPOOKS LIST (Sparks' Permanently Ongoing Overview of Kooky Shit)

People claim to have witnessed supernatural phenomena for the following reasons:

(1) They're trying to deceive others (*I know I'm not lying*)
(2) They've been deceived by others (*By Catholic Church? Unlikely*)
(3) They have deceived themselves (*?????*)

It hurts me to write a third entry on the list. Physically hurts me.

What the hell to write in that last set of brackets? A steadily blinking cursor awaits my verdict as whisky ravages my gullet.

Scientific logic has backed me into a corner I thought I could avoid.

If someone claims to have seen a ghost and they're not lying, or being lied to by others, then they must have somehow lied to themselves.

Hey. Hear that grinding noise? Those are the tectonic plates of belief, shifting under my feet.

The latest email salvo arrives from Astral Way. I've ignored his messages for days now, because the man's become aggressive, bordering on abusive. But tonight I think "What the hell" and open this one.

Astral tells me that the Hollywood Paranormals' experiment will begin in six days, and that I'm "seriously a damn FOOL for missing out on covering it, or even potentially becoming a part of it." You sense smoke rising from his keyboard as he furiously types, "This will be THE most prestigious twenty-first-century investigation into the human mind's ability to conjure up a ghost."

The human mind's ability to conjure up a ghost.

If I believed in fate . . .

Astral goes on: "Furthermore, IF you agree to join us for

this experiment and give it the full exposure it warrants, we will grant you some VERY valuable information regarding your supernatural YouTube video. After conducting intensive studies, we have concluded WHERE in the world it was shot, narrowing it down to an area of less than FIVE SQUARE MILES."

I was already sold, but now I'm solder. My fingers are a blur.

"Hi, Astral. Calm down, mate. I'm coming."

Alistair Sparks: "There follows a transcript of a conversation recorded by Sherilyn Chastain on 7 November 2014. She has claimed the conversation took place with Jack at Lantau Island's Ooh La La bar."

(Beach waves and bar chatter in the background throughout.)

SHERILYN: So, Big Man. Here's my challenge to you. You get to choose its fate. If you're so very *certain* I'm full of shit, then just say the word. I'll wash the bottle's contents in salt water and destroy the spirit. On the other hand, if you're not a hundred per cent sure, then spare its life and I'll try to help it move on.

(Long pause.)

JACK: Last chance. Have you ever *seen an actual ghost*?

SHERILYN: I can't *answer* that. The things I've seen could be *labelled*—

JACK: Kill it.

SHERILYN: Jack, listen, don't do this. Sit down. I'm sorry I lost my temper, okay? It's just, you're not being honest, and—"

JACK: Just kill it, Sherilyn.

SHERILYN: Jack, there's something you should know about that video. Something about the words. (Pause.) And hey, don't you want my verdict on the *book*?

JACK (Walking away): I was being stupid, the other day. Just jet lag, that's all. Get rid of the book too. Burn the rest of it yourself, with fucking sage or something.

SHERILYN (Raising voice): That book really *is* from the future. (Pause.) Jack, did you hear me? The book's from the future and it does mention your death. (Pause.) Jack! Run all you like, but it's still true. (Long pause. Sherilyn sighs. The sound of a bottle being dragged along a table.

Sherilyn's voice lowers to a mutter.) Come on then, mate. I'm so sorry. Let's get you in the water.

CHAPTER SIX-SIX-SIX

(Eleanor: Very important note—please delete any and ALL earlier mentions in this manuscript of the words "Adramelech," "Mephistopheles" and "Baphomet" on the soundtrack of the YouTube ghost video. Afterwards, check and recheck to make sure that NO mention of these words remains.)

I jerk upright on the sunlounger, the moment I realise Bex is crying.

My ringing phone woke me half blind and glistening beside a kidney-shaped swimming pool. This was no great surprise, as it's where I fell asleep after lunch and the kind of Bloody Marys that might kill a lesser man. Less anticipated was the book-shaped hole in my new tan, thanks to *Conjuring Harold: An Exploration of Psychokinesis* being splayed across my pecs. During the first twenty-four hours of my stay here at West Hollywood's Sunset Castle Hotel, I've absorbed half of this account of the seventies experiment that the Hollywood Paranormals plan to emulate. Can't be bothered to read more. Books were way too long back then.

Professor Stanley H. Spence wrote this thing. He was one of the eight Toronto parapsychology researchers who conducted the Harold Experiment back in the day. Semi-impressively, Spence will be flying down to join us for the experiment, acting as "impartial observer and advisor," according to one of Astral's overexcited emails.

When the phone wakes me, it's 5:21 p.m. PST on 11 November. Onscreen beneath the incoming number, the words "BEX MOB," together with a still photograph of a laughing, drunken redhead in Brighton's Bar Revenge, tell me it's Bex calling, from eight hours ahead of me, GMT. Time travel.

Funnily enough, when I answer, she sounds drunk and might actually *be* in Bar Revenge. Yes, I'm pretty sure that's an untalented karaoke gentleman in the background, struggling to match the frenetic pace of Beyoncé's "Crazy In Love."

And at first, I think Bex is laughing.

"Why do I do it? Why do I fucking do it? Tell me!"

"What's going on?"

More sobbing. "I'm such an idiot," she says. "Crazy In Love" becomes muffled, reduced to bass notes, and I hear traffic. She must have gone outside. Sitting here in the sun, I do my best to picture her at 1:22 a.m., standing distraught among bouncers, smokers and snoggers, while the Palace Pier sits dark and skeletal across the roundabout. Perhaps, nearby, a lone seagull tugs at batter-coated chicken bones on the roof of a parked Ford Fiesta.

"Bex, what's happened?"

"What is it with you guys? If you do want to commit to someone, why'd you feel the need for one last freedom-fuck? If you need that, then why bother committing?"

I do my best to sound devastated. "Oh God. Honey, I'm so sorry to hear that. Who did he—"

"Some slut-bitch *slut* with a slutty profile pic. She messaged me about it and I confronted him and he eventually admitted it and I dumped him. Oh, social media, it's so great. It *connects people*." Her fury collapses back into bitter sobs. I can just about discern the pumping bass notes of Girls Aloud's "Something Kinda Ooooh."

I know Bex needs a good friend here. She needs to be told that Lawrence probably just had a dumb fear spasm on the eve of moving in with her. That people do silly things when they're afraid. That *she's* the one he wants to move in with, as opposed to Slut-Bitch Slut, who probably just looked great after five pints.

I know I should tell her to sleep on it and, if she really loves Lawrence, to sit down and talk things through with him tomorrow.

"What a huge cunt that guy is," I tell her. "He never deserved you."

More sobbing. "God, this is pathetic. You got a new flatmate yet?"

"Yes," I say, intending to follow this up with the triumphant sucker punch of "You!," but before I can do so, she lets out a pained wail.

"It's . . . you," I say, flatter than planned.

"Oh, right," she says, controlling herself a little. "Then that's something."

I still have one of those perky, light-headed hangovers that make everything seem less real and more possible. "Hey," I tell Bex, "why don't you jump on a plane and come out here? I'm doing this stupid experiment thing and there'll be a fuck-ton of downtime. We could . . . hang out."

A stunned pause. "How . . . how much would the flights be?"

I give her a rough estimate, conveniently leaving off the taxes, fees, airport charges and carrier-imposed surcharges. She starts crying again.

I haven't experienced such a strong yearning since I emptied my study five years ago to turn it into her bedroom. I want her to move in with me all over again. Year Zero, Day One. Yes, she'll move into my big West Hollywood hotel room and I'll ease her pain. And mine. So I tell her I've loads of air miles saved up. I tell her I'll cover her return trip. I tell her not to worry about a thing. And once she's here, if she's okay with it, she can crash in my room free of charge. Because that's what friends are for.

She agrees to the trip. Says she could fly out in three days. Oh God, she says, maybe this is exactly what she needs to move on.

Beneath all her burbled gratitude, I can make out the bass notes of "Celebration" by Kool & The Gang.

I only allow myself to sing it when I come off the phone.

The roof of the Sunset Castle is lined with stone turrets, just like you want it to be. The hotel was built 105 years ago, but it's new to me and I approve. This place has just the right amount of swish, and it towers over a stretch of Sunset Boulevard that I love. The staff are slick and helpful, treating me with the respect to which I'm accustomed. I'm unhappy with the mineral water brand in my minibar, but am in the process of having that rectified.

Servers glide discreetly around the pool area with trays, delivering drinks and club sandwiches. I stop one and order a celebratory mojito. He's wearing shades, so I can't tell whether he's staring at the paler rectangle on my chest where *Conjuring Harold* made its mark.

The YouTube video is a big boy now. The likes of Kim Kardashian and Tom Cruise have helped propagate it via social media, to the extent that it is now ripe for parody. There are multiple versions of it on other people's YouTube accounts. One of these rather predictably replaces the audio with the *Ghostbusters* theme tune. Another pulls a similar trick, but dubs in audio from *The Blair Witch Project*, so that actress Heather Donahue is heard snivelling and crying as if it's her filming in the basement. When those blackened feet float around the corner at the camera, poor Heather screams herself hoarse: "*Oh my God, what is that?*" By far the most widely shared bastard-isation of the video, though, employs visual trickery to place large fluffy slippers on the apparition's bare feet. The kind of fluffy slippers with big claws. Giant Muppet flippers.

All fair enough, and mildly amusing, but triggering a pop culture phenomenon doesn't advance my investigation. By now, several people have noticed the boiler room plug socket and messaged me about it. Depending on my mood, I'll either reply, "Wow, thanks!" or "I posted about this days ago, jackass."

I hope the Hollywood Paranormals' experiment will shed light on why I saw Maria Corvi in Hong Kong, but somehow I doubt it. My main objective is to glean their intel on the video, then serve my time on their nine-day project across two weeks. The Harold Experiment was quite a sceptical affair, in that it sought an alternative explanation for ghostly sight-ings—namely the human mind's potential ability to conjure up a "ghost." We'll soon see if that's possible. You can probably guess where my bet would go.

Astral Way and his Hollywood Paranormals could be about to hand me the biggest lead on this YouTube video since my plug socket epiphany. But let me tell you: if they intend to take me for an idiot, there'll be hell to pay.

Noon the next day, I find Astral wedged into a booth at the Sunset Boulevard branch of Mel's Drive-In. It's a small West Coast chain of fifties-style diners specialising in "home-style cooking." Each table boasts a mini jukebox.

Social media means never having to wonder how new contacts will look. Astral looks exactly as he does on YouTube, Tsu, Facebook, Google+, Gaggle, Goodreads, Pinterest, Kwakker, Reddit, Switcha Pitcha, Spring.me, Skype, Ello, HelloYou, Zoosk, Whatsapp, Wikipedia, WordPress, Quora, Kik, Uplike, MySpace, MyLife, MSN, Blogspot, Badoo, Bebo, Academia.edu, About.me, App.net, Itsmy, Instagram, Influenster, Twitter, Tumblr, Telegram, TripAdvisor, Flickr, Flixster, Friendster, Foursquare, Line, Last.fm, LinkedIn, LiveJournal, StumbleUpon, Streetlife, Spotify, Slated, VaVaVoom, Viber, Vimeo, Vine, Vig, Classmates, Match, PlentyOfFish, OkCupid, eHarmony, ChristianMingle and no doubt Tinder and/or Grindr. He's a disproportionately confident six-foot hippy, with bold red shades propped up on his head. A late-twenties lummox, maybe five years away from being winched out of his bedroom to the nearest hospital. He wears a red baseball shirt with the number forty on it, unbuttoned to showcase a tangle of silver charms and medallions, not to mention a tantalising hint of side-boob. Big black shorts, with a wallet chain that could strangle a rhino. When he waddles to the restroom later, I'll notice how a thick, sweaty ponytail of dirt-blond hair clings to his back.

As I walk up, the guy's cold blue eyes flick from his phone to me. I say hello and offer a hand for him to shake. He doesn't shake back, so I scoot into the other side of the booth and match his death stare, second for weird second.

For a moment, I think he's going to slump forward on to the table with a knife handle sticking out of his back, as people do in movies when you meet them in a public place having been promised key information.

"I'm waiting," he says.

Like it's the most obvious thing in the world, he says, "I'm waiting for an apology."

Damn you, Maria Corvi and whoever made the YouTube video, for conspiring to make me meet this oaf.

"What exactly do I have to apologise for?"

"Y'know, other reporters would have jumped at the chance of joining us for this experiment. But you blew me off for the longest frickin' time."

Pushing that unsavoury mental image aside, I tell him, "I'm not a reporter: I'm an author. I'm also a broadcaster."

He half laughs, half grunts. "Who isn't?"

"Why didn't you invite one of *those* reporters, anyway? Why nip at *my* heels?"

"This was a real bad idea," he growls, looking disgusted with me, with himself.

"Listen," I say, employing tact solely because he hasn't told me yet where the video was shot. "Took a while, but now I'm interested, okay? Here I am. Interested and also hungry." With that, I offer his last chance of a handshake from Jack Sparks.

He relents and grips me with a clammy paw, tight enough to make joints pop.

"Thank God for that," I say, withdrawing the hand and picking up the lunch menu, scanning the beers. "So where was the video shot?"

"What made you change your mind about joining us?" he asks, still not happy. "The video info? Not the experiment, or our status?" This man's ego just won't quit. I feed him some flannel about how his experiment will be perfect for the book. Astral obviously knows about the Italian exorcism—social media means never having to bring anyone up to speed—but I'm not about to tell him how the Great Hong Kong Corvi Mystery influenced my LA trip.

The way Astral orders food speaks of high maintenance. When it arrives, we're talking about my SPOOKS List and I show him how it currently looks. "I cannot believe," he says, his mouth a heinous washing machine full of mashed bread, beef, cheese and pickle, "that you don't have a fourth entry on that list. Not even the *possibility* that ghosts are real."

I shrug a big so-what. He snorts and takes another bite before he's swallowed his first. "Man. So you don't think ghosts are even *possible*."

"What do you care?" I say, chewing, my fingers and lips smeared with sauce. Blue cheese, orange buffalo. "Your experiment isn't even about real ghosts, right? I'm interested in what the human brain's capable of."

He nods his ham-hock head. "Psychokinesis. That's the process of using the mind to—"

"To influence stuff without touching it," I cut in. "I'm not a total newb."

"So you'll know what a thought form is too," Astral says.

As it happens, I do. A thought form, also known as a tulpa, is a non-physical entity created purely by thought. If it hadn't been for Maria Corvi in my room, I would never have entertained this pie-in-the-sky madness. But now, I'll confess to mild experimental curiosity. In the seventies, Astral tells me, when Professor Spence's Toronto group created their own thought-form Harold, he started rapping on their table and moving it around.

"So they made Harold up from scratch, right? And they thought he was a manifestation of their own psychokinesis. I haven't read the whole book—did he ever actually appear?"

What I'm asking is, you slobbering hippo: did Harold ever materialise like, say, a thirteen-year-old girl in a hotel suite?

Astral places his ten-dollar behemoth burger down with both hands, shaking his head. "But hey, that was the seventies. When we put sharp modern minds together, who knows? We might see our ghost."

"Even if we do create a fake ghost, though, won't that disprove the supernatural?"

Astral just keeps on shaking that head. "Psychokinetically produced entities and actual ghosts are not mutually exclusive. Why would they be?"

The Hollywood Paranormals met through social media six years ago, "united by the common goal of making scientific discoveries in the parapsychological realm." A cursory glance at their YouTube channel, on which they regularly pose and preen at various investigation sites, suggests they were also united by the common goal of making names for themselves and bagging a cable TV series.

"Thanks for watching. Please comment and subscribe. ☺"

The son and grandson of Episcopal ministers up the coast in bullet-riddled Oakland, Astral claims to have seen three "spirits" during the Hollywood Paranormals' tenure—although of course none were captured on video. "Every damn time," he laments to me, "we were shooting in the wrong frickin' direction. I feel like spirits are camera-shy. Maybe the camera really does capture souls, like some folk believe, so they run scared. Which makes *your* video very interesting to me."

Astral believes the video genuine. "I've watched it a whole bunch of times. Our guy Pascal's really into it too, as you'll . . . Ah! The man himself."

A short, smiley guy, his skin the colour of a latte, slides into the booth beside Astral. The French-Canadian's round steel-rimmed specs cling to a smooth shaven head. He has a tablet tucked under one arm and looks excited, which may account for him being caked with sweat. I can see my face in his forehead.

As Pascal swipes at his screen, my anticipation grows: part of the Great Video Mystery is finally about to be solved. Astral gruffly reminds me that the Hollywood Paranormals "need to get full credit for this. You need to post the news straight after and promote us as agreed. You also need to—"

"Yeah, all right, all right," I snap. "Let's see what you've got first." I'm apprehensive, not least because the video's provenance will dictate where my journey goes next. For all I know, it could have been made in some Mexican drug cartel war zone.

Pascal, bless him, launches a PowerPoint presentation.

Each of the slides consist of two pictures.

The first picture on each slide is a still from the video. A magnified close-up of some device on the basement wall. The second picture is a product page from a manufacturer's website.

"This junction box," Pascal says, indicating a still from the basement, "is the product of only one company." He points to the picture next to it: "Steinberg Appliances Inc., okay? You can see the logo in the video, right there. See? And this pressure gauge here is also the product of one company—Bloom

& Bloom Pressure. Look real hard and you can just about see the logo back here in the still."

Colour me somewhat impressed. No one, not even me, thought of this stuff. Pascal goes on to link several more items seen on the basement walls to these same two manufacturers. Steinberg Appliances Inc. and Bloom & Bloom Pressure.

"So what does all this mean?" I ask, as we reach the umpteenth slide. Admirable though all the sleuthing is, I yearn for the big punchline.

Pascal and Astral look so pleased, they could just about fuck each other.

"Both of these companies," says Pascal, "are real old-timers. They only fit their equipment in person, locally. They don't franchise or even ship out. So—"

Astral leaps in to steal Pascal's thunder, heavy on the gravitas. "These companies . . . only supply Los Angeles."

"Whoa," I say.

"And not just that," adds Pascal quickly, "but they only supply one area."

They exchange glances, then say it together on the count of three: "*Hollywood.*"

"*Whoa,*" I say.

While thinking, *Hmm, that's quite the coincidence.*

It's disconcerting that Dr. J. Santoro looks like the smarmy one from *Die Hard.* The corporate weasel with the big white teeth, thick side-parted hair, and beard. The guy who ends up chewing a bullet. From the moment I lay eyes on Santoro, I pledge to myself that if he says anything like "Jack, *Booby*: I'm your white knight," I will leave without further comment.

Dr. Santoro does offer reassuring and orthodox elements

you want from a psychiatrist. The sterile white-walled room, with few distractions except a box of tissues, some plastic cups, a water cooler and a bowl of wrapped peppermints. His voice is a Zen master's. His suit and spectacles complete the picture. My chair doesn't recline and is uncomfortable, with broad, flat wooden armrests. But I never liked the look of those horizontal shrink chairs that make you think "dentist."

You know what's less reassuring and orthodox about Dr. Santoro's office? The pit bull.

Sharon is a big grey pit bull terrier, with a splash of white on her chest and paws. She pants constantly, rolling out her tenderised meat-carpet tongue. A cage sits in one corner of the room, in case a client dislikes dogs. This whole office, a small rented space in a nondescript Burbank building, reeks of Sharon.

Just as human bodies are ninety per cent water, so psychiatrists are ninety per cent ears. Santoro lets me talk for as long as I want. Which would normally suit me, but I'm mainly here for his input. It's only fair to see what psychiatry, as a branch of science, reckons about how I came to believe I'd seen Maria Corvi that night in Hong Kong.

I also tell Santoro how, ever since Hong Kong, my brain has decided to lay a recurring dream on me.

I find it fascinating how the supernatural infiltrates your head, even when you reject such concepts. Just as cold germs go about their work, regardless of whether you believe in them.

Every night, I drive alone on some remote two-lane highway. The dash clock always reads 3:33 a.m., which mirrors the time in the real world. There is no moon.

This highway could be anywhere. Or at least, anywhere that

ever plays host to thick mist which hangs as far as headlights can see. At times, this mist makes the tarmac and the grass verges appear white as snow.

Every night, I see the silhouette of a person up ahead. They're standing in a hitch-hiker's pose with one arm up.

Roaring closer, I see that this person is a smiling Maria Corvi. She's a phantom much like the "ghost" in the video, her transparency inconstant, in flux. She wears her blue smock as seen in Italy and Hong Kong.

Her eyes, fixed on me, are bright yellow and piercing.

Her hitch-hiker arm swings, loose as a scarecrow's in the wind, to point off along the road ahead.

Each time she mouths the word "Enjoy," she whispers it directly into my ear. Her breath curls against my eardrum.

In my rear-view mirror, Corvi shrinks steadily back into obscurity, still pointing, jaw working. The mist enshrouds her until it's all I can see.

Dead girls in the rear-view mirror may appear more real than they are.

And when I focus back on the road ahead: shit! There's Maria again. Standing in the middle of the lane, no more than two white lines away from my front bumper.

Bug-eyed and terrible, bleached white by the headlamps. Seeming to relish the prospect of fatal impact.

Every night, this makes me jump.

Every night, I wake before I hit her. Then I laugh it off and go back to sleep.

As is so often the way with shrinks, Dr. Santoro seems most interested in what he perceives to be the root of the story. As I tell him what happened on Halloween, his forehead cracks with thought. "You say you became convinced Maria Corvi was purely an actress. By the end of the exorcism, I mean. How convinced were you, exactly? A hundred per cent?"

I nod, to hurry him along and to see where he takes this. Sharon backs up and presses her anus against my bare left leg, just above the ankle.

Santoro consults the notepad on his lap. "You say Maria regurgitated pieces of metal, including nails."

I nod him along some more, wincing at the feel of Sharon's anus and rearranging my legs.

"And she went off in an ambulance at the end," he adds.

"Well," I say, "that was the end of the narrative presented to me. I didn't actually see the ambulance leave."

Dr. Santoro uses interlocked fingers to create a small church in front of his chin. Two forefingers erect a steeple, which taps his nose as he mulls. I wonder if he's doing this on purpose, to help me reimagine the scene. "So you believe the paramedics were also bit players in that scenario."

I shift in my seat, feeling judged. I suffered more than enough thinly veiled ridicule in rehab, and now that feeling's back. All this for two hundred and fifty bucks.

"I hadn't thought about that," I say. "Is it important?"

The flesh church and steeple remain as he mulls some more.

"It could be that some part of you—perhaps a part you're unaware of, deep in the well of the mind—believed either that Maria Corvi was demonically possessed . . ." Here, he sees my face and blows the flesh church apart, turning it into one insistent forefinger. "Or that she was mentally ill and being exploited by the Church."

I humour him by considering these ideas. "The latter, at a push," I finally say. "That was my belief at one point during the exorcism. But actually possessed? No way, José." Dr. Santoro blinks a couple of times, and I fleetingly wonder if his J initial stands for José.

He keeps asking questions, but I eventually get the truth out of him: he thinks I'm guilty over Maria Corvi. He thinks some uncharacteristically kind part of my brain feels guilty for not checking up on her well-being. For all I know, he points out, she could have died of blood poisoning in hospital. He thinks I'm aware of this possibility, even if I don't outwardly feel it. After all, he notes, in my recurring dream she does appear as a ghost.

Dr. Santoro thinks that my guilt, perhaps coupled with the lingering after-effects of hallucinogenic drugs, caused my brain to project an all-singing, all-dancing Maria Corvi into my Hong Kong suite.

It's a theory, I'll give him that.

"So," I say, assembling my own flesh church in mockery of his, "you believe the human brain is capable of creating a three-dimensional person, right in front of you."

Ha. Yeah. Let's see how *he* likes it.

Sharon peers up at me with the eyes of a disapproving old crone.

Dr. Santoro just smiles. Not a thin smile hiding gritted teeth, but a properly laid-back Californian white-toother. "I've been in psychiatry for over two decades. I've learned that it's rash to underestimate the capabilities of the human brain." The wall clock ticks softly for a while, at seven cents per second, before he adds, "You mentioned you were asleep before the incident. Sleep is when the brain processes everything. It's when we delve deepest into that well."

"If Maria was a guilt projection," I say, "then why did she say,

'Enjoy,' rather than something sarcastic like 'Oh, thanks for checking up on me, dickhead'?"

Sharon emits a low whine. Santoro gestures for the dog to trot his way on her stubby legs. "I guess you could interpret what she said as sarcastic. 'Enjoy your glamorous journalist's life, while I'm dying in this hospital bed.' You know, that kind of thing."

I want to tell Santoro how vivid Maria Corvi seemed. Her movement. Her voice. Blue threads dangling loose from the hem of her smock. I even suffered smelling her breath. Having said that, every time I picture her, standing there with that nightmare face, the detail does fade. Even just five days later, she's fuzzing around the edges.

They say you don't directly remember things you see. Instead, you remember a memory of a memory of a memory of a . . .

The mind plays Chinese whispers with itself.

I keep talking, trying to find holes in Santoro's theory. To tear it apart. Two minutes before the end of our session, though, he lunges in for the kill.

"So what would you say is a viable alternative?" he says, stroking the back of Sharon's head, just above the collar. "If not a real person, or a guilt-based hallucination, then what did you see? A *ghost*?"

And then Dr. Santoro gives me the kind of rational, pitying look I've laid on true believers for years.

The Chrysler 200's dashboard radiates that sun-baked plastic reek.

Parked out in Santoro's car lot, I google "Maria Corvi hospital." If I hadn't walked away from that church believing it all to be *The Truman Show*, I would have done this a lot sooner. The way Santoro sees it, of course, I harbour guilt whether I believe it's justified or not.

I expect to find, if anything at all, a record of Corvi having been admitted, treated and discharged on Halloween. The Italian daily newspaper *La Repubblica*'s website soon whips the rug out from under me.

Maria Corvi went missing from the ISMETF Hospital on 31 October, just two hours after I last saw her. Two people were found dead in a broom cupboard on her ward.

A male nurse called Pio Accardo had his throat slit. Maddelena Corvi had been stabbed thirteen times. Traces of rust were found in the wounds on both bodies.

Countless radio songs melt into one as I stare at a palm tree.

Seeing Maria Corvi referred to in a newspaper—and seemingly as a murderer—makes her seem so much more . . . real. Surely the Catholic Church wouldn't stoop to faking deaths— or sacrificing real people? Okay, even I know that last idea's crazy. *(Eleanor: Happy? Good. Still wouldn't put it past the bastards.)*

I obviously know who poor Maddelena was, but another Google search summons Pio Accardo, a real twenty-three-year-old with online footprints. A selfie with other staff members here; a blog post entitled "The Best & Worst Things About Hospital Work" there. In one happy photo, he clutches a rolled-up university graduation certificate and wears a laurel leaf crown that I can't now help but think of as a wreath.

The *Repubblica* article is dated 2 November, and I can find no follow-ups. Other sites carry much the same details, but some run a quote from your friend and mine, Father Primo Di Stefano. "I did my very best to rid the poor girl of the spirits within. It is with deep regret that I concede my efforts were not enough. Please treat Maria Corvi with extreme caution as the demon inside her is clearly now in full control. I shall pray for her mother and Mr. Accardo to find safe passage to heaven."

So, then. Murder. And the Grim Reaper ain't done yet.

Just hours after I learn of Maria's Halloween rampage, my phone rings in one of the downstairs aisles of Amoeba Music. Surely the world's biggest record store, this place is the size of a football pitch. Just wall-to-wall physical media.

I'm studying the cover of Slayer's 1986 album *Reign In Blood*, to which I gravitated during my teenage thrash metal phase. It always worked well for anger, although to Chastain's mate Fang it probably sounds like a chill-out album. The artwork depicts a goat-headed Lucifer being paraded through hell on his acolytes' shoulders. It's such a clichéd portrait of the Devil that it makes me chuckle now.

The middle-aged man on the phone has a strong Italian accent. I've never heard his voice before, and there's background commotion, office buzz.

"Who am I speaking to, please?" he asks.

At first I think he's a cold-caller. "Don't you know? You just called me. Jack Sparks. Who's this?"

"I'm Inspector Cavalcante, with the police here in Rome. May I ask your relationship to Antonino Bonelli?"

"I don't know that name. Why are you calling?"

"I am afraid Mr. Bonelli was found dead yesterday. He apparently did some translation work with you on . . . let me see here . . . October the thirty-first?"

Christ.

"Tony?" I say, pushing *Reign In Blood* back down among

the other records. "I knew him as Tony. Yes, I met him for the first time that day."

The inspector casually explains that he's calling because Tony had spoken about me "a great deal" to his wife before he disappeared five days ago. Interrogation paranoia makes me explain, a little too hurriedly, how I haven't returned to Italy since leaving on Halloween night.

Tony left a suicide note at home, in which he wrote, "Hell is having no control. She controls me now, so I must do the right thing." And get this: the note carried a charming post-script: "It's all Jack Sparks' fault."

Even worse: Tony's wife had contacted the police on 5 November to allege that he was sexually abusing their young son. My fault, really? That's a new one.

As Cavalcante tells me how the investigation is only just beginning, how they "just want to establish the basic facts," I lay eyes on someone at the other end of this long aisle. Someone who looks very much like Tony.

He just stands there, looking at me, wearing the same leather jacket Tony wore in Italy. It glistens. Somehow looks wet, as does his hair.

It's stupid, I know, but I walk towards him anyway.

Connections, connections, so seductive.

"How did he die?" I ask.

A pause. Then, "Mr. Bonelli was found in a river outside the city. Can you think of any reason why he would say it was your fault?"

"None at all," I say, squinting at this Tony lookalike, drawing closer.

"Did you have any more contact with Mr. Bonelli after that day at the church?"

"None whatsoever."

I bump into a pink-dreadlocked skater girl glued to her phone. When I duck past, ignoring her insults, the Tony lookalike is no longer there. The spot where he stood is marked by a puddle of greenish-brown water on the floor.

I fend off more of Cavalcante's questions, while staring at the puddle.

"Hey," I say, just before he hangs up. "Do you know anything about the Maria Corvi case? Has she been found?"

"I cannot discuss other cases, I'm sorry."

I try explaining that I'm a journalist, but that doesn't help at all. I consider telling him about the link between Tony and Maria, then stop myself. Because, after all, what exactly *is* that link, apart from them having met for a couple of hours?

"Why do you ask?" Cavalcante adds.

"Oh, I just saw it in the news," I say, then hang up as a cute Amoeba employee with a vintage bob arrives to deal with the puddle. She squeezes that gloopy shit-green mess from mop to bucket, mouthing, "What the fuck . . ."

My thoughts exactly. The fallout from the Italian job no longer amuses or fascinates me. Those people have actually started to mess with my head, both in dreams and the real world. For a moment there, I actually thought I saw a dead man in a record shop. And if I can make that mistake, anyone can.

This is how people lose themselves. How they wind up setting fire to themselves, so that the police trying to bust into their compound will never learn the cult's secret rites. Or worse, how they wind up handing their life savings to Sherilyn Chastain.

I decide to forget the Maria Corvi clan. Let's get real: this stuff would be great for a true-life murder book—maybe one I'll write myself some day—but there's nothing supernatural going on. It's a dead end.

Maria Corvi is a teen psycho who should have been placed in the care of someone like Dr. Santoro a long time ago. Tony Bonelli is . . . was . . . a disturbed paedophile who ended up doing the right thing.

Only one point of interest remains: why I saw Maria in Hong Kong. Maybe a second chat with Santoro, or even the Paranormals' experiment, will help explain how my brain produced her. If not, I'll just have to blame the drugs and get on with my life.

Either way, from this moment forth, Maria and Tony and all those other sideshow mutants are squarely in my rear-view mirror.

Onwards!

Alistair Sparks: "Google has confirmed that Jack Sparks' laptop was used to search for the following terms on 12 November 2014, hours after Amoeba Music employee Kate-Linn Kasey recalls mopping up 'a heinous mess.'"

maria corvi news

maria corvi update

maria corvi latest

maria corvi found

maria corvi arrested

maria corvi dead

tony bonelli dead

antonino bonelli dead

antonino bonelli suicide

inspector cavalcante police real?

trusted combat magicians for hire -sherilyn -chastain

reasons for seeing ghosts

help with ghosts devil supernatural

am I cursed

Alistair Sparks: "The following is an extract from Rebecca 'Bex' Lawson's personal diary, dated 12 November 2014."

Fuck a duck, Diary: I'm off to Los Angeles!

I feel . . . how do I feel? Good and bad.

The good part's obvious. I can't remember the last time I accepted this kind of charity, but I feel no guilt. Jack and I both know he owes me. I mean, it's not like I looked after him during his Year of Drugs for any kind of reward—I did it to keep the stupid sod alive. But it was a really trying time that still haunts me even months later. A return flight to Hollywood and we're even!

The bad? I'm still gutted about Lawrence. A tiny bit of me wonders if I should have given him another chance. I never had him down as a cheater, but it was tragic how he denied it for a while, even when I had evidence. So the rest of me keeps telling that tiny bit to shut up. If the guy needed One Last Fling before moving in with me, what would he be like after a few years? And if we married? Mum's right: forget him. Just forget him.

The only potentially bad part of this LA thing? I know Jack likes me.

The funny thing is, he thinks he's so subtle that I'm totally oblivious to this.

He doesn't believe, for one second, that I notice the glances at my tits. And how he sometimes holds eye contact for longer than a friend should.

I also doubt Jack remembers the many times he's tried to make a clumsy move while wasted. The old Arm Around the Shoulders routine, followed by the old Coming in for a Kiss routine . . . He forgets all my brush-offs. He's a lab rat that can't remember getting electrocuted every time it presses Button A. Luckily, I'm good at defusing those occasional situations. I know he'd never ever get pushy or grabby—he's more pathetic than anything else.

Hopefully, the worst of all the attempted seduction stuff is behind us, in that Year of Drugs, starting last June. The guy was a mess, coming back to the flat at all hours, waking me up. Sometimes, of course, I'd get wasted with him too (just drinking and smoking tiny bits of personal weed, in the unlikely event that the police end up reading this).

I saw desperation in Jack. So much desperation. He really wanted, needed, to lose himself. I never figured out what happened last year to leave such a big, gaping black hole, but his tower of confidence crumbled right in on itself. I never asked why and even in his darkest hours he never told me.

Whatever made him want to spend his days mashed out of his head stayed buried deep. So deep that he probably couldn't access it himself. I wondered if it sometimes came out at night. I'd pass his door and hear him saying, "Sorry, sorry, I'm so sorry," in his sleep. Which was strange, coming from a guy allergic to apologies.

Sometimes I even thought he wanted to die. When I had to call him an ambulance, I wondered whether he'd deliberately OD'd.

I'm still amazed he believes I don't read his books. Of course I bloody read them—they've got me in them! Ha, no, that isn't the only reason, but it does make me laugh the way he pretends to be in love with me in print. He's really dined out on that one. And of course, the most hilarious thing is how he presents me. He gets my basic personality right, I suppose, but the book version is a bit "manic pixie dream-girl." When his fans meet me, they actually expect me to be (a) a redhead and (b) a fitness instructor! What's wrong with (a) good old brown hair and (b) running the south-coast wing of a car-hire company?

Exactly when did ginger hair go, in guys' minds, from being the subject of playground taunts to this big fantasy thing?

And did I once stick some orange dye on, because I felt like an extra bit of fan attention at one of Jack's book signings?

No, Diary: you did that, shut up.

Best of all, in every single Sparks book I'm seen walking around the flat in my underwear, pouting at nothing. Some dirty-mac weirdo shuffled over to ask me about that at a signing. The guy looked gutted when I told him how the reality was a great big fluffy dressing gown covered in coffee stains. He didn't want to hear how our flat's central heating hardly ever works.

Jack's a good writer and I do feel proud to live with him. Sure, he lost his way creatively with the drugs book. It already seems to be his most popular, but that's mainly because rubber-neckers are queuing up to watch him implode. I just hope this supernatural book will set him back on the rails, even though I don't understand why he's doing it. You don't see Richard Dawkins or Prof. Brian Cox travelling the world in search of ghosts, do you? It makes no sense, just like that whole thing with the medium, which I believe I've yet to document in these pages . . .

After he came back from Italy and we went on the pier, I was all excited to tell Jack about this American medium woman who was performing in town the very next night. I thought she'd be a no-brainer for his book—talk about low-hanging fruit! Her show was a ten-minute walk from our flat and he could've ripped her to shreds. Maybe tried to interview her afterwards. So I was amazed when he didn't go for it. And not only that, when I asked why, he kept changing the subject and even got a bit snappy. Weeeiiirrrd.

So here's this unstable, vulnerable, inexplicable guy who fancies me, even though the real me apparently isn't fit for his readers' consumption. I'm going to LA to spend a couple of weeks with him. We're sharing a hotel room. You can't tell me he doesn't hope something's going to happen.

As you know, Diary, I fancied Jack when I first moved in. But then you get to know someone. I don't mean his personality's bad, even if he is basically an arrogant prick. I just mean . . . you see socks on the radiator. You come to see this person as a mate. And in a coldly self-preserving way, you know that if you did hook up and it all went wrong, you'd need to find somewhere else to live.

So I don't see Jack in that way any more.

Hmmm. Do I?

No, I don't.

I definitely don't.

I probably would go for a rebound something, but it shouldn't be with Jack. It mustn't be.

I just wonder what kind of state he's in. Did he suggest I come and see him for my sake or his?

Oh Diary, you great big bundle of paper and ink. You're therapeutic, but no substitute for a friend. You give no advice whatsoever. Wish I hadn't alienated all my mates while loved up with Lawrence the Unfaithful.

In two nights I'll be there.

Two. Nights.

So, Los Angeles. What have you got in store for me?

CHAPTER SEVEN

My hand is a rocket, shooting high as it can go.

"I want to name the ghost."

All heads jerk my way.

I can't decide who's the most affronted. Astral's cheeks are red, but that's nothing new. So it could be the blustery half-Mexican guy—the one I call Dragon Lord (2,080 followers) because I can't be bothered to memorise his name. Seven Hollywood Paranormals is just too many.

Perhaps Obligatory Goth (3,452 followers) takes the most offence. All hoity-toity intellect in a black Betsey Johnson dress lined with safety pins, she mimics me by raising a skinny arm sleeved with screaming ghost tattoos. "This isn't a classroom," she says.

Actually, I think the Waster (78 followers, hasn't posted in four months) steals the pissed-off crown. That balding, beer-bellied, middle-aged mess. Spittle flies from his mouth as he clumsily demands to know why I should choose the ghost's name. His stupid voice echoes Barney, that guy glued to Moe's bar in *The Simpsons*.

The whole experiment will take place in this small and barely air-conditioned meeting room, with its bracing view of a smog-choked freeway. In this building, you hire spaces by the hour. Whenever I want to smoke, which is often at the moment, I have to ride the lift seven floors down. Still, Astral insists, "A professional experiment requires a professional environment. When we post pictures and selfies, it's vital that the background has the correct look."

We sit within a circle of technology. Besides the expected camcorder on its tripod ("We put no footage online until the experiment's done," Astral dictates, "but posts and updates are fine"), various blipping, flashing, humming, ticking machines feed off plug extension boards. Remember shoving spare electrical parts together as a kid and make-believing they were proper, working sci-fi equipment? That about sums up this tech. Pascal (735 followers) and Dragon Lord have summarised what each device does, but I was too busy blanching at the prospect of spending a total of nine days here. I suppose this contractual obligation is worth the lead on the video, but it's only thinking about spending every night with Bex—starting tomorrow evening when I meet her at LAX—that keeps my pecker up.

The room smells of takeaway. On our round table, beside the phones, the tablets and the netbooks, sit subs and soda and crisps and even a burger/fries combo. Guess who brought the fast food? Astral, the human washing machine. It's like he gets off on people watching him masticate.

Just ten minutes after our lunch meeting yesterday, the big galoot had divulged certain details of the conversation to his 8,341 followers. Social media means never having to write your own minutes. As agreed, I've given the Paranormals their precious public credit for the video revelation. Every hundred cycles of Astral's busy lower jaw, regular as clock-work, these people consult their phones to check how my influence has boosted their popularity. As if they'll ever be in my league.

The Waster bleats on about how I should have more respect for group decisions, until Astral wisely cuts across him with more diplomacy: "I do think it would be best if we stick to making decisions as a group."

Dragon Lord arches a smug eyebrow my way. "There is no 'I' in 'team.'"

"No," I reply. "But there *is* a 'u' in 'cunt.'"

This very nearly derails the whole experiment before it begins. For a start, there's a Gatling gun salvo of tuts from Professor Stanley H. Spence (no online presence). The seventy-nine-year-old flew in from Toronto yesterday, and you sense that Hollywood is not the best fit for him on any level. Brilliantly, he's the very image of an old-school American professor. He has the spectacles, the smartly trimmed white beard. Even the leather patches on the elbows of his tweed jacket. No bow tie, though. If he stops tutting, I may buy him one.

Pascal cracks up, his laughter behind one cupped hand drowned out by uproar from Dragon Lord and Obligatory Goth. There is aggressive finger-pointing from the Waster and insistence from ministers' boy Astral that such profanity has no place here. None of which stems my territorial pissing.

"Listen," I say. "I'm going to name this ghost. We can collab-orate on the rest."

There's a great deal of what Sherilyn Chastain would call

negative energy in the room. Dragon Lord breathes more fire over me. Most of the others study Astral, waiting for his response. Willing him to stand up to me.

With one paw buried in a bag of Cheetos, Astral blows out a long, cheesy breath.

"What would you like to call our ghost?" he says, triggering more irritation. I catch Pascal still amused. He doesn't give a shit. I like Pascal.

Thinking fast, I pull something from the ether.

"Mimi," I say. "We'll call it Mimi."

You'd swear all air has been sucked out of the room.

In space, no one can hear you ask Jack Sparks why he picked such a stupid name.

"*Mimi*," Dragon Lord says, with the face of a fox being forced to lick shit off a wire brush. Which makes me all the more determined to stand by the name. Astral knows to pick his battles carefully. Without Sparks, the experiment's visibility would be zero. With Sparks, there's a ready-made crowd, downloading *Conjuring Harold*, learning what the seventies experiment was all about and anticipating this reboot.

So I win my battle and Astral outlines the remainder of today's task: creating Mimi's character. She can't be based on any real person. The whole point is that she's fictional, "a product of our gestalt consciousness."

The first few times, whenever Astral and others say "Mimi," they draw the word out, with resigned expressions. After that, the name becomes part of the furniture. Thanks to the weak air con, no one has the energy for sustained sarcasm.

Having named the spook, I take little interest in the rest. And the process hardly grips everyone else. If the prospect of a ghostly manifestation in this room is the Hollywood

Paranormals' idea of heaven, then manufacturing the ghost's details is the long, hot car journey required to get there.

Harold, the imaginary ghost dreamed up by those crazy Canadians in the 1970s, was a married English aristocrat and all-round big girl's Cromwellian blouse. When his gypsy mistress was burned as a witch, Harold killed himself in a fit of guilt over having allowed it to happen. Thankfully, room consensus deems historical figures pretty dull. Our Mimi turns out to have been *born* in the 1970s, only to die, we quickly decide, in the early 2000s.

"Maybe she was in 9/11," offers the Waster. A faded The Truth Is Out There T-shirt suggests he holds dumb conspiracy theories about the tragedy. "She was bringing her husband some lunch when it all went down."

Obligatory Goth rolls her eyes all the way up to her drawn-on eyebrows. "Or maybe she, you know, *worked there.*"

When we reject the Waster's World Trade Center suggestion, he folds his arms tight and stares at his trainers. The man could only look more idiotic if his red baseball cap had a little twirly spinner on the top. He regularly fidgets with the insulin pump hooked to his waist. Lately, this device has been malfunctioning, feeding too much insulin into his bloodstream. Because of some alarmist article the Waster read online, he believes his noisy neighbour is hacking into his pump via Bluetooth and interfering with it, trying to put him into a coma.

The Waster's neighbour simply must be trying to kill the Waster, because the whole world revolves around the Waster.

"Mimi was a drug addict," states Obligatory Goth. "The bassist in a big rock band, who fucked the frontman and got into all kinds of—"

"But then we have to decide who the big rock band was,"

Astral warns, "and suddenly it's not so fictional any more. Let's stay vague."

Flashing those killer eyes of hers, Hot Mama (5,051 followers) says Mimi was a gifted singer and psychic who visited Kenya and got beaten to death for being a witch. She adds that this might connect our Mimi "rather nicely" to Harold, as a tip of the hat. Fun trivia: Hot Mama was once a contestant on *American Idol*. You'd never know this, because she only mentions it twice-hourly.

Dragon Lord says Mimi was a cinema usher who caught a bullet to the brain during a random shooting spree.

When the Waster emerges from his sulk, he says Mimi played her music too loud. Her neighbour complained repeatedly until finally he shot her dead on her front driveway.

Astral thinks Mimi was a competitive eater who appeared at big events across America, only to one day choke to death when two hot dog buns filled her windpipe.

The seventh and quietest Paranormal, Soldier Boy (2,672 followers), is the kind of crew-cut jock who would have beaten the stuffing out of the other members at school. Having returned from Laghman Province three weeks ago, he looks dazed and hunkered back inside himself, as though real life is a bit much. Running a hand over his buzz cut, his biceps stretching the sleeves of his old American Eagle T-shirt, he says Mimi was blinded by an IED in Afghanistan, then committed suicide after a few months of PTSD back home.

I tell everyone how Mimi was a journalist who set out to write a book in which she travelled across America on a pogo stick, only to get flattened by a ten-ton truck.

None of the ideas are well received. People debate, then argue. Professor Spence notes that "In the original Harold

Experiment, Harold was actually created by one nominated outsider," but his words are lost in the mayhem.

Of course, our phones slow the whole process down, but that's just the way it is. When Astral sees an online report that a disturbed man has climbed the Hollywood sign, we all scan social media for reports, then watch live feeds of police negotiators trying to talk the guy down. The air hums with invention as we try to think of the funniest online comments to make. Needless to say, mine is by far the best, even if some spectators find it distasteful given that the guy jumps and dies.

Professor Spence clears his throat loudly. He notes that focus is "absolutely key" to this experiment and that there were no websites or smartphones in the seventies. The only answers to his points are more screen taps and swipes, along with the unabated hiss of more live-streaming footage. This, in case Spence hasn't noticed, is not the seventies. Not some restaged period piece. As the old man struggles to comprehend the strange new era in which he finds himself, I wonder when this lone time traveller will tire of us.

Like most things generated by committee, the character we finally sketch out for Mimi is beige. Something about how she's an office worker trapped in a loveless marriage who somehow ends up dead. Then we head off to celebrate in a bar. The professor declines to join us, his consternation palpable.

The menu flaps in my hands, literally a newspaper without the news. It lists hundreds of food items across so many big pages. Hinge this monster open and you can't see anyone or anything else. Which proves handy when you want to hide Dragon Lord's permanently disgruntled and punchable face.

"Didn't see that sucker punch coming with your YouTube

video, huh, man?" he crows, from behind the page I'm examining dedicated to tacos. "Made in Hollywood, baby. Made in Hollywood."

The life and colour of Barney's Beanery swirls around our table. It's a bar with a restaurant or a restaurant with a bar, depending on your needs. A really fun place, with retro arcade machines at the back. I vow to beat the living shit out of Dragon Lord later. On Donkey Kong.

Pascal asks if I'm happy now that I know where the video was shot. He wants everyone happy, all the time, but I don't have an easy answer. At first, I doubted the little guy's conclusion, but then I took a closer look at his PowerPoint presentation, right there in the booth at Mel's Drive-In. I checked out the companies' websites for myself and it all tallied.

Now I've had a day to think about it, the video's origin isn't such a big coincidence after all. I mean, if I'd gone to Helsinki or Guam and the video turned out to have been shot there, my brain would've fallen out the back of my head. But Hollywood, land of fiction? Not so surprising.

"Hollywood makes it so much more likely that the video's fake," I tell Pascal, as the others earwig in. "It's probably a fucking viral, for *Paranormal Activity 17* or something. And I'm the mug who's been conned into promoting it."

Bullets of opinion whizz past my ears. Like Astral, both Hot Mama and Soldier Boy believe the video genuine. Dragon Lord, the Waster and Obligatory Goth, cynics after my own heart, laugh and tell me it's "totally" man-made. It's not even as advanced as viral clips they've seen in which a golden eagle snatches a kid in a park or an ape takes an AK-47 off a bunch of African soldiers and promptly goes apeshit. CGI, they say, is now so sophisticated that anything can be achieved.

My video, in comparison, would be "a cakewalk," whatever the hell a cakewalk might be.

Pascal perches on the fence, saying he's reluctant to make a definitive call, but something about it undeniably "spooks" him. Sherilyn Chastain's love child, ladies and gentlemen.

The Paranormals love to talk. At any given point, at least two of them are jawing off at the same time, in the same conversation. Words collide, chopped into useless salad. Throw a huge character like me into the mix and you have cacophony. I tend to trip the conversation up anyway, because these people do that American thing. That thing where I start talking in an English accent and they do a double-take. They pay extra attention, as if I'm actually speaking Russian.

The Beanery gets blurry. As booze levels sky-rocket, everyone talks over everyone else. I'm not sure how to take it when Obligatory Goth recommends I try Arrogant Bastard ale, but it's a mighty 11.2%, so I'm happy enough.

I can barely remember how I get back to my hotel. I only recall getting into an argument with Dragon Lord, quizzing Soldier Boy about war and enjoying some mutual flirting with Hot Mama, whose amazing booty-hugging dress helps me forget about Bex for a while.

My first session with the Paranormals has been just about tolerable. Even if I'm now even more convinced that the Mimi Experiment will involve nine people sitting in a room for as many days, staring at fuck-all.

Alistair Sparks: "The following is an excerpt from an early draft of Elisandro Alonso Lopez's planned ebook, The Mimi Experiment: The Truth 'N' Nothing But.*"*

World needs to know how crazy Jack Sparks really is.

I never wanted him to join the experiment. I got talked over, then outvoted. Astral pushed for it big-time, saying we needed to take our group "to the next level of visibility." Being in Sparks' new book was supposedly the key, because he's some big-shot Brit writer and has like 260K followers (but only follows thirteen people back, including Richard Dawkins and Ricky Gervais). No one except me and maybe Lisa-Jane seemed to consider the fact that Sparks is an atheist, which is about as closed-minded as you can get. Maybe God doesn't exist, who knows, but why do people like Sparks feel such a burning need to slap their chips down by the roulette wheel? Makes no sense.

This fucking guy.

I don't know whose bright idea it was to invite him to the after-session drinks at the Beanery. Probably Pascal's. Just from the obnoxious way Sparks insisted on naming the ghost, it was obvious he wouldn't gel with us on a social level.

The guy was already drunk during the session, but then he gets wasted when we all hit the bar. He keeps dabbing a finger on his gums and also hits the restroom a lot. Nothing suspect there, right? And he wonders why we can't understand half of what he's says, when he's so clearly wasted. Starts talking about "bloody Yanks." We all feel embarrassed for him, but keep the conversation alive.

We try to ignore him dropping a glass, then leaving us to alert staff. We try to ignore his clumsy attempts to hit on

Ellie, not knowing or caring she's with me, saying how she's "a really hot mama." We try to ignore him yelling in Johann's bad tinnitus ear, "You just got back from a war—why are you hanging with these losers? You should be off your tits in a brothel!"

Myself, I try real hard to stay polite when he makes fun of my oriental dragon shirt, then asks me where he can score some coke. Because I'm half Mexican and so obviously *must* have big-time contacts along the border.

This fucking *guy*.

I don't know which idiot orders him an Arrogant Bastard, because it sends the prick into space. He interrogates us endlessly about his dumb YouTube ghost video, which I kind of suspect he filmed himself as a publicity thing, but I hold back on saying so. We try to offer opinions but he steamrollers over us. Why ask questions then not listen to the answers?

The real problem starts when he asks about "the three words on the video." There's a pause, then Lisa-Jane asks what he means, and Sparks just says the same thing again, like it's obvious.

Ellie says, "Oh, you mean the camera person saying 'Oh God' and whatnot?" Sparks, all aggressive, he says no, he doesn't fucking mean that. He says he means the three separate words: one spoken at the start of the video, another halfway through and the last one right at the end.

We just stare at him, like he's trying to test us.

I say, "Are these words subliminal?" That gets a laugh, so the crazy Brit slams a palm into the table, spilling Ellie's drink.

"No!" he says, "They're not subliminal. They're the opposite of subliminal." Then he says the three words, but he's so trashed we can barely understand them. He adds, "They're all demon names. Why am I having to tell you guys? You should know this stuff."

We just keep staring at him.

This fucking guy.

Then he's waggling a finger, looking us all in the eye one by one. And he's laughing, which comes as a relief to the more sensitive among us. He says, "Hahaha, you guys. Very good, well played, you got me!" Pascal and Ellie start to laugh along, but Astral pulls his big leader thing and shuts them down.

"We honestly don't know what you're talking about," he tells Sparks. "I've watched that video many times, full volume, and the only words spoken are 'Oh God . . . this is it,' like Ellie says."

But Sparks is still laughing, still waggling that finger, as a big pizza arrives for everyone. "Fuck you," he says, slurring, grinding his molars, pulling out his phone. "That's right— haze the new guy. This is a sorority initiation thing, yeah? What's all that sorority stuff about anyway? What a pack of bollocks."

Then he's asking his followers. Takes him five whole minutes to tap out, "Hey! The Scary Video. What do you make of the 3 words at start, middle and end? Adramelech, Mephistopheles and Baphomet?"

So we sit there, waiting for the response. Ellie isn't eating the pizza because she's too tense. I wink to reassure her, but I know she's thinking, "I have to spend *two weeks* with this imbecile?"

I check out the responses to Sparks' post. It's one never-ending column of question marks.

"Huh???"

"What words??"

"All I hear is 'Oh God, this is it,' dude?"

"WTF?!??!"

"Haven't heard those words. Played it again. Still don't hear them??"

"This a joke?"

Let me tell you: as Jack Sparks reads through these replies, we watch smoke gush from the volcano, expecting the worst. He grips his phone so hard, his hand shakes. Then, before anyone can stop him, he erupts. Heaves the table up, trying to flip it. Our pizza slides off and slops on the floor. Sparks screams in my face, I can't even remember what he says. I scream back and the security guys are coming over. Astral gets up to intercept them, but they practically walk through him to manhandle Sparks and me. Jack's shouting all this stuff about "fucking liars" and shit, all the way to the kerb, which his ass hits hard. Security know me, so I don't get the kerb treatment, but I do get kicked out of my favourite night spot.

This.

Fucking.

Guy.

Astral and Lisa-Jane talk to security, trying to explain, but I'm still not allowed back in. All I can do is watch Sparks lying on his side on the kerb, and he's crying. Actual tears on the guy's face. He's like, "What the fuck, what the fuck, no no no . . ." all fear and snot.

The others come out to join me and someone calls a yellow cab. By the time it arrives, Sparks is sitting upright on the sidewalk, playing the YouTube video on his phone. He thrusts the phone at us, asks, "Hear that? *Do you hear that?*," then drags his finger across the screen to rewind it yet again.

But we hear no words.

We help him to stand then put him inside the cab, his clothes all peppered with cigarette butts. He doesn't resist, his face still wet. We give the poor driver a twenty and tell him to keep the change, just to take this pain-in-the-ass the short distance back up the hill to his chichi hotel.

As the cab pulls away, we hear Sparks inside. We see the blue light of his phone screen. "Hear that?" he asks the driver. "You hear 'Adramelech'? For fuck's sake, listen again!"

Through the rear windscreen, we see the silhouette of the driver shaking his head. Raising a hand to tell Sparks to knock it off.

The seven of us stand on the sidewalk, watching the cab blend into traffic. Wondering what just happened. Tomorrow, Astral will wake to a garbled email threatening us all with "severe legal action" if we mention those three devil words on the video. Sparks says he'll deny ever having heard them. He'll also tell his followers how he was only kidding about the three words—of *course* they're not on the video, ho ho ho. Try to pass it off as "a social experiment."

"Well," says Lisa-Jane, sparking up a smoke. "I think we can do without that guy."

"No," says Astral. "He stays."

"What?" says everyone else.

"He has to stay," says Astral.

We are dumbfounded.

The big guy finally confesses over stiff drinks in the next bar. Before coming out to LA, Sparks agreed to fund most of the experiment. He's covering half the meeting room rental and our new equipment, plus Professor Spence's flights and accommodation. I have no idea why, and neither does Astral, but he reminds us that our two Kickstarter campaigns failed horribly. Few people care as much as we do about some experiment from the seventies. Although one day soon, it'll be a very different story. After this experiment, man, we'll be paraded through the damn streets on people's shoulders.

Until that day, all of us are stuck working jobs that just about cover our rent, food, gas, little else.

So . . . yup.

Turns out we can't change our lives without this fucking guy.

CHAPTER EIGHT

When this many notebooks slam shut this hard, they make the sound of panicked birds flapping away.

As I pull up a chair, Eduardo Sánchez, Daniel Myrick and four colleagues jolt, checking my hands for weaponry. They look surprised and somewhat affronted. But quite frankly, if they didn't want anyone to know in which Melrose Avenue café they were having this development meeting, they shouldn't have publicly posted a shot of the menu. Upon seeing that post, I shrugged off the hangover and motored straight here. After all, Sánchez and Myrick created a great horror film which convinced millions that three student film-makers really did go missing in the woods of Burkittsville, Maryland. Who else could possibly be my number one suspects in The Great YouTube Video Mystery?

Ignoring the polite protests of "Sorry, that seat's taken" and the "We're kinda having a meeting here," I plonk my phone between Sánchez and Myrick, then tap the screen into life.

"Do we know you?" Sánchez says, almost as bristly as his beard.

"You've probably read me," I tell him. "I'm Jack Sparks and I won't keep you long."

"Shall I have someone come over here?" someone nervously murmurs to Sánchez, looking around the café.

I start the YouTube video playing. "I just want to know if you made this," I tell the duo. "It seems very you."

From this point, curiosity takes over. Necks crane. Chairs squeak as people shift position. Myrick even repositions my phone to get a clearer look.

About twenty seconds in, the film-makers shake their heads as one.

"Sorry," says Sánchez.

"You got the wrong guys," says Myrick.

I look them in the eyes for a long moment, drawing upon the Larry David school of lie detection. "So you never saw this video before? This definitely isn't a *Blair Witch* thing?"

They're so palpably perplexed that I'm forced to believe their denials. My number one suspects are hereby off the hook. I exit to the sound of notebook pages fluttering back open.

The first thing I did today, after breakfast and ibuprofen, was zap the same email over to eighty-two local film and TV production companies. These are not exclusively companies based in the Hollywood district. Just because the video was filmed somewhere in Hollywood's 3.51 square miles doesn't mean the prodco responsible is based there. They could be anywhere in LA. Of course, they could technically also be based anywhere in the world, but I'm trying not to think about that right now. Chances are, the video was shot by locals.

In these emails, I've included a link to the YouTube video and asked if the recipient was responsible for making it. Worth a try.

While motoring over to the second production company on my Personal Visits list, I ponder the internet's latest reactions to the video. Some of which have been big.

Several people have publicly announced that "my" scary YouTube video has stopped them killing themselves. They believe it to be real, you see, and therefore proof of an afterlife. Armed with this knowledge, life no longer seems so pointless and depressing.

This is good news. There has, however, been a flipside, as there always is with behaviour based on abstract concepts. Fifty-five-year-old Elspeth Cook from Phoenix also believed the video to be real and therefore proof of the afterlife. She too made a public announcement. "Armed with this knowledge," she wrote on her blog, "I now have the courage to put an end to the pain [of her lymphatic cancer] and ascend." She killed herself three days ago, with a Xanax overdose.

This is terrible news. I'm already assembling my potential lawsuit defence.

Listen, it's not *my* video. I didn't create it, no matter what some people think. And it has spread so very far, embedded here, there and everywhere, that it's unlikely Elspeth Cook even saw it on my YouTube page.

Obviously Elspeth Cook and her family have my sympathies too.

Sherilyn Chastain is emailing and phoning, trying to re-engage. Trying, in other words, to claw her way back into my book. She still claims she has something "pretty bloody important" to tell me about the video, and I still have zilch interest in knowing what that is. I'm deleting all written missives and voicemails unread and unheard.

When my thoughts turn to Astral Way, my foot hits the

accelerator. This guy makes me want to blow the whole experiment off. In an email this morning, he tried to put me in my place about Barney's Beanery. Yes, Astral still has a lot to learn about dealing with me. Nobody, but nobody, puts Jack Sparks in the corner or anywhere else.

So what if Hot Mama turns out to be Dragon Lord's girlfriend? How was I to know?

So what if I asked Dragon Lord an apparently inappropriate question?

So what if it all got heated at the end?

The Hollywood Paranormals strike me as extremely self-centred. They want everything to go their way. They want everything to play out according to their own petty little sensibilities, in their own microcosm.

They're going to have to learn to accommodate different points of view.

Specifically, mine.

My fingers are slime-yellow. I'm coated in this thin toxic oil, outside and in. I'm sick of cigarettes, but can't stop.

Bex is too thrilled to kill me for smoking at our Rainbow Bar & Grill patio table. We're watching the sun set over Sunset and knocking back Jacks in honour of Rainbow regular Lemmy from Motörhead, who reportedly can't drink that stuff any more, doc's orders. Through an open door back into the bar, you can see the great man beneath his Stetson, funnelling cash into a fruit machine and drinking red wine. Platinum records and photographs crowd the walls around this living legend, conjuring the ghosts of dead ones. This is where Marilyn Monroe and baseball star Joe DiMaggio met for their first date, back when it was an Italian restaurant.

Granted, he beat her up and she divorced him, but still, they were here.

Despite her eleven-hour flight, Bex has that whole "just out of a relationship and determined to look extra-great" thing going on. Flame-red hair more lustrous than ever. Make-up immaculate, not that she needs much. Pouting for Britain. Low-cut top, high-cut denim skirt. Even if she looked a total mess, mind you, I'd be happy to have her here. I'd forgotten how good her very presence feels around me.

Her bulging suitcase sits beside our table. After a day of overzealous security guards and denials from the likes of Blumhouse Productions, Twisted Pictures and Ghost House Pictures, I ended up having a few too many drinks to drive, so told her to get a yellow cab here from LAX. Which was a shame, as I missed out on a potentially romantic airport moment.

From the moment Bex sprang out of the cab for a big hug, she has been utterly enchanted with LA. This woman just stepped through a cinema screen into *The Wizard of Oz* (get out of my head, Sherilyn Chastain) at the precise moment it switches to Technicolor. The only words she's said so far are "Amazing," "Jesus," "Fuck," "Wow" and "Yes, definitely a double."

Not only has Bex just arrived in America for the first time, she must now endure the tragic tale of Translator Tony. Head trip, right? Except I can't get her to listen. "I'm really sorry," she says after a while. "I just zoned out again." She drains her glass, ice clunking against her nose. "So you don't actually *believe* you saw this dead guy in the record shop?"

"It was just some guy who looked like him. Tony just has . . . *had* . . . one of those faces you recognised, you know? He was an everyman." Which is bullshit, given Tony's monobrow and tombstone teeth, but it gets me off the hook.

"An everyman who fiddled with his kid." She puts the glass down and looks around for a server. "My God, that was strong."

"They don't mess about with spirits in LA," I say. "Unless they're the Hollywood Paranormals." I follow this with a "Boom-tish!," knowing the joke will trigger Bex's bad-joke face. She doesn't disappoint me. "Tony hardly seemed the most stable guy when I met him," I add. "He was smoking his head off, scared of his own shadow."

Bex is distracted again, ordering us more drinks, fumbling with dollar bills, peering at them to work out what's what. It's okay, I tell her: it's on a tab, we pay at the end. My insides turn green as she eyeballs a passing long-haired guy who looks a lot like the rock guitarist Zakk Wylde. I start to wonder if my cape-swirling, moustache-twirling scenario to lure Bex to LA and exploit her break-up doldrums has been ill-conceived. For reasons best known to herself, she doesn't see me in that way and she never has. All these girls I've gone out with, over-loving me to the point where I've had to let them down gently, and yet to Bex I am rubber-stamped "Mate," "Flatmate" and "Chopped Liver."

When Bex realises I've stopped talking, her eyes flick back from The Man Who Might Be Zakk. "So, yeah," she says, vaguely. "Tony was a bit of a mess, then."

Disheartening. When an incoming call buzzes my pocket, Bex greets my universal sign language for "need to take this call" with nonchalance—she has a new drink and some eye candy. Guy candy. One drink into her holiday, I'm dispensable.

A male Italian voice fills the line. Not Cavalcante. And surely not any other detective, unless they're somehow calling from the bottom of a lake.

This voice is angry and . . . *wet*. Each syllable *swims* into the next.

"Jack. Jack, is that you . . ."

This guy sounds familiar in a way that creeps me out. "Who's this?"

"You know who. Tony, the translator guy."

I don't know what my face does at this point, but it wrenches Bex's full attention back to me.

"Jack, you bastard," says this alleged, supposed Tony. With a throat full of gurgling drain water, he says, "You screwed my *life*."

Hand on heart, at first I think he says "*wife*." When I ask him to repeat himself, it sounds no better.

The guy must be using some kind of voice-filtering app: every breath is a dripping sponge, clenching and unclenching. "I'm being punished," he says, "and it's all because of you."

My rationality finally snatches back the reins. "Oh, very good. The dead guy phones me up. Spooky! Well done, mate— you do sound like Tony. Not bad at all."

His voice trembles as he says: "She can do anything, Jack. Anything. She can take you anywhere, any time she likes."

"Okay . . . who's *she*?" I say, feeling stupid for even playing along. "The cat's mother?"

"She left hospital, then came for me, to control me. To make me *do things* . . . oh my God. My own son. I had to free myself. But even now I'm not free, and this is all your fault, you *bastard*."

I guffaw down the line and wink at a puzzled Bex. "So *Maria* turned you into a filthy paedo? I thought that was my fault."

"I saw you in the record store, Jack. Has that happened yet? And then the bathroom. It was cruel, but I had a chance to get even and I took that chance. What is the date?"

I gulp bourbon, the words "record store" echoing around my skull. Bit weird, that. Either this maniac was there in the store, or it's a lucky stab in the dark. Either way, I've had enough of him.

"A big shout-out," I say, "to whoever ends up listening to a stream of this wacky prank. Check out Jack Sparks dot co dot uk and buy a T-shirt."

"Tell me what *date*," snaps the caller.

"I'll tell you to fuck off."

A storm front of menace rolls back into his voice. "Better watch out, Jack. You gonna get what you deserve."

"Ooh, a speedboat?"

A bubbling inhalation, a saturated outbreath . . . and when he speaks again, the voice changes entirely. My ear fills with the deep, dark tones of Maria Corvi.

"*In your dreams*, Jack Sparks."

The phone line dies, taking her prickly laughter with it.

Bex drums the table, waiting for news. Two fresh drinks sit beside the others.

I can't speak for a while. I light a cigarette, while trying to get this stuff straight, to work it all out. Finding myself at a loss, I settle for leaning back and blowing twin smoke plumes through my nostrils.

Bex raises her glass, solemn. "Let's get hammered."

So there's a guy out there pretending to be someone who killed himself. A guy who threatens me, doesn't know what day it is and does a nice sideline in impersonating Maria Corvi.

I knew this book would attract cranks, but on this level? It's astounding what some people will do for a supporting role in a Jack Sparks book. For all I know, "Inspector Cavalcante" and this latest joker may even be the same guy. Some wag who caught wind of the Italian exorcism drama and decided to have some fun. The stupidity hurts my head.

I nod furiously at Bex as we clink drinks. "What could possibly go wrong, Miss Lawson?"

Bex leans forward to whisper her reply. I want it to be "Well, we could end up in bed." Instead, of course, she says, "That guy over there—do you think it's Zakk Wylde?"

Come 3:33 a.m., my head is a rotten melon with a machete handle sticking out of it.

I wake from the usual Maria dream, my surroundings monochrome.

Beside me on the bed, there's a long black shape.

Bex is lying on her back on the crisp white linen, fully clothed. Just as I am.

Behind the air con's churning whirr lies a different sound. Takes me a while to work out that Bex is snoring.

I clamber off the bed with a grimace, then pad through to the bathroom and stand in the doorway, flicking a switch. The sound of electrocuted flies heralds striplights blinking into life and scorching my retinas. Lumbering in, the vinyl-plank floor cool under my bare soles, I thank my past self for taking the time to stockpile potent stateside painkillers. I dry-gulp what I imagine the maximum dose to be.

As I perch gingerly on the side of the bath, willing the pills to work, a flashback montage rises up through the gallons of booze we sank at the Rainbow and beyond. Polaroid moments resolve themselves.

Me and Zakk Wylde both grinning dutifully as I photograph him with a delighted Bex on the patio.

Some guy in a white vest yelling along the Sunset Boulevard

sidewalk because we left Bex's suitcase behind on that same patio. "You wanna get your shit blown up, man?" asks this crowned king of rhetoric.

Me telling Bex how Hunter S. Thompson lives on through me.

Bex telling me some stuff about Lawrence. God knows what.

Both of us taking it in turns to ride a rotating mechanical bull at the Saddle Ranch restaurant. Howling with laughter as it hurls us on to the heavily padded ground. Beer after beer, always with a JD chaser. Because them's the rules.

Me telling Bex how much I resent Hollywood using the video to hitch a free ride on my back.

Christ. Hungry tongue-kissing on Sunset Boulevard, my back against a wall. Bex's body heat radiating though me. Two adults regressing into drunk teens, the picture completed by my hands clamped on Bex's denim derriere. A toothless old woman hobbles by, lugging carrier bags stuffed with junk. She says, "If I were you, I'd buy a gun first." Her strong Southern accent makes it sound like "If *ah* were *yoo, ah'd* buy a *gern* first."

The two of us laughing about the old woman all the way back to the hotel, the lust spell broken.

Shrieking at traffic, jaywalking outrageously. Furious horns parp.

That's where my memory pinholes shut. We must have crawled up here and passed out.

"Jack . . ."

An urgent whisper from nearby. I fully expect the bathroom door to frame a confused Bex, her hand outstretched for painkillers . . .

Instead, the doorway remains a static rectangle, framing only the wall outside.

I step out of the bathroom, still expecting to bump into Bex.

But she's still in bed. Still snoring.

She said my name in her sleep! Surely a good sign, along with all that kissing.

"Jack . . ."

That same whisper. An icy shard of sound, cutting through the air con. Or is it actually part of that endless drone? A sonic quirk, cheating my ears? Fools call me self-obsessed all the time, but am I really so far gone as to hear my own name whispered by an air-con unit?

"Jack . . ."

Well, I'm now sure about one thing.

I'm facing the bed and yet the whisper came from behind me.

I swing around and home in on a sickly strip of yellow light. The one that runs beneath the entrance door.

Two telltale black smudges interrupt the yellow. Two giveaways that someone is standing right outside my door.

Our door.

I picture Maria Corvi out there. Can't help it. The deranged, starry-eyed Maria Corvi, whispering my name.

I saw her in Hong Kong, so why not in LA?

Connections, connections, so disturbingly plausible.

Behind me, Bex's fragmented breath.

Above me, cool air rushes from slatted vents.

Before me, that door, still with those smudges beneath it.

With a head this sore, I'm in no mood for nonsense. I soon cover the short distance to the door.

And yet . . . and yet I hesitate to peer out through the spyhole embedded beneath the Fire Emergency map.

"Jack . . ."

My name flits through the wood at me. Yes, through the wood for sure.

Is this another hallucination, waiting to happen? When I look out through the spyhole, will Maria Corvi's yellow eye glare back at me, wide, glinting, accusatory? She's missing and could even be dead. Is this my guilt resurfacing? And if so, could I really still feel guilty about a double murderer? I know what Dr. Santoro would say . . . basically any old balls to back up his pet theory.

Oh, fuck this.

I shove my eye right up against that tiny brass ring.

Nothing and no one stares back through the fish-eye lens. This room's at one end of an empty corridor, which stretches away, lined with doors, the straight lines curved. All that downlighting on the walls may seem pleasantly subtle and boutique-stylish in the evenings, but it now looks downright sinister.

I try to remember how tall Maria Corvi was. If she was standing outside, right up against the door, would I be able to see her?

Maybe not.

I step back from the door, far enough to review the yellow strip.

Two smudges, still there.

An involuntary shiver gets the better of me. Now, I don't *believe* Maria Corvi is standing out there, dead or alive. It's just that steeping yourself in supernatural concepts makes these thoughts rise from primeval depths. You find yourself fearing what countless ancestors feared before you, ever since the first ambiguous shadow was cast upon a cave mouth's wall.

The irrational fear gene lives on in us all. It's irritating, but these things need to be handled the same way as when you've taken a bad drug. Simply tell yourself how these crazy thoughts and anxieties are just down to the drug, nothing else.

Then arm yourself, just in case.

Damn all those airport security scans that rid you of potential weapons. The best I can muster right now is a full bottle of room-service Cabernet.

Moving in slow motion, I grip the smooth doorknob.

I'm torn between opening the door fast, which might wake Bex, or taking a more gradual approach, which would give a homicidal teenager more time to decide exactly where to skewer me with a rusty nail.

With one hand, I make a caveman club of the wine bottle. With the other, I twist the doorknob.

There's a heavy-duty grinding sound as I swing the door open.

No one's outside. Why yes, I do feel stupid, thanks for asking, but at least Bex is still asleep. I put the bottle down, then step outside.

Closing the door hushes the room's air con, leaving a stark silence out here. Only TV talk-show murmurs can be heard from one of the other rooms.

What am I doing? I'm still drunk and really should be sleeping it off. I suppose I want to find an actual real-life person who, for reasons best known to themselves, has decided to whisper my name through my hotel room door.

I want to know why I keep seeing and hearing things that make . . .

"Jack . . ."

. . . no sense.

This new whisper (which does sound like Maria if you

think about it. Or Translator Tony. Or Camera Boy. *Hush, stupid lizard-brain*) comes from the far end of the corridor.

My bare feet slap the carpet as I run towards it. Never expected to be led away from our door, so didn't grab shoes, but I can't resist this siren call. Halting at a T-junction, I consider my options.

To my left, the silver glint of room-service trays outside every third door punctuates a long strip of carpet. At the very end of this corridor, I squint back at myself from a full-length wall mirror.

To my right, the corridor passes more doors and a bulky ice machine half buried in an alcove, before hitting another junction.

"Jack . . ."

Decision made. I hurry off to the left, following the sound. My mirror image stomps towards me, growing larger, its body language more determined.

Two turns later, the corridor broadens into a square space prettified by vased flowers. Two lift doors along one side and a fire door on the other. My name gets whispered from beyond the fire door and so I burst through it, determined to catch the fucker out.

The stairwell's stone floor freezes the soles of my feet. Brightly lit stairs coil down six floors. No sign of movement anywhere. No sound of footsteps.

And yet the sporadic whispering continues below, leading me down ever faster until I'm taking three steps at a time. Risking broken toes to get ahead of the game. Because that's how this feels, like some kind of teasing childhood game, a playground rerun. If someone wants to press my buttons, they're pressing well.

Down, down I go. Up, up goes my heart rate.

At ground level, I'm confronted with a door marked "Lobby." I sit back on a low step and catch my breath. My T-shirt's stuck to my back. When I flex my shoulder blades, they squelch. Still, the headache's gone.

"Jack . . ."

This from the other side of the lobby door, obviously.

Can you see where this is going? You probably can. You're smart: you're reading a Jack Sparks book, for Christ's sake. But I still have no clue.

I palm open the door and enter the super-chic lobby, where the faux-marble floor does little to warm my feet. Across the other side, at reception, a tall, blond receptionist chats to someone out of sight in a back room. Some bloke in an evening jacket and jeans, probably a night-owl guest or drug dealer, is slumped on one of the artfully misshapen sofas, engrossed by his phone.

The adjoining bar area lies dormant and dark. Its fancy metal stool legs jab skywards, furniture dreamed up in an H. R. Giger power nap. Moonlight stroking shelved bottles of vodka and gin and . . . oh, who cares.

I'm just killing time on the edge of it all. Head cocked at an angle. Hair an asylum-escapee mess. Shoes nowhere to be seen.

Listening, waiting . . .

Waiting . . .

"Jack . . ."

I track the voice past fountains that spurt dutifully even at this hour, lit with garish blue and pink light, into a short corridor branching off the lobby. It ends with a service door, wedged open by a bucket and mop.

"Jack . . ." says that infuriating voice, from the darkness beyond the door.

Maybe I am Scooby-Doo after all. Maybe this is the janitor fucking with me.

I steal a look back to the lobby. From here, I see no one and no one sees me. I drag the heavy door wider open, step over the bucket and duck inside.

Ancient wooden steps cascade down. The light switch doesn't work, but the bottom of the staircase is dimly lit, so I grip the glossy wooden handrail. These chips in the rail's varnish surely mirror the state of my sanity in pursuing this.

I test each new step with one foot before applying my full weight to it. Which seems so wise but does me no good. Halfway to the bottom, the meat of my right sole sinks down on to something sharp, skewering the muscle. I bend double, panting, dog drool oozing from my mouth. Standing precariously on one foot, I pinch out the drawing pin, its tip wet.

Once the staircase is behind me, subdued overhead light leads the way into the hotel's shoddy underbelly. These hot, rough-walled service passages smell dank.

With each new step I survey the concrete floor, for fear of more pins. Or worse, broken glass.

"Jack . . ."

My shadow jerks and contorts on the wall as I pick up speed.

Soon, there's no more light to guide me, so I fire up the trusty Zippo.

The damp heat becomes more imposing and I notice a few pipes on the right-hand wall. Ten steps later, those pipes multiply to imitate the London Underground map. I see a junction box. Gauges with flickering dials.

A penny rolls in from the shadows of my mind, ready to drop.

Up ahead, the passage is set to widen. The right-hand wall of pipes ends at a corner.

The low hum of a generator draws louder, closer with each step.

At the end of a ceiling-cord hangs a bare bulb, caked in dust that dulls the light it gives out.

I am gooseflesh.

I'll admit that something unnameable prevents me from going on. Something clenched and fearful in my guts. Utterly ridiculous but true.

After a few deep breaths, I hold up the Zippo and stride around the corner.

The penny lands, spinning wildly.

I am standing in the boiler room from the video.

There's no one else here with me. No humanoid shape on the ground. No ethereal figure looming over it. Of course not.

There's just that pattern of pipes and gauges and boxes on the walls, which makes my head swim with déjà vu.

I take it all in for some time, just *staring*, as sweat trickles into my eyes. The Zippo grows hot in my hand.

The only sound emanates from that generator, relentless.

My trance is broken by something in the corner of my eye. Something that looks a lot like a big shadow, flitting in front of the lift door.

Of course, when I refocus over there, all is still. Just a trick of the—

From behind me comes an urgent rattle of footsteps.

I swing around, my gooseflesh developing gooseflesh of its own.

The Zippo flame reflects in two pairs of wide eyes.

The first pair belongs to a tall, blond guy with a name badge pinned to his grey waistcoat. This, then, is Brandon, who was manning reception. Behind him stands a short Hispanic woman clutching a bedraggled mop as a defensive weapon. Apparently the Sunset Castle doesn't deem maintenance staff worthy of name badges.

"Told you," she mumbles to Brandon, looking me up and down. Lingering on my dirty feet.

Brandon spreads his hands palm up, calm but firm. "Sir, why exactly are you down here?"

"That," I tell him, "is a fucking good question."

Part
Two

CHAPTER NINE

Bad things happened since I last wrote.

Blood all over these sheets.

Blood all over me.

I need help.

I keep expecting to hear the grunts of LAPD officers out in the corridor. Expecting the door to burst inwards.

It took so much focus to call Sherilyn Chastain on the phone. My hands have this Parkinson's quake, and when she picked up I could barely talk properly.

In the back of my mind, those infected words kept going round and round. Those words that wanted to splurge out through my mouth. Out through my fingertips on to the keyboard, then on to the screen.

The thing wants me to let go and just type those words forever. This is worse than drug addiction. Surely you can only carry such a weight for so long before your knees buckle. But I must not bend.

I won't get the better of myself! I won't.

Sherilyn stayed calm on the phone, which really helped. She kept her voice all steady and told me to breathe deep.

She knew all this would happen. She must have, because she tried to warn me. Why didn't I listen when she told me to abandon the Mimi Experiment? Because I'm a fucking idiot and I've brought all this on myself. And others. Oh God, oh God.

Between some of these keys—between the Q and the W, and the K and the L—there are these little canals of blood. Beneath them all runs a lake. This whole thing may as well be written in blood, ha ha! Laughing feels good, feels important, got to play it down, got to stay fucking calm here.

I cannot let me get the better of myself.

Sherilyn said she'd take the next plane over. I was so pathetically grateful I cried.

And while I wait, I'm going to write exactly what went down. Because no matter what happens to me now, there has to be a record. And I'm afraid this thing inside will regain full control, this time forever. If that happens, I'll have no objectivity left. I'll be a big bag of meat writhing around in a secure facility, screaming those words and nothing else.

Up until now, I've described real events while distorting certain truths.

I've played down the drugs.

I've made no mention of the fear, the tears, all that slow-boil nausea in my guts.

I haven't told you the real reason I'm writing *Jack Sparks on the Supernatural.*

Let me go back to what happened after I found the boiler room. Three, maybe four nights ago? Since then, I haven't been able to write anything up because it's been Mimi during the day, Bex at night.

I have to relive exactly how I felt and thought at the time, no matter how stupid and blinkered it now seems. But now I can be *honest*, both with you and with myself. There's been so much I haven't been willing to admit even to myself. Bravado may feel like a shield, but when you're telling yourself lies, it becomes a prison.

I really hope this writing focus keeps me stable for the next twenty-four hours, until Sherilyn gets here. It may also help me process all that has happened.

And the thing inside had better stay hidden, or I won't hesitate to use the blade again.

"Tell me why I shouldn't dial 911, you little cock-sucker."

Marc Howitz is sharp and angular, from his attitude to those potato-peeler cheekbones. This room is power drunk, even for a hotel manager's office. Marble desk, cold marble floor, everything else varnished and polished to within an inch of its life. Sitting there in his Versace, the guy thinks he's Scarface.

Dawn light bleaches its way across soulless wallpaper. That jobsworth Brandon brought me straight here after finding me in the basement, so I've had no time to dream up any bullshit to feed Howitz. I'm still utterly stunned by the video's boiler room *just so happening* to be tucked away in the bowels of this hotel. I feel afraid and confused, just like Tony Bonelli.

Was that really him on the phone last night? Of course not. *Yeah, just keep telling yourself that.*

I exaggerate to Howitz how I've spent months trying to

track down the origin of the YouTube video, then lie about how "sheer gut instinct" led me to the Castle's basement tonight. When Howitz realises I've hit the end of the story, he leans back in his brown leather manager's chair and chews it over. His mouth literally chews. He's drawing this out, enjoying it.

"I'm disturbed," he says, his voice made of ice, "that somebody filmed in an extremely private area of our hotel without permission. And you say it's some kind of . . . *ghost* deal. Do I look like I believe in ghosts?"

I tell him I don't believe in them either. I rub tiny pieces of basement grit out from between my toes, hoping he doesn't notice my grey footprints on his nice floor. I also hope he can't smell my booze-pickled breath or see coke flakes in my nose hair. You didn't really believe I'd shunned cocaine since rehab, right? Since Italy it's been every day, getting worse and worse. This week, I've been starting before lunch.

When he asks to see the video, I feed him the Google keywords. He sags and rotates ninety degrees to his monitor, aggrieved that there's no aide present to do this tiresome manual work on his behalf.

Just before he clicks "Play," I ask him to tell me if he hears any words on the soundtrack. Because that's something else I didn't tell you, reader—no one else can hear those three words. Just me. I didn't tell you, because I thought I was going mad. I could hardly avoid telling you about Maria Corvi in Hong Kong because it was such a pivotal moment, but somehow those three demonic words were worse. More unnerving. Insidious. And now that I've *gone* mad and everything's gone so badly wrong, it really doesn't matter any more. (*Eleanor:*

please forget what I said earlier about deleting those three words from the book. I'm sorry. And for the record, I'm really very sorry for the way I've treated you.)

"Adramelech," says the voice on the video, loud and clear. The voice that sounds like Maria Corvi.

Howitz says nothing about "Adramelech" or "Mephistopheles" or "Baphomet," because of course he doesn't hear them.

"'Oh God, this is it,'" he announces at one point. "I heard someone say, 'Oh God, this is it.'"

"Yeah," I say, downcast.

Howitz talks at me, but I'm too busy wondering yet again how it's possible for audio on a video to only be heard by me. I'm wondering if there might be *any* other people on the planet who could hear this. Maybe people with the same rare blood type? What bullshit. I don't even know what my blood type is.

"Open your fuckin' ears, Mr. Sparks. I *said* that this most certainly is our boiler room area on the video."

"Thank you for confirming that," I say, trying to sound patient. Yearning for another line, just to keep me awake. A busy day lies ahead.

"So you don't know who shot it?" says Howitz. "Because it would have involved trespassing, just as you did tonight."

"Let's build on our common goals: we both want to find out who shot this thing. But I'll need your help."

Howitz smacks the flat of his palm against the desk. "Trespassing is a felony. For all I know, you could have intended to blow up my hotel."

My brain stalls, searching for a way to reroute his power-trip hysteria. "What if one of your staff shot the video? You must have at least one budding film-maker. Maybe an actor?

Someone who would break your rules in a heartbeat if it meant raising their profile."

He scowls, but something dawns behind his eyes. Discomfort with the idea of one or more of his super-obedient, fawning staff members going rogue and filming dumb spooky shit in the basement. I doubt it's true, but I've planted the seed.

"Let me interview your staff," I say, "and see if I can dig anything up."

"You're testing my fuckin' patience, Sparks. I never even heard of you."

"Ghosts are great for business. I found this video and sent it viral—two million hits since Halloween. Tom Cruise and Kim Kardashian posted about it. Jay Leno joked about it! So if the Sunset Castle becomes connected with this thing . . ."

Howitz scratches at his designer stubble, annoyed by his own temptation. An internal phone rings so loud it jumps an inch off his desk. To this guy, I'm no longer a potential terrorist, just an irritating distraction from the day's workload. He holds both hands up. "Fuck it, whatever. Johnson and Gonzalez just clocked on: go bother them instead. You retards were made for each other."

As I leave, verbal gunfire blasts out after me. "Just stay out of that damn basement, or I'll have your nuts on my wall."

Walk far enough around the Sunset Castle's perimeter and you discover the dark side of the moon.

Unlatch the gate marked "Staff Only" next to the swimming pool, then walk through and keep walking until you reach the hotel's glamour-free side, hidden from the Sunset Strip and most of the rooms. Huge rusty pipes worm out of the ground and plug into the brickwork. Waste bins the size of Sherman tanks exude foul fumes.

This is where Johnson and I sit, halfway up some pockmarked steps. I didn't know how many Castle staffers I really wanted to interview, but when Johnson turned out to be the boiler room engineer, I made a beeline for him. He was easy to find, what with the faded brown maintenance uniform and callused, grubby hands ready for any job on earth.

Johnson accesses the boiler room from here, using the ancient, grime-caked service door. "Wow, this is crazy," he says, pouring me some bitter coffee from a flask. "Being interviewed—and by a Brit! I love the British. Do you write about boilers for a living or what?"

He's pushing fifty, but his eyes are new and alive. It's hard to tell whether this is because, finally, someone wants to listen to him. Before I can even sip my coffee, he surprises me with a light-bulb moment. "Ever write about ghosts?"

Wary of leading the witness, I smother my surprise. "Why's that?"

And pleased as punch, he says, "Do I got a ghost story for *you*."

I'm wondering if he'll tell me a tale set in Albuquerque or somewhere equally random, but no. Dialling his voice down to a whisper, he says, "There's a ghost. A ghost right there in the boiler room."

I remember the shadow I half saw last night, and quiver. My aim with this chat was just to verify that no ghosts had been witnessed down there. Yet here's Johnson, defying expect-ation.

"I've been contracted to work that boiler room for five years now. I also do the Standard, the Best Western along the way

. . . and lately things have changed here at the Castle. I've *seen* stuff. A shadow that moves by itself, without being linked to nothin'."

I twirl a forefinger around, urging him on. He taps a couple of cigarettes from a pack of Lucky Strikes and hands me one, then lights us up.

"When I'm down there, it's just me. While I'm regulatin' those boiler levels, everything else is still. But lately, if you'll excuse the profanity, I see shit in the corner of my eye, y'know? I see movement. I see the black *move*. And when I turn to look, there's this blur of activity, real fast. Shit goes back to normal, as still as . . . as still as . . ."

He grasps for a suitable simile for very still things. I have no interest in waiting for the result, so jump in: "Could it be rats?"

"They'd have to be fuckin' giants, man!" His laugh turns into a tobacco cough and he thumps his chest. "Excuse the profanity. I'd hear those suckers, for sure. Besides, I'm good with the traps and the poison. Always have been."

"How about human intruders? Kids?" I nod over at the service door. "That doesn't look too secure to me."

He blows smoke out through both nostrils. "It's secure enough, man. And when I go down there, I always lock the door behind me. Before you ask, whenever I've seen this shadow thing . . . the other door, the one that leads up to reception? That's been locked too."

"When did you first see these shadow movements?"

His brows furrow. "What's the date now? November fifteen? I wanna say . . . first time I noticed this stuff was two weeks back. If you wanna know the truth, having a ghost here is pretty cool. Spices the job up some."

I walk away, thinking Johnson an untrustworthy imbecile. His testimony doesn't fit the narrative growing in my head, so I discount it. Journalism at its finest, oh yeah.

Bex, beautiful Bex, is all bunched up in bed, watching *Good Morning America* in the dark, with water and a half-empty strip of painkillers. "No more JD, ever," she says, from a Medusa mass of red curls. "Ever."

Straight away there's a weirdness between us. I can't tell whether she remembers us kissing last night, or whether only I remember it and I'm behaving differently, which is in turn confusing her. So I play it safe and make out nothing happened, while coaxing her down to breakfast.

Out on the rear terrace, beneath a maroon marquee, she marvels at the view south across the city. I don't tell her that the further south you go from here, the more likely you are to get ripped apart by gang crossfire.

"That was a good effort for a first night," she says, over bacon, eggs and black coffee.

"Remember much?" I ask, keeping it breezy.

She forgot her shades, but sadly her eyes give nothing away. "More the first part of the night. After that . . . not so much."

Our moments of public indiscretion went straight to her brain's trash folder. Damn it. Still, Bex forgetting is better than her remembering and waking up horrified.

Once she's had coffee and laughed at me pocketing miniature Tabasco bottles from our table's ramekin (we have a whole basket of these things at home, from U.S. hotels), I decide she's ready for the big video news.

For a while, her mouth just sticks in an "O" shape.

"You came to Hollywood," she says, "where the video turned

out to be made. And you stayed in this hotel . . . where the video turned out to be made."

I watch her thoughts race as she tries to figure this out, spearing thin, dark bacon strips with her fork.

"So," she says. "Did you choose this hotel yourself?"

"Ah," I say. "*Ah*. Now that's the thing."

CHAPTER TEN

Seven floors up in Culver City, Professor Spence uses a handkerchief to dab his shiny forehead as he finally speaks his mind.

"I had no idea this whole experiment would only last the two weeks I'm here! My group meditated for twelve months. And . . . y'know what, I gotta say, can nothing be done about this damn AC?"

"There were no direct results from your period of meditation, sir," says Astral across the table. "Reading your book, it really strikes me as a misstep. The good stuff came afterwards, when you changed your approach."

"But the meditation," says Spence, "was valuable groundwork for what happened later. I strongly suggest the group doesn't skip it. At least give it a try."

Elisandro, the one I used to call Dragon Lord, clucks his tongue. "I really don't know what we'd get out of that."

Attitudes towards Professor Spence are divided. Most of the Paranormals reserve a basic level of respect for what the man did in the seventies, while believing the Mimi Experiment needs to take a far more contemporary approach. Only Ellie (formerly Hot Mama) and Pascal hang on his every word. And me, I couldn't care less whether Spence is here or not. The guy's doomed.

"One of the reasons we spent so long meditating," Spence persists, "was to think about Harold. About his character. We focused strongly on him for that whole *year*. I gotta say, I have strong reservations as to whether you've got this Mimi character clear in your heads. You're rushing into this thing."

The professor's words may as well hang in the air in wobbly Comic Sans before tumbling into a big broken pile. He sighs, purses his lips. I suppress a chuckle, glad that the old fart's attempts to pointlessly elongate our experiment are being shot down. (Looking back now, of course, I know I was idiotic, just like almost everyone else around the table. We were the architects of disaster.)

With Spence rudely overruled, the group plunge straight into what was the second phase of the seventies experiment: Waiting For Our Ghost To Show Up.

After Spence and Co. spent a year meditating and trying to get their Harold spook to appear, with no tangible results, they considered giving up. They then became inspired by British parapsychologists who had explored psychokinesis (or PK, as it's known). Those Brits, who had in turn been influenced by the atmosphere of Victorian séances, suggested elements that would encourage PK phenomena. Belief was vital, they said. But at the same time, an easy-going, relaxed atmosphere would be much more likely to produce results than intense meditation.

"So we'll just hang," says Astral. "Professor Spence, could you remind us of a few things you used to do?"

Spence raises his eyebrows: oh, so *now* we want to listen. "Well," he says cautiously, "we told jokes, we sang songs, we chatted to each other. Sometimes about Harold, but not always. We kept it varied. Sometimes we recited poetry."

"Thanks, Professor," nods Astral, mashing nachos on spin cycle 6. "So we'll do all those things from today."

"Maybe lose the poetry," mutters Elisandro.

"Hey," says Ellie, giving him a playful elbow jab. "I write damn fine poetry."

"Oh," he says. "Is *that* what that stuff is." He slaps an arm around her back. "Kiddin,' babe." I stare at the guy, thinking how sick he makes me.

Spence notes that his seventies group placed objects and pictures related to their Harold character around the room. Fencing foils, sweets, antique cushions. It was, he says, all in the name of "helping us picture the character with the utmost clarity."

His words barely sink in, because no one really listens any more. People only care about what they're going to say next. Our default mode: broadcast.

Lisa-Jane (Obligatory Goth) asks Professor Spence for three words that describe the atmosphere fostered by his seventies group. He ponders this, as if holding a non-existent smoking pipe in one hand, then says, "Convivial. Carefree. And gay."

A ripple of childish laughter. I chuckle along with everyone else at Spence's antiquated use of the word, even though bewilderment, realisation, hurt and alienation cross his face, in that order. The man really is a relic here, and yet he is the sole voice of reason in this room.

No one listens any more.

Only when it's far too late do our ears open wide.

The whole getting-laid-back thing proves awkward for the group. The Paranormals are not your typical Californians. They're caffeinated misfits on society's touchlines. So the process of creating a convivial, carefree and gay atmosphere in this sterile, corporate room feels contrived to say the least. And when it's not contrived, it's plain wrong. Howie the Waster's rants about his allegedly homicidal neighbour may be heartfelt, but they hardly encourage the right vibe.

We discuss Mimi's threadbare life story, over and over. Her drab existence as Seattle office worker and unappreciated wife, brightened only by her connection with co-worker Jeremy (Jeremy! I did not suggest this name). Their eyes would meet across the office each day. Snatches of forbidden contact, building to something. Mimi's death, as it happened. Because in the dead of winter 2004, a truck flattened her as she ran across the downtown area for a secret rendezvous with Jeremy. See ya, Mimi. And hooray for my truck suggestion eventually being used. Elisandro and Howie are especially keen on the scenario. Reading between the lines, I'd say they've both been cheated on and Mimi's their whipping girl.

Our story might be corny junk, but Mimi is now the boulder from *Raiders of the Lost Ark*. She's rolling and there's no easy way to stop her and rethink what she's all about. We must stick to the character we've created. Besides, we're dying to get to the interesting part.

So we skim over the specifics of Mimi's loveless marriage to some austere guy who Johann (Soldier Boy), in a rare moment of lucidity, decides to call Ivan. The marine is still all jumpy and spaced out, but slowly eases up as the unfurling fiction of Mimi leads him away from reality. Maybe this is what the experiment means for Johann: sheer escapism. I never manage to get him to open up, but I also never try all that hard.

Between Mimi chats, we're all far more comfortable talking about ourselves and our interests. I tell everyone about my stupid attention-seeking pogo-stick journey from Land's End to John O'Groats. Then it's my turn to zone out while the others say something or other. But now, in this hotel room, as I play the audio file I recorded during that session, I find myself more inclined to listen.

Her big brown eyes wide, Ellie talks about natural remedies. Says she got all that from her grandad, back in New Orleans. "He was a medic in the Navy. Always kept his medical box full, even after he left the gig. We called it Grandpa's Dispensary. When me and my sisters was kids, you daren't talk about a cut or nothin', because then the iodine would come out."

Elisandro is the only one engaged as he drones about what he's learned of digital projection during his time working at the local Arclight cinema. Astral entertains only himself with talk about some "cool new chain" that's sprung up locally to rival In-N-Out Burger. None of us give two shits about Johann's ambition to front a series of fitness DVDs, having been inspired by Shaun T's *Insanity* series. Still, these monologues present a good opportunity to check social media.

By the end of the afternoon, nothing supernatural has happened. The table remains un-rapped. Professor Spence hasn't spoken since we laughed at him. As I watch the old academic approach the lifts at a speed belying his age, my instinct is that he won't be back. And I'm right. Tomorrow morning, he'll check out of his hotel and fly back to Toronto at his own expense. A decision that almost certainly saves his life.[1]

The Hollywood Paranormals will never mention him again.

Before anyone else can leave, I announce my big news. "Last night," I say, "I discovered that the YouTube video's boiler room is in my hotel."

Leaning themselves forty-five degrees back, unblinking, they all do a great impersonation of people caught in a wind tunnel. I swear it's almost convincing.

My paranoia, you see, has mushroomed into suspicion. When I first told Astral I was coming to LA, he shot back a link to a pre-filtered list of "cool" hotels. Which seemed very kind and helpful at the time.

Guess which hotel, at the top of that list, was by far the most appealing and most reasonably priced?

Yeah. Exactly.

Astral, the fat magician. Forcing that card on me like a pro.

As I stand before the Paranormals, I believe they shot that video themselves. Maybe they have a confederate at the Castle. Maybe Johnson isn't half as stupid as he makes out.

When the Paranormals caught wind of the Italian exorcism and my new book's theme, they pounced upon their chance for a big publicity drive. Pascal hacked into my YouTube and dumped the video there, then Astral launched his tireless campaign to draw me to LA. Probably had a Plan B if I didn't

---

1 Professor Stanley H. Spence would die three days later in the early hours of 18 November, after falling down stairs at his Toronto home. Despite what certain sections of the internet might have you believe, there is no reason to doubt the coroner's eventual verdict of "accidental death." Upon arriving home, Mr. Spence had written a polemic article railing against "the YouTube generation and its catastrophic emphasis on self-expression over learning," which would be published posthumously in *Time* magazine. —*Alistair*

choose the Sunset Castle. Some plan to get me there anyway, so I'd make my big discovery. They also managed to get me to fund most of the experiment. I'd never have admitted that before, but now who cares? The Mimi Experiment was far more important to me than I'd let on. I really needed to know if I could have imagined Maria and the smoke cloud in Hong Kong.

The story they want to tell is pretty dumb, which just makes me feel all the dumber for literally buying into it. Journalist becomes obsessed with scary video, only for some *spectral force* to draw him to the very hotel where it was filmed. Enter the Paranormals to save the day and dispel the Sunset Castle phantom! Not to mention piggybacking on my fame and followers and bank account. All afternoon they've badgered me for online "signal boosts" and shares and all that crap, but I've started ignoring these requests.

"Astral Way invited you to Like his page Astral Way."

Ignored.

"Lisa-Jane Spinks invited you to Like her page Lisa-Jane Spinks."

Ignored.

"Elisandro Alonso Lopez invited you to Like his page Elisandro Alonso Lopez."

You get the idea. Anyway, I decide to play along with their little storyline, just to see where it goes next.

"Can I interest you guys," I ask, "in conducting a séance in that boiler room tonight?"

The words "Hell yeah!" soon lose all meaning.

"Pretty sure I can get it straight with the manager," I say. Then I add innocently, "Unless any of you know anyone at the hotel?"

Everyone looks blank.

Good work, guys. Oscars all round. But I want to bust through your defences and make you confess. Because for all your pseudo-scientific trappings, people like you give others false hope.

As I stand before the Hollywood Paranormals, I want this book to end with them fully exposed and the internet's most authentic-looking ghost video debunked. I want these people on record, telling me how they shot the video and what they hoped to achieve.

I don't know it, but I've become Sully Strong.

Remember Sully Strong, from chapter six of *Jack Sparks on Gangs*? The guy I tried to talk sense into during our moonlit alleyway chat, sitting on two upturned crates. The Detroit Crips guy who thought he was a noble warrior, fighting the good fight, bulletproof 4 life. A hardcore rebel who rejected any other value system. When in fact he was just a glorified serial killer whose days were numbered.

I don't know it, but these are the levels of self-denial at which I now operate.

My hair is a freeway fright wig when Sherilyn Chastain calls the car phone. I drive everywhere with the Chrysler's hood down, even in November. Feeling in the mood for humouring crazy Sherilyn—this woman who in just a few days' time will represent my final hope of salvation—I actually pick up.

"Jack, I've seen the posts and blogs about this experiment. Don't do it. Seriously. Pull out."

"What's the matter, Shez? Don't want the Paranormals taking up more space in my book than you and your scary bottle?"

"Stop projecting your attitudes on to me, you idiot. This is about you and your safety. Don't you feel it, Jack? This crash course you're on?"

I hammer my horn and swerve around a Daimler that has bolted through a red light. "Wanker!" I shriek back over my shoulder, then don't bother to tell Chastain I didn't mean her.

Her tinny, digitised voice persists. "It started with the exorcism, Jack. And trust me, it's far from over. Have you realised yet, about the words on the video?"

It takes me a while to answer. "That's just the drugs. I've fucked my brain. Thought I saw Maria Corvi in my hotel room in Hong Kong too. Now, if you don't mind, I'm driving."

My finger hovers over "End Call," but something stops me. Even here, in my state of blinkered arrogance, some shred of sense lingers. I want to hear what Chastain thinks about me seeing Maria.

"It's not the drugs and you know it," she says. "The video, seeing Maria again, this experiment—they're all linked. Listen, before you burned the book . . . did you read the chapter about you?"

My focus blurs in and out. I clamp my hands on the wheel and try to hold it together. I didn't dare read that chapter. I only read Di Stefano's foreword, which referred to my existence in the past tense. That was enough to freak me out on the flight back from Rome. Half of me still thinks the book's a sick prank, but combined with a plane and the smell of burning, it launched a panic attack. Wish I'd never changed my mind about torching the whole thing in my Brighton bedroom.

If that chapter survived the Zippo flame, did Chastain read it? Does she know how I'm supposedly going to die?

I punch "End Call."

Chastain redials three times, but I ignore her and retreat into my cosy shell. I tell myself once again how Chastain is a con artist trying to win back my trust. Maria Corvi may be a killer, but she's not possessed by Satan. Tony Bonelli probably isn't even dead, let alone making threatening phone calls. The YouTube video was the work of a bunch of manipulative ghost-chasing LA dicks. The Mimi Experiment's just good fodder for the book.

And I can safely forget about the three words only I hear on that video.

Everything's fine.

My self-preserving world view is safely back in place. This is how most people get through their lives, and I can hardly blame them.

If you thought my excuses for not investigating the hospital murders and Maria's disappearance were feeble, you were right. I tell myself the same justifying, reassuring crap I told you in these pages, but the idea of returning to Italy scares me. From the moment Maria Corvi somehow followed me to Hong Kong—actually, from the moment she said "Enjoy your journey" through Tony's mouth—I wished I'd never met her. I felt like I'd *activated* something and now the walls of the world were closing in.

I plaster over these lurking fears with bravado. Thick layers of bravado that do their damnedest to smother the Nirvana lyric, "*Just because you're paranoid / Don't mean they're not after you.*"

Remember how I wrote that I wake up laughing off the recurring dream? Pure bravado. Every night at 3:33 a.m., without fail, that dream reduces me to a quivering mess. Can't get back to sleep without pills and fat vodka slugs.

The Exorcist has always terrified me. Even the cover of Slayer's *Reign In Blood* unnerves me.

I think of ghost trains as fear aversion therapy. I could never face one of those things without Bex to hold on to.

Until Bex arrived in LA, I was sleeping with the lights on. Told myself it was so I wouldn't hurt myself while stumbling to the bathroom drunk.

In fact, I've been telling myself that since adolescence.

The lies we tell ourselves. Comforting justifications, designed to try and fill the holes in us.

I may have reassured myself that the church exorcism was *The Truman Show*, but my bones still felt cold inside.

I may have given myself all manner of explanations for Maria's appearance in that Hong Kong suite, but when she vanished into the floor, I cried tears of confusion.

I may have told myself that Dead Tony Bonelli's phone call was an online prank, but I've still never felt so alone while surrounded by people.

And of course, I've written all these reassurances down.

While lying to you, I reinforced the lies I told myself.

The numbing power of cocaine works wonders for bravado. Without a noseful, I could never have followed that voice down to the boiler room.

More than anything else, though, my secret mission keeps me going. Keeps me investigating, instead of running back to Brighton and hiding under my bed. The mission I'm finally ready to reveal to you when the time comes.

As I cruise over to see Dr. Santoro in Burbank, I might still be cushioned by denial, but deep down, marrow deep, I know Sherilyn's right to warn me. What's going on isn't solely the product of psychological *connections, connections*. I did start something on Halloween. Speaking from a watery grave, Tony Bonelli told me I'm going to get what I deserve. And according to the pages of a Father Primo Di Stefano book that shouldn't yet exist, what I deserve is death.

But hey, Jack, just keep driving. Keep snorting the chemical euphoria. Keep bullishly posting online about how the supernatural doesn't exist.

Everything's f-i-n-e.

During the session, my full metal jacket of denial stays tight despite Santoro's best efforts. I've only turned up because I want to see if there's a rational explanation for "Adramelech," "Mephistopheles" and "Baphomet," but of course he knows where the real meat lies and starts gnawing at it.

"How would you characterise your childhood?"

"I wouldn't."

Santoro also failed to get me to talk about my parents during our first session. Today, I refuse to discuss Maria Corvi too. I know I should open up, I really do, but I can't handle it. *I would*, I tell myself, *but not on two hours' sleep. Maybe next time.*

Sully Strong would be proud.

Sharon the pit bull is present again. Funnily enough, as I write this up on a bloodstained hotel bed, documenting all the amusing things she does during the fucking session no longer seems important.

"Everything's connected," says Santoro. "You've obviously no obligation to talk about your childhood. But it is analogous to visiting an osteopath with a bad neck, then not letting her touch your shoulder blades. It all links together."

Connections, connections.

"Like I said, I want to talk about the video. Remember, the—"

"The YouTube video, yes," cuts in Santoro, referring to his notes. This is the world we live in now, where even your shrink won't let you finish a sentence.

After I explain about the three words only I can hear, I feel like he has no clue what to tell me. "I guess you realise that these are the names of devils?"

Off my nod, he adds, "How do you feel about the Devil?"

"Same way I feel about God," I say, wondering if I'm exhibiting any of the giveaway micro-expressions that tell experts you're lying. "They're just imaginary friends for adults. Or imaginary enemies."

"But does the *concept* of the Devil scare or disturb you?"

Maria Corvi, the puppet, rising from the dusty church floor.

Maria Corvi, the hitch-hiker, whispering "Enjoy" through the mist.

Maria Corvi, speaking each of those three words on the video—shut up, shut up.

But you know it's her, don't you. The girl of your dreams.

You know.

Shut up!

I swallow down the dread. "Concepts are just . . . concepts."

Three dollars' worth of clock ticks are augmented by the tap-tap-tap of Santoro's pen on his notepad. Now that I've noticed this habit of his, each tap becomes a hammer to the skull.

"What kind of voice is it?" he asks. Sweat clams up my palms: is he reading my mind? "Male, female? Young, old?"

"I don't know." I just want this over with. Can't stop thinking about my next two lines of coke, white and fluffy as angel wings.

Santoro frowns at his pad again. Tap-tap-tap. And I just know he's making the connection. That's what shrinks do. They piece together a narrative, just like journalists or believers in the supernatural.

"Does the voice sound at all like Maria Corvi?"

Shut up about M**** C****, Santoro, or I'll Die Hard *you.*

I contort the muscles in my face to feign surprise. "Hmm! Hard to say."

Get out, Jack. Get out of here and never look back.

Tap-tap-tap. "Are you hearing any other voices at all, outside of the video?"

Oh, here we go. The voices. Shrinks love those voices.

What about the calling of my name that led me down to the boiler room? God, let's not make this worse. I've already admitted to hearing three words that shouldn't be heard. Devil words, at that. The wacko klaxon is blaring.

Voices. Brain scans. Disease. Schizophrenia. Tumours.

Calm as a baby lamb, Santoro talks about referring me to a medical centre. I could just walk into one of these centres myself and pay, apparently, but he knows a really good one. He's saying "strictly routine tests" and tapping that fucking pen as I push myself up to stand on numb clay legs and stagger for the door.

Yes, I get up and walk away. I walk fast until I can no longer hear Santoro calling my name and asking, "Don't you want to find an explanation for all of this?"

I walk until gulping LA's toxic air seems to save my life.

Because when the chips are down, walking away is the one thing you can rely on Jack Sparks to do.

CHAPTER ELEVEN

I find Bex upside down against the wall of our room with her legs spread wide.

Her face is caked in sweat. Her biceps and triceps quiver under the pressure of supporting her lower body. This is nothing new—I'm used to wandering into rooms back home and finding her contorted into some improbable position, keeping herself lithe and limber. In fact, this feels worryingly familiar. We're already tipping right back into platonic domesticity.

I greet her, then nip into the bathroom. When there's a chance someone might hear, the trick is to flush the toilet then quickly snort the powder up into your sinuses before the water settles. The kind of sneaky little ritual that makes coke-heads think themselves extra clever.

With ever-impressive mastery of her body, Bex peels out of the handstand and rights herself. Maria Corvi crawls back into my thoughts, that macabre puppet rising from the church floor, but I swat the vision aside for the tenth time today. I'm way too good at burying things. Guilt and shame a speciality.

Pupils dilating, dopamine levels soaring, I plonk myself on the bed amid the wrappers of luxury snack items that once sat in a basket on the minibar.

"Sorry," Bex says. "The hangover made me eat a load of shit today. Nothing to do with me. It was the hangover. It also made me watch a load of shit TV."

"Haven't you gone out at all?"

"Made it to a magazine stand after lunch. Apart from that, thought I'd wait for you."

Hope surges through me again, as much as I try to anchor it. There's nothing worse than misplaced hope.

"Well, listen," I tell her. "We're going to start the night in a seriously glam location."

"Really?"

"Oh yeah. Big on the atmosphere. It's *hot*."

"Way cool," says Astral. Sweat drips from him as he points at the bare hanging light bulb. "*The Evil Dead*, man."

The Paranormals nose their way around in the gloom, doing a stand-up job of pretending they've never been to this basement before.

"You see so much more than in the video," marvels Howie, limping over to touch pipes, dials, everything, as if visiting the BBC's TARDIS set. "I hadn't even noticed that damn elevator door."

Only Bex's reaction seems genuine. Rather than being disappointed to find we were coming down here, she's full of wonder, taking it all in. She stays close to me, though, wary, having believed the video to be real from the moment she saw it.

The smell of Lucky Strikes wafts down from upstairs, out

by the bins. Rather than seeking Howitz's permission, I just lied to Johnson in a conversation like this:

"We need to hold a séance down there tonight with some ghost experts. Mr. Howitz asked me to square it with you."

"Oh, he did?"

"Yep, he wants to make you official co-ordinator."

I don't care about Johnson's job security.

After unlocking the service door, Johnson led us down crumbling stone steps. Johann and I helped him carry a beaten-up dining table from a storeroom to the boiler area. The others separated a ceiling-high stack of plastic conference chairs. Johnson hovered, angling for an invitation to stay, until I suggested he get some air. I said he'd be the first to hear if we got results. "Just don't touch no dials," he called over his shoulder, ambling back up to the subdued evening light.

And now I just stand here, watching the Hollywood Paranormals do their shtick. I'm reminded of their YouTube efforts, in which they descend on supposedly haunted venues across America. Parapsychological superheroes assembling.

"I definitely feel a presence here," claims Astral, leaning on the rickety table with both hands. "Felt it from the get-go, soon as we came down those steps." His colleagues concur.

"Hella cold down here, for a boiler room," says Johann.

More agreement, followed by Ellie noting that there are no windows. Bex is weirdly quiet: I sense their observations are spooking her, clamming her up. I give her a wink, and her brave smile touches me.

Lisa-Jane screws the Mimi Experiment camcorder to its tripod, although I expressly forbid the group from uploading footage without my say-so. Pascal and Elisandro rig up all the other toys.

Ellie beams as she produces a battered and sun-faded Ouija

board. "And of course we got this. Been passed from generation to generation in my family."

For a while there, I tell them, I thought I was going to
write a book about the supernatural that didn't feature a Ouija
board. I come across as typically aloof, but the war in my head
feels familiar. This is the same conflict I felt when Bex suggested
we visit an American medium back in Brighton. I know the
Paranormals are about to put on some kind of show here—the
culmination of their master plan. My head knows it will all
be laughably fake. But my pounding heart is somewhere else
altogether as I join the others around the table, being sure to
sit next to Bex.

I don't know what I'm more afraid of: the séance unveiling
a real ghost, or being suckered into these people's lies.

Blame my secret mission.

Astral squats on a stool at one end, casting himself as banquet
host, positioned so that he reaps the lion's share of camera
time. I even overhear him instructing Pascal to adjust the
camcorder to frame him better. As usual, it misses me altogether,
which is perfectly deliberate on their part.

"We need to *open our minds*," Astral announces, his eyes
swivelling my way, "so that we might connect with the presence here. Are we ready?"

I nod, playing along with the game they created. Waiting
for them to trip up.

All our forefingers converge on the planchette, the wooden
pointing device with its round transparent window. All the
better for seeing which letters the spirit selects. We've formed
a tight circle of fists around the window. I'm right-handed and
Bex is a leftie, so our thumbs touch. I curl mine around hers
and squeeze, telling myself it's for her benefit.

All around us, small lights blink. On the nearby monitor screen, a flat line solemnly awaits irregular activity.

Astral closes his eyelids with a theatrical flutter. "We seek an audience with the spirit here. We have seen you in a video and are very interested and intrigued. And so is the internet."

Is he going to tell the ghost how many hits and unique visitors it's attracted? *Hey Casper, your Google ranking's awesome, dude.*

Everyone remains very still. The only sound comes from the analysis machines and that enduring generator hum. The only movement I'm aware of is the tiny tug of Bex's thumb on mine. I wonder if she's excited or regretting this. And I wonder about my own place on that spectrum.

"Are you here with us?" Astral asks of the dark. "Please answer via the board. *Are you here?*"

At least a thousand coke-fuelled heartbeats later, the planchette begins to move.

While I feel I'm exerting no pressure myself, I've read up on the scientific explanation for a moving planchette: *the ideo-motor effect.* Involuntary, unconscious motor behaviour initiated by the mind, whether you realise it's happening or not.

In this case, of course, the planchette is simply being moved by seven other people—I'm excluding Bex—who have planned the outcome of this little charade.

It edges away from its starting point at the top of the board and slides down into the alphabet.

I follow Pascal's gaze over to his gadgets. The flat line has begun to spike. "Electromagnetic energy up ten," he reports. "And a temp drop of ten."

"I feel that," says Ellie. And it does feel colder. I peer at the

Paranormals' machines, wondering if one of them covertly pumps out cold air.

The planchette stops moving when its window displays the letter "I."

Everyone says the letter out loud, softly. Then we wait for the next.

The planchette moves again. But instead of shifting to another letter, it remains on the same one.

It sticks on the letter "I."

Circling it slowly, ever so slowly.

Astral clears his throat. "Is this the first letter of your name?"

At this point, I think I get it. The planchette is about to head over to the word "YES," which is helpfully provided on this board along with "NO" and "GOODBYE." I undercut the tension by murmuring how handy it would be to have an "OMG" and a "LOL." Only Bex and Pascal laugh.

The planchette keeps moving, but doesn't deviate.

It keeps on circling the "I."

For the longest time, Astral tries to coax more from the boiler room spirit.

He asks for the spirit's age when it passed over. Where it was born.

Is it happy to communicate? Are we doing anything wrong? There's no response.

I . . .

I . . .

I . . .

When we finally call it a night, some of the disappointment flooding the basement is secretly my own. Where was the performance, the theatre? The climax of the Hollywood Paranormals' cunning plan?

"So have you ever received just one letter before?" I ask Astral, in a rare instance of me talking to him directly.

"It's usually all or nothing," says Elisandro, speaking for him. "You either get no response or, like, reams of info."

"Just one letter," puzzles Howie. "Why that letter? Why 'I'?"

Johann shrugs. "Maybe it really is the spirit's first initial. Maybe it got stage fright."

Astral heaves his bulk off the stool. "We could try again in a few nights."

Ah, so tonight marks the start of a long game. It might have seemed too instant, too convenient, if our alleged ghost started yapping right off the bat. Victorian mediums periodically claimed the dead weren't co-operating in order to lend their own amazing powers more credibility when the spirits *did* play ball.

We loiter in small groups, speaking in hushed tones. The world's most lo-fi cocktail party. Lisa-Jane and Johann feed me all kinds of crap about their previous Ouija escapades. I barely hear any of it, because I'm looking around the area. Noticing how even the extra lights we've set up can't penetrate the dark in some of the corners.

Then I focus on Astral and Bex talking, off by themselves, near the lift door. They're too far away for me to hear them, but Astral's leaning against a dirty wall, striking a pose, as if chatting her up.

Ha, I think to myself. *Good luck with that, fat boy.*

Nightfall. The Sunset Strip is all car headlights, bright neon tubing and lofty spotlit hoardings. Bex and I are waiting for an electronic cross sign to let us over Sunset so we can reach Carney's—a fast-food place installed in a single yellow train carriage just off the road.

I should've waited until I'd eaten before doing more coke, but the urge overcame me, post-séance. Needed to steady myself and top up my certainty, or my denial, whatever you want to call it. And now I'm not hungry at all.

Bex claims she wasn't creeped during the séance. "The basement's scary, but these Paraglider people or whatever they're called, they just want to be in your book. They all have that look in their eyes, like they're auditioning for *Big Brother*."

"*Thank you*," I say. "So I'm not going mad." As we reach the other side of Sunset, I add, "If you weren't scared, then why were you so quiet?"

She doesn't answer, and I notice her funny little smile.

"It was weird," she says when I ask again. We're heading up three steel steps into Carney's. "I went all shy! I don't usually get like that."

I don't know what she means. "Why shy?"

Long pause. "What's that guy's name? Is it Astral?"

Red-hot nails poke my guts. "Yeah . . . so what?"

And Bex laughs. "You want me to spell it out?"

We're standing in front of the service window inside the train carriage, where a guy in a Carney's T-shirt and cap greets us. "Welcome to Carney's. Can I take your order?"

I ignore him. "Yeah," I tell Bex. "Please do spell it out."

"I think he's kinda hot, okay? A hot hippy."

Those red-hot nails rupture soft tissue inside me, freeing a wave of resentment.

"You are *kidding*, right?"

"He's got nice eyes."

"You guys gonna order?" says one of the two muscle-vest guys waiting behind us.

"Yeah," I say. "I'll have ten cheeseburgers and ten fries."

Bex boggles at this. "Did you just say ten?"

"That's right," I say, the drug smothering any sense of how loud I am. "If that's what it fucking takes, I'd better bulk up."

An atom bomb detonates in my head. It's so stupid and shameful, but I walk the length of the train carriage, then head back down on to the street, leaving Bex behind.

I stalk back to the crossing, swearing aloud, with steam blasting from my ears. Thinking how it all makes sense in a sickening way: if you stuck a pump up Zakk Wylde's rectum and inflated him, he'd look like Astral.

Tyres screech to a halt as I march across. Horns blast.

When I reach the other side, that mad old woman from last night—twenty-four hours ago, when anything seemed possible—is passing by. She eyes me as if for the first time. "If I were you . . ." she begins, only to cut herself short. Probably because I look equally deranged. No point preaching to the converted.

"Jack!" comes the cry from back across Sunset. "Jack?"

I didn't walk away to make Bex follow me. I did it because walking away is what I do. There was a time in my life when I managed to stop doing this—while tracking down and interviewing gang members for a book, for instance, and having guns and knives pulled on me—but it was only really for my benefit. Big social issues to make me look bigger and more important. I've never cared about gangs. Or, for that matter, about magicians being set on fire in the Dominican Republic, people blaming homosexuality on demons, anorexic Filipino girls being killed by botched exorcisms or any of that stuff I mentioned.

I've never cared about anyone who isn't Jack Sparks.

There's a smoking pit where my empathy should be.

Last summer, my life took a turn. Ever since, I've been at

odds with myself, because the system I built no longer offers what I need. I knew the only way I could kick drugs would be to write *Jack Sparks on the Supernatural*.

You don't understand and I can't expect you to. I haven't explained myself properly, not yet.

By the time Bex catches up, I've locked myself in our hotel room's bathroom.

She sounds equal parts pissed off and confused. "Since when do you go off on me like that? You back on the powder, or what?"

"Yes, I am," I say, pulling the two-gram wrap from its zipped partition in my wallet. "And I'm going to do a shitload more."

"God, so all that rehab was for nothing? I only said I quite liked that guy—what's it got to do with you anyway?"

I use my Amex to separate a bump of coke from the rest, then chop it up beside the sink.

I slice lines as Bex questions me through the door. Her voice fades, even as it rises in pitch. I just focus on the powder. It's really good to focus. These days, my thoughts are so conflicted that I'm coming apart. I want to fire my brain into orbit and leave everything else at ground level.

Two snowbound airport runways await my attention on the porcelain. I tug a dollar bill from the wallet and roll it up.

Bex's yell manages to register. "Jack! *What exactly is your problem?*"

I growl and sling the dollar tube in the sink. Leaving the coke behind, I unlatch the door and fling it open in one motion. Bex takes a few steps back, tense, ready for anything. When I see her fear, it neutralises the verbal burns I wanted to inflict. I hold the door frame and fumble for words, for the right accusation.

"You don't even remember what happened last night, do you?" I say. Off her reaction, which looks disturbed and uncertain, I add, "Or are you just so bloody ashamed?"

At first Bex seems to rack her brains for what I'm talking about. But that's not it. She's assessing the situation and girding herself.

I must suddenly look as vulnerable as I feel, because she walks to me. I flinch as she places both hands on my hips. Such human contact feels strange. Nice strange. Great strange. Her hands stay in place as her eyes meet mine.

"I thought *you* forgot," she says.

And then we're kissing. Deep, unleashed.

Hands on buttons and zips.

A blitzkrieg of the senses.

I'm not going to describe anything else that happens tonight. As a member of the YouPorn generation, you can imagine it yourself. But most importantly, my work has already exploited this woman enough.

Yes, let me get the truth about Bex down. I'm far beyond caring what Erubis Books thinks about me saying this.

I've never been in love with Bex.

Lust, yes, love, no.

From the moment five years ago when we met and she moved in, my balls have done the thinking. But I knew it would make a better story if I loved her too. I also thought it would be better if she was a fitness instructor rather than . . . oh God . . . rather than whatever it is she actually does.

I knew I was an egotistical prick. I also knew that people might tolerate me more if I showed a softer side, even if it didn't exist. So I wrote my fake unrequited love for Bex into *Jack Sparks on a Pogo Stick* and people responded well. Almost too well. Most of the Amazon reviews ignored all the sweat and the painfully compacted vertebrae I'd suffered for that dumb road trip, and wrote instead about me and Bex. About how they wanted to see if we'd ever get it together. People lapped that stuff right up, even if they didn't normally buy the kind of books I wrote. At book signings, guys asked if I'd shagged her. Girls asked if they could be her friend.

So I kept the thread going through the books that followed. If I was dating someone else, I struck it from the record. Even if we had slept together, I wouldn't have said so in my books. Because then the whole will-they-won't-they appeal would die. We journalists eliminate whatever dilutes our chosen story, while keeping—or adding—what makes it pure. When Bex dated other guys, I became Yearning Jack in the pages of *Jack Sparks on Gangs*, then Heartbroken Jack in *Jack Sparks on Drugs*. Most readers believed Bex was the cause of my drug rampage, which was a great way for me to cover up the real reason.

There's no question that I *should* have been in love with Bex. And I always loved her as a person and as a friend. But my overriding urge has been to fuck her brains out. The more unobtainable she was, the more she became an achievement I wanted to unlock. A VIP lounge I could never access. Yeah, grim. I used her as a character in my work to cast me in a more favourable light. Because if someone as funny and cool as Bex gave me the time of day, even to the extent of living with me, then how bad could I be? Thank God Bex didn't read those books, or she might have been creeped out by this flatmate who seemed so smitten.

I've never felt capable of love, or really understood it. My dad laid down the template: never look back. Move on, cold as Christmas. Don't get tied down, don't even think about what you're leaving behind.

In the cavernous archives of my mind, my dad is the faintest presence. Barely a shadow. Sometimes I catch an evocative smell or feel a resonance I suspect is linked to him, because I can't place it anywhere else. Or I'll detect negative character traits in myself that I can't ascribe to Mum. But that's it.

Oh, he tolerated having one kid—especially a golden boy like Alistair. But when the second screaming bag of shit and piss popped out, I was the straw that broke his back. Rationally, I may now suspect that's not the whole truth, but emotionally it's too late. I'm programmed. You can rationalise a baseball bat, but it still drastically changes the shape of your head.

Three years, eight months and seventeen days after I was born, Dad stole off towards the sunset, never to be seen again, at least not by us. Mum burned all photos of him on the garden barbecue when I was four. I still remember how that smoke smelt and what it did to the back of your throat.

I swear my first memory is the noise our mum made the day she realised her husband wasn't coming back. She locked herself in their bedroom and made these slaughter noises. The sound of animals being carved up alive.

Alistair and I were in the living room, hearing all this. I was too young to understand what was going on, but I clearly remember him giving me this *look* before he went off to knock on the door and see if Mum was okay.

Oh God, that look.

Hear that? it said. *Do you hear our mother howling her head off? You made that happen. You're the reason our dad left.*

This baseball bat is my earliest memory.

Family life only rode downhill after that. There were some

good times, but mostly Alistair resented me, and I suppose I resented the extra time he'd had with Dad. One night, when Mum had sunk a bottle of red, she yelled through my bedroom door, saying how she wished she'd never had me. I was seven.

I could barely remember Dad's face, but apparently I didn't need to. All I had to do was look in the mirror. Naturally, out of me and Alistair, I had to be the one who resembled him.

And my mother could barely look at me.

I was all those barbecued photographs made flesh, back to haunt her.

CHAPTER TWELVE

Inside this howling body tube, this roaring tunnel of moulded white plastic, there's far too much peace. Way too much alone time.

Can nothing be done to make an MRI scanner less of a coffin?

Last night, I didn't have the Maria dream. I didn't wake until the morning, with Bex's bare heat curled around me. Happiness has been a stranger for some time, but this morning he and I were on nodding terms.

Those fat lines of coke called my name from the bathroom sink. With one sweep of my hand and a spin of the tap, I washed them down the plughole. Straight away I felt the addict's pangs of regret, but I'm determined to straighten up. To gain true perspective on everything. It's time to stop taking the easy way out.

So here I am. Doing what the doctor ordered, with a rubber panic-bulb in one hand. Wanting, needing to rule out the possibility that something's wrong with my brain.

But a full-body scanner is a tough place for a man who likes to forget. All I can think about in here, in the grip of cocaine withdrawal, are bad memories and death. Guilt and shame.

Last summer. Alistair becoming more terse with each new voice-mail.

"Jack, I really think you should come back to me."

"Jack, I don't know what you're doing, but we need to talk."

"Jack, what the hell's wrong with you?"

Endless emails from him too, most of which I ignore. Some of which I read through slow ketamine eyes. Fast cocaine eyes. Heavy-lidded bong eyes, on the other side of the cosmos.

Delete, delete, delete.

The nurse's soft voice mercifully interrupts. She speaks into my headphones from out there in the world of the living. "You'll feel a scratch on the back of your hand. Just a little imaging solution, as we discussed."

If there's a hell, it's full of people locked in coffins, alone with their thoughts and their worst memories.

My mother sitting at a slatted wooden garden table. Her hand shaking as she lights a cigarette.

Me, driving through rain, Alistair yelling abuse.

As a needle pricks my vein, I start to freak inside this caco-phonous tomb. I want to squeeze the panic-bulb. I want the Zippo, but it's in the jacket I was told to remove.

The nurse must spot my restless, twitching feet, because she returns to my ears: "Just another twenty minutes, Mr. Sparks. Please, try to go to your happy place."

I don't think I have a happy place. This possibility makes me ache.

I try to imagine sitting on a beach. Which, given the noise

levels, inevitably becomes a beach next to a construction site.

I change channel to sit in a noisy pub with unlimited free drinks and multiple lines of cocaine chopped out on the bar. I imagine being loaded, buzzed up, feeling like The Man.

That doesn't do the job either. Which cranks my anxiety, until I realise a pub is not my happy place—it's my escape route.

Bex's face takes centre stage. No beach, no bar, just our Brighton flat. We're on the big fat yellow sofa. She holds my hand and stares into my eyes, then tells me everything's all right.

Through the year of *Drugs* and beyond, Rebecca Lawson has been my anchor. My flesh-and-blood cocaine.

But how I've used her. I've seen her, over the years, as a body to be conquered, as a crutch, as someone to manipulate.

I'm going to make it all up to her.

Hey, maybe this could be something solid, something secure.

Maybe, even if I can't feel love, this could be an actual, proper relationship.

"Thank you very much for coming in," says Roger Corman. I'm literally on the edge of my seat in his San Vicente Boulevard office, wondering what he's about to tell me.

When I came out of the med centre, unsure how to feel about the three-day wait for results, I was surprised to find a voicemail from Corman's PA, asking if I was available to meet. I phoned back fast. The octagenarian is a legend in independent film-making, having been responsible for over four hundred movies, which often tick the horror genre box, like *Piranha* (1978) and *Children of the Corn* (1984). He gave the likes of Francis Ford Coppola and Jack Nicholson their first breaks.

He's also a marketing genius, hailing from that generation that really knew how to use trailers to sell a picture, regardless of whether everything in those trailers was in the finished article.

In person, he's genial and dapper in a black suit and white shirt. His New Horizons Picture Corporation was one of the companies I'd emailed about the video, but the only one that has asked me in for a meet. Everyone else has now responded, on the phone, by email or in person, with variations of "No, we did not make the video, you gigantic freak."

After all this searching, will it turn out that Roger Corman shot the damn thing?

"I'd like to discuss this YouTube video with you," he says across his desk, voice soft. He's writing notes on a yellow legal pad. Reading upside down, I can see the capitalised heading "GHOST VIDEO."

I grip the arms of my chair as he says, "This thing has gained a great deal of hits on YouTube. It's a very powerful piece of film-making, don't you think?"

I can control myself no longer. "Did you make it?"

"Oh," he says, with a chuckle. "Oh. I was about to ask you the same thing."

What I feel here is a bizarre relief. "No, I kind of found it. Or it found me. Someone put it on my YouTube account."

"I see. So you don't own the rights to it?"

"No."

We keep talking for a while, but I can tell that, from Corman's point of view, the meeting has already served its purpose.

Reading that legal pad upside down, I see he's written "PUBLIC DOMAIN???"

★   ★   ★

I stride into the Culver City experiment room with my head held high. Buoyed by a weird combination of sex, Roger Corman and the death of a recurring dream.

All the way here, I've pep-talked myself. I can't control all the bad things I've done these last few years, but I can control what I do *now*.

I can still turn this day around, and every other day that follows.

I can get to the bottom of what's going on with the video, with the Paranormals, maybe with my own paranoia.

I can make things work, really work, with Bex.

Everything's fine and that's a fact.

Astral soon dents my titanium. He takes me aside and says, "That girl Bex, man . . . Is she with you?"

My reaction is pure knee-jerk. "Yeah, she is."

"Cool," he says, nodding furiously. "Hey, you did good there, buddy."

"Thanks," I say. "I'll treasure that note of surprise forever." Then I give him just enough cold, dead eye contact to communicate that this subject is closed. Of course, I know Bex isn't *with* me, but there's no way I'm letting Astral barge in.

I sit and fume over his impudence as the others crack on. Pascal musters the gall to speak at length about how quantum physics has made time travel all the more likely. "It's possible," he says, "that what we see as ghosts are in reality time travellers. It could be that séances are a safe way for them to communicate with us." This notion is greeted by much earnest nodding and stroking of chins—as is Ellie, when she broaches the idea that this experiment could potentially attract a "genuine passing spirit."

These sycophants congratulate Astral on a social media

competition he's running where the winner gets a follow-back from him. An idea he copied from me. The team are also "excited for" a local radio interview Astral and Elisandro did about the experiment. An interview I never knew was happening and which probably doesn't even mention me.

Checking my phone, I discover that my social media accounts have all disappeared.

Just . . . gone.

When I try to access them from my phone, the log-ins no longer work.

Speechless, I stare at the screen. I will it to change. A brand-new suspicion blooms: can this sabotage be sheer coincidence, the day after I refused to boost the Paranormals' profiles any further? Is Pascal the friendly computer genius avoiding eye contact, or am I imagining that?

I cycle through apps and sites, hitting the same buttons again and again, but the results stay the same. The cornerstones of my online profile have been demolished. Only YouTube remains.

These people leeched me for followers, many thousands of followers, and now they've shut me down. Anyone invested in following the experiment can only get the skinny from them. The Paranormals jumped up on my shoulders, then gagged me. The one guy in the experiment who's going to question it all.

I'm falling through a void. My cheeks are red-hot chilli peppers.

Everyone else keeps on delivering monologues about themselves.

I am Mount Vesuvius, circa AD 79.

Just as I'm about to let rip and roast them, that's when the table starts to move and the face appears in mid-air.

★   ★   ★

"A face? What do you mean, a fucking face?"

Here's Bex on a high stool beside me at the Sunset Castle's Tiki Bar, out by the pool. She's demolishing a pina colada, still very much in holiday mode. Not to mention WTF? mode, now that I've mentioned the face. The moving table means nothing compared to the face.

"And in *mid-air*?"

I'm still rubbing my bruised jaw as I nod, then tell her what I'm about to tell you.

Lisa-Jane is saying how she once sent Marilyn Manson a vial of her piss, when one corner of the table rears up all by itself.

The words curl up and die in Lisa-Jane's mouth.

You can sense our collective pulse.

"Okay," Astral intones, a tremor in his voice. "Let's just keep on talking, guys."

I abandon my chair and squat down, trying to find an angle where I can see everyone's knees at the same time. I observe how the table shifts from standing on two legs, to one, back to two.

Catching my perplexed expression, Lisa-Jane sneers. "Time to open your mind, huh?"

"If opening my mind involves trusting you," I say, "then forget it."

Her nostrils flare. "Meaning . . . what?"

"LJ," snaps Astral, more imperious by the minute. "Let's stay focused here. What did you do when the pee overflowed on your fingers?"

I sit back down beside the others. All our fingertips rest on the table's surface as it rises and falls in unexpected places.

When one leg lands heavily on Howie's alleged gimp foot, his howl of pain is lost among our excitable whoops.

Yes, *our* whoops. I kind of get swept away. Might as well enjoy this bullshit while dismantling the Paranormals' reputation. Do the others look delighted because their specially doctored magic stunt table is functioning well? Yes. Could we achieve this same movement on any table, anywhere? No.

This particular table must conceal small motors. Tiny gyroscopes. Remote-control receptors, accessed by someone's hand buried in their pocket. Or it's controlled by an outside accomplice, monitoring everything through a camera hidden in one of Pascal's gadgets. We live in an age where you can use a smartphone to switch on your central heating from the other side of the world. Or, according to Howie, induce a fatal insulin overdose via Bluetooth. Making a table move is no kind of stretch.

Lisa-Jane nods over at the camcorder: "Please say we're rolling." Pascal nods.

I'm pretty sure Ellie sees the face first.

I think she says, "Oh my God, guys, *guys* . . .," but it's hard to be certain because the moment is so very shocking and she's soon joined by everyone else gasping, swearing and fumbling for their phones.

Chills rush up my arms. This floating face is looking directly at me.

It's suspended high enough so that most of us have to crane our necks. Same size as a human head, and with a human face, but genderless and strange.

I mean, it has two eyes, two ears, a nose and a mouth, but the nature of each element keeps changing. Slowly, fluidly, continuously. The eyes switch from brown to blue to green.

The ears, nose and mouth change size and shape. Even the colour of the skin is restless, darkening and lightening.

The only constant is the attitude this apparition gives off. It grins.

Not what you'd call a benign grin, either. This grin is more "Yeah, I'm here, motherfuckers, and now the fun starts." The eyes gleam. Mimi looks as pleased to see us as the Paranormals are to see it.

Is this supposed to be the same Mimi we created? It doesn't even look like a woman. Although, thinking about it, we never bothered to discuss how Mimi looked. We just wanted results. Bragging rights.

Our first instinct is not to communicate with this entity, but to capture it.

"Sweet mother of God," says Astral, stabbing sausage fingers at his phone screen. "I need to get a picture to Fox News." Elisandro tilts the camcorder upwards on its tripod, homing in for Mimi's close-up. Pacing around in circles, Ellie says she's going to call *American Idol* host Ryan Seacrest.

I couldn't say how I feel. My stomach does a figure-eight. *What is this thing?*

It's the same push and pull of emotion I've felt while writing this whole damn book. That same internal war. As everyone else's phones make their digital photo-snapping sounds, I don't know where to look. I'm transfixed by the floating face, while trying to work out where the holographic projector must be. Even though holograms only work in dark rooms with special lighting rigs. Could this be some new, cutting-edge holo tech? Is that even possible? What kind of hologram were Tupac and Michael Jackson?

If the Paranormals have seen this spectre a hundred times

during dress rehearsals, their acting is once again exemplary. While they gush and drool and photograph the face, I'm almost more tempted to photograph *them*, to document how genuinely blown away they appear.

When I get it together to take my own photograph of Mimi, I discover what the others are realising. When I tap the screen to zero in on the face, the little focusing square doesn't materialise. You'd swear there's nothing there to focus on . . .

"Fuck," breathes Johann, goggling at his screen. "It's not showing."

I snap Mimi, then join everyone else in examining our camera rolls.

We've taken a whole bunch of pictures of the ceiling and the ceiling alone. Elisandro's shoulders heave as he reviews the camcorder footage, which doesn't show the face either. He then channels all his zealous steam into an attack on me. "There you go, Mr. Big-Shot! That's why there aren't more real ghost videos."

Astral beats him to the punch. "Yes, some of these things *don't come out on film*." He says this unhappily, because he now has nothing to send Fox News.

The Mimi face beams down, as if enjoying the friction.

"Why's it looking at me?" I wonder aloud.

"It's not," says Astral. "It's looking at me."

"Bullshit," says Howie. "It's looking straight at *me*."

Everyone else says the same. Mimi is somehow looking at all of us at once, which makes me feel ill deep inside. Do we all need MRI scans? I certainly need some cocaine and a tequila slammer.

"Mimi," says Lisa-Jane, her cool evaporating, those drawn-on brows urgent squiggles. "Is that you? Nod if it's you."

Astral growls and opens his mouth to reprimand Lisa-Jane for taking control. Then his mouth stays open when the Mimi face nods its head.

Everyone cheers. A team who just scored the winning goal.

Contact has been made.

Discipline gives way to chaos, as people fire questions up at the face.

Ellie: "Are you really the Mimi we created, or are you a spirit passing by?"

Johann: "Is there life after death?"

Pascal: "Are you a time traveller?"

Howie: "Can you confirm that my neighbour is trying to kill me?"

I want to ask a question too, but everyone's so loud and my throat is sandpaper and there's a jackhammer pulse in my temples.

Everyone yells questions up at Mimi. Pure word salad.

Elisandro puts his hands together, then jerks them apart: "Stop!"

Mimi vanishes into thin air. It doesn't blip out, but rather melts away.

Something desperate ignites me. Something that believes Mimi is a real ghost. I flash my teeth at Elisandro and snarl, "Oh, nice work, dickhead."

Elisandro launches himself across the table and clocks me one on the jaw.

I grab him and topple back blind, losing my balance, dragging him down with me, white hot with hate. Before we hit the ground, my knuckles slam into something small and round and hard in a sea of soft flesh. Elisandro makes a glottal choking sound as his falling body weight smacks the wind from my lungs. He wrenches himself away in panic, crawling off across the carpet. Ellie stoops, her arms outstretched to intercept him. Mother and toddler.

"Asshole," she spits at me.

Johann's eyes are molten grey steel. His whole body flexes as he steps towards me, pauses, mutters some admonishment to himself, then joins the others crowding about Elisandro. I just loll around on the carpet, winded, checking that my jaw still works.

Elisandro clutches his throat and croaks as Ellie cradles him from behind.

This transient physical pain feels secondary to my mental anguish.

The push and pull.

Science sweeps in to provide a crutch, just as it has since I was five years old. I'm reminded, with as much impact as Elisandro's fist, that this experiment actually isn't good fun. Neither is my determination to expose them for making the video.

All of this is tearing me apart.

The firestorm of fear and rage at the back of my throat engulfs the room. "You think I don't know this is all total bullshit? You really think I've been going along with this *utter crap*?"

Our astonishment after seeing Mimi invests this war of words with an electrical charge. Forked lightning flashes out of me as I accuse the Paranormals of rigging the whole Mimi Experiment. They deliberately alienated Professor Spence, I say, because they knew he'd see right through the artifice when the table started moving. Probably because he and his own bunch of fakers had employed the same tricks in the seventies. So they'd wanted him on board at the start for the PR cachet, then just blanked him till he walked.

Astral's face turns purple as he tries to bellow me into submission, while Lisa-Jane screeches that I'm "a paranoid coke-head prick," but I just keep repeating myself until the full force of my disgusted bile sinks into their dumb heads.

"And I know full fucking well," I tell them, my forefinger a jabbing gun, throat sore from shouting, "that you stupid shits made the YouTube video. And now it's all going to blow up in your faces."

Bex stirs a straw around in her new pina, making the little umbrella fall out.

"Oh dear," she says. "So much for the whole stealthy-playing-along thing."

"Yeah," I say, tonguing a cracked tooth. "That's gone for good."

"So all this stuff happened this afternoon? What did they say when you accused them of making the video?"

"Oh, there was a whole load of shouting and big eyes and American stuff, until we all got tired of fighting. So we shifted to this other meeting room—one without a table—and made a circle with our chairs, talking it out like adults."

She's getting impatient. "And the outcome?"

Despite my nagging need for coke, I'm unable to suppress a smirk. "I pissed them off even more."

"You'd better be kidding," says Johann. The others, even Pascal, are equally aghast.

"I'm serious," I say. "Either we relocate the whole experiment, or I'm out. I won't even include this farce in the book. And you'll have to sell your arses on Hollywood Boulevard to fund the rest."

Howie scowls at my ignorance. "*Hollywood Boulevard*. You

mean Sepulveda." He then looks relieved when Lisa-Jane breaks the silence.

"How exactly do you think we achieved the illusion of a floating fucking head today, Jack? I'm so psyched to hear this."

I shrug. "Who knows what your fancy gadgets do?"

"I'd be happy to talk you through it again," says Pascal. Even my favourite Paranormal's gone all passive-aggressive.

"Listen, man, this is so counterproductive," says Astral. "We just made our biggest ever breakthrough. We should all be celebrating, but here's you, peeing all over it." He spreads his words out slow and thick, believing me stupid. "Now you listen up. We did not make that video."

My hands curl back into fists. "People have killed themselves because they think the video proves the afterlife. Your little self-promotion stunt has cost lives. You've given people false . . ." The words catch in my throat and I have to compose myself before I choke up and lose it altogether.

"Come on, Jack," says Pascal. "You've got the wrong idea here. We need to patch this up and move on."

"Well," I manage, "I'm offering you a way to do that. I believe you've rigged that meeting room and that table, somehow, some way. So tomorrow, we move to my friend's studio up in the hills. Big Coyote Ranch. We use a brand-new table you've never even seen before and your equipment stays unplugged."

I silence their protests with a raised finger. "At least for a while. And then we see what happens. If we still experience phenomena like today's, I'll be stumped and converted. Everyone wins."

Enjoying the barrel I have them over, I hammer my proposition home. "Now if that isn't scientific, then what is?"

Grudging acquiescence rumbles around the room. Elisandro gets up, hurls his chair against a wall, then goes to stand outside.

"And one last condition," I tell the others, with special emphasis on Pascal. "A fucking important one. You undo whatever you've done to my social media."

Pascal looks genuinely mystified.

Bex drops her bombshell question as we walk along Sunset towards the House of Blues. I didn't want to go out tonight—I'd much rather we stay in and punish the bedsprings. All that lost sleep hangs heavy on my eyelids, and I'm jonesing for my twin fixes of cocaine and social media grandstanding. Alcohol seems a poor relation.

"Have you been telling people we're a couple?" she asks, springing it on me fast. A panther strike from the bush.

I grind to a halt so fast a granite block may as well have sprung up in front of me. "Who said that?"

Turns out Astral friended Bex today. He did this knowing that my social media's up the creek, so I couldn't see his sly move. Then he messaged Bex and oh-so-casually asked how long she and I had been a couple.

"So you told him we're together?" she asks.

"What did you say back?"

"Answer the question."

Every cell in my body wants to hunt the guy down and beat him. "Well, how would you feel if I had told Astral that?"

"Jack, how many times do I need to say 'Answer the question' before you answer the bloody question? Did you tell Astral we're together?"

"Only because he asked, to see if the way was clear, the big sleaze."

She smirks awkwardly. Half laughs. "Let's . . . not go changing our relationship status just yet, yeah?"

My self-esteem plunges on a bungee cord.

"Oh God," I say. "Of course not."

"Would you mind if we go back to being mates?" she adds, reworking the bungee cord into a noose. "I think of you as one of my *best* mates, and I don't want to mess it up for the sake of, you know, a holiday . . . thing."

"I totally get that," I say, unable to grasp how the future I'd begun to imagine for us could be rejected. "Never thought anything different."

We wade on through pale yellow pools cast by street lamps. Stunned into silence, I check social media as a reflex, only to be reminded that most of my accounts don't exist. It's so infuriating, not being able to put myself out there. Ideas for great posts keep hatching, then flying around my skull with nowhere to go. A hard ball of unfulfilled self-expression festers in my gut. My followers probably think I'm dead. I plan to start new accounts everywhere, but these things take time. Now that Bex has poured cold water on us, I no longer feel like shooting a new YouTube video tonight—it's so much harder to hide your misery on those things.

The rest of the night is a dying dog, but we get by. It helps that the hot and noisy House of Blues has bands onstage, something to watch. When potentially difficult silences sweep in to consume us, we swat them away with words, any words. Trite observations about strangers. We both know we're avoiding the issue of what sex has done to us, but some conversational barriers may as well be granite blocks.

As the drinks go down, some of our old rapport returns, even though it feels forced. "If you *had* to have sex with an animal," Bex asks me, "which would it be?"

I can't think of anything funny to say.

She thinks her own answer over. "I'd have to go for a giraffe, because I wouldn't have to look it in the eye."

Our dinner server becomes excited about our nationality. "You guys are from England?" he exclaims. "Hey, do you know Neil Yates?" We stare at him, somehow keeping it together. Bex covers her mouth with her hand. The guy walks off baffled, still believing England to be a small village.

Tonight I sleep on the sofa, while Bex takes the bed. For the second night running, I don't dream of Maria, which is wonderful. If she still has some problem with me, what's she waiting for? It feels like the curse has lifted. Perhaps the curse was only ever cocaine.

Despite Maria's no-show in my dreams, a whole horde of angry imagery crashes around my head till morning. Not content with sabotaging my online presence, Astral has wrecked me and Bex before we even had a chance.

Which makes this personal.

Until tonight, I'd wanted to expose Astral Way and the Hollywood Paranormals.

Now, I want to destroy them.

CHAPTER THIRTEEN

Pascal aims my phone so I can see myself on the screen. I've instructed him to do it this way, so I can have absolute control.

"Bit to the left," I tell him, snatching at one of the infernal insects that buzz non-stop around us. "Bit more."

Pascal prods his specs back up on the bridge of his nose. "I promise you, Jack. We haven't done any of this stuff you're accusing us of."

"I said a bit more to the *left*. There. Ready? Three . . ."

Onscreen, behind me, you can see the sawn logs that comprise Big Coyote Ranch's roof. You can see most of the front porch, ideal for sitting down to play banjo. This place may look rustic, but inside there's a million dollars of studio tech.

"Two . . ."

Offscreen, behind Pascal, lies a hazy panorama. A row of boulders mark the cut-off point where this broad crest sweeps deep into forbidding stony gulfs shared by other hills. Uncomfortably steep roads snake back down towards the distant metropolis. From here, the City of Angels resembles several grids pushed together in an irritatingly arbitrary fashion.

"One . . ."

Sitting high off Mulholland, the ranch occupies several acres, with few neighbours. Ever since the global crash, record companies have sent their bands to less glamorous locations, and Big Coyote's owner, my expat mate Rod, has reeled against the ropes. This week, no one's recording at all, so he's handed me two sets of keys and left us to it. He's one trusting guy, Rod, but then we go way back to the late nineties, when an influential *NME* article of mine put Big Coyote on the map.

". . . Action."

Hearing the beep, I strap on my web face and launch the spiel. Because I'm convinced Bex will change her mind, today I'm still powered by caffeine and caffeine alone. Maybe the whole relationship status thing temporarily threw her. Best to stay off the Charlie, even though I'm strung out. This morning I was so tempted, I even got that chalky taste in the back of my throat, as if my body had generated an emergency supply. But if I can't have coke, I can at least bask in the light of a million YouTube eyes, while dealing Astral a blow to the kidneys.

"So I'm up here at Big Coyote Ranch," I tell the camera, "with a ghost-hunting group whose name escapes me. I've moved the Mimi Experiment from Culver City to the Hollywood Hills, to rule out any trickery from them. Never trust a true believer, even if they do claim to be a scientist. Let's go inside and see the new table we'll be using. Oh, and see if you can guess which of these people is Jabba the Hutt in disguise . . ."

Pascal follows with the phone as I walk through the front doors, which are flanked by vending machines, two glowing sentries. Star and cameraman, we cross the spacious reception lounge lined with empty black leather sofas and dotted with flight cases containing the Paranormals' equipment. The group sit around our new square table, staring daggers. Of course, they perk right up when they realise they're being filmed. Oh yes, they try to establish themselves as real characters.

I seize the chance to humiliate them. These people who think they can whitewash me out of the Mimi Experiment coverage like some dirty little secret. Circling the table, I play up to the camera, taking the piss, quizzing them. I ask Astral if he feels any affinity with Jabba the Hutt. Johann about the importance of physical fitness to the dead. I ask a subdued Howie whether his neighbour has killed him yet. Caught in the headlights of the internet, they maintain fixed grins, even as their faces redden and they shift from one buttock to the other.

Astral's grin drops clean off the moment filming ends. "You done?"

"No, *you're* all done," I say, restraining myself from physically assaulting him as I snatch back my phone from Pascal. "Hope you've planned your defence. 'Oh Jack, we can't believe it, Mimi didn't appear this time—and it's your fault for changing location!'"

Astral mumbles something I can't hear, and I ask him to repeat it. Ellie jumps in: "You can be damn sure nothing'll happen if we just trash-talk for hours. Convivial and carefree, remember?"

"Oh yeah, sure," I say. "Because you're all the very *opposite* of uptight."

Ellie flops back in her chair, overplaying her exasperation.

"Everyone's hands where I can see them," I say. "And the equipment stays inside those cases."

Lisa-Jane's eyes are only happy when they roll. "Sure thing, Ghost Cop."

As the others begin a stilted conversation, Astral fixes his poisonous gaze on me. He finally hates me as much as I hate him. I stare back until he looks away.

I examine my phone to check YouTube's reaction to my new exclusive Big Coyote Ranch report. I have the phone set to auto-upload everything I film, because I can't conceive of needing a second take.

I blink at what I'm seeing, as if blinking will solve the problem. The new clip has failed to upload, because my YouTube account no longer exists. Someone has obviously hacked into my account and deleted it.

Around the table, people stiffen as my enraged glare hammers into them all.

The table lurches upwards so hard that we jerk our hands away. It leaves the floor and keeps rising until it smashes into the ceiling.

As plaster chips rain down, we leap to our feet and stagger back with our chairs. The table stays up there, motionless, its surface jammed against the ceiling. Sir Isaac Newton's nemesis.

For once, nobody speaks.

Shock and awe.

When it leaves the ceiling, this table doesn't just fall, it throws itself down. The legs bash the carpet so hard that the whole thing ricochets off at an angle.

One leg punches Astral in the paunch. Winded, he struggles to hold the table still. It bucks and rams a corner hard into his mouth, shattering teeth and freeing blood.

Elisandro and Johann leap over to help tame this wild horse.

Something catches my eye, up by the ceiling.

Mimi is back.

Or whatever the hell this thing might be.

The insane floating face now has a real edge to it. A spiteful edge that makes me forget to breathe.

"Holy God," says Howie, seeing Mimi too. Everyone else thinks he's talking about the table situation.

"Mimi," says the face. "Mimi."

I wouldn't know how to describe the voice. Distorted, not quite human. Like the ever-changing face, it's neither male nor female.

Everyone gawps up at the apparition, shaken by our baby's first words.

Our attention is split between that face and the table, which thrashes harder, challenging the combined efforts of wiry Elisandro, ripped Johann and man mountain Astral. The three men shake and strain as they fight to control it.

Elisandro shoots a glance at the rest of us. "Any time you like. Any time."

"Won't do no good," barks Johann. "This thing's *insane*."

We onlookers don't move or make a sound. Gripped by a silent, rising hysteria.

"Mimi," says the face. "Mimi, Mimi, Mimi."

Blood dribbles from Astral's mouth to his chin to the carpet. Five words come out of him as one: "Can'tholditeveryoneout!"

Lisa-Jane, Ellie, Pascal, Howie and I snap out of our stupors and run for the nearest doors. I never saw Howie move so fast. As we go, the Mimi face breaks into a staccato yell. "Mimi! Mimi! Mimi! Mimi!"

Ellie and I duck through a door and end up in a corridor lined with framed gold discs, the others having taken a different route. I look back into the lounge through a fist-wide gap in the door. It's a surreal sight: three men wrestling with a table, while a disembodied face hovers above them.

Astral, Johann and Elisandro count to three, then scatter fast.

"*Mimi!*" The scream hurts my ears even at this distance. "*Mimi!*"

When the trio abandon the table, it pivots up on to one leg and becomes a deranged spinning top. Gaining speed, it's a diamond-shaped blur.

I step aside as the three of them come barrelling through the door, one by one. They pile up against the opposite wall, a profane car wreck.

I hurry to close the door behind them, in case the table decides to give chase.

The last thing I see inside that room is the Mimi face, up by the ceiling. Silent now, but still grinning fiercely at me.

I slam the door so hard that Big Coyote feels set to cave in on us.

Elisandro grabs fistfuls of my shirt and hauls me around in a semicircle arc until I'm up against a wall.

While he's barking right in my face, trying to get a rise, I must look catatonic.

I can't hear a word he's saying.

I can't feel a thing he's doing.

All I can think about is how Mimi behaves nothing like your typical thought form.

I remember the question Ellie asked, back in Culver City. *Are you really the Mimi we created, or are you a spirit passing by?*

Only I saw the smoke cloud in Hong Kong. Only I saw Maria Corvi in my hotel room and Tony Bonelli in Amoeba Music. When it's just you seeing this stuff, doubt springs eternal.

This time, there were eight of us. All seeing the same ghost, under brand-new conditions beyond the group's control.

Elisandro glowers and frowns, as a big smile splits my face open.

It feels like my secret mission, the one so secret that only I know it exists, may be destined for success.

Yes, I may finally have found evidence of the supernatural.

CHAPTER FOURTEEN

THE SPOOKS LIST (Sparks' Permanently Ongoing Overview of Kooky Shit)

People claim to have witnessed supernatural phenomena for the following reasons:

(1) They're trying to deceive others
(2) They've been deceived by others
(3) They've deceived themselves (Guilt projection? Tumour?)
(4) Group psychokinesis has produced crazy, inexplicable results (TBC)

Having been denied the reaction he wants, Elisandro unhands me as roughly as he grabbed me, his face twisted in disgust.

I sag back against the corridor wall, spellbound by new possibilities.

Finally, I know the Paranormals can't be rigging the experiment. Not unless they've hired Steven fucking Spielberg.

We're way past the point where this can be pretence. The table knocked some of Astral's teeth out. But more than that, everyone's reactions just felt so right.

All those reactions felt so right back in the church too, didn't they? And on the boat in Hong Kong. You just didn't want to accept it, because you were scared. Scared of the unknown, scared of looking stupid. You wanted to be the aloof, dry, above-it-all journo. The big celebrity atheist.

I still believe the Paranormals made the YouTube video. It was their breadcrumb trail to get me to take part in a genuine experiment. And I still know full well that they've cut my comms. Did they delete my YouTube channel to destroy the evidence, knowing I'm on to them? These people are still not my colleagues and can't be trusted.

We all reconvene in Rod's office. The Paranormals are so wired, they don't even notice full-frontal *Hustler* pages on the walls. I'm sharing a constricted space with seven bug-eyed aliens from the Planet Freakout. I'm thrilled too, but am at pains not to show it. I want to know more, so much more. I have to be certain.

We stop and listen every few minutes, just in case that table's still on the move. No one acknowledges this fear, but it's a fixture.

Seven variations on "So do you believe us now, asshole?" yank my mind back to the room. "Yeah, whatever, get over it," I tell them. "Something very unusual happened in there. Something's definitely going on."

Hearing this, Elisandro makes mock prayer hands and whispers at the ceiling.

"But could that have been a collective hallucination?" I say.

Astral studies two of his own teeth in the palm of his hand. The sleeve of his hockey shirt drips with blood, his tongue glistens red and his speech is all messed up. My heart fails to bleed.

"Hell of a hallucination," he says, only it comes out as "Herruva harrucination." I'll spare you the rest of the phonetics. "Remember: the Harold Experiment never made Harold appear or speak. We've gone far beyond."

Yes, that's good. Beyond is good.

Ellie fusses around Astral. Having delved into her grab bag of potions, she dabs something inside his mouth that makes him wince. "Man," says Elisandro. "Could be stitches." Astral's only reply is a groan.

"Mimi *could* be a time traveller," begins Pascal, only to get talked over by Johann: "Maybe we really did make ourselves a psychokinetic entity. And a sparky son of a bitch at that."

A subdued Howie sits forward, elbows on knees. "I don't mind saying it scared me," he tells the floor. "That got way out of hand real quick."

"Like I said, Mimi just didn't like the change of location," Elisandro argues, unable to let go of his beef with me. "Maybe she'll settle down."

The room seems unsure about this. "We should maybe put the experiment on hiatus," offers Pascal. Unusually persistent, he raises his hand to quell the protest. "*Just until* we know more about what we're dealing with here."

"How will we know what we're dealing with," I say, "unless we carry on?"

Astral jerks his mouth away from a wet ball of cotton wool in Ellie's hand. "Ow. For once, I agree with Jack. But let's vote."

Elisandro jumps in. "Hands up if you think we should stop the biggest damn thing that ever happened to us."

"That's right, mate," I say, purely to annoy him. "Keep it nice and neutral."

Still studying the carpet, Howie raises his hand. Encouraged, Pascal follows suit.

If I have to, I'll break each dissenter's arm. I must see what happens next. Quite apart from my own private motive, this could actually now become a world-famous experiment.

Maybe, given time, we'll discover a way to capture Mimi on film.

I crave cameras. Big-branded TV news cameras. CNN, FOX, ABC, NBC, CBS. I'm already planning clothes that will complement their onscreen logos.

"Guess we don't need the other side of the vote," says Elisandro. "You guys are outnumbered."

Howie yanks down his hand as if something burnt it. Pascal fiddles with his wallet chain, stealing nervous glances at people.

"We carry on," I say, excited about the next step.

"Not today we don't," says Elisandro, leaping at the chance to contradict me, even when we broadly agree. "The big guy needs ER. I'll drive."

When I break the news that the only way out is through the front doors, via the lounge, we all feign tough nonchalance.

"So there's no back exit?" says Ellie, nonchalantly. "No problem."

"It'll be fine," says Lisa-Jane, nonchalance itself as we all approach the lounge.

"It should only move when we're in session," says Pascal, whose nonchalant facade is thinner than most, since he hangs back behind the rest of us.

We find the table aping Battersea Power Station. Motionless, on its back, legs up. The Mimi face is nowhere to be seen. As much as its appearance has galvanised me, I dread the next encounter. Something about that thing, that creature, disturbs me no end.

Without trying to make it look like we're edging along the wall furthest from the table, we do exactly that. Single file, never letting the table out of our sight, and above all nonchalant, until we reach those front doors.

The sun's last hurrah bathes LA in a shocking pink. Those wonky, shiny grids now seem to demonstrate character. The insects' hum feels life-affirming.

I can't wait to see Bex. Even if we are only friends now, I need her.

Elisandro and Ellie lead Astral to their Honda Civic, while Howie limps off with Lisa-Jane. People have been taking turns to give Howie a ride, because the big bad neighbour allegedly slashed his tyres and he can't afford new ones.

We rev our engines. Then we nod and casually wave goodbye, as if we're all going to see each other again.

I grunt myself awake on the sofa.

Across our room, a fully clothed Bex slams her suitcase lid in a bid to close it. The case flows over with stuff and she becomes more irate with each new attempt.

I've woken from a dreamless sleep into a nightmare in which Bex is preparing to leave.

My too-bright phone screen tells me it's half one in the morning. I can't have been asleep long. What the hell's happened? I was dog tired again, so we had a leisurely drink, a Chinese and a sensible early night. Still awkward, but getting less so. And at times, there were signs that she still liked or even wanted me.

I told Bex that the day's Mimi session had been the same old woeful fakery. I said how I was looking forward to exposing the Paranormals in this book. I could tell she knew there's something strange about me these days. She wanted me to spill, but the thought of having to explain my secret mission glued my lips together.

Bex bangs the suitcase lid down again. My mouth, furred with dead Merlot, takes a while to log on. "What you doing?"

No answer. But the fury in her eyes confirms she heard perfectly well.

"Hey." I swing my feet off the sofa, down on to the soft rug. My near nakedness makes me feel all the less sure of myself. "Did I do something wrong?"

The hand-grenade smirk she tosses in reply reminds me of Maria Corvi in the church, looking back at me from the stained-glass window.

I know something you don't know, fucker.

"Bex, why have you packed?"

"I'm going to a different hotel, then back to Brighton, then you'll never see me again." Face flushed, she abandons her struggle with the case. Then she nods at my laptop, which sits open on the desk. "That thing goes into screen-saver mode after a while."

I don't know where she's going with this, but my stomach seems to have worked it out before me.

"And when it's in screen-saver mode," she goes on, "you've set it to play a lovely little slideshow from your Pictures folder."

Porn! She's seen porn. But Bex doesn't hate porn, does she? No. Only the choky-slappy stuff, and I'm not even into that.

"So there I am," she continues, "coming back to bed from the loo, half asleep, bit pissed, when I see a picture of a girl."

My blood temperature goes into freefall.

"And oh my God, it's *only* the same girl who fucked up my relationship with Lawrence. The exact same picture that was on her profile, too. And so I wonder to myself, 'Hmm, why would Jack have that on his computer? Did she try it on with him too, or what?'"

I'm trapped under ice.

Having squeezed out some bile, Bex sets about closing her suitcase with a more level head. She spots the jeans poking out and shoves them back in.

"You should put a password on that lappy," she says. "I looked around and found this Notepad file with—*shock, horror*—a draft of the same message this non-existent catfish bitch sent Lawrence."

I claw up at the ice, but my lungs have frozen solid. Can't speak, can't breathe. Can barely even see.

"So I cried quite a lot and was sick," she adds, with a casual sing-song delivery. "Then I had a good old think." This is the worst part of all: the thought of Bex crying and heaving as a result of my insane deceit, while I slept peacefully on.

There's the sound of cloth ripping as she zips her case shut.

"Didn't take long to make my decision," she says. "Then you woke up, so you know the rest. Bye, Jack."

She sets the suitcase upright. In my current state of mind, the telescopic metal handle is a dynamite plunger. I don't trust my legs to support me if I stand, so I just surrender, hands raised. "I'm so sorry. I fucked up badly, but don't go."

Bex rolls her belongings towards the door. Realising that sorry won't cut it, I switch tactics. Hammering on the ice, desperate for air. "But listen! He still arranged to meet her. This girl. Even if this girl didn't exist, he was still up for it.

And he shouldn't have been, because you're amazing. So you have to take that into account! He was still a cheating *bastard*."

Bex flips the safety lock on the door. "You think I'm going back to him? God, your brain is so binary. So fucking black and white."

She's fresh out of script. All those lines she rehearsed while I slept, they've been said, and now her voice is lined with hurt. "I'm going home to a new life. You're right, I don't deserve a cheating bastard. And neither do I deserve a conniving, devious prick."

The door opens with that deep ratcheting sound and an airlock hiss.

Bex doesn't even glance at me as she leaves.

CHAPTER FIFTEEN

By the time Elisandro calls, I'm a different man, chock-full of cocaine and the contents of the minibar. I've yelled out of the windows at guests having breakfast below and I've bombarded Bex's mobile with calls and texts, which have been ignored.

My voicemails and messages started off apologising. Then, as the coke took hold, warping my perspective and making sleep impossible, I told her she was crazy to "throw it all away" over this. Finally, when I really peaked, she was branded terrible names for abandoning me when I need her.

I am beyond stupid.

In the dead of night, I came to regret touring the Paranormals' social media profiles. At 2:51 a.m., Astral posted a photo of him and Bex in a hotel bar. She looked uncomfortable to be having her picture taken, and he looked triumphant, with one arm around the back of her seat. The post's only words were "Good times. ☺"

Spiralling out of control, I phoned Bex, then Astral. When neither answered, I texted them all manner of abuse.

This must be why Elisandro's calling: to pick yet another fight. Because today's Mimi session isn't until 1 p.m. By my reckoning, I should still have three uninterrupted hours of hedonism and self-loathing.

"If you're calling on Astral's behalf," I snap at him, "you can suck it."

Straight away, his wavering voice rings alarm bells. "Something horrible has happened. Howie's dead."

"He's *what*?"

"Me and Ellie went to pick him up—we were gonna have breakfast . . ."

I sit heavily beside a window, trying to comprehend this.

Seven Hollywood Paranormals is just too many, says a shadow voice somewhere in my head, making the rest of me uncomfortable.

"So his neighbour did it?" I ask. "With the pump, the Bluetooth?"

All I hear is traffic and Ellie sobbing. Then Elisandro pushes the words out. "Howie was decapitated."

Someone seems to have cut the strings that work my mouth.

"We haven't called 911 yet," Elisandro is saying. "I guess we're in shock. Howie gave us a spare key a while back, so we went in to see why he wasn't answering the door . . . and we found . . . Oh God. It was like his head had been . . . like, *ripped* . . ."

Back on my feet, disoriented, I work the coffee machine as if I really need more uppers. "Does everyone else know? In the group?"

"Haven't got hold of Pascal yet."

Something about Pascal's name forms an ominous connection that I can't quite grasp. "Where are you?"

"Melrose, not far. Want us to pick you up?"

"Yeah, I'll be outside. And please keep trying to reach Pascal."

The worried note in my voice infects his. "Okay . . . See you in ten."

I hurry into the shower. As hot water rocks me, all I can think about is Howie's head disconnected from the rest of him.

Not just disconnected.

Ripped.

When someone says, "Mr. Sparks," I'm striding across the foyer with black coffee in a paper cup and a coke wrap in my wallet. The idiot's idea of being ready for anything.

Marc Howitz is standing outside his office door with his hands on his hips. "A *word*, please."

I suspect this word is probably going to be "séance."

"Maybe later," I say without breaking my stride.

"Hey!" he shouts, as I pile into the revolving door.

I slide into the back of the Honda, wincing as another coffee spill torches the webbing between my thumb and forefinger.

Into his phone, Elisandro says, "You got hold of Pascal yet, man?"

Ellie, all streaked mascara, points at the phone and mouths Astral's name.

"Ask him where Bex is," I tell Elisandro, who waves a shut-up hand at me. "Okay," he tells Astral, winding up the call. "I'll let you know if we find him first." Then he stares through the windscreen into the middle distance.

"Fine, I'll call Astral myself," I say, raising my phone to my ear.

"Don't," says Ellie. "He's as upset as we are."

Needing to make sure Bex is okay, I speed-dial Astral. When he doesn't pick up, I punch the back of Elisandro's seat. He, in turn, punches the dashboard. "Jesus, Jack! Cool it or get out. Astral said he left the girl at her new hotel, okay?"

"Did he leave her this morning or last night?" My question sits there for a beat, a loaded gun.

"Please can we focus?" says Ellie. "Pascal's not answering his phone, email, nothin'."

Pascal lives half an hour away in North Hollywood. When I tell them we should drive there right now, my concern is again contagious. "Oh my God," says Ellie. "You don't think . . . ?"

The tremor in my raised hand undermines the attempt to placate her. "Let's just stay calm and get over there."

Without another word, Elisandro pulls out into traffic and puts his foot down at the first opportunity. Coffee splashes my chest, but I barely notice.

The act of pushing Pascal's front-door buzzer seems to slow time itself. The wait drags on and on and on.

All the way here, we've kept our spirits up, saying how silly we're being. How Howie's death has understandably rattled our cages. Clearly, we're just making connections (*connections, connections*) that aren't real. While all the time, underneath all this mutual reassurance, we know two things.

Howie's head can't have been ripped off by anything human.

The only two members of the group who voted to stop the Mimi Experiment were Howie and the resident of 1033 Tanowen Street, North Hollywood.

We share tight smiles as we wait for Pascal to open up. I stockpile oxygen in my lungs specifically so that I can let it all out in one big burst when the guy's little round face appears in a window. I might not have known Pascal long, but I like him a great deal more than I did the Waster.

Three, four, five hits of the buzzer and still no response. Ellie holds the button in until the battery dies. Shielding my eyes from the sun, I peer at the upper windows of this small detached house. I toss a handful of tiny stones to drum on the glass. A big old gas-guzzling station wagon slows as it passes, the po-faced old woman at the wheel making no attempt to conceal her curiosity.

Pascal lives alone, Ellie tells me, as the station wagon trundles on its way. Mostly bought this place with inheritance cash.

We steal around the side of the house. Elisandro monkeys himself up and over a tall wire gate, then opens it for Ellie and me. By this point, we couldn't care less what the curtain-twitching neighbours might think.

All the windows on this side of the house show thick blinds pulled down. The path leads to a modest backyard, with garden chairs and a plastic table.

Locked patio doors afford views into a wide lounge area. We press our faces against the glass, hands cupped around our temples to block out the sun.

I see a La-Z-Boy chair, a big flat-screen TV, a stack of video game consoles. A whole wall of shelves hold DVDs, Blu-rays and some old-school VHS in oversized cardboard cartons.

Then I notice something else at squinting distance on the far wall. Can't work it out. Elisandro makes the high keening sound of a dog. I squash my nose against the window pane, trying to make sense of what I'm seeing.

Looks like a mass of thick pinkish-red organic matter stuck to the wall. Ground beef or something, spread a few inches thick.

Then I notice the wallet chain hanging from the mess. The shredded material that was once clothing. The blood that still drips down the wall beneath all this, pooling on the carpet.

One detail brings the whole picture together: the frame of Pascal's spectacles, sparkling in a lone ray of sun. The thin metal has been mangled along with the rest of his body.

"Oh God, no," I say, my stomach churning. That poor guy.

Elisandro's dog sound becomes a wail of despair.

Ellie doesn't understand what we're reacting to. We try to get her away from the windows, but she just keeps looking until her legs buckle.

Seeing a good man who's been spread across a wall isn't the worst of it. No, the worst is the realisation, in the back of my mind, that this book will sell more than the others put together. *Maria killed people after I met her, which was good value, but now I'm right here as the murders happen. Right in the thick of it.*

All this while two fellow human beings weep and retch by my feet.

This isn't the first time I've managed to disgust even myself.

A ping in my pocket. Bex has finally responded to the text I sent on the way here, begging her to confirm she's okay (read: alive).

The text says: "Do not contact me again."

I'm so glad she's away from all this, but the idea of never seeing her again makes me want to prostrate myself beside Ellie and Elisandro.

CHAPTER SIXTEEN

The Mimi table sits where we left it in the reception lounge, except now it's the right way up. Eyeing the thing with the caution it deserves, we move on, calling out for the others. When no one calls back, we start to fret.

The serpentine journey up to Big Coyote took twice as long as usual. Ellie kept having to tell Elisandro to slow down, dry his eyes and concentrate on the trail. It was like being driven by an old married couple.

I snorted a couple of crafty bumps off my hand around the back of Pascal's place. The other two saw me do it, I suppose, but were too busy tugging their hair and sobbing to moralise. I really felt the need to sharpen up—to mentally record every second of whatever came next. And after two more bumps in the back of the Honda right before we enter the studio, my brain is filming in 4K.

Turned out that Ellie and Elisandro weren't beyond self-preservation. Just as they had after finding Howie, they dithered about whether to call 911. *Will we be implicated?* they wondered, wringing hands. Station Wagon Lady witnessed us ringing the buzzer, but didn't see us go around the back. There was fraught debate on the pros and cons. Finally, a call to Astral broke the bad news, then made the decision for us: we would all meet at the ranch, then work out what to do. We could call in the murders from there, no problem.

Yeah. No problem. How very idyllic.

We eventually find the others dotted around a "live" studio room, right at the back of the building. To reach it, you thread through a control room. Dominated by a wide console bank lined with buttons and dials, the control room's where you tend to find producers, engineers and dominant band members. One wall is made entirely of toughened glass, including the door halfway along it. Through this we see Astral, Lisa-Jane and Johann among the live room's microphone stands and amp stacks, their eyes puffy and bloodshot.

Lisa-Jane sits on the floor, her back against one of the padded walls. Johann stands with his arms folded. Since the guy's probably seen friends blown up, you'd think him harder to faze, but even he looks shaken.

Astral is sitting the wrong way around on an armless revolving chair, his mouth stuffed with gauze. Seeing me through the glass wall, he looks away. I clamp my teeth together. Anything to stop myself launching into a rant about Bex once I get in there.

Right up until I pull the glass door's handle, it looks like the trio are just mouthing words to each other in silence. Once you break that soundproof seal, their voices leap out at you. No one says it in words, but you sense everyone's way more cut up about Pascal than Howie.

"How did Pascal go?" Johann wants to know, switched on, the most engaged I've seen him.

Ellie and Elisandro gaze at their shoes, so I grasp the nettle. "You don't really want to know."

"Don't tell me what I want," warns Johann. "What are we dealing with here?"

"Howie and Pascal weren't killed by a person," says Ellie. "Couldn't have been."

"And they were the only two who voted against . . ." adds Elisandro, trailing off when the others nod. They already made that deductive jump.

No one tries to say these deaths could have been a coincidence. Not even me. *The Truman Show*'s over and I'm not in Kansas any more.

Astral tugs the gauze from his mouth so he can speak. "Mimi doesn't want to go, now we've created her. We pulled her out of thin air and she's alive in some way . . ."

"Maybe she's a real ghost, like Ellie said," I say, trying not to sound too hopeful.

Astral signals for me to keep my voice down. He looks around at the walls and out through the glass into the control room. He says, "We kinda thought she might not be able to hear us in here, but you never know."

He doesn't appreciate me laughing in his face. But it's a funny concept: the idea that a ghost, a psychokinetic entity or whatever Mimi is, couldn't hear you in a soundproof room.

Astral's chair squawks in protest as he swivels to face me full on. "Fuck you. Two friends are dead here."

"All right, mate!" I say, totally out of line. "I didn't kill 'em."

Astral heaves himself off the chair, thunderous. I want to fight him, so I stick my dukes up, but Johann jumps in. "No! No more of this shit. We stick together." Testosterone trickles from every pore as he points at me. "*You* watch your mouth."

I preferred Johann when he was adrift with PTSD. No one tells Jack Sparks to shut up, especially when he's feeling chemically indestructible. "Okay, meathead," I say. "So what next? We carry on, yes?"

Lisa-Jane pinches her eyebrow piercing and stretches the skin until it looks set to rip. "I don't think carrying on is a good idea," she says.

"Keep your voices low," Astral reminds everyone.

"But if Mimi wants to carry on," I say, "surely that's the safest thing to do."

"We can't let our own creation hold us to ransom," argues Lisa-Jane. "Let's end this."

"How do you un-create something?" I say. "May as well try not to think of a blue elephant. First thing you think of is—"

Astral interrupts: "Well, we need to find a way."

"Hey," says Johann, "this might be stupid, but—"

"I'd put money on that," I say, coke-leery, loving how Johann wants to kill me but can't, because jail.

"*But,*" he carries on, "Mimi only appears when we're all together, right?"

"Obviously not," I say. "Look what happened during the night."

"Johann's got a point, though," says Ellie. "Maybe we don't all have to be in the same room. But if we're in the same area, maybe even the same city, the PK circle stays intact."

"So if we get far enough away from each other . . ." Astral ponders.

"You're clutching at straws," I tell them. "Pulling rules out of your arse."

"Shut your mouth, you wise-ass junkie cretin," Lisa-Jane spits.

When the prospect of separation makes Ellie and Elisandro

hold hands, I feel my first tug of emotion towards them. I don't like it. Cold cynicism is so much safer.

"Let's try," says Johann. "We get as far away from each other as possible, then figure this out online."

Lisa-Jane rubs her temples with both hands. "Shit, shit. My job, my mom, the dogs . . ."

"I'm sure we can soon come back," offers Ellie, ever hopeful.

"I'll take you to your place," Elisandro tells Ellie, "and you can pick up your car."

Everyone stands. Johann talks about Aspen, Colorado; Lisa-Jane her brother's place down in San Diego. Me? I'm not going anywhere. I vent my frustration on a nearby guitar, punching a discordant twang out of its neck.

Astral is saying something typically controlling—something about how Ellie and Elisandro need to go their separate ways at the *very first* opportunity—when evil creeps into the room.

"Mimi," says a small voice amid our chatter.

"Mimi," it says again.

My spine tingles as I follow the source of the sound.

And there's Mimi's face, emerging from the front of an amplifier stack right where the Marshall logo should be.

The face looks younger this time, paler too. The sly, sharp smile burns right through me.

Hi! You all thought you could escape, didn't you?

Everyone else has fallen silent. I know they're all equally transfixed by the face.

It.

"Mimi, Mimi!" says Mimi. Its eyes widen as it leaves the amp stack and hovers before us.

The boulder from *Raiders of the Lost Ark*.

That smile evaporates into rage.

"Mimi!" comes the scream.

We all bolt for the door to the control room.

How I wish I could claim gallantry. Lisa-Jane's ahead of me, so I grab her waist and swing her aside to clear my path to the door.

Getting there first, Astral grapples with the handle, but it needs to open towards us. So his bulk blocks its path and we're all piled up behind him.

Lisa-Jane swings a chair at the glass wall, but it bounces clean off and smacks her in the face.

Mimi's next scream hurts my ears. I fill my hands with Astral's doughy back-fat and shove, as if I can somehow force him through the closed door. Yelling at me and Astral, Elisandro pushes Ellie ahead of him, squashing her breasts into my back. Lisa-Jane tries to force herself in front of everyone, also yelling, her nose bloody.

This is when the first person dies.

Johann's severed upper torso slams against a Marshall stack, having been thrown there. His eyes are all whites, rolled up in their sockets. Gravity sucks him down to the carpet, where he falls to one side, a discarded toy.

Makes sense, says my inner voice, even as I stare horrified at the dead man. *Kill the strongest first.*

Someone throws up.

Someone else, probably Elisandro, punches me twice in the back of the head, filling my vision with comets and stars. Astral shouts how he can't get the door open and how everyone needs to get back.

"Mimi! Mimi!" Each scream is a needle to the eardrums. Elisandro punches my head again and my hearing cuts out, making all this commotion distant and distorted.

Astral rams himself backwards, using his weight as a weapon, until we all do the domino topple. Yanking the door open, he disappears into the control room. As I spring back up, Lisa-Jane darts out after him.

Two pairs of hands push me hard from behind. I stumble over the door's threshold, sheer momentum carrying me until I trip and fall. The control room carpet rises to slam into one side of my face.

Ellie and Elisandro trample over me. I wheeze as a foot jams into the small of my back, then watch their fleeing heels shrink.

My hearing snaps back into play, but I can't hear Mimi.

I use one side of the console desk as leverage to haul myself upright.

The glass door must have hydraulic-hinged itself shut.

Through the glass wall, in the live room, Johann's legs remain upright, rocking gently from side to side in bloodied khaki shorts. Absurdly, my first thought is that it's an amazingly realistic special effect. The knees give way and the legs collapse.

Mimi stares at me, hanging immobile in the centre of the sealed room. The shifting mishmash elements of the face have changed once again: more feminine, strangely familiar. The lips are a heartbeat, spasming open twice each time to silently scream her name.

My back jangles as I hurry towards one of the exit doors.

When I steal a last look back, Mimi has disappeared. As unnerving as the spider that scuttles out of sight beneath your bed.

Sure enough, when I dash headlong into a corridor where gold discs flash past on either side, two simultaneous screams ring out. One is Mimi again, but the other comes from Ellie, whose back has somehow become stuck to the ceiling above a junction up ahead. She flails about, but the plaster holds her firm.

"Mimi, Mimi, Mimi!" comes the howl, but I can't see the face anywhere.

Elisandro sprints back to the junction, appalled, like he's only just noticed Ellie is no longer beside him. I'm still running towards them both and really want him out of the way.

"Help me get her down," he shouts. Before I can respond, something truly horrendous happens: Ellie gurgles, and her head pivots—or is pivoted—to one side. The skin of her neck stretches until bone bursts out.

Some of the blood catches Elisandro on the face. He makes sounds that remind me of my mother upstairs after Dad left home.

I'm about to reach Elisandro and sprint on by, when the arcane magnetism holding Ellie against the ceiling is revoked. Her body falls, forcing me to slam on the brakes or end up beneath her.

It's a small mercy that Mimi's howls mask the awful crunch of impact.

That horrendous ghost face is suspended in a corridor off to my left. The face has changed yet again, and I shudder as I finally recognise my mouth. It's mainly masculine now . . . and do I see Astral's eyes in there? Other people's features, too. The Mimi face is a collage, but there's no time to ponder, not with Elisandro grabbing my arm and yanking me back around to face him.

"Help her! Please help her."

"She's dead, mate, I'm sorry."

"Mimi! Mimi! Mimi!"

"But we can't leave her here."

"She was dead before she hit the ground. Come with me."

"Mimi! Mimi! Mimi! *Mimi-Mimi-Mimi!*"

Painfully aware of the phantom flying right for us, I try to drag Elisandro away, but he digs in his heels and won't let go of me.

I slam my forehead into his, sending him reeling, then make my dizzy escape.

From up ahead in the reception lounge, I hear Astral's voice and see his and Lisa-Jane's shadows flit across the carpet. I speed up, desperate to see the sky again.

Behind me, Elisandro roars incoherently at Mimi until he's abruptly cut off. Truly dreadful sounds ensue. The sounds of human disassembly.

Sprinting into the lounge, I'm greeted by the smashing of glass. The fallen vending machines now form a barricade across the front doors—Mimi's work, no doubt—and so Astral has heaved a chair out through a window. He and Lisa-Jane hurry towards this new exit.

And then there were three. If these two die, I'll be the only survivor. The sole storyteller. And then everyone will listen, no matter how much I talk.

Being appalled by these thoughts doesn't make them go away. I've had similar daydreams before: about being on the receiving end of a terrorist attack, for instance. Maybe not involved enough to get hurt, but just enough to have an engrossing story to tell. Just enough to get people's eyes and ears glued to me for years to come.

I'm sick, I know.

"Careful," Astral warns Lisa-Jane, kicking at some of the glass fangs that jut out from all around the window frame. As if a little broken glass is cause for concern right now.

Lisa-Jane is saying, "Not gonna die, not gonna die," over and over.

The corridor with Ellie and Elisandro's corpses has fallen all too silent.

Astral helps Lisa-Jane climb up on to the window frame. "Hurry up!" I tell them, hopping from foot to foot. Flooded with the buzz that only impending death can bring, I'm looking around for another window to smash when—

"Mimi! Mimi-Mimi-Mimi!"

The sheer volume makes me clutch my ears. Astral struggles to keep both supportive hands on Lisa-Jane's back. She's standing on the interior window ledge, clutching the top of the frame. Hesitant, unsure how best to exit, she glances at the remaining glass fangs. "Not gonna die, not gonna die . . ."

The face now floats above the table in the middle of the room. Always the centre of attention.

When Mimi screeches again, it's twice as loud. A sonic shock wave that weakens my knees.

"*Mimi!*"

I'm sorry. There's no nice way to put this: Lisa-Jane's head explodes.

The sound isn't what you'd expect: it's more a hideous "clack" of bone. An eyebrow piercing rebounds off my chest, along with other stuff that makes me gag.

She went faster than the others. Maybe even painlessly. These are the kind of details that will break me worldwide. (Shut up, you fucking monster.)

Lisa-Jane's limp body falls back from the window into Astral's arms, leaving him clutching her, lost in horror.

There's no feminine component left in Mimi's face. What hangs over the table now is a continuously alternating composite of me and Astral.

Mimi stares at me, but I know that Astral sees the same face staring at him.

An idea skitters through my head, about how he and I could somehow work together to get rid of this thing. Then I remember his YouTube video con. I remember all his sly manipulation. I remember last night's post: "Good times. ☺"

Only one of us is getting out of here alive.

My lizard brain somehow grasps the situation as Astral lets Lisa-Jane tumble to the ground.

"Mimi, get him," he calls. "Kill him, so I can be the last."

Yeah, he's grasped it too.

Mimi comes at me. Insane eyes glinting, shrieking its name.

Then it changes course and hurtles right back at Astral with astonishing speed.

"*Mimi-Mimi-Mimi-Mimi-Mimi!*"

Astral opens his mouth to yell something, but the ghost face punches right through his navel and flies out through his spine, devastating everything in between. It leaves a gaping hole wide as a saucepan lid.

There's an almighty snapping sound, and Astral's body arches at a deeply wrong angle. Gargling, he claws at the cavernous ruin below his ribs. Incredulous, fading fast.

That's Astral for you, crows my inner bastard. *Spineless. I could always see straight through him.*

And yet, by the time his big head hits the carpet there are tears in my eyes. The do-or-die lust for survival is eclipsed by the enormity of all these lives extinguished.

Mimi hovers steadily my way, beaming, victorious. It now wears my face and my face alone.

"Mimi," it says, with my speaking voice.

"Okay," I say through a tight throat. "It's over. Whatever you are, just disappear, all right? Just *go*."

"Mi–mi," it says, still coming my way. "Mi–mi."

And for the first time, it strikes me that it's not saying "Mimi" at all.

It's saying, "Me. Me."

Mimi was the name I chose. Outwardly arbitrary, but at some level . . .

"Me, me," says my own gliding spectral face. "Me. Me. Me. *Me*."

I back away from it, bumping hard into one of the toppled vending machines.

There's no time to reach the broken window. So I make a break back towards that corridor, desperate to find another exit. Anything to get away from Mimi.

What am I doing? Just embrace it. Let it in. I was born to be great, no matter what Mum and Alistair thought. (No, no, this thing is evil.)

Electrified by panic, I rattle a door handle on a side wall, only to find it locked.

"Me. Me. Me. Me. Me."

I slap a hand over the lower half of my face, when I see and smell what happened to Elisandro.

I have never run this fast in all my life, but it's not nearly fast enough. My own voice draws closer.

"Me. Me. Me. Me. Me."

I duck around a corner, heels hammering along a new stretch of carpet . . .

. . . which leads up to the feet of a teenage farm labourer.

Maria Corvi stands with her arms scarecrowed out, crucifixed out. Blocking my path, solid and corporeal, ten steps ahead of me. As usual.

Her face says it all. The gleeful vindication of someone who has devoted time to engineering a special surprise.

Those yellow eyes blaze with delight.

The rictus grin gloats.

My skin rears up all over, wanting to evacuate my bones.

"Me! Me! Me! Me! *Me!*" shrieks the voice behind me, so loud, so close.

"Enjoy," mouths Maria, savouring the moment.

Something hammers into my back, driving me up into the air so hard that my head whacks a light fitting.

Next thing I know, I'm back on the ground and my vocal cords and my mouth are saying stuff, even though I haven't asked them to.

"I, I, I, I, I," they're saying.

"Me, me, me, me, me," they're saying.

A rising tide of alarm forces me creakily to my feet. What's happening?

Maria and the ghost face are nowhere to be seen. My mouth jabbers on, unauthorised.

"I, I, I, I, I . . . me, me, me, me, me . . ."

I try to shut my mouth through sheer force of will, but that doesn't work. So I try using my hands, but my jaw's too stubborn. I may as well be attempting to stop an industrial piston.

I try to stay centred. The mortal remains of Ellie and Elisandro remind me that at least I'm still alive. I just need to figure out what's going on.

I tell myself to breathe and think. No mean feat when your mouth has gone rogue.

What is this?

"Me, me, me, me, me," says my mouth, as I stagger back towards the lounge.

Is it shock?

"I, I, I, I, I," says my mouth, while I head for the broken window, trying not to look at Astral or Lisa-Jane.

Is it cocaine psychosis?

But of course, as always, no matter what I tell myself, I know the truth. Mimi is now inside me. Inside my head.

"Myself! Myself! Myself!" says my mouth, louder and with greater force, as I carefully climb out over the window frame, down on to sun-soaked grass.

Wind ruffles my hair as if trying gamely to assure me that *everything's fine*. Crickets persist with their reedy chorus as if nothing untoward has happened. I do my best to adopt their mindset.

Just relax, relax . . .

Then I remember how I don't have a car here. So I have to climb back into the building and fish around in Astral's wet shorts for his keys. The poor guy gazes up at me. Lights off, nobody home.

"Me! Me!" I yell down at him.

Without my permission, my foot kicks him hard in the ear.

Only when I try to jam the key in the ignition do I realise how very badly my hands are shaking.

Experimenting with my new condition, I send a defiant neural signal to my mouth, telling it to say "I'm fine, there's nothing to worry about." This command is ignored. My mouth resolutely keeps up the "Me, myself and I" routine.

About halfway down the track, this automatic speech evolves. I say new things, still entirely beyond my control. I find myself saying, "I'm great," "You love me," "I fucking rule," "Worship me" . . . you get the idea.

Admittedly, I've said these things before. But now they pour out incessantly without my brain's conscious participation. It reminds me of the time curiosity led me to try Viagra. Hated it. Despite my cock's resemblance to a baby's arm holding an apple, I didn't actually *feel* turned on.

So I'm in this car that isn't mine, rolling down treacherous trails towards the City of Angels. I'm telling no one in particular how brilliant I am, non-stop. And I'm crying.

"I am superb!" yells my voice, thanks to wind from my lungs that I didn't want to contribute and a mouth I would dearly love to seal.

Slowly but very surely, I start to believe my own hype.

Whoever coined the idea that if you say something enough you'll believe it never expected it to be true in this context.

Yes, at some point, my brain flips and fizzes and gives in. It becomes so much easier to go along with this than to remember all that terrible, violent death back up the hill. In fact, I start to enjoy it. Forget cocaine: this is way more powerful, intense and all-consuming. This is downright phenomenal.

All those thoughts about fame reaped from the death of others, which felt so atrocious back at the ranch? They now feel gorgeous.

I have no guilt, no shame, no restrictive feelings whatsoever.

As a dark force gains dominion over my soul, embers of my former dread still glow, but these are dim, out of reach inside myself, irrelevant.

I spy Maria Corvi standing on the roadside, just as she used to in the dream. She points ahead, smiling, wholly surreal in blazing sunlight.

I smile right back. Ecstatic to have wandered straight into her trap.

"*Every time you go away,*" sing Hall & Oates on 95.5 KLOS FM, "*you take a piece of me with you.*"

I give Maria Corvi the thumbs-up and drive on by, jabbering about how I'm the king of everything.

Alistair Sparks: "Brandon Hope is a thirty-two-year-old hotel recep-
tionist from Santa Barbara, California. On the afternoon of 18
November 2014, one hour after the killings at Big Coyote Ranch,
Hope was working at West Hollywood's Sunset Castle Hotel when
a guest caused disruption . . ."

ALISTAIR SPARKS: Please summarise what happened in
    reception that afternoon.
BRANDON HOPE: I feel nauseous even talking about it,
    considering what happened afterwards. But okay . . . In a
    nutshell, that deeply sick individual Jack Sparks whipped up
    a little storm.
ALISTAIR: Were you a hundred per cent positive this man
    was Jack Sparks?
BRANDON: Oh, you know, I'd rather not get involved in
    that freaky stuff. All this internet speculation has been such
    a pain in the ass. I had to leave the Castle because so many
    crazy people called and emailed and even turned up in the
    lobby, getting in my face. Listen: far as I'm concerned, unless
    this guy has an identical twin brother, he was Jack Sparks.
ALISTAIR: And you say you first met this guest when you
    and the cleaner Arlette Ortiz discovered him in the hotel
    basement in the early hours of 15 November?
BRANDON: Let me tell you, he didn't seem so damn sure
    of himself that night. First time we laid eyes on him, there
    he was in the boiler room, blinking against my torchlight
    with this stain on his pants. This big wet map of Italy, running
    down one of his pant legs.
ALISTAIR: You believe he'd urinated in his trousers?
BRANDON: So I told him he shouldn't be down here and
    he looked like he was searching for this great snappy

comeback. Then he just said nothing and shrugged. He looked pretty shaken and glad to get out of the basement. But then, three days later in reception, he was suddenly acting like Harvey fucking Weinstein. I don't know if it was drugs or whatnot, but he marched up to reception with these big hard eyes, determined to have me upgrade him to a deluxe suite. This was right after he refused to tip our valet Pierre and instead proclaimed he'd won an award for writing. Like Pierre could feed his kids with that knowledge.

When I said no to the room bump, Sparks banged his fist on my desk and raised his voice. All the classic spiel came out. All the stuff I already heard a million times. Didn't I know who he was, he could have me fired, yadda yadda yadda. He had this freaky stutter all of a sudden, but only on certain words. Must've said "I" about a thousand times. Then the guy crossed the line, and I'll admit, it did faze me. He asked how I'd like to be skinned alive and covered in salt. The guy said this smiling and without blinking, like he was inviting me to a dinner party or something. So I assured him the deluxe suites were taken, but offered him a room service meal with our compliments. In my head, I was comparing the dollar value of that meal with the value of getting him away from me. Oh my God, totally worth those eighty-two bucks.

ALISTAIR: Your colleague Ruth Adler, who delivered the meal to this guest's room, declined to be interviewed. But she has stated that he threatened her too, right?

BRANDON (Sighs): She got out real quick.

ALISTAIR: Why?

BRANDON: Well. She told me . . . she told me Mr. Sparks

picked up the steak knife and made . . . obscene demands.

ALISTAIR: So given that this guest directly threatened yourself and another employee, did you not consider calling the police?

BRANDON: Oh, thank you so much for asking: I really needed the bonus guilt. Ruth didn't tell me about her experience straight away—she told Mr. Howitz. But what do you want me to say? Did I fail to act on the murderous psychopath in our hotel? Yes, as it turned out, I did. But honey, I meet these people every day. That's Hollywood.

CHAPTER SEVENTEEN

Thank God, the room service girl flees, deathly pale, before I can force sex on her.

I shrug off the disappointment and sit cross-legged on the bed with the room service tray laid out before me. Stuffing my face with juicy T-bone, eating with my mouth wide open, meat slapping meat, I tell myself how smooth and inconspicuous my return to the hotel has been. And I actually believe it.

The room is swamped with shadow. No lights, because I no longer have any reason to fear the dark. Whatever lurks there will be inferior to me.

As I wash down all that blood-red beef with a flood of fifty-dollar wine, oh my God, that's when I get a text from Bex.

"Hey," she writes, "is my passport there in the room? Think I may have left it behind."

This pleases me. The woman who rejected Jack Sparks—*Jack Sparks!*—is still here in America. No doubt still in LA. My sly, bright snake eyes conduct a brief search of the room. But to my foul new way of thinking, it doesn't matter whether the passport's here or not. I can tell her it's here, can't I?

After all, she'll never use it again.

Bex clearly didn't realise she only existed for my benefit. But now she's of no benefit to me at all . . .

Deep inside, Real Me snaps to attention, desperate to snatch back the reins. Real Me wants to call Bex and warn her to stay away. Real Me wants to arrange to have her passport couriered to her. Or better yet, left somewhere for collection, so I can't possibly know where she's staying. I can't trust myself any more.

But Real Me can't access the steering wheel. Real Me is bound and gagged across the back seats.

I'm paralysed, fighting for air.

Locked inside this enforced caricature of myself.

The steak knife's blade glints approval as I mentally compose a reply to Bex, telling her to come and get her passport.

Yeah, come and get it . . .

Remember, whispers Real Me, sneaking the message past Mimi's defences, syllable by syllable. *Remember . . . remember what Sherilyn told you about Aleister Crowley. The straight razor?*

"Yeah, I, I, I, I, I remember," I say aloud, picking up my phone. "Some crap about cutting yourself to control ego. So what?"

So cut yourself.

I pull a face. "Why would I, I, I, I, I want to do that?" I say, while thumbing out the text to Bex.

Purge yourself. Control Mimi. Save Bex.

Still typing, I say, "You expect me, me, me, me, me to save that fickle, ungrateful little whore, who chose Lawrence and Astral over me, me, me, me, me? No way."

Do it now.

"Nah. That would really hurt. Loads more fun to use the blade on Bex. I'm thinking of really drawing the process out. I, I, I, I, I think I, I, I, I, I would enjoy that."

The text complete, I'm about to hit "Send."

You know how your body sometimes jerks awake, having pulled back from the journey into sleep? That's what happens right now. A bolt of pure instinct compels me to drop the phone and grab the steak knife. With the other hand, I pull up my T-shirt, exposing my midriff.

Before Mimi can stop me, I drag the serrated blade across and split the skin.

I shake and hiss and sweat as the blood beads up. My eyes water.

This dribbling stripe of torn flesh is a victory for Real Me, who gains more control and makes me do it again, a notch higher.

The whole world pivots around the pain.

"Stop this," says Mimi through my mouth. "I, I, I, I, I am precious."

Scared of Mimi regaining leverage, I cut myself again and again until my torso presents a column of horizontal slit mouths. A ladder of red rungs from navel to neck. My crotch and the sheets beneath are slick with blood.

Hoping it's safe to stop, I gasp and roll on to my back, relieved to recover my true personality. Even though instinct tells me Mimi is a grotesque amplification of my darkest impulses. Yeah, Mimi embodies the Jack who destroyed Bex's relationship and anticipated my career boost as the Paranormals were murdered one by one. Mimi is that foul ego, cranked up. The thing inside Maria Corvi hijacked our experiment in order to twist that dial to eleven.

I know I've won the battle, not the war. This is only remission. I know this because Mimi whispers from a crawlspace at the back of my mind.

Mimi whispers, "me," "myself" and "I."

Mimi whispers, "You know you want me, me, me, me, me back."

Tinnitus from hell.

It takes all my self-control not to burst into tears when Alistair answers his phone. If I can't call Mum, then he'll have to do.

"It's me," I say. "Jack. I really need help."

"How dare you," he fires back. "How *dare* you."

His contempt leaves me stunned as the line dies. I call back three times, no reply. Badly needing someone who cares about me and can help, while realising how few people fit that bill, my thoughts go to Bex . . . only to recoil for her own safety. While Mimi skulks in my head, I need to give Bex a very wide berth. Just can't trust myself.

When I call my agent, at first he says nothing at all. There's only background office chatter and phones ringing.

"Hello?" I say again. "Murray, I really need help."

Before he hangs up, his voice is cool and clipped in a way I've never heard before, even when I've pissed him off royally. "Do not call here again."

Sitting with the phone warm against my ear, my thoughts race. Am I already a fugitive: a mugshot on the wall behind a newsreader? Have the bodies been found at Big Coyote Ranch? Surely not this soon. And I'd hardly be difficult to trace. Why hasn't a SWAT team crashed through the windows? Nope, there's no way Alistair and Murray know about Big Coyote. Alistair has resented me since Dad left, then hated me for the last year or so. Murray has finally decided I'm more trouble than I'm worth. I've torched through any goodwill I once merited.

Should I call Dr. Santoro? No, he's strictly an appointment-only guy. Doesn't give a shit.

Then Sherilyn Chastain springs to mind. She probably loathes me as much as Alistair does, but it dawns on me that only she can help. She understands my situation. She even tried to warn me before it all happened.

When Sherilyn answers her phone, I'm curled up on the floor. Sweat oozes out of me, despite the rattling air con. Down here on the scratchy carpet, hugging a blood-spotted white towel to my mutilated chest, I am a child running to mama. A child limping home after falling from a tree.

The golf ball wedged in my throat makes it hard to speak. "Everything's gone wrong. Everything."

A deep breath at the other end. "Okay. Stay as calm as you can, take a moment, then define 'everything.'"

I tell her about Big Coyote. I tell her I'll give her all my money if she cures my head and makes sure Mimi never comes back, but she doesn't seem to listen. Just says she'll take the next flight out of Auckland.

With my breath far from calm or deep, I ask how long I'll need to hold out before she arrives.

"Try not to think about that, Jack. Depends on flights, but at least twenty-four hours."

"Don't know if I can wait that long. Don't know if I can cut myself any more."

"Just focus. Have you written about what happened? That might help keep Mimi at bay. Email me what you already wrote so far. And only cut yourself again if you really feel Mimi coming back, okay? Avoid arteries."

"Sherilyn," I say, gripping the phone so tight the casing creaks. "I know Maria made this happen. The thing inside her, is it the—"

"Jack, I need to book flights. Just keep yourself together."

I don't even have time to thank her before she ends the call.

I stay on the floor until Mimi starts whispering again.

"You know I'm coming back," it says. "Just a matter of time. And you know it'll feel *good*."

I heave myself up and over to the laptop. Yes, I'll follow Sherilyn's recommendation and write. Surely that's twenty-four hours of work right there. Then she'll arrive to help me and everything will be *fine*. Once I'm back on an even psychological keel, I'll approach the LAPD and try to explain what went down at Big Coyote Ranch.

Yeah, good luck with that, Future Jack. Future Incarcerated Jack.

So here I am. Twenty-four hours later, I'm all up to date with the book, but everything's not fine. Not fine at all.

I'm still waiting for Sherilyn.

Mimi is a shark threading its way up from the black depths.

The blade stopped working about an hour ago, maybe because I'm so very tired. I I I think Mimi regains a foothold whenever I I I nod off over the laptop, even for a few seconds. And sometimes when I I I type words like me me me or myself myself myself, I I I can't stop typing them and sometimes I I I can't help saying them either. Over the last few pages, I've clawed back control and deleted these extra words, but now I I I'm leaving them in, to show you.

It's getting worse and worse. I I I I have a nasty feeling that updating this book may have helped me me me me focus on something, but it's also essentially all about me me me me.

Which means it's also all about Mimi.

Which has paved the way for her to come back.

Can Sherilyn help? I I I I probably don't deserve her help. But I I I I'm going to take it anyway, because I'm selfish. We all are, right? It's survival.

That's right, isn't it?

It's what I I I I keep telling myself myself myself myself.

Can't spent the rest of my life trapped inside myself myself myself myself.

Oh please, please let Sherilyn help.

Mimi rises. I I I I slip back under the waves.

My med centre MRI results just turned up in a text.

Their scans showed my brain has only "very mild" damage from drink and drug abuse.

To see that result when I'm so deeply unstable makes me me me me me weep. And I I I I I can feel myself changing fast, really fucking fast, oh Jesus, hey, I I I I I texted Bex and told her she can come and collect her passport any time she likes, ha ha! She replied and said she'll be over in thirty minutes, ha ha ha ha ha! Okay, Sherilyn, I'll email this over now to make sure you're all up to date. I'm sure you'll *love it*.

Someone's knocking on the door. Better go :D

CHAPTER EIGHTEEN

Finally! A chance to write again. I hope I live long enough to tell you everything that's happened since Mimi came back.

I'm in a great deal of physical pain, but it's amazing what you can achieve when you need to write your epitaph. To think I used to put off writing because I had a fucking cold.

Things have been way beyond bad, which I expected, but also really kind of wonderful, which I did not.

As I write, this is the fortieth day since Halloween. I worked it out. Not Day Forty in a way that anyone would credit, but Day Forty nevertheless. Thanks to a Good Samaritan, I'm holed up in a warm bed, but you won't believe where and you especially won't believe what day it is.

Let me tell you the story anyway.

I'm steeling myself, and so should you.

Blood squelches against my bare behind and the backs of my thighs.

This bed's top sheet is soaked with blood. It's mostly the

blood I shed while trying to keep Mimi out, but some of it isn't my own.

Marc Howitz knocked on my door at the worst possible time, just after sundown, when Mimi had regained control. I'd already taken selfies of me all bloody and posted them to a newly opened social media account.[1] I'd suffered the public humiliation of asking Richard Dawkins for a "signal boost," only to be ignored because I don't really know him. Mimi did not appreciate being blocked.

When I opened the door, there was Howitz outside, positively throbbing with wannabe gangster rage. He told me how he'd fired Johnson after catching wind of my séance. And what was this crap about me harassing his room service maid? He wanted me to leave right now, publicity or no fuckin' publicity.

I hauled him inside the room by his tie and punched him senseless. Then I used the steak knife to saw through his windpipe. His blood felt hot on my face as I dragged him into a closet. By the time I'd wiped the knife clean on a curtain, the spluttering sounds had stopped.

That's how the act of killing Marc Howitz felt to me. That simple, that cold. Howitz was a problem that needed solving. He wouldn't stop talking and doing things, so I had to stop him talking and doing things.

I'm so very sorry.

As I sit back down on the bed, Mimi is disgusted by all the Crowley cuts I inflicted on my bodily temple while trying to tame it. Real Me has nothing to say, because he's unconscious in the boot of the car, his head wrapped in electrical tape.

---

1 No trace of these photographs, or this account, has ever been found online. They may have been intercepted and deleted by the provider, but no records exist of this. —*Alistair*

Someone pushes a keycard into the slot outside my room. That awful grind of metal cylinders and chambers as the door bursts open.

Bex's face appears in the widening gap. She freezes at the sight of me nude and criss-crossed with red. I had got a great deal of Howitz's blood on my clothes, so decided to strip. In addition to the infected ladder on my chest, freshly seeping cuts mat the hair on my forearms, hips and upper thighs. The rest of me has been daubed with fingerprints, palm prints, miscellaneous smears.

She's in her blue hoodie and jeans, the suitcase behind her. For a moment, I think she's moving back in, to save me from myself.

If only.

"Jack, what the fucking hell?"

I smile reassuringly, the steak knife's wooden handle gripped behind my back. "Don't worry. It's really not as bad as it looks."

Bex rejected me. Me, me, me. She must pay the price.

I indicate the waste basket under the desk. "Threw the passport in there a while ago, but feel better now." I gesture down the length of my body as if unveiling a piece of art. "Turned the anger inward, that's all, and now feel super-calm."

Processing all this, she frowns hard. "What did *you* have to be angry about?"

My serenity is borrowed from the Archangel Gabriel himself. "Nothing. Nothing at all, I now realise. Please come in."

Leaving her suitcase jammed in the doorway, Bex breaches the threshold with caution. "You're really not well."

Her gaze roams compulsively along the highways of my body. Touring the slits, the pus and the scabs. It's a while before she speaks again. "What happened to the experiment? No one's posted since yesterday. I tried calling Astral . . ."

I tighten my grip on the knife handle. A sinister old Sisters of Mercy song springs to mind: "*And she looked good in ribbons . . .*"

"Don't worry," I say. "Jack Sparks is fine." I lie back on the bed, to encourage the idea that I'm relaxed and benign. The blood down there sucks at my back.

Bex is just reassured enough to finally remove her attention from me. On her way over to the waste bin, she says, "Jack Sparks needs an ambulance. And talking in the third person? I see you're doing *great* with the coke, you fucking dick."

I hinge upright with a barely perceptible slopping sound, then spring off the bed and land beside Bex. She's stooped, peering into the bin and saying she can't see the passport.

I kick the legs out from under her so she lands on her back. With the benefit of height, it's horribly easy to drag her across the floor by her ponytail. Too shocked to make a sound, she punches at my legs and groin. Slapping her buys me a few seconds to get her on to the sofa, face up. The same sofa upon which, according to my current deranged state of mind, she cruelly made me sleep.

My knees pin her arms down so that I can take my time showing her the steak knife. She shrinks herself as far into the sofa as the firm padding will allow—anything to put more distance between herself and that thing. She is two big eyes in a nest of hair, tracking the knife as I move it in slow, tormenting arcs.

"Oh Jack," I say, in a grotesque parody of her voice. "Jack Sparks. You always talk about yourself all the time, but now you're going to listen to me."

I intercept her scream by shoving my free palm over her mouth. She tries to bite, but I'm safe as long as I keep my hand outside her lips.

I lean in until only my hand separates our mouths. "Oh Jack, Lawrence wants me to move in with him. Isn't that great, Jack? Isn't it?"

I straighten back up, still straddling her, and bring the blade down across her upper thigh. Slashing through the material of her jeans, then the skin.

Waking up helpless in the car boot, Real Me screams along with Bex.

"Good times, yeah?" I say, punching her as she freaks out.

Her face wet with tears, Bex rocks her pelvis up, desperate to dislodge me and making it harder to keep my hand clamped over her mouth. The idea of shutting that mouth for good springs so easily, so casually to mind. Like Howitz, she's a problem to solve. Death is the obvious solution to this person who doesn't value me nearly as highly as I value myself.

And as Rebecca Lawson squirms helplessly beneath me, I glide my sharp steel down to where quivering tendons ride taut in her neck.

Her face says: *How did I not see this coming? How did I misjudge this so very badly?*

And also: *Is this really the end? But that can't be right.*

"Haunt me," I tell her.

The blade meets the gulping bulge of her throat, and darkness descends.

Alistair Sparks: "There follows the transcript of an audio recording made by an app on Sherilyn Chastain's mobile phone. Dated 19 November 2014, start time 11:02 p.m. PST."

SHERILYN CHASTAIN (Incomprehensible speech): . . . with another woman?

(Pause.)

REBECCA "BEX" LAWSON: Is that thing recording?

CHASTAIN: Yeah.

LAWSON: In that case: no, I haven't. And, er . . .

CHASTAIN: Sorry, mate, I'm being totally inappropriate. Jet lag just really gives me the horn.

LAWSON: He's . . . twitching and stuff.

(Jack groans.)

CHASTAIN: Yep, waking up. Here we go. You ready?

LAWSON: Not really.

CHASTAIN: Just remember our goal here, okay? Remember the *tactics*.

LAWSON: Yeah.

JACK: What . . . what? No. No fucking way! Set me, me, me, me, me free.

CHASTAIN: Sorry Jack, not gonna happen. Your mate Rebecca's good with knots.

JACK: I, I, I, I, I decided you should die and so you should be dead. Why aren't you dead?

LAWSON: Well, sorry for the incon-fucking-venience. Cheryl said she'd follow me up here, just in case, and—

CHASTAIN: It's *Sherilyn*.

LAWSON: I thought she was some mad person stalking me from Facebook. Still not entirely sure.

CHASTAIN: I saw her in pics you'd posted, Jack, then managed to grab her in the foyer. You didn't reply when I called from the airport, so I had a feeling Mimi might be ruling the roost.

LAWSON: Took your time getting in here, though.

CHASTAIN: *You* try finding something hard enough to knock a guy out, but not hard enough to crack his skull.

LAWSON: You should've just cracked his skull.

CHASTAIN: You don't mean that.

LAWSON: Have *you* ever thought you were about to die?

CHASTAIN: Too many times to count.

LAWSON: Jesus, ow, ow.

CHASTAIN: Leave that leg alone—it's just a scratch. Look at *this* guy.

LAWSON: He did all that to himself.

CHASTAIN: Well, in layman's terms—

JACK: Untie me, me, me, me, me and I'll kill you both faster, I, I, I, I, I promise.

CHASTAIN: In layman's terms, he was trying to control his own ego.

LAWSON: What? His own ego? What?

CHASTAIN: Listen. What the Mimi Experiment did, it projected Jack's ego and turned it into a psychokinetic entity.

LAWSON: How can a scientific experiment do that?

CHASTAIN: Usually it can't. But with a great deal of help from darkness . . . Jack's ego was combined with everyone else's to form a gestalt being. When that being came under threat, it rejected what it saw as the inferior parts of itself and came home to possess Jack.

LAWSON: You really are mad, aren't you?

JACK: My hands . . . they want to do terrible things to both of you.

CHASTAIN: You're only human, mate. (Laughs lightly. Pause.) I find humour can help in these situations. So, Jack, listen: when you were in rehab, did you complete the fourth step of recovery?

JACK: Go fuck yourself.

CHASTAIN: Discharged yourself in the end, didn't you. Thought you were fine.

JACK: I, I, I, I, I *was* fine. Nothing gets the better of Jack Sparks.

LAWSON: Apart from the challenge of achieving a hard-on.

JACK: You shut your mouth! Shut your filthy lying *mouth*.

LAWSON: And you wondered why I called the whole thing off. You limp-dicked loser. You're not even a man.

(Pause. Someone walks across the room.)

CHASTAIN: Now, Jack . . .

JACK: Get out of my face, Chastain.

CHASTAIN: Tell me the first thing that ever scared you shitless. Tell me now.

JACK: Why should I, I, I, I tell you anything?

CHASTAIN: Because then I might set you free. And then you can kill us. You'd enjoy that, wouldn't you, so play along like a good little boy and let the real Jack talk for a while. (Pause.)

JACK: Sherilyn, you're here, thank fuck!

CHASTAIN: *Talk*, Jack, before Mimi shuts you down again. What was the first thing that scared you shitless?

JACK: The black hole.

LAWSON: Huh?

JACK: The cloakroom in the middle of our house. My brother shut me, me, me, me in there. There, I, I, I, I told you. Now let me, me, me, me go.

CHASTAIN: I told you to let the real Jack *speak*, if you want to be *free*. So stay in that cloakroom for me. Let the real Jack picture himself there now. Why are you afraid?

JACK: You irrelevant specks of dirt. I'll make you beg for death.

LAWSON: Bit dumb, isn't it, being scared of an empty cloakroom? What do you have to cry about in there?

JACK: It's dark, you idiot, so dark. Can't see a single thing. Remind me, me, me, me: why aren't you dead? You should be dead.

CHASTAIN: So what do you do in this room, besides crap your nappy? Do you bang on the door? Ask your bro to let you out?

JACK: Both. Then I, I, I, I realise he won't open up any time soon and I, I, I, I start crying. As I'm banging on the cloakroom doors, begging Alistair, he shouts that he hates me, me, me, me because I, I, I, I made our dad leave. He says I, I, I, I can cry until I'm sick and die in the cloakroom for all he cares.[2]

CHASTAIN: Why does he think you made your dad leave?

JACK: I, I, I, I don't like this. Get the ropes off.

CHASTAIN: If you don't answer my questions, you can die on that *chair*, for all I care.

(Pause.)

JACK: Him and Mum always thought Dad left home because of me, me, me, me. They didn't *say* I, I, I, I was to blame all that often, but it was obvious from the way they treated me, me, me, me. And I, I, I, I . . . started thinking they were right. Dad left because I, I, I, I was this horrible, ugly, screaming little nightmare kid.

---

2 This is absolutely and categorically untrue. My foreword provided the correct account. —*Alistair*

CHASTAIN: I can see how he'd regret not aborting you. (Pause.) Now close your eyes and put yourself right back in that darkness. What happens after you realise you'll be in there a while?

JACK: I, I, I freeze. Just so scared. Chills all over me, me, me. The worst part is when I, I, I feel something else in the room.

LAWSON: *Feel* something?

JACK: I, I, I hear it, moving about. Smell it too, maybe. There's all these pictures in my head: about a million different versions of how this thing might look. I, I, I stop calling to Alistair, because it won't do any good, but I, I, I also can't speak. There are coats hanging up and I, I, I feel around for my mum's.

LAWSON: Why?

JACK: She smokes and she always has lighters everywhere. So I, I, I feel in the pockets and find a Zippo. I, I, I remember how she worked it, so I, I, I copy her and flip the wheel. I, I, I want to see this thing and face it. Make it more . . . knowable.

CHASTAIN: Makes sense.

JACK: But when the lighter comes on, turns out I've set a coat sleeve on fire.

CHASTAIN: Do you get to see the thing in the dark?

JACK: No, it was never there. It was just something I, I, I imagined in the dark and in the corner of my eye.

CHASTAIN: You quite sure about that, Toto?

LAWSON: *Toto?*

JACK: So then I, I, I panic, because the coat burns fast. The smoke makes me, me, me cough. Can't breathe, nowhere to go.

CHASTAIN: So what happens? Because sadly, you didn't die that day.

JACK: Alistair sees smoke coming out from under the door. He pulls me, me, me out of there, yelling for Mum. She comes in from the garden all groggy and Alistair tells her I, I, I barricaded myself in the cloakroom and set it on fire.[3] She swears her head off, fills a bucket in the kitchen and chucks it in the cloakroom. Me, me, me and her precious Alistair get checked out for smoke inhalation in A and E, then she brings us home and slaps me, me, me hard around the face.[4] I'm grounded for two weeks after that.

(Pause.)

LAWSON: Best way to treat a needledick like you.

CHASTAIN: How do you think this affected your thoughts on the supernatural?

JACK: I, I, I . . . don't care.

LAWSON: Is this Real Jack or Evil Jack?

CHASTAIN: Hard to tell. Mimi keeps clawing him back. (Pause.) How did you feel about the unknown, growing up?

JACK: That everything could be explained away. Literally explained away: kind of . . . banished. You just had to shine a light on it. Science helped me, me, me deny so much fear. Mum was this big hardline Catholic, so I, I, I reacted against that too. I'd get back at her by talking about the big bang and stuff. And if science didn't help, I, I, I had the Zippo. Still take it everywhere.

(Pause.)

CHASTAIN: Did you by any chance misplace that Zippo when you—

3 Untrue. —*Alistair*

4 Again, untrue. Our mother never, ever struck either of us. —*Alistair*

JACK: Came to your place, yeah.

CHASTAIN: You cried in the bathroom like a stupid little baby, didn't you, until you found it in your pocket. (Pause.) For the benefit of the recording, Jack is nodding.

JACK: It panicked me, me, me. Can I, I, I get out now? I, I, I feel better.

CHASTAIN: No, Mimi still has a good grip. But nice try.

JACK: I'll rip your guts out, you know that?

CHASTAIN: Proves my point.

(Pause.)

LAWSON: Why don't you tell us the real reason you've been writing this stupid book?

CHASTAIN: Oh, I worked that one out. He's been looking for the supernatural—it's the only explanation that makes sense. But what I don't know is *why*.

JACK: I, I, I don't want to talk any more. And I, I, I don't want to hurt you now, so you should let me, me, me go.

LAWSON: Very convincing, Sir Ian McKellen.

CHASTAIN: How do you get on with your brother now, and your mum?

(Long pause.)

JACK: Won't talk any more.

LAWSON: Do you have any idea how much I'd enjoy pulling your bandages off and rubbing this stuff in?

JACK: Don't you dare.

CHASTAIN: What's that—Tabasco?

LAWSON: Oh, I dare. You were going to slit my throat, Jack. I wet my pants. I almost died in soaking wet pants.

CHASTAIN: One last try before he gets the sauce. Jack, how do you get on with your brother now, and with your mum? (Pause.)

JACK: I, I, I don't. Well, I, I, I don't get on with Alistair because the two of us clashed even more as we got older. He hates me, me, me now. And my mum always loved him a thousand times more than she loved me, me, me. Was it my fault I, I, I looked like my dad?

(Pause.)

CHASTAIN: You're using the past tense—did your mum die? (Pause.) Jack is nodding. How long ago?

JACK: I, I, I don't even know exactly when. That's how fucked I, I, I was.

CHASTAIN: Explain? (Fifteen-second pause.) Jack, explain.

JACK: I, I, I think I've lost too much blood. Feel faint.

CHASTAIN: No you don't.

LAWSON: Did she die last summer? Is that why you started the drugs?

(Pause.)

CHASTAIN: Jack is shaking his head.

LAWSON: Right. Which bandage comes off first? Eeny meeny—

JACK: Two Junes back . . . Mum asked me, me, me and Alistair to visit her, together. I, I, I was this big-shot writer and I'd won an award. Thought I, I, I was brilliant, but . . . Going back to Suffolk was this big inconvenience. I, I, I hadn't seen Mum in a couple of years and Alistair in even longer. So I, I, I turned up at this house where Alistair and I, I, I grew up—the house with that bloody room. Alistair and I, I, I kept it all very civil for Mum's sake, but there was this weird moment between us when she was off in the kitchen.

CHASTAIN: And what was that?

JACK: Oh, he found some excuse to lead the way through the cloakroom. He made a point of holding the door open for me, me, me to follow. He peered over his specs at me, me, me, with this kind of butter-wouldn't-melt, questioning look. Like: "Can you handle this now?" I, I, I really wanted to be all nonchalant, but I, I, I couldn't face going back in there, so walked the long way around instead. And when I, I, I saw him on the other side, he was wearing this cruel little smile.[5]

LAWSON: He got the better of you again, even as an adult. Because you're weak.

JACK: Me, me, me, Alistair and Mum went into the back garden and sat down at the table. I, I, I remember the slats on the tabletop. Even, like, the grain in the wood. Birds were calling to each other and you could smell all this freshly cut grass. But then there were dark clouds and that kind of . . . heavy feeling in the air before a storm. Mum lit up a cigarette and she told us . . . (Pause.) She told us she had motor neurone disease and wasn't going to live all that much longer. (Pause.) Maybe Alistair already knew, or suspected. Him and his wife and kids still lived locally. From the moment she opened the front door that day, something was wrong. Her speech was off and it looked like she had to make an effort to swallow. She'd asked Alistair to make cups of tea for us, which was unheard of. She always did that. When I, I, I bothered to visit, anyway.

CHASTAIN: How did you feel when she broke the news?

JACK: All I, I, I remember is . . . I, I, I remember all these splashes in my tea, from raindrops. Then . . . er . . . er . . . I, I, I . . .

LAWSON: What did you do, Jack?

CHASTAIN: Quick! Mimi weakens with every word of confession, so spit it out.

---

5 I did not. All untrue. —*Alistair*

JACK: I, I . . . got up and walked out. Ran out, actually. Then I, I got in my car and drove back to London.

LAWSON: You did what?

JACK: Alistair shouted at the back of the car, telling me, me to come back, shouting "Coward!" There was this flash flood pissing down, but I, I could still hear him for what seemed like miles. I, I told myself I'd left so Mum didn't see me upset.

CHASTAIN: But you were just a coward, weren't you? Jack's nodding.

JACK: I, I ran when she needed me. Just like Dad did. I, I was terrified. The thing about believing in science, about being an atheist . . .

CHASTAIN: It means death isn't a door. It's a brick wall.

JACK: Yeah, yeah. And . . . oh God . . . I, I didn't want my life to change. I, I wanted to keep my lifestyle and my precious fucking career. I, I didn't want to be looking after . . . (Voice falters) and all that stuff . . . So I, I drove back to London so fast. And on the way I, I decided my next book would be *Jack Sparks on Drugs*.

LAWSON: Oh. Right.

JACK: Yeah.

CHASTAIN: Your mum's dying, so you fuck off into oblivion.

JACK: Not consciously. I, I just threw myself into the book, calling it research.

LAWSON: And what dedicated research it was.

JACK: I, I ignored Alistair's voicemails and emails. I, I even ignored a call from Mum. Sherilyn? I, I feel weird. Has Mimi gone now?

CHASTAIN: Did you see your mother again before the end?

JACK: By June this year, I, I was at my worst, totally fucked up.

LAWSON: You were unbearable.

CHASTAIN: Did you see your mother before she—

JACK: I, I remember you bringing me the post one day, when I, I was in bed.

LAWSON: Yeah?

JACK: The windows were wide open, but reading this letter, the room still felt too hot. Alistair knew voicemail and email hadn't worked, so he sent me, me this piece of paper with his big, angry handwriting. It said something like "Mum died last week. Funeral next Monday. Call me if you even care."

CHASTAIN: Did you go? (Pause.) Jack's shaking his head.

LAWSON: You didn't go to your own mother's funeral.

JACK: I, I went into shock, like I'd re-entered the Earth's atmosphere. The guilt and shame got so bad, drugs couldn't paint over them. I, I didn't care so much about Alistair, but Mum . . . I mean, she hadn't been perfect by a long shot. Most of the time she made me, me feel so shit that I, I had to invent reasons why I, I was okay. You know when you're a young kid and you just say the opposite of whatever anyone says to you? Well, that's how the confidence, or the arrogance, whatever . . . that's how it started. Mum or Alistair would tell me, me, that I, I was stupid and I'd just say I, I wasn't, as an automatic reaction. Whatever they said I, I was, I, I told them they were wrong. And as I, I got older, I, I started to believe it. That confidence became my kind of default position: I, I was right and everyone else was wrong.

I'm making Mum sound bad, but that's not the whole story. She was my mum, you know? She worked two or three jobs, the whole time me, me and Alistair were growing up. She worked herself into the . . . ground. And at the end of her life, when I, I owed something back, I, I deserted her. To think of her . . . this strong woman stuck in bed, getting more ill every day, more scared, more paralysed . . .

CHASTAIN: And wondering if her younger son would ever come back to say goodbye . . . (Jack sobs for twenty-eight seconds.) So . . . after your mum died: was this when you went to rehab?

JACK: Pure masochism. I, I wanted to confront myself, what I'd done, while I, I was sober. To punish myself. And once I'd cleared my head in there, it was just unbearable. I, I became obsessed with saying sorry.

LAWSON: You said it in your sleep.

CHASTAIN: Saying sorry to your mum?

JACK: Must've been.

LAWSON: But for whose sake would that apology be? Your mum's or your own?

CHASTAIN: Selfish by definition, wasn't it? Because as far as you were concerned, you wanted to apologise to a dead woman, in a world you believed offered no afterlife. A world with no ghosts.

JACK: Well . . . I, I started to wonder . . . you know, if there might be something out there. Just . . . something after death. I, I remembered the thing in the cloakroom, for the first time in ages, and I, I drew hope from that. But—

LAWSON: I thought you said there *was* no thing in the cloakroom?

JACK: But I, I was scared of wishful thinking, too. It's like . . . the fear of hope. Misplaced hope. That's the worst thing: misplaced hope. I, I was so scared to leave the grid, you know, to leave science behind, because it meant—

CHASTAIN: Facing the darkness again. Got it. So that's why you wanted to write *this* book?

JACK: I, I could keep my public face. I, I could set out on this journey with this book, keep myself going with money . . . and . . . er . . . oh God . . . I could search for life after death.

LAWSON: Bloody hell! You hypocrite.

CHASTAIN: Imagine Dawkins writing *The God Delusion* while hoping to convince himself there's a creator.

LAWSON: So what were you going to write if you found evidence for the supernatural?

JACK: Well . . . I, I . . . (Pause.) I was going to keep it to myself. I had to keep that public face. My persona. My . . . my brand. (Lawson makes vomit noise.) In the book, I'd explain any kind of phenomena away as bullshit. But I really wanted to find a sign. Some sign that one day I'd either see Mum in the afterlife, or be able to contact her.

CHASTAIN: Jesus, you're unreal, you know that? All those believers you've mocked, calling them dumb, demeaning them. And yet you've been sliming around, trying to find what they already had.

JACK: Yes.

CHASTAIN: You cowardly, weak, selfish sack of shit.

JACK: Yes. Yes I am. (Pause.) I can speak properly again. Has it worked, has Mimi gone?

CHASTAIN: She seems to have fucked off, yeah. We've been stripping you of psychic armour, Jack. Getting to the core of you and purging all that ego, so Mimi had nothing left to cling to. A full transcript of this recording absolutely has to go in your book. Got that?

JACK: Is this revenge then, Sherilyn? Not that I'd blame you.

CHASTAIN: If I wanted revenge, Jack, I'd still be in Auckland getting first-class head.
(Recording ends.)

CHAPTER NINETEEN

Bloodless flesh valleys loop around my wrists and forearms. These marks inflicted by the girls' makeshift ropes are small fry compared to the Crowley cuts. And the sum total of all this pain, in turn, is nothing compared with what's about to happen.

Sherilyn had arrived with bandages and Band-Aids. These cover half my body. In their hurry to incapacitate me, the women left me nude. Understandable.

As I wince my way back into my T-shirt and other scattered clothes, I'm flooded with something alien. I think it's called gratitude. So much gratitude to these two angels who led me out of the dark cave.

Yet when I hug Sherilyn, she becomes rigor mortis personified and soon withdraws. Bex can hardly look at me, let alone brook physical contact. I try so clumsily to embrace her, the apologies spilling out of me, but she backs off, raising both palms. Those hands shake, but her voice holds firm. "Jack, I didn't want anything more to do with you *before* you tried to kill me."

She does, at least, understand that I wasn't myself, or the regular me, because she says she won't press charges.

Oh my God.

Howitz.

The memory of killing him is so hazily dreamlike that I've almost convinced myself it never happened. Then I open the closet door, just a crack, and his cloying reek slithers into me. I see him slumped in there. Bug-eyed with fallen coat hangers on his lap, his throat an obscene red-toothed grin.

The sight whips the breath out of me. I click the door shut and lean back against it clutching my chest, my heart thumping the palm of my hand. I look around the blurry room to check no one saw, which feels like such a Mimi thing to do.

I should tell Bex and Sherilyn what happened with Howitz. I just can't bear the thought of their faces changing when they realise they've helped a hands-on killer, even if he was possessed at the time.

Turns out Bex missed her flight home today—yesterday now, since it's long gone midnight—because of that passport. She's even more pissed off when I tell her I never really had it.

My heart skips a beat when she mounts a search of her own.

I watch as she opens doors and hauls out drawers.

Drawing nearer to Howitz's resting place each time.

Cold-sweat shivers spur me into action. Self-preservation wins once again. Have I learned nothing?

Yanking open the nearest wardrobe, I'm relieved to spot Bex's passport on the floor. When I hand it over, she stuffs it into her suitcase without a word. Announcing she's heading straight to LAX after a shower, she disappears into the bathroom and jams the latch shut.

Which leaves Sherilyn Chastain and me. Her hair now a dark green mess, Sherilyn splays herself across the sofa. "Tired as a cunt," as she puts it. I know how she feels. I bury the strong urge to ask her about Maria Corvi and that book from the future which details my death. She's clearly still recovering from the last favour she did me. I'm supposed to be the new, selfless Jack.

"How much do I owe you, Sherilyn? Do you take PayPal or—"

She sweeps a limp hand across the lap of her jeans, waving me off. "If you wanna know the truth, I did this for me as much as you."

Off my quizzical look, she says, "Three months ago, I messed up a job in London. Really fucked it. Not good. Then the Lengs' little girl got hurt in Hong Kong because I made a mistake."

Silence between us as I take this in. "So I'm your karmic equaliser?"

She nods, her eyes half open.

"Thank you anyway, Sherilyn."

"You already thanked me."

"It doesn't seem enough."

"Fuck off, Jack. I don't have the energy for embarrassment."

I push myself, force myself, to pose a question I don't necessarily want to know the answer to. "Did *you* read the chapter about me in Di Stefano's book?"

Without skipping a beat, she shakes her head and says, "You torched that whole section. Now, a couple of things you need to know. Number One: slip back into selfish ways and Mimi will slip back into you."

Should I tell Sherilyn about Howitz right now? I really should tell her.

From the bathroom, the shower's white-noise hiss.

"Number Two: people only see what they want to see. The unconscious mind is great at filtering out stuff that fucks up the status quo. Now that you've been purged of so much ego, you may finally see the dead. Or ghosts. Or whatever model you want to place on that kind of energy."

"Christ," I breathe. "Yeah. I want to see an actual ghost. A real person, a dead person."

With her eyes shut, Sherilyn points down with both fore-fingers. "You're probably in the right place, mate."

It takes me a while to catch her meaning. I stare at the floor like an amnesiac, trying to work it out. Then my jaw drops. "What if the Paranormals didn't really make that video?"

She drowsily shifts a cushion behind her head. "Tell you something: if they did make it, they did a pretty fuckin" good job. A video where only you could hear three words on the soundtrack?"

My stomach rolls. "Yeah. Any idea what those three words mean?"

"They mean someone or something is fucking with your head."

Maria.

"But why those three words?" I ask. "Why those three demons?"

Sherilyn bucks right off the sofa, back in the room. "Ah! Yeah. I worked that out, somewhere over Niue Island. Wrote it down on a scrap of paper." She pats her pockets, then heads over to search through zippered sections on her suitcase, which sits beside Bex's. "Somewhere . . ."

"Could you maybe just tell me?" I say, trying not to sound ungrateful.

"Best if I show you. Found it."

As she hands me a page from a complimentary Air New Zealand notepad, that's when the world turns to shit.

A slaughterhouse howl rips out of the bathroom.

A raw expression of agony, terror, shock.

I hope my death will at least erase this howl from my memory.

Sherilyn and I stiffen, then race to the bathroom door. I get there first, rattling the handle and of course finding it locked from the inside.

A second howl cuts off abruptly, making bile rise in my throat.

Before I can kick the door, Sherilyn slams her own heel into the wood, knocking it off the latch. And we're in.

Into the room fogged with steam.

The room where the shower door is still shut.

I wrench that door open, in time to glimpse something red and unthinkable being sucked out of sight, down through the wrecked shower tray. Down through a jagged star-shaped hole, as if something punched up through it. Blood, so much blood, overflows and splashes my bare feet, just before the rest swirls down into the star with a loud glug.

Sherilyn hauls my numb mannequin self aside. Staring at Bex's blood on my feet, noting strands of her hair curled around my toes, I'm dimly aware of Sherilyn swearing and spraying her aerosol around the edges of that star. I want to ask what just happened, but can only mutter, "Bring her back," until my attention is stolen by what's happening in the sink.

Through the steam, you can see the greenish-brown water that fills the bowl, leaves floating on its surface. Somehow alive, this water rises above the rim without spilling a drop, then sculpts itself into a crude human head. One single brow appears above the eyes. Filthy water forms jagged teeth in an open mouth, which speaks with the same thick gurgle I had in my ear at the Rainbow Bar.

"Hell," Tony Bonelli tells me, "is having no control."

Tony's head collapses, vanishing fast down the plughole. When only the leaves remain, Sherilyn abandons the shower tray and rushes over to spray the sink. Then she does the same to the toilet bowl and every other inlet in the room.

I'm sitting on the floor, unsure how I got down here, quite unable to stand. Sherilyn has to grab me under the arms and pull me backwards across the tiles on my backside, until we're no longer in the bathroom.

On the way out, I ask, "We can get her back, right?"

And all Sherilyn can say is, "I'm so sorry."

Doesn't matter how long I sit down here on the floor, rocking forwards and back, sucking cigarettes right down to the stubs: the tears don't come.

How can you be expected to shed tears over something you can't accept? Something so ridiculous, so impossible?

I brought wonderful, kind, supportive Bex to Los Angeles. I brought her here and she's ended up . . .

I might as well have killed her myself. God knows, I tried.

The mind recoils. Cannot process. As if I'm standing at the foot of Everest with my face pressed against the bare rock, trying to see the whole mountain.

All the questions I aim up at Sherilyn contain the word "why."

Why does Tony hate me so much?

While spraying the gaps around the bathroom door, Sherilyn gives her opinion. Based on the working draft of this book I emailed her, she thinks Maria Corvi victimised Tony for translating my words in the church. My mocking words. Guilt by verbal association.

"Oh," is all I can say to that. And then, "Oh God, why can't Maria just forget me?"

Standing on a wobbly chair to spray the ceiling air con, Sherilyn says, "Because you laughed, Jack. During that exorcism, you stole the limelight. This thing inside Maria demands to be the centre of attention. It demands fear and respect. And it always gets the last laugh."

"Bex had nothing to do with this," I growl, fighting myself into my shoes, keeping the blood and hair on my feet. "It's me Maria wants." I roar into the ether: "It's me you want!"

Someone thumps on the wall from an adjoining room, and I scream abuse back.

"Jack . . ."

It's that voice again. The whispering voice that leads to the basement.

"Do you hear that?" I demand of Sherilyn. "My name being whispered?"

Spraying plug sockets, she just shakes her head.

"Jack . . ." says the voice.

I'm up on my feet, then out the door, marching through corridors, propelled by rage. Sherilyn calls after me, wanting to know where I'm heading. The basement? If so, she says, I have to wait. She needs more time to prepare.

As the lift doors close on me, I yell at her not to follow.

A breathless Sherilyn finds me at reception. I'm pointing across the foyer to the basement entrance door and ordering some designer-stubbled guy, not Brandon this time, to give me the key. Stubble Guy blanches and reddens, then snatches up a landline handset and hits one number. Then he tries another extension and says into the phone, "Ruthie, where *is* Howitz?"

I reach over the desk, grab the handset and slam it back on to the cradle in a jumble of curly cord.

"Out, or I call the cops," Stubble Guy says.

"Hey!" comes the cry from some night owl across the foyer. This anvil-headed thirty-stone black guy leaves his sofa. As he strides towards us, he looks twice as big thanks to his reflection in the polished floor.

While all this is going on, of course, a disembodied voice still whispers my name.

Sherilyn eyeballs the approaching vigilante, while easing a cosh out of the lining of her small backpack. "Come on, fellas. No one wants this to get ugly."

Balling his fists up tight by his sides, Stubble Guy doesn't even blink. "You need to leave right now."

I yank my T-shirt up and bunch it around my neck so Stubble Guy can see my ruined torso. All those Band-Aids stained pink from blood, green from pus. All the places where dressings have fallen off, revealing testimonials to a sick mind.

Fishing a key out from under the desk, Stubble Guy hands it over the same way he'd dish out a quarter to pacify some raving street loon.

Sherilyn slides the cosh back into its secret compartment.

Flickering bulbs test my nerve as we prowl the service corridor, down where the air gets warmer and wetter. The beckoning voice has fallen silent.

This burning anger feels useful. So much easier to get to grips with than, for example, massive grief or unbearable loss.

"Had to leave half my bloody stuff upstairs," Sherilyn grouses.

"I told you not to follow me," I say. "I just want this over with. Something wants me to come down here, and it sounds like Maria's voice."

"I can't just let you hand yourself over, Jack."

The darker these passageways become, the more fear saps my resolve. I dip into my pocket where the Zippo usually sits, only to find it empty. I stop walking, not knowing what to do or say.

Sherilyn jerks her head around. Feline, alert. She utters a migraine moan, then shoos something invisible away with one hand.

"What's going on?" I ask her.

"Just got a psychic strike."

Standing beside me, Sherilyn is a silhouette, profiled by limited light from the main boiler area up ahead. The sudden cold feels unnatural: an abrupt change of season. This time I can't blame the Paranormals' equipment. My God, what if they really didn't make that video? It's strangely comforting to touch the rough, sweaty surface of the nearest wall.

"What's a psychic strike?" I ask her.

"Whatever this thing is, it knows it's got company. Probably detects me, so it's lashing out. So you're gonna stay here while I secure the area. No arguments."

I agree way too fast. Like she said during the ego-purging ritual, I'm a coward. I totally wanted her to follow me down here.

From her backpack, Sherilyn takes the aerosol, some kind of figurine and a zipper bag of something. Handing me the surprisingly heavy pack, she says, "Hold this for me and don't move."

I fight the dread as her clomping footsteps become taps,

then barely audible clicks, which merge with the generator hum as she disappears around that internet-famous corner.

I'm waiting in darkness.

My hand goes to that Zippo pocket again.

Waiting in darkness.

It pointlessly explores that empty pocket.

Waiting in darkness.

My heartbeat is improvised jazz played with gong hammers.

Then I remember what's in the other pocket. A crumpled piece of paper . . . wrapped around my phone.

Waiting in darkness.

I pull out the phone and unlock it. I bathe in the feeble blue light while glancing skittishly around in case it reveals something terrible.

Sherilyn gave me this sheet of Air New Zealand notepaper upstairs, before hell rose up from the sewers. I unfold it by phone-light, struggling to remember what it was even supposed to be.

This is what she wrote:

ADRA **ME** LECH

ME PHISTOPHELES

BAPHO **ME** T

Sherilyn's voice comes back along the passageway whip-crack loud, stern as a lion tamer. "Oh, no-no-no. Stay back. You stay back or you'll get some of this."

When she speaks again, she's muffled and under duress. The sudden fear in her voice tightens my skin.

There's the dull sound of something or someone hitting the ground.

"Sherilyn?" I call. "Sherilyn, are you all right?"

No reply.

The generator drones on.

I so badly want to run. Yes, run like my dad did. Run like I always do. But this woman travelled across the world to save me, even if she insisted it was really to save herself.

No matter how counter-intuitive it might be, I shrug on Sherilyn's backpack, then force myself to walk towards the boiler room. I might be acting brave, but my lungs hitch when I try to call Sherilyn's name again. Best to let them focus on breath. As long as they're firing white mist out in front of me, I'm alive.

I start filming with my phone. If there really is a ghost, I want the whole world to see. For once in my life, I want, need to achieve something positive. Maybe this thing will defy photography like Mimi did, but I have to try. So I'm edging along the wall with the pipes, approaching that corner, heart pulsing in my mouth. Every single part of me feels heavier, more solid than it should.

If this ghost is waiting around the corner for me, I may as well confound its expectations. So I crouch and crawl. As I do this, something knocks on the door between my unconscious and conscious minds.

I slowly extend my phone around the bend, down low, millimetre by millimetre, then carefully follow it with my head so that I can see the screen.

I gasp. *How is this possible?*

Across this open area, Sherilyn Chastain lies prone on the ground. I can't see much of her, thanks to all those heavy shadows, but I know it's her.

I know all of this.

All of it.

Standing over her is a dark humanoid figure, facing away from me. This figure fades slowly in and out of view.

Only its bottom half is visible on my screen.

I look past the phone at the scene itself, as if to confirm this insanity.

At first I tell myself this is just history repeating itself.

But I know the truth. Oh yes, I know.

"Oh God," I whisper. "*This is it.*"

I am Camera Boy.

I duck back around the corner with a spine full of ice, keeping half of that terrible scene in frame—the exact same terrible scene I've witnessed hundreds of times before, along with a million other people.

This is too much to take. It's bending my head and I have to get out of here. Bravery crumbles and the survival instinct kicks in, telling me to move.

The viewfinder shows that the dark figure is now facing me. It must have slowly turned around while I was freaking out. Of course it did. I know this off by heart.

I can't see the figure's face and now I really, really don't want to.

As I scramble backwards away from that corner on my arse, I know what's next.

Jesus Christ, it's coming for me.

The sheer inevitability only makes it worse.

The figure glides fast around the corner, heading right for me, black feet hanging.

As I haul myself upright, a scream catches in my dust-dry throat.

The spectre's face is charred and cracked. The mouth a skeletal grimace.

Oh, but the eyes. Oh God, those eyes, full of torture. Dragged along for the ride whether they want to be here or not.

This is not just a grotesque parody of my own face.

It *is* my face.

Of course it is.

I half expect to find myself glued to the ground, like in all the best nightmares. Instead, gazelle legs launch me into action.

And I'm running through darkness, beneath bulbs that have finally given up.

I'm crashing into walls I don't remember and can't foresee.

I don't hear the spectre, but I know it's there. Flitting behind me.

Soundless, deathless.

I fall on to the staircase that leads up to the foyer. I scramble up these steps on all fours, thinking nothing of the splinters gouging my hands.

Please, please, just let me get back up into the light. What can this thing do to me up there, where there's people and life and open space?

"Don't go in there," rasps a sick version of my voice from behind me.

I glance back and see my dead self coming up the stairs.

I see the whites of my dead eyes.

Blind in the dark, I slam into the closed door and mount a crazed fumble for the handle. I'm fully aware that if some prick's locked the door, then I'll die, either by my own ghost's hands or through cardiac arrest.

"Don't go in there," my voice repeats, close, so close.

Dead breath frosts the nape of my neck.

I heave open the door and swing myself through it, rocked by a head rush and an intense flash of red light.

I slam the door behind me, but I'm not standing in the corridor back to the hotel lobby. I'm in total fucking darkness.

All aboard the ghost train.

I keep hold of the door handle, as if a phantom couldn't glide through solid wood if it chose to do so.

I pray for help, for light.

This door handle feels different. It used to be metal, but now it's wood. And it feels overwhelmingly familiar. The shape of it, the grooves . . .

Please, please, please . . . if there's any kind of God, then *let there be light.*

Nearby, a metallic clink and grind.

A tiny flame erupts.

I think my prayer has been answered, until I see the side of a young boy's face.

The boy clutches a burning Zippo lighter, trembling so much he's a blur. The dancing flame highlights tears rolling down his cheeks.

In this cramped space, I see the coats hanging right beside him. One of which he has set on fire.

"Jacob?" says Alistair, his muffled voice coming through the door I just entered. "Stop winding me up, you ugly little shit."[1]

Rooted to the spot, seeing my open mouth reflected in the shiny new brass of the Zippo, I silently *will* my five-year-old self not to sense my presence.

But of course, the boy's eyes dart this way, as far as they can go.

And he whimpers.

It's inevitable.

The boy so wants to be brave. He wants to turn and face

---

1 An entirely fabricated quote. —*Alistair*

the unknown. He's desperate to look and see nothing at all, so that everything will be fine.

Yet he can't move a muscle and he's wetting himself.

Because he knows damn well he sees me in the corner of his eye.

This moment will scar him forever. It will drive him to smother all doubt. To bury so much as the possibility that he saw something in this room.

Quite apart from the fear, he wouldn't want to give his brother the satisfaction.

As I step forward to hug this boy, a green explosion blinds me.

CHAPTER TWENTY

Cold soil devours my body temperature. Blades of grass squash themselves against the side of my face. Birds chirp and sing.

Hands, my hands, are wrapped around my head, shielding me from sunlight. Sherilyn's backpack forms a protective shell.

It feels so safe to remain foetal, blind and still. Seeing and feeling are overrated.

Yet my brain is a relentless angle-grinder, sparking questions.

How was it possible for me to meet my own ghost in a basement?

How was it possible for me to film a video I'd first seen twenty days beforehand? (I'm sorry, Paranormals, so very sorry, for accusing you of making a video I was somehow destined to make myself. And I'm even sorrier, Sherilyn, for leaving you down there.)

And how in the blue caterwauling fuck was it possible for the presence my young self glimpsed in that Suffolk cloakroom to have been my adult self?

Images parade before my mind's eye. Terrible iterations of

me. My face on the shrieking airborne Mimi. My face on the charred basement spectre. My face on a traumatised child then known as Jacob.

Jacob Titherley, my birth name.

I withheld one detail about Maria Corvi. About her parting shot to me in Italy via that bastard Bonelli's mouth. She didn't say, "Hey, Jack Sparks. Enjoy your journey." No, that would have been too simple, too easy. She said, "Hey, *Jacob Titherley.*"

All the abominable events since, I realise, have been about me. Someone, or something, has said: "You want it to be all about you? *Coming right up.*"

"Me," hidden in the three words on the video that only I could hear.

Myself, dead, blackened, my eyes brimming with despair, starring in the video I'd watched so many times.

"I," endlessly circled on the Ouija board in that boiler room.

This must be how a mouse feels as a cat plays with it, prolonging its demise. I'm on the journey advertised by Maria, my life mounted on rails. If Maria hadn't appeared in my Hong Kong hotel room, I wouldn't have read Astral's umpteenth email and so would never have gone to Los Angeles. If I hadn't become obsessed with the video, my paranoid relationship with the Paranormals might never have reached critical mass, ending their lives. I've been manipulated every step of the way.

I still have no idea where I am. Only that I'm outside and it's suddenly day.

I fear I'll open my eyes to some vast, barren hell. Nothing would surprise me.

Only when my memory dredges up a shower tray full of blood am I motivated to do anything, if only to kill the image. Because if I start to cry for Bex, I know I might never stop.

So I heave myself into a sitting position, groaning at the pain from one hundred Crowley cuts. I pull my legs to my chest to form a protective front against whatever awaits me.

Then I open my eyes.

There is no hell. Not here, anyway. Beneath an ashtray sky, dense grey woods stretch out to a horizon crowded with hills. (*Eleanor: I'm trying so hard to write as well as I can, despite the pain. I truly want to be remembered as a good writer. It's all too easy to question my own judgement now, so if you see anything bad, please change/remove. I trust your discretion.*)

I'm on a grassy cliff edge, the height of two trees. All that forbidding woodland looks too dead and dour for this to be California. But why should I be back there? Only just now, I seemed to be in Suffolk in 1983. Tony Bonelli's words come back to me: "She can do anything, Jack. Anything. She can take you anywhere, any time she likes."

Any *time* she likes.

The trees are bare and gnarled, reaching skyward, as twisted as . . .

As twisted as arthritic fingers.

Oh God, no, surely not. Lots of landscapes look this way. I could be anywhere.

Except I'm mounted on those rails. There's a deranged rhyme and reason behind all of this.

I shuffle myself around on the cold soil and see the back of the church.

The building towers over me. Steeple pointing to the heavens. Stained-glass window translucent in a renegade shaft of sun.

As queasy as I feel, it's weirdly reassuring to have found a familiar landmark.

My phone, I realise, is still gripped tight in my hand. It reveals the time to be 2:36 p.m. . . . . on 31 October.

Halloween. The same Halloween I'd believed to be firmly in my rear-view mirror.

A dull pressure squeezes my skull as I take in the scene depicted by the window's coloured glass. Jesus on the rocks. Father Primo Di Stefano's words echo back from the memory vaults: "It is Christ during his forty days in the wilderness."

I lasted twenty days after Halloween. And now I'm twenty days back. No prizes for guessing the total.

Best not to think about myself in the same light as Jesus Christ. Talk about playing into Mimi's hands.

A laugh rings out inside the church. This volcanic eruption, this hysterical belly hoot, stops me in my tracks.

This laugh sounds exactly like me.

My skin prickles as I stare up at that window, then hurry towards it.

Beneath the glass, missing bricks provide footholds as I haul myself up.

"*Signor!*" says a voice from inside that sounds exactly like Father Primo Di Stefano. "Please, what are you doing? Show some *respect*."

I grip the towering window's ledge and take one more step up, so I can peer in through the glass. As I cling to the rough masonry, my quads and calves shake under the strain.

From this vantage point, the simple altar and pulpit sit in the foreground, then a sea of pews rolls back to the furthest wall. Just past the altar stands Father Primo Di Stefano, side on to me. His assistants Beard and Beardless flank Maria Corvi, each holding one of her arms.

I don't linger on these people for long, being drawn quickly to three more sitting five rows back.

There's Maria's mother, Maddelena. Back from the grave.

Then there's the man I used to call Translator Tony. Back from the grave.

That guy sitting between the pair of them? That's me. Grinning and clapping, with my hands held above my head.

I don't know if you've ever looked at your past self through a window, but it's disconcerting. The effect is so very powerful that your brain falls over itself to find an explanation. I must be looking at my reflection, it suggests. Or maybe I'm watching a video on a big screen. Or maybe that's not Jack Sparks in there.

This is not the first time my brain has told me lies.

Maria's raggedy head now faces my window, her eyes glued to mine, full of sunlight.

Her knowing expression intensifies. *Ah, hello Future Jack. How's that journey working out for you?*

Past Me's own attention shifts my way. From memory, from direct experience, I know he wants to figure out what the funny actress girl is looking at.

The idea of making eye contact with Past Me brings the cloakroom to mind. Soulquake! I shove myself away from the wall and land on my back with a gasp.

Anxiety threatens to drag me under as I run through everything I know, or think I know, about time travel. Why didn't I listen to Pascal's speculation back in Culver City? The little I know about time travel has been derived from fiction. I doubt having seen the occasional episode of *Doctor Who* can help me right now.

One central tenet feels instinctively right: meeting Past Me would be bad. If we were to touch or even talk, the world might explode or implode or something. Anti-matter and matter. I actually laugh at this. A hysterical outburst from a man lying on the ground behind a church while a previous version of himself carries on watching an exorcism inside, oblivious to his timeline looping the loop.

This is fifty shades of fucked-up.

I stop laughing when I consider I might be dead. Could I be a ghost? Is this death? I'm comforted to feel warmth in my neck, then a pulse. But might a dead person *feel* alive to themselves? What if the thing looking out through Maria Corvi's eyes can see me, but no one else can?

I remember the ghost in the basement, back in LA. Or *forwards* in LA, depending on how you look at it. *That* surely was, is, will be my ghost. My future ghost. Unlike me, it was transparent, fading in and out of sight. Then I remember it was badly burnt, and I suffer another anxiety spike.

My thoughts spiral this way for some time, until my scatter-shot breaths deepen and the panic subsides. I decide I must act.

Inside the church, Father Di Stefano cries out in pain. Ah, that must be Maria regurgitating the nail into his leg. How did I ever think that was fake? I really was just shielding myself from reality. A lifetime ago.

What to do? How about if I dare speak to Past Me and tell him to abandon this book? What if I tell him to apologise profusely to Di Stefano and especially Maria? If I undo the offence caused by that laugh, might it undo all the horrors to come?

Maybe I'm being given that second chance.

What are the rules here? I'm doing what I accused the Paranormals of doing: making them up as I go.

After pacing a shitload of circles, psyching myself up, I make my way around one side of the church.

The first thing I see, upon clearing the corner of the building, is Tony Bonelli. He's standing a good distance away towards the front, where the cars are parked. He's smoking and hasn't seen me yet. But a lurking memory tells me he's about to.

Sure enough, he spots me standing back here by the cliff edge and nods casually. I expected him to be horrified or at least afraid, but of course to him I'm the same Jack he's working with inside. At this distance, he's unlikely to notice I'm wearing a different T-shirt. The jacket's the same, these are probably the same old jeans. He can see neither Sherilyn's backpack nor the bulk I've gained from all the bandages and pads under my clothes.

Blazing, I stomp towards him. My hands twitch in anticipation of the soft flesh of his throat, eyeballs, anything they can get. I want to make this fucker suffer for what he did to Bex, even though he hasn't done it yet. Even though he will no doubt be driven to it by madness.

Bonelli frowns, takes a step backwards. He's about to say something, probably to ask what's wrong, when Past Me emerges from a side door. Gripped again by nameless fear, I duck back around the corner of the church, out of sight.

I hear Tony gasp, startled, and remember how peculiar this moment was for Past Me. I thought the guy had been rattled by the exorcism, when in fact his reaction to seeing my homicidal doppelgänger was pretty natural. I'm surprised he didn't run away screaming.

What the hell am I doing? Forget Bonelli, forget revenge, forget fear: I need to change this timeline. Right now, it's running exactly as it did before. I prepare to round that corner once again. This time, I'll make a difference. I'll get Past Me's attention and tell him everything I know. The universe will not implode.

Let's go.

"Hello, Jacob," croaks a young girl's voice from over my shoulder.

There, right behind me, stands Maria Corvi. Her hands clasped demurely in front of that blue smock, a big smile on her face. She'd be quite the jolly picture if her own blood and stomach acid weren't still smeared around those lips, along with flecks of rust. Yes, she'd almost look human without the cracked facial skin and those pus-yellow eyes.

Those eyes of hers, with actual hellfire dancing where the retinas and optic nerves should be. No trick of the sun after all.

She places her forefinger against my lips. The broken-nail finger, wet with blood. Her rotten-kipper breath infests my sinuses. "It went well in there, don't you think, Jack? I do love saying all that Bible stuff the priests want to hear."

I wonder if she's about to let me in on a joke. To pull back the curtain on the real Oz. The actual *Truman Show*. And when she does this, I'll somehow be magically off the hook. Bit of fun, no harm done.

This is, of course, a prime example of misplaced hope.

With a tiny left–right motion, her finger smears vile liquid on my lips, then withdraws. I seize my chance. "Are you . . . Are you who I think you are?"

Mock-innocent now, coquettish, Maria says, "Mamma will soon call for me. I would so hate to worry her."

Maddelena Corvi. The mother who was right about her daughter being possessed. The woman with hours left to live.

"Listen," I say. "I'm sorry for laughing, okay? I'm so very, very sorry."

I recognise Maria's mannered shrug all too well. It's the one I employ when I want to pretend I don't care.

"I take it all back," I persist. "I know who you are. You're real, and I'll tell the world."

From inside the church, Past Me's voice rings out loud and clear: "There's no such thing as the Devil!"

Maria's laugh is faint in her throat.

"Maria?" calls Maddelena from inside the church. Maria's sickly eyes dart to follow the sound, and her mouth hatches open. From the back of her throat, loud and clear, comes the rich ticking sound of a grandfather clock.

The sense of a trapdoor beneath my feet breeds desperation. "I want to live. I've learned so much. Please forgive me."

Maria tilts her head to one side, looks up and places one finger on her chin. As if actually considering the idea.

Tick-tock, goes the back of her throat. *Tick-tock.*

Maddelena, her voice a paper aeroplane on the breeze, calls her daughter's name again.

Tick-tock.

"Please," I say, "at least spare Bex. Rebecca Lawson. She didn't deserve that."

Sorry, Sherilyn. I'm so sorry. I have seconds, just seconds, to make my case.

The ticking stops when Maria speaks again. "Nothing to do with me. Entertaining, however. Did you hear her bones, the way they broke down in that pipe? Bex's broken bones."

My eyes sting with tears of nausea, of blind hatred. I reach behind myself and feel around for the secret compartment in Sherilyn's backpack.

Maria's eyes twinkle. "Of course, my little Antonino wanted to kill *you*. I couldn't have that. But you should throw your pets the occasional treat."

My probing fingers find the compartment empty.

"You won't see Tony again," says Maria, with a giggle. "I sent him way back through history. Oh, the fun he'll have."

What would a cosh achieve anyway? I'd only be harming the thirteen-year-old girl this thing occupies.

Actually, no.

No. I promised myself I wouldn't lie to you again: I'm not paralysed by the fear of harming poor blameless Maria Corvi. It's fear full stop. The kind of fear you feel when confronted with true evil's glacial gleam. The kind of fear that warms, then soaks, the crotch of my jeans while I barely notice.

Maria reaches into a pocket in her smock and produces the cosh.

Looking for this, Jack? Naughty naughty.

My stomach shrinks as I back away from her. Maria follows, cruel smile fixed, dropping the cosh back inside her pocket.

My mad brainwave is born more of outright despair than logic. I know Maria created Mimi, using my and the Paranormals' combined ego power. But perhaps if I could bring Mimi back, deliberately wake her, she might protect me. Perhaps I could turn Maria's creation against her.

"I am perfection itself," I tell Maria, trying my hardest to convince. "Unstoppable. The greatest writer who ever lived. I just spent forty days in the wilderness. I am He. I am *Jesus Christ!*"

Mimi's hovering face fails to appear. Nothing happens at all.

Maria's bestial features rearrange themselves into something like pity. "Oh Jacob, you really haven't been paying attention. Mimi and I are very close indeed. In fact, we're inseparable."

Her right hand shoots up to clamp itself around the left-hand side of my neck. My flesh becomes hotplate bacon, hissing and sizzling against her palm.

Maria pouts and purrs. This tidal wave of pain, fine wine to her.

I can make no sound. There can only be submission as I sink to my knees and plunge into black.

Next thing I know, I'm denied the privilege of unconsciousness. I'm on my front, being dragged along the grass by a fistful of my hair. Every few feet, the hair rips out in Maria's hand and my head thumps the ground. She tosses the torn clump aside, grabs another fistful and resumes the process.

The wooden cosh sits between my teeth, its round end wedged against the back of my throat, choking me, ensuring I breathe only through my nose.

As I'm being scalped and beaten senseless, I can smell the bubbling pizza pepperoni that now passes for skin beneath my jaw.

I reach out for Maria's legs, but my fingertips never so much as brush them.

Is that the sound of me finally mustering a scream? No, it's an ambulance siren, drawing closer.

This thirteen-year-old girl hauls me towards the cliff edge. It's astonishing how very fragile we all are. Bring just enough mayhem to someone, beast them to perfection, and suddenly a fatal fall feels like mercy.

Somewhere in the background, Maddelena says, "Maria? *Dove sei, la mia bambina?*" But she won't save me. Because this has already happened and I've got the message now: I can't change anything. It's already done and so am I.

Maria says something triumphant. Forgive me, but I'm so rigid from the massive anticipation of violent death that I don't even hear.

She shoves hard, the grassy soil falls away and gravity claims me.

CHAPTER TWENTY-ONE

So I wake spread-eagled in the rough arms of a tree, with no idea of what's what.

My left leg sends intense distress signals. Something's very wrong there.

God knows where the cosh ended up, but I can still taste the wood.

I can only tell what's up and what's down from the way my blood drips. The body's natural compass.

Yes, according to the blood from a new gash across my forehead, not to mention several freshly reopened Crowley cuts, I'm hanging upside down.

Everything's hyper-real. Leaves and branches in such high definition. Rainbow dewdrops. I suppose cheating death does this to the perception.

For who knows how long, I just bleed and try not to faint. Then I remember Maria Corvi's voice emerging from Tony Bonelli's mouth: "I'll be back in a few hours, okay?"

A curious statement at the time, but one that now waves a red flag.

Maria is being taken to a hospital from which she will then escape. Poor Maddelena Corvi, poor Pio Accardo. And poor me, because Maria will return to finish the job.

I can't stay here awaiting the *coup de grâce*.

I engage my gut muscles and curl up to wrap my arms around a bough. My left leg spits wrath. Cold sweat breaks out all over me and my vision swims. To avoid another blackout, I bite my lip until my own blood mingles with the reddish-black gloss Maria left behind.

This leg is screwed below the knee. The skin's intact, but the foot points to two o'clock instead of twelve. Putting any kind of weight on it makes me retch.

Having to drop the last few feet down to the ground doesn't help. I land on my good leg and lean heavily against the trunk behind me, Sherilyn's backpack crunching into the bark. Knowing I can't walk by myself, I seize a thick branch and bend it down. The thing protests and warps into a U before snapping off where it meets the trunk.

Leaning against this ad hoc crutch, I take experimental steps away from the tree. It's slow and agonising, but I can move.

When I cautiously touch the burn on my neck, a sticky glob of melted black flesh comes away on my fingers. Pledging not to do that again, I thumb the blood from my eyes and look around. I'm at the foot of the cliff face, on the edge of the woods. Since Maria plans to return to the church, I must get away from it as quickly as possible. More than anything, I must reject the notion that fate has me in its jaws, no matter what I do. That way lies defeat.

Through the trees, I see snatches of horizon, interrupted

by hills. As I mentally trace a route through to those hills, a familiar beep sounds in my pocket.

The phone's front glass is cracked, but it still works. A pop-up notification tells me that ten per cent of the battery power remains.

Behind this lies a second notification: "Your video *Untitled* has successfully uploaded to YouTube!"

It takes me far too long to work out what that means. What video? My head feels so light. My injuries are the sworn enemies of logic, memory, common sense. The stuff I need in order to survive.

Of course. It's *the video*. The video I filmed in the Sunset Castle's boiler room, before being wrenched back to 1983, then forward to this Halloween. Since the data reception here is woeful, the forty-second clip must have taken an age to auto-upload, draining the battery as it went.

And now, Past Me will see the video at Rome airport and embark on his dishonest quest. He'll set out to debunk the video, while secretly hoping to discover it's real. Puzzling through all this inflames my brain and slays my concentration. On my third step into the woods, I stumble and wave one arm frantically to avoid a fall.

I'm forced to move and think at the same time, despite being unfit for either. Hungry for distraction, I count my torturous, shambling steps. Only after two hundred and fifty do I allow myself to look back.

The church and cliff have been reduced to patches of green and grey, visible between snarled boughs. All these bare trees afford me less shelter than they might, but the distance I've covered is at least something. An achievement. I try really hard to forget how I'm unlikely to evade a being that can manipulate time itself. *Don't think about that. Just move.*

The Motörhead song "Killed by Death" barges into my head. The one where Lemmy rasps, "*I ain't gonna be easy, easy/ The only time I'm gonna be easy's when I'm killed by death.*" It's not poetry, that's for sure, but it's apt. I ain't going down without a struggle. I'll do whatever I can to complicate this hunt. My ego got me into this, but it may also help prolong my life. One aspect of ego is hard-wired: the urge to survive. Sometimes you just can't help being selfish.

These are your pain receptors and you'll do anything to stop them firing.

These are your lungs and you'll do anything to keep them pumping.

Hating myself for failing to confront Past Me, I decide to put it right. I tap in my own phone number, then hit "Call."

Phoning yourself is obviously a mad thing to do. But against every law of physics, perhaps with the exception of select quantum theories, there are now two identical phones in the world. Not to mention two Jack Sparkses.

The line connects, the other phone rings and I answer. Or, rather, Past Me answers.

For the time it takes a butterfly to flap its wings, no more than that, I hear the thrum of a running car engine. Then an ungodly electronic Aphex Twin shriek bursts from the earpiece, making me punch "End Call." And oh God, I feel dumb. Really should've seen that coming, since I've already *lived* the other side of this.

Okay, so phoning Past Me causes some kind of endless freak-out loop. The universe can't cope. Writing off the whole idea, I jam my branch into the dirt and hobble onwards.

The signal dies, so I switch off the handset to save battery. Of course, by the four hundredth step, I've realised what I should have done with the phone, but it's too late. Retracing all one hundred and fifty laboured steps back through angry thorns to the area with signal would undo all my hard work. I can't shake the feeling that Maria Corvi's already on my tail, so I vow to wait until I reach higher ground before turning it back on.

Each step is a real undertaking. Each new stride rams the tree branch up into my armpit until the skin breaks. All this bleeding is about as good for energy as the descending sun is for morale.

The heavens are a dull, muted red. Every shadow in sight, stretched to breaking point.

I dread nightfall. Oh, how I dread it.

Every ten steps, a single raindrop explodes on my patchy scalp. Then every five steps. Then every one. When swollen clouds finally let rip, my clothes become dead weights. The once crisp and parched woodland floor now sucks at my good foot. I pause to crane my head back and enjoy the moisture on my tongue. I truly savour it trickling into the back of my throat. A small mercy, which seems so big.

I seek shelter at the foot of a wide, knotty trunk. Sitting down harder than I'd have preferred, I hiss as I stretch the bad leg out before me. Just need five minutes' rest, then I'll go back at it.

When I revive the phone, its signal fluctuates between nothing and a single bar. Having managed to keep the Big New Idea in my head, I fire up the YouTube app. From my list of uploaded videos, I select *Untitled* and delete it. This strikes me as an ingenious plan, ensuring Past Me never gets to see the video. And you probably think you're really clever for knowing what's wrong with that plan, don't you? Yeah. Hobble a mile in my shoes with a microwaved bag of shit for a head, a club foot, a gashed forehead, a cauterised neck, half your hair missing, Crowley cuts, blood squelching under your one good heel and a pissed crotch. Then we'll see how smart you are.

I realise my mistake shortly after deleting the video. Because, yes, Past Me is already at the airport and has already seen the damn thing. Me deleting it only gets his hound-dog nose sniffing harder.

Phone battery status: five per cent. The thought of becoming too weak to press on through this darkening maze, with no link to the outside world, fosters panic. Panic, in turn, summons adrenalin, which sharpens me up. I need to do something that isn't already part of the programme. Something that doesn't slot so neatly into the jigsaw already established.

I need to call someone for help. Someone who isn't me.

A concept that, again, must sound so simple to you. To me, it's a revelation. The last thing I think to use a phone for is a phone call. These days, you phone a person and they assume someone's died.

I've no idea how to call the local police, and it'll take too long to find out. So I can try Alistair. Sure, we hate each other. The mama's boy might hang up on me again, but he might also take me seriously this time and organise a rescue.

This is when a genuine, forty-two-carat revelation swells my throat to the width of a drinking straw.

Oh my God. Right now, *Bex is still alive*. She's no longer dead in the depths of the Sunset Castle, clogging the drains. She's still in Brighton, high on endorphins, thinking everything's cool with Lawrence. And everything might stay that way if some manipulative shit doesn't break them up.

I could call Bex and tell her to never, ever go to LA.

I could save her life.

I could save her from me. From Tony.

Phone battery: four per cent. The handset's over two years old, so its power ebbs all too fast.

I have only one guaranteed call.

One stark choice to make.

I can call Alistair and save myself, or call Bex and save her. Either or.

All around my tree, rain hammers the ground.

That hard-wired survival thing I mentioned earlier? Here's where it really kicks in, whether I want it to or not. Somewhere in my brain the hypothalamus is going crazy. No doubt Mimi, the goddess of self-preservation, is curled around it, helping the natural process along.

I want to live. My God, I so want to live.

On my own messed-up timeline, Bex has already died. She's gone and the world didn't end. But if I go, the world may as well end from my point of view. I've seen evidence of an afterlife—*my* afterlife, even—but what kind of existence was that? That blackened boiler room thing seemed to be my future ghost trapped, gone insane. Hopefully that will be a temporary stage—a penance. But what if there's no actual afterworld, with the accent on "world," beyond that? What if we all just become electromagnetic echoes clinging to earth?

When the battery hits three per cent, I ditch all this contemplation.

As I prepare to speed-dial a number, a trilogy of vivid mental images present themselves to me in one split second.

Moments later, the line connects. The other phone rings for an excruciatingly long time before someone picks up.

"Hello, Dolly," says Bex. "You're in Greece, aren't you?"

I was totally going to call Alistair. Then I remembered Bex's face as I pinned her to that hotel room sofa, deranged, waving a knife around. All that misplaced hope and trust registering on her face, in those wet eyes. *Is this really the end? But that can't be right.*

I remembered Bex beside me on the big fat yellow sofa. Holding my hand, staring into my eyes and telling me everything was fine.

I remembered Bex the first time I ever laid eyes on her. Climbing down from the gym cross trainer, coated in sweat. Motivated and happy, with a whole normal life ahead of her, until I slunk cockily over to say hello and ensure her doom.

These memories resurfaced at precisely the right time. Well . . . the right time for her, the wrong time for me.

Hearing Bex's voice jams my throat right up. There's so much I want to say, but battery limitations dictate that I say none of it. I must warn her right off the path to her death, while my dwindling supply of lithium-ion allows it.

"End that call," Bex says sharply, before I can speak. "Hang up now."

And I'm confused. Because now Bex's voice is different, and it isn't coming from the phone. It's coming from the ground directly ahead of me.

Straight into my ear from the phone, from Brighton, Bex is saying, "Hello? Have you pocket-dialled me, dickhead?"

A pool of blood has formed in the sodden earth, one step beyond the shelter of the tree. The blood seems to dance, as raindrops trigger tiny explosions across its surface.

From the centre of this pool rises the horizontal face of Rebecca Lawson. Nose first, then lips, forehead and chin. Finally her baby-blue eyes break the surface, gazing skywards, misty as old glass marbles, unblinking against the downpour. Having risen no more than two inches, her face resembles a desert island surrounded by choppy red sea.

All my pain blurs into irrelevance.

Fireworks scorch, swirl and whistle in my guts.

I end the call, cutting off Living Bex, my eyes locked on Dead Bex. As I crawl towards the blood pool, a whole flood of emotion threatens to break through the dam I've maintained since she died. Amid all the intense joy and amazement, there's so much guilt, not to mention unease at how very alien, how very macabre she appears.

"This is you, isn't it?" I blurt, stupidly.

When Dead Bex replies, I fully absorb the change in her voice. It's more melodious, and carries a new accent, unlike anything I've heard. "We get to come back when there's good reason," she says. "Unfinished business. Or someone trying to prevent your death. Genuine reasons like that, we call XXX."

She doesn't actually say "XXX," or anything like it, but I wouldn't know how to start spelling the actual word. It's a fresh new alien sound from somewhere beyond the alphabet. A word I doubt the human voice box could even produce.

I'm on all fours at the pool's edge. Rain lashes the back of my head as I stare down at this impossible apparition. Questions form in my head, then fall apart. So many questions, jostling for pole position. Yes, I saw Tony Bonelli after he died, but that felt like Maria's doing. Yes, I saw my own future ghost, but that felt impossible to comprehend. This, on the other hand, feels like the universe raising the curtain on its ultimate secret.

I settle for gushing, "So there's definitely an afterlife?"

Rain steadily washes the blood from Bex's face, revealing the bluish-white skin beneath. "Better call your brother before that phone dies."

"Is it like heaven, or—"

"Forget all that stuff," she says. "People waste their time guessing. You're just worms, Jack, trying to picture what's above the soil. The reality is way beyond you."

I don't remember my exact response, but it hinges on incredulous swearing. For the first time, her eyes move and lock on to mine.

"Listen," she snaps. "I appreciate you finally manning up and putting yourself second, but I don't want to be saved. Call your brother instead."

As the implications sink in, my mouth is a big dumb open hole. "Hold on . . . that means . . . this afterlife is *so* good, you . . ."

"I'm fine with having been sucked down a three-inch-wide pipe to get here, yeah."

Ashamed, I bow my head. While Bex might be content with her new life, the fact remains that I cut her old one short. "I'm so sorry," I tell her. "For everything. I'll make it all up to you."

"No need," says the face in the blood.

An idea jolts me. "Have you . . . have you seen my mum over there?"

"Yeah, sure, Jack, I've seen your mum. Oh, and I saw *Neil Yates* too."

Bex's cloudy lemonade eyes appear indifferent as her acid sarcasm burns me. She says, "You know why most of us don't hang around? It's all *this* shit. All the questions. People wanting you to pass on messages and apologies. People desperate to say stuff they should have said to the living. I don't even know your mum's name, Jack. You never talked about her. Too busy going on about yourself."

My emotional dam strains and creaks. A thick crack appears across it. "Give her a message for me?"

"Tell her yourself when you—"

"Bex, please! I want her to know I'm sorry."

"Call. Your. Brother."

Bex's eyes swivel to the sky once again. Then the island of her face begins its slow, smooth descent back into the blood.

That's when my dam bursts. Those fireworks in my guts become a record-breaking New Year's Eve display. My tears are indistinguishable from the blood and the rain. Half blind, I lurch down and hold a palm against Bex's grave-cold porcelain cheek. And I tell her I love her.

I tell her this over and over. First time I've said it to someone and meant it, let alone said it more than once. Sobbing my head hollow, I gabble at the submerging dead woman, saying sorry until her face is no longer there to be held.

As the tip of her nose sinks out of sight, I yell, "Did you hear me? Please say you heard. *I love you.*"

The aching silence seems to last a whole lifetime, before her words bubble back up.

"Fucking funny way of showing it."

The blood pool seeps off into the soil, finally submitting to the downpour.

I roll over on to my back and gawp crazily at the darkening sky.

The phone in my hand is soaked through. A total brick.

If I hadn't tried to save Bex, I might have saved my own neck.

But for once in my life, I wouldn't change a thing.

Out here in the black heart of the woods, exactly four hundred steps towards nowhere, I clamp my teeth into an idiot grin.

As the rain eases off, I cackle and whoop.

THE FINAL SPOOKS LIST (Sparks' Permanently Ongoing Overview of Kooky Shit)

People claim to have witnessed supernatural phenomena for the following reasons:

(1) They're trying to deceive others
(2) They've been deceived by others
(3) They've deceived themselves
(4) Group psychokinesis can produce results
(5) Supernatural phenomena are real
(6) The afterlife is real
(7) Satan is real
(8) It's all fucking real. We're just too wrapped up in ourselves to see it

By the light of a pale moon, I rifle through Sherilyn's backpack. There are all manner of magical items. And a netbook. This thing will contain the latest version of this book I emailed her. If I can just get out of this rain and find somewhere to write, I can finish the damn thing.

Last thing I'll ever do.

It is Halloween, after all. I know how this works.

Until recently, I'd never have dreamt the world could keep turning without me.

The moon melts away behind a bank of cloud, painting these woods black. I can no longer see my hand in front of my face.

My imagination ensures that every grotesque, contorted tangle up ahead is Maria Corvi, waiting patiently for me.

At the very bottom of the backpack, my fingers close around smooth brass.

Without having to see, I know it's the Zippo. Sherilyn must have packed it for me, then forgot to hand it over.

I squeeze the lighter in my hand while hauling myself to my feet.

I plant a slow kiss on the warm brass casing.

Then I toss it away and walk into darkness.

AFTERWORD BY ALISTAIR SPARKS

Inspector Tacito Vivante's phone call came through on the morning of 13 November 2014.

I was getting dressed in the master bedroom of my Suffolk childhood home, which Chloe and myself had inherited from my dear departed mother. That afternoon, I was scheduled to run twenty kilometres for MND (Motor Neurone Disease) Research. As soon as I heard the tone of Mr. Vivante's voice, however, I knew I would not be taking part.

At midnight on 31 October, Italian fire services had arrived at a location two miles east of the church where Jack had witnessed an exorcism that day. A small cottage was ablaze at the foot of the hills, and despite the firemen's best efforts, there would be no survivors.

One of two badly burnt bodies was identified as the cottage's seventy-five-year-old owner, Sergio Acierno. Horrifically, Acierno had been crucified against his own kitchen wall by rusty nails, then received a third to the forehead.

It took the Italian authorities longer to confirm that the

other remains belonged to Jacob Titherley. The process had been delayed by his nationality, his pseudonym and the process of securing dental records from Brighton. Jacob's sole cause of death had been incineration, although his body exhibited other wounds consistent with his accounts in this book.

When Vivante broke this news, I sat heavily on the bed, where I stayed for hours, half dressed in running gear, until Chloe arrived home from work. I had expected drugs or alcohol to take my brother's life for some time. Yet the impact of him dying like *this* knocked me off my feet. It was made all the more poignant by sitting in the very bungalow where Jacob and I grew up together.

Jacob had been found in the bedroom of the cottage, where the police believe Mr. Acierno had granted him a place to rest and improvised a makeshift splint around his left leg. While the fire immolated the bed and much of the room, a netbook computer remained untouched on the floor. Small-town superstition blended all too easily with tabloid hyperbole when one "inside source" told *La Repubblica* newspaper, "The computer lay open on its side, with a perfect circle of untouched floor around it. The screen, the whole thing, it remained utterly unmarked by ash."

That netbook was taken into police custody along with other items from the scene. I have been legally advised not to attribute blame, but it is a fact that *Jack Sparks on the Supernatural* then leaked on to the internet in its raw, unedited form.[1] Starting off in the web's darker, more esoteric corners, the

---

1 This text was missing the transcript of Sherilyn Chastain and Rebecca Lawson's supposed "ego exorcism" of Jack. However, because the "SherilynBexJackConvo.mp4" audio file was also leaked, some devotees created their own inferior, typo-ridden "fan edit" of the book, which added this material. —*Alistair*

torrent file spread slowly before gathering speed. By the time Jack's death was officially announced on 19 November, the internet seemed to explode. Many fans rounded on me, ridiculously blaming me for Jack's decline—even for his death—and making my online life a misery for months to come. Meanwhile, the British press conspired to make my real life a misery too.

Jack's death, when coupled with his leaked book, suited whatever your agenda happened to be. If you were an anti-drugs campaigner, then Jack Sparks had finally suffered an inevitable mental breakdown, murdered Mr. Acierno, then burned down the cottage himself. If you were a true-crime aficionado, then Jack and Mr. Acierno had fallen foul of the psychotic Devil-worshipping teenager Maria Corvi. If you were a believer and/or a subscriber to *Fortean Times* magazine, then you took Jack's account at face value and *Jack Sparks on the Supernatural* became compelling evidence for everything from the afterlife to time travel.

Myself? I have no agenda and much prefer to stick to the facts.

Fact One: Jack was unable to face up to our beloved mother's passing, either before or after it happened. Despite what he thought, I never held this weakness against him, but this book clearly expresses his lingering grief and guilt, exacerbated by drug addiction. I suspect this toxic combination warped his previously held scientific views, creating psychological inconsistencies and extreme delusions. Which leads me on to . . .

Fact Two: Jack died on the night of 31 October 2014. Ergo, he could not possibly have experienced the twenty days that followed, as "documented" in the book. Unless we open a whole other kettle of worms and posit that Jack did not actually write *Jack Sparks on the Supernatural* himself (a rabbit hole down which endless internet essays have disappeared), he must have written the book way in advance of his death, perhaps even in tandem with, or directly after, *Jack Sparks on Drugs*. I believe he researched real people like Father Primo Di Stefano and the Hollywood Paranormals in order to create a credible narrative. A narrative that, while wildly fanciful to the point of madness, ultimately seemed to confirm the afterlife. Wishful thinking all the way. This book is fantasy fiction rooted in autobiography, much like *Fear and Loathing in Las Vegas*, the best-selling 1971 novel by Jack's writing hero Hunter S. Thompson. Nothing more, nothing less.

Fact Three: for many years, the scientific sceptic and former magician James Randi has offered one million dollars to anyone who can prove their psychokinetic powers. The prize remains unclaimed. With or without the Devil's help, the Hollywood Paranormals did not create a psychokinetic gestalt entity formed of their own egos that ultimately destroyed them. Such a concept is absurd.

Fact Four: the Devil is a part of Christian mythology, having been invented by man to keep other men in line. And not even the wacky world of quantum physics has begun to prove the ludicrous concept of time travel. So Satan most certainly did not send my brother off on some sadistic, time-warping forty-day journey in order to teach him a lesson about ego and certainty. Contrary to so much fan theory, my brother was not sent two years forward in time at Rome airport, just so that he could buy *The Devil's Victims*, only to be whisked back again. And neither did he have a panic attack on a flight out of Rome while some "future" incarnation of himself died in a burning cottage thousands of feet below. I have no idea who stewardess Isla Duggan dealt with on that Rome–Gatwick flight, but it was manifestly not my brother.

Ever since my brother's death, hundreds of blogs, essays and articles have agreed with the above facts, while an equal number set out to dispute them. How the latter group love to cite "evidence" that supposedly contradicts the facts. They point out that the LAPD found traces of Jack's DNA at the Big Coyote Ranch murder scene. Not to mention all those eyewitness reports of "Jack" during his supposed twenty days after Halloween, from Brighton to Hong Kong to Los Angeles. One theory, more than any other, has gained traction while attempting to explain such alleged inconsistencies.

The Impostor Theory suggests that one mentally unstable person—perhaps an obsessed fan and/or a Satanist—acted out the key events of *Jack Sparks on the Supernatural* between 31 October and 20 November. They somehow gained access not only to a draft of the book, but to Jack's personal effects such as his laptop and passport. Perhaps, some theorists offer, this impostor stole them from my brother before murdering him and Mr. Acierno. Certainly, the Italian police have yet to prove their own thesis that Maria Corvi committed these murders, and the teenager remains missing as I write. The impostor, it is said, may also have planted Jack's DNA up in the Hollywood Hills.

The Impostor Theory would admittedly explain *someone* having stayed in Hong Kong and Los Angeles hotels under the name Jack Sparks; the Hollywood Paranormals group having worked with *someone* who was never captured on film in any of their session footage; and Sherilyn Chastain having met *someone* who to this day she insists was Jack Sparks.[2]

As I recently told the *Sun* newspaper and *Closer* magazine, the fact that I actually spoke to someone impersonating my brother has lent grist to the the Impostor Theory's mill. After Jack's agent Murray Chambers and I learned of Jack's death, Murray alerted me to the fact that someone had been posting on Jack's social media accounts since Halloween. Together, we fought to have all these accounts shut down and deleted. YouTube was the last site to comply. Cruel hoax phone calls from West Hollywood were then made to Murray and myself within minutes of each other on 18 November. Just as described in the book, a voice admittedly similar to Jack's begged us for help. We both hung up in shock and disgust. On reflection, of course, we could have kept this impostor talking, but hindsight's twenty-twenty.

Editor Eleanor Rosen and I elected to insert the segments of additional material between certain chapters for two reasons: (a) to provide extra value for those who bought this official book over the inferior torrent file; and (b) because some of these segments could be seen to track the impostor's activities. But of course, you are at liberty to interpret the material as you choose. To each their own.

The last year has seen dramatic changes in my life. Defying

---

2 In case you were unaware: Miss Chastain eventually made a full recovery after being assaulted in the Sunset Castle's boiler room in the early hours of 20 November. Miss Chastain insists her prone body is depicted in the widely circulated YouTube video featured in the book, even though this is impossible. Tragically, of course, nurse Pio Accardo, Marc Howitz, Rebecca Lawson and all seven members of the Hollywood Paranormals were murdered in a manner broadly consistent with the descriptions in *Jack Sparks on the Supernatural*. The translator Antonino Bonelli did also commit suicide, seemingly in the wake of allegations of his incestuous paedophilia. —*Alistair*

all social media trolls, I became outspoken in urging the paranormally and religiously minded to turn to science. I also signed up for my TV debut as the host of a forthcoming documentary series for the Sky Living channel. I do not think of myself as a natural celebrity, but the opportunity was rather thrust upon me. By all accounts, I also seem to have shown aptitude for the work.

Entitled *Alistair Sparks Debunks the Devil*, the series sees me adopt my brother's surname as a mark of my deepest love and in order to keep his name alive. It will also address some of the theories surrounding his demise. In the first episode, you will see the pilgrimage I made to West Hollywood's Sunset Castle Hotel with Father Primo Di Stefano in tow. Regardless of what I believe, Jack seemed to fear that his spirit would end up trapped in the hotel's boiler room for eternity. So as a gesture of respect, I had Father Di Stefano perform a simple rite intended to help Jack move on. It was a very profound, personal and private experience, which you can see in full in Episode One.

The recent release of Father Di Stefano's book *The Devil's Victims* triggered a great outcry among some of Jack's fans. They felt Mr. Di Stefano was "cashing in" by appropriating the book title Jack had used in *Jack Sparks on the Supernatural*. Mr. Di Stefano denies this, "in the strongest possible terms," insisting he had planned to employ this title for years.

One passage of *The Devil's Victims* has provoked shock and sorrow in Sherilyn Chastain and a portion of Jack's followers, for reasons I reject. This passage documents our joint visit to the Sunset Castle and the days that followed. Perhaps if you buy into the supernatural, then this passage lends Jack's story some form of coda, but it's not my cup of tea. Still, in the spirit of giving something back to Jack's fans, who have suffered such uncertain heartache, I shall include the passage here, by kind permission of Chiesa Books.

As I knelt on that dirty floor in the middle of the hotel boiler room, I tried not to let the TV cameras affect my ritual. I commanded myself to focus only on the spirit of Mr. Jack Sparks, whose soul I believed to have been kidnapped by that execrable fiend Satan and imprisoned here. Mr. Sparks and I may have had our differences during the brief time I met him in life, but he is God's child like any other, and so deserved saving.

Despite my concentration being momentarily broken by a highly frustrating incident when the producer asked if I could pause while one of the cameramen switched batteries, I successfully made contact with Mr. Sparks' essence.

Mr. Sparks was melancholy at first, fearful that we might enrage his "master." Then he became excited when I told him I had the power to set him free. I did just as I had promised and spent the rest of my time in Los Angeles feeling blessed for my ability to help people.

Then came the vision.

The most powerful vision I have suffered in three decades.

It struck a full week after the ritual, while I was walking across a cobbled square in Vatican City. It consumed me to such a degree that it was all I could see and hear. I was forced to stop dead in my tracks. Two onlookers phoned for an ambulance, fearing I had suffered a stroke or suchlike.

I beheld a distressed Jack Sparks, in his spirit form, drifting east through the sky from the Californian coast, across America. He struggled limply and tried to resist, but it was no good: some dark agency compelled him. This cast a terrible shadow upon my soul, because I knew I had failed. Rather than my ritual freeing Jack Sparks, it had merely prompted the Devil to relocate him.

As Jack Sparks flew east, his human spirit form disintegrated, until he resembled dark tempestuous smoke.

Overlaid on this image was a green clock face, its hands spinning forwards at speed, over and over again.

I saw Jack Sparks' spirit stop on England's east coast.

Then the clock face became red. Its hands spun backwards, back into the past, as unholy winds swept Mr. Sparks further east, until I saw him crossing Asiatic waters . . .

Finally, all of these images faded away and I saw only one thing.

One new image. A cryptic sight that puzzles, intrigues and concerns me deeply to this day.

It was a small bright-red glass bottle with no lid, floating in the sea. The contents lost forever.

The last six months of filming have seen me interview people everywhere from Los Angeles to Waco to the Gaza Strip to Lusaka to London to Rome. Now that all those air miles are behind me (until Series Two, one hopes) and my work on this book is done, I feel I have completed an emotional journey.

Perhaps because of all the strife surrounding my brother's death, however, I found myself unable to fully grieve for Jacob until this very morning. While rifling through a box of our childhood photographs and playthings, I chanced upon a small wooden donkey. The kind you operate with your thumb. When I made that donkey's legs crumple, I am not ashamed to say my face followed suit.

Despite my new-found media profile, I hope I can now focus on being a husband and father once again. In recent weeks, my wonderful daughters Xanna (nine years old) and Sophie (seven) have worried me somewhat. To my dismay, they read the pirated version of *Jack Sparks on the Supernatural* that was passed around between school friends. As a result of the book's account of the cloakroom in this bungalow, both girls began to dream about seeing "Uncle Jack" in there. Over the last few days, these distressing nightmares have bled into their perceived waking reality, as is so common in the young. The girls have made outlandish claims, such as having heard Uncle Jack laughing from inside the cloakroom. Patently, my children have been just as disturbed as Chloe and myself by this horrendous affair, but I am determined to restore calm to our home.

Despite the trauma of losing my brother, domestic life must go on, with all its reassuringly earthy chores. The refrigerator needs a new light bulb. The garage needs a clean. My family need and deserve my full attention once again.

I hope to see you over on Sky Living.

Until then, as I say on the show: keep it rational.

NOTE FROM THE PUBLISHER

While the majority of Jack's media accounts have now been deleted out of respect after his untimely passing, at the request of his fans, we have left select parts of his site www.jacksparks.co.uk online as a place for his followers to share memories and theories about the events leading up to his death. Please feel free to visit and pay your respects.

ACKNOWLEDGEMENTS

This novel was fuelled by help from many people, not least my agent Oli Munson who believed wholeheartedly in this story from its birth as a mere paragraph, my editor Anna Jackson whose input, enthusiasm and trust has been utterly invaluable and everyone else in the wonderful Orbit team.

I'm hugely grateful to Sarah Lotz, John Higgs, Rebecca Levene, Esther Dickman, James Moran and William Gallagher for their reading, razor-sharp thoughts and encouragement. Big salutes go to Ian "Cat" Vincent, without whom Sherilyn Chastain would be a far less convincing combat magician, and to Dijana Capan, without whom she'd be less convincingly Australian.

Other great and helpful folk: Dave Morris, Ray Zell, Oliver Johnson, Peter Brain Taylor, Daisy Campbell, Phill Barron, Benjamin Cook, Scott K. Andrews, Greg Taylor at the *Daily Grail*, Andrew Smith, Shardcore, Steven Barber, Natasha Von Lemke, Sparrow Morgan, Ian Richardson and everyone else on Facebook who fielded incessant questions about cars, MRI scans and other things I know nothing about.

A highly appreciative nod goes to A. R. G. Owen, Iris Owen and the other Toronto researchers who conducted 1972's the Philip Experiment, which became the Harold Experiment for the purposes of this book. I would encourage any interested readers to hunt down their non-fiction account *Conjuring Up Philip: An Adventure in Psychokinesis* (1976).

Last but definitely not least, massive respect to film-making legends Roger Corman, Eduardo Sánchez and Daniel Myrick for agreeing to appear in this book as themselves. That still blows my mind.

extras

orbit

meet the author

Photo Credit: Amy Terry, Take Aim Photography

JASON ARNOPP is a British author and scriptwriter. His background is in journalism: he has worked on magazines such as *Heat*, *Q*, *The Word*, *Kerrang!*, *SFX* and *Doctor Who Magazine*. He has written comedy for BBC Radio 4 and official tie-in fiction for *Doctor Who* and *Friday the 13th*, but *The Last Days of Jack Sparks* is the first novel, which is entirely Jason's own fault (though some may prefer to lay the blame on Jack...).

interview

Did you always want to be an author?

This seems to be the case, because *Doctor Who* inspired me
to write my own comic strips based on the show from the
age of four. Yeah, *Doctor Who* has a lot to answer for. By
the grand old age of twelve, I was writing and illustrating
prose stories starring my own characters, which my very cool
headmistress turned into bound books, and then installed
them in the school library. Looking back, that was the first
real validation of my stuff: the kind of justification that us
desperately needy writers all crave, to enable us to crawl to
our desks each morning. A few years later, rock journalism
swept me off on a great big tangent for about a decade. But I
suppose I was still telling stories.

***What have been your most memorable moments as a jour-
nalist?***

My favourite trip abroad was probably joining Manic Street
Preachers on their Japanese tour in 1994. My favourite rock
interview was a drunkenly fractious semi-confrontation
with legendary metallers Pantera in a Baton Rouge beer garden. My favourite non-rock interview was *Doctor Who* legend Tom Baker in and around his Sussex home. In terms
of memorable *moments*, though, I've received death threats;

been surrounded by enraged, gun-wielding security guards in Vatican City; and found myself tangled up in a 1993 tabloid front-cover story about a TV celebrity. I should probably tell you more about those things someday on my blog.

How have you found it working on tie-in fiction for such popular shows and films like Doctor Who *and* Friday the 13th?

It's great fun when you actually love the properties, as I do with both *Doctor Who* and *Friday the 13th*. You get to play with long-established and utterly iconic toys. The only real downside is that you're only borrowing those toys and so there are certain things you obviously can't do with them. That's why it's also great to create your own fictional toy boxes, because then you have total freedom.

What advice would you give to aspiring writers?

It's healthy to understand that there are no magical, secret shortcuts. Don't pay good money to anyone who claims to offer any—and when given writing advice, treat most rigid absolutes with a healthy degree of caution. Read a lot, write a lot and resist the burning urge to show your stuff to pivotal industry folk until it shines like a thousand suns. Stop worrying about how you could never do what other authors do. Chances are, they couldn't do what you do either, because you're completely unique. So be yourself and explore your own weird preoccupations through compelling stories. If you ever feel stuck or intimidated, write with the attitude that no one will ever read it. Because then you'll probably create your best work.

extras

Do you hate social media?

No! Not today, anyway. I engage with it on a daily basis, but admittedly there's a love/hate thing going on. I love the way it allows us all to connect faster than ever before. And I hate the way it allows us all to connect faster than ever before. Good and bad things come of those speedy connections, and I'm kind of astonished by all the binary certainty that social media seems to encourage. I do constantly wonder what the internet has done to our brains. But all things considered, I suppose I'd prefer to have social media than not.

What's coming up next for you?

I'm working on my second novel for the mighty Orbit, which is provisionally entitled *Jack Sparks: Ha Ha Suckers, I'm Alive*. Just a bit of fun there. But yes, the second novel, for sure. I've also been releasing free books via JasonArnopp .com, in the form of stand-alone short fiction, and plan to continue this behaviour. Lastly, I intend to keep spending money I don't really have on old-school VHS films. All of this, while I'm dressed as a goat and shrieking Satan's name every 666 seconds. Obviously.

introducing

If you enjoyed
THE LAST DAYS OF JACK SPARKS,
look out for

FELLSIDE

by M. R. Carey

*You will find Fellside somewhere on the edge of the Yorkshire
moors. It is not the kind of place you'd want to end up, but it's
where Jess Moulson could be spending the rest of her life.*

*It's a place where even the walls whisper. And one voice belongs
to a little boy with a message for Jess. Fellside will be the death of
you—if it doesn't save you.*

1

It's a strange thing to wake up not knowing who you are.

Jess Moulson—not thinking of herself by that name or any other—found herself lying in white sheets in a white room, overwhelmed by memories that were predominantly red and yellow and orange. The colours merging and calving endlessly, out of control, billowing heat at her like she'd opened an oven door too quickly and caught the full blast.

Someone had just been talking to her with some urgency. She remembered the voices, low but coming from right up against her face.

Her face . . . Now she thought about it, her face felt very strange. She tried to ask one of the women in white who came and went why this was, but she couldn't open her mouth very far, and, when she did, she wasn't able to make anything happen beyond a few clicks and rasping sounds which hurt her in coming out.

The woman leaned in close and spoke very softly. She was younger and prettier than Jess but still managed to wear an air of authority. For a moment, Jess didn't even have any kind of reference point for what this person might be. A nurse or doctor seemed most likely, but in the utter disorientation of those first few minutes it seemed possible that she was some kind of nun—that the crisis Jess was going through, against all the evidence, was a crisis of faith.

"You won't be able to talk for a few days yet," the woman told her. "You shouldn't even try. There was a lot of damage to your lungs and the tissues of your throat, and they won't heal if you put strain on them."

Nurse then, not nun. The damage was to her lungs and throat. Her soul might well be intact, although it didn't really feel that way.

Jess made a shrugging gesture with the arm that didn't have a drip in it. She wasn't shrugging the information away; she was trying to ask for more. But the nurse either misinterpreted the gesture or ignored it. She walked on without another word.

Jess was left feeling not just frustrated but afraid. The nurse's expression as she looked down at her had been very strange. There had been compassion there, but also something that looked like reserve or caution. Did Jess have some disease that was communicable? But in that case, why get so close?

She didn't worry about it for long though. There was something in her system that was pulling her endlessly towards sleep. She gave in to it—a surrender that was repeated on and off through that first day. Her conscious periods were short. Her sleep was shallow and haunted by whispers in what sounded like many different voices. Her waking brought the same questions every time as she clawed her way up out of the darkness like a swimmer hitting the surface just before her lungs gave out.

Where am I? How did I get here? Who's thinking these thoughts? What was before this?

It wasn't just the one nurse who was careful around her. They all seemed to have their issues. Jess kept hoping that one of them would answer the questions she couldn't ask. It seemed like this should be something that got covered in Nursing 101. If a patient wakes up from severe trauma, you start by filling her in on the basics. "You've had a very nasty accident," say, or "You were mugged and rolled and left for dead outside a tube station."

Almost a clue there. A thousand memories twitched at those words. Tube stations had been a feature of her life, so London was probably where she lived. But there was nothing in her mind to back up either the accident or the mugging hypothesis. There was just a hole—the outline you might leave if you cut a paper doll out of a sheet of newspaper and then burned it or threw it away. She wasn't Jess for now. She was the suspicious absence of Jess.

When she did start to remember, she got that same sense of blank confusion all over again, because she was only remembering earlier awakenings. The first day hadn't been the first day after all. She had been here for much longer than that, drifting in and out of consciousness, living in a single fuzzy moment that was endlessly prolonged.

The earlier wakings had been different from the more recent ones. Her disorientation had been overwhelmed back then by desperate, uncontainable hunger. She was an addict (when those memories came back it was in an almost physical surge, as though her compressed mind were snapping back to its accustomed shape) and she had needed a fix. Had needed to feel okay. One time she had pulled herself out of the bed and crawled most of the way to the window, drip and all, intending to climb out of it and slip away down to the Hay Wain on a heroin run. Through the window there was a view of sky and tall buildings—no way of knowing how far away the ground was. But Jess had been prepared to try until the women in white embargoed the idea.

Remembering all this now brought the craving back, but it was dulled. Manageable. The hunger wasn't strong enough to pick her up and shake her. It just sat in a little corner of her mind, politely requesting attention.

That in itself was scary. With the memories of her addiction had come another set of memories, pushed to the surface of her mind by the force of some internal pressure. She'd got clean before, just once in her life, and the process had been a dark streak of misery obliterating days and weeks. If she'd been through cold turkey again, lying in this bed, then she must have been here for a very long time.

The weird feeling in her face frightened her too. It was as though her flesh didn't belong to her. As though someone had given her one of those cosmetic masks made of fragrant mud and then forgotten to scrape it off after it hardened.

On the third day she tried to sit up. Women in white came running and pushed her down again. "I want a mirror," she told them in a bellowed murmur like the world's worst stage prompt. "Please, just bring me a mirror!"

The women in white swapped uneasy glances until one of them reached a decision. She went away and came back with a tiny compact from someone's handbag. She held it so Jess could look up into her own face looking back down at her. It was a nasty shock, because she really didn't recognise it.

This wasn't the amnesia. She knew what her face should look like, and what she was seeing now wasn't it. Oh, it was a reasonable facsimile that would fool a stranger—and when it was at rest it didn't look too bad. Well, yeah, actually it did. There was thick swelling around her eyes as though someone had punched her a whole lot of times. The skin was taut and shiny in places. And she was fish-belly pale, as if she'd spent a year or two living like Osama Bin Laden in a cave in the side of a mountain.

But when her face moved—when she tried to talk—it turned into something from a nightmare. The right side of her mouth was unresponsive, deadened, so the more animated left side tugged and twisted it into a parade of grimaces. The symmetry disappeared, and you realised that it had never really been there at all.

"Okay?" the nurse holding the compact asked. Gently. Probing the wound.

Jess couldn't answer. There wasn't any answer that covered how she felt.

Some of the recent past came back to her in her sleep that night. The whispering voices were still there, as though a hundred conversations were being held in the space around her head. With them came a sense of vulnerability, of lying exposed in some big open space. She wasn't alone: a multitude surrounded her, invisible. So many that there wasn't enough room for them all to stand: they were folded around and over her like hot treacle poured out of a pan.

Jess hadn't dreamed since she was a child, but images came and went nonetheless. She held her face—a tiny version of it—in her hands, and then parted her fingers to let it drop. Again and again. Sometimes when it dropped there was a rustle or a tinny clatter from far below her, sometimes no sound at all.

Then the fire came, rising up in front of her.

Climbing in at her mouth.

Nestling inside her.

She woke shivering in the warm hospital room, chilled by her own slick sweat. A breath was caught halfway up her throat like a solid thing, and she had to spit it out piecemeal, in quick, shallow gasps.

"What happened to me?" she croaked at the nurse who came to take her temperature and blood pressure in the morning (smell of breakfast heavy in the air, but Jess was nil by mouth so the smell was as close as she was going to get). "There was a fire, wasn't there? Tell me. Please!"

"You should—"

"I know, I know. I should get some rest. But I can't until I know. Please!"

The nurse stared at her for a long time, hanging on the cusp of saying something. But all she said finally was, "I'll ask the doctor." She tucked Jess in, folding the stiff cotton sheets with the brusque efficiency of an origami black belt.

"Please," Jess whispered again, saving it for when the nurse's face was bent down close to hers. She thought it might be harder to say no at that range.

And it seemed she was right. "Yes, there was a fire," the nurse said reluctantly as she smoothed out the last creases from the sheet.

"Where . . . was . . . ?" Jess asked, feeling only a few hot twinges in her throat this time. As long as she limited herself to monosyllables, she could ace this conversation.

"Your flat. Your flat caught fire when you were inside. When you were . . . not able to move."

When I was high, Jess translated. I set my flat on fire when I was high. Who does that? Only someone intent on ruining themselves and everyone around them.

Her mind treated her to a slideshow. A resin statue of a Chinese dancer with a flute. A lampshade shaped like a hot-air balloon with two waving fairies in the gondola underneath. Her folk CDs. Her books. Her photo albums. All gone?

"How . . . bad?" she asked.

"Very bad. Really, you should try not to think about it. It's not going to help you to get well."

The nurse retreated quickly. It seemed to Jess that she wanted very much to get out of earshot before she was made to field any more questions.

And at that point another slide clicked into view.

John.

His face, his name and a sense of what the face and the name had meant. Oh Jesus, if John was dead! Panic flooded her system, only to be followed a moment later by a wild and slightly nauseating surge of hope. If John was dead . . .

She sat up before she even knew she'd decided to. She couldn't sustain it though, and slumped right back down again, sick and dizzy.

She had to know. She husbanded her strength so she could ask, and tried to shore up her non-existent stamina with an exercise regime. She could only hold her weight on her elbows for a few seconds before falling back on to the sheets, but she worked on it at intervals through the morning, determined each time to beat the previous time's total.

Consultants' rounds were at eleven. The doctor walked past Jess's door without slowing, followed by a bustling line of medical students who—each in turn—peered in with big round eyes as though Jess was a model in a porn shop peepshow before hurrying on to rejoin the crocodile.

Right then.

God helps those who help themselves. Jess hauled herself out of bed and slid her feet down on to the floor. She worked the cannula out of her wrist and let it fall. The loose end drew a ragged red line across the white sheet.

It wasn't easy to get vertical, but once she did, she was able to translate her drunken sway into a forward march just by picking the right moment to raise a foot and put it down.

She headed for the door at action-replay velocity, taking about a minute and a half to cover twelve feet. Getting through the door was more of a challenge, because she accidentally knocked it with her elbow and it started to close on some kind of spring mechanism. She had to lean against it to keep it open as she negotiated the narrowing gap. Then she was through, the door swinging to behind her, and for a moment she thought she was free and clear. But that was because she was looking to the right and the swelling around her eyes left her with no peripheral vision.

From her blind side a hand came down on her arm, just below the shoulder—not heavily or tightly, but it stopped her dead all the same. A voice said, "Ms. Moulson, I'm going to have to ask you to go back inside."

Jess turned. It took a lot of small movements of her feet. The woman who was facing her now was not in white, but in midnight blue with a bright yellow tabard. She was a policewoman, no taller than Jess but a fair bit stockier and more solid, and presumably (unlike Jess) not so weak that a stray breeze would knock her over. Jess sagged, checkmated in a single move.

And appalled and confused all over again. Why was there a policewoman here? Was she under guard? And if she was, did that mean that she was under protection or under restraint?

That was such a big, yawning chasm of a question that it eclipsed, for a few moments, the question of what had happened to John.

"Why?" she croaked. That was a little vague, but it would have to do.

The policewoman frowned. She had dark, freckled skin that made Jess flash on the memory of her own face in the mirror—her unnatural pallor, like something that lived under a stone.

"You're under arrest. Didn't you know that?"

She did now. That had to count as progress. She managed another "Why?"

The other woman's expression changed, but only for a moment—a cloud of doubt or concern drifting across it and then disappearing as quickly as it had come. "For murder, Ms. Moulson," she said. "The charge against you is murder."

She closed in on Jess, as though she intended to herd her physically back into the room. Jess stood her ground, more out of bewilderment than belligerence. Murder? she thought. Whose murder? Who am I supposed to have . . . ?

"You'll have to go back inside," the policewoman said. "I shouldn't even be talking to you. I'm the one who's meant to keep other people from talking to you."

"Who . . . ?" Jess panted. The corridor was yawing like a ship at sea. She couldn't move, although she might make an exception for falling down.

The woman's hand came out and took her arm again. She leaned past Jess and pushed the door open—effortlessly, one-handed. Jess could have thrown her full weight against it right then and that feeble little spring would have been too much for her. "Please, Ms. Moulson," the policewoman said. "Go back inside now. I'll tell your lawyer you're awake, the next time he calls."

But Jess had come way too far to back down. "Who?" she whispered again. "Who . . . dead? John? Was . . . John?"

"Your lawyer will fill you in," the policewoman promised. But when Jess didn't move, she sighed heavily and shrugged. "It was a little boy," she said. "A ten-year-old. It looks like it may have been an accident, but that's not for me to say. You set the fire, and the charge as I understand it is murder."

She had both hands on Jess's arm, one above and one below the elbow, and was trying to turn her around. But no part of Jess was communicating with any other part now. Her upper body moved, her hips twisted, her legs stayed exactly where they were.

There was only one ten-year-old boy who she knew even vaguely. His name popped into her head from nowhere, and her lips shaped it although no sound came.

Alex.

Alex Beech.

She was aware of falling. But the floor, when she got to it, recoiled from her as though she was something unpleasant to the touch.

2

Alex Beech was the boy upstairs.

Upstairs where, exactly? It began to drift back into Jess's mind in clotted, disconnected pieces.

The first piece looked like this.

Coming home late one evening from the bookshop where she worked to her flat in Muswell Hill to find this skinny little kid sitting out on the stairs—the flight that led up from her landing to his—dressed in a vest and underpants. Feet bare in the November cold, on stone steps that were chill even in summer. His blond hair was darker underneath, as though he bleached it. And his face looked too small to sustain that crazy, free-form mop.

"You okay?" Jess asked.

The boy nodded but didn't speak.

From above him came shouts in two different voices, bass and soprano. The door of the upstairs flat was closed, but the phrase "always been your fucking problem" came through clearly in a falsetto yell. That was the mother. Then "Don't start! Don't you bloody start!" from the father.

Jess hesitated. You couldn't invite someone else's kid into your flat, could you? Certainly not without letting their parents know. However innocent your motives were, it wouldn't fly. She almost talked herself into it but chickened out. She made cocoa instead and brought it out to him. Chocolate flakes and marshmallows. All the trimmings.

The next time she looked out, he'd gone. The mug was where he'd been sitting, on the seventh stair from the bottom. It was empty.

That first encounter set the tone for all the others. They were allies of a sort, but they only ever met in no-man's-land. On the stairs. And they only ever talked about banalities.

"How was your day?"

"It was okay."

"You want some cocoa?"

"Yes please."

Apart from that, she followed Alex's adventures at a distance. Heard his mum and dad cursing him out—seemingly whenever they took a break from cursing each other. She knew his name was Beech because their mail lay out on the table in the hall some days, waiting to be picked up. And she got the *Alex* from a thousand shouted commands and reprimands.

"You've got a pet," John said the first time he saw the boy. "Did he follow you home?"

"That's not funny, John."

"I'm not laughing. Honest, Jess! I think it's cute. What does he eat?"

She had to admit that she didn't know. But the next time Alex camped out on the stairs, she brought him a sandwich as well as the cocoa. "It's cheese," she said. "I don't know what you think about cheese. But it's there if you want it."

He seemed to think that cheese was acceptable, by and large. He ate the sandwich, apart from the crusts. And their relationship entered a new phase. Jess thought of it as comfort and supply.

Still no talking, though. Just "How are you?"; "I'm fine." She thought about sitting down next to him, striking up a proper conversation. So is school going well? Do you have a favourite sport? A best friend? Do your parents only shout at you or do they hit you too?

"You want to keep your distance from that," John warned her. "I mean it, Jess—it's trouble you don't need. If he tells you he's being abused, what are you going to do? Call the police? They'll start looking into us too, and find out we're using. We'll go to jail."

John still called Alex her little pet, but he didn't laugh any more and there was a nasty edge to his voice when he said it. He seemed to feel that the whole thing had gone beyond a joke.

Jess went ahead and had the talk with Alex anyway. John Street wasn't her conscience. He was the anti-Jiminy Cricket, always egging her on to darker and crazier things. This time she decided to pretend she had a better angel.

"Only once," Alex said when she asked him if his dad ever got physical with his reprimands. Jess had no idea what to do with that. She suspected that one smack or punch always led on to n, where n was a large number. But it wasn't exactly a smoking pistol. Not enough to justify an anonymous tip-off to child services, or an ugly altercation on the upstairs landing. And her batteries were low in every way that mattered. If there was a confrontation, she would almost certainly lose.

She gave Alex her number—made him put it into his phone. "If you ever need someone," she told him, "you can call me. Or just come down and knock on the door. I'm usually home."

It didn't ever happen. And after a while she forgot about the promise—forgot she'd ever even made it. The addiction was lying like an iron bar across her brain right about then, and it was getting worse with each day that went by. Alex was one of the last things to go, but he faded out in the end along with the rest of the world. She went sailing away to a sunny, squally island where the population was three: herself, John Street and heroin.

At first, that was as far as Jess's memories would take her. But she kept on dipping her bucket into that deep black well and hauling up more and more details. When the psychiatrists appointed by the court to test her mental faculties asked her what she could remember, she tried her best to tell the truth, but the truth changed from one session to the next. She could see in their eyes that they thought she was faking her amnesia.

Then her lawyer (also court-appointed, set in motion by the magic of legal aid) arrived like a fox in a henhouse and sent the psychiatrists packing. His name was Brian Pritchard. He was exactly Jess's height, which made him quite short for a man, and grey-haired, even though he couldn't have been more than forty-five or so. The hair read almost like a statement—of gravitas and moral rectitude. "My client isn't ready to talk about these traumatic events," he told the shrinks in cold, clipped tones. "And by God you'd better not try to use those assessments in court if you haven't got a consent form to go with them!"

But they did have a consent form. Jess was signing everything that was put in front of her, collaborating with every legal process, being as helpful as she could. That was what innocent people did, and she was sure in her heart she was innocent.

Pritchard did not approve. "You've been arrested and charged," he told her waspishly. "In an ideal world the police would still be vigorously pursuing their inquiries, but we don't live in an ideal world, Ms Moulson. If you hand yourself to them on a plate, they will take you and pick you apart and wipe their fingers clean with the laws of evidence. And in the meantime they will not be exploring any other possibilities, because exploring other possibilities takes effort. So please, as a favour to me, treat everyone who *isn't* me as your sworn enemy until your trial is over."

Jess glanced at the man who had accompanied Pritchard on to the ward. A skittish little junior solicitor or clerk whose role was to hand his boss pieces of paper when they were needed and who scarcely ever spoke. When Jess met his eyes, he blushed and looked away.

"Oh, I don't mean Mr Levine," Pritchard said. "You can treat him as landscape."

On that first visit, Pritchard took Jess's statement about the night of the fire without comment or question. On the second, the next day, he brought her some newspaper articles and printouts from internet blogs in order, so he said, to give her a better idea of what she was up against.

Inferno Jess: "I know nothing!"

The woman at the heart of tragic ten-year-old Alex Beech's death is being treated at London's Whittington Hospital both for her physical injuries and for memory loss. Yet doctors have found no evidence of brain damage or psychological trauma.

Pritchard seemed to be trying to provoke her into some kind of response, but all Jess could give him was exhaustion and despair, occasionally peaking into dull amazement.

"They might as well just come right out and call me a murderer!"

"They'd be very happy to," Pritchard said. "But they're mindful of the sub judice laws. Most of them use the word 'alleged' quite liberally. Alleged murderer. Alleged crime. The magic ingredient in unfounded allegations. Some have taken to calling you 'the Inferno Killer', in quote marks. They have a star witness, by the way. You should brace yourself, because it's going to get unpleasant."

"Who? What witness?" But she knew.

John. John Street. Of course.

"Don't let that prey on your mind," Pritchard advised her. "I think he's their weak link, to be honest. I'm delighted that they're leading with him. I'm sure we'll get to the truth. Now let's go over that statement of yours and see which parts of it are fit for purpose."

Not many, it turned out. Time and again the lawyer took Jess to task for stating as truth things she could only know by implication. "You were out of your head for large parts of the evening, yes? Then please don't make assumptions about what you didn't see and couldn't hear. Your role here is to state the facts. Let me worry about the truth."

"They're the same thing!" Jess protested, but Pritchard shook his head.

"The facts are in the outside world. You can verify them with your senses or with objective tests. The truth is something that people build inside their heads, using the facts as raw materials. And sometimes the facts get bent or broken in the process."

"I'm not going to lie," Jess said.

"You misunderstand me. I'm not asking you to. I'm asking you to stay with the facts, where you're on safe ground, and stop lunging off towards something dim and distant that you're thinking of as the truth. That's a dangerous voyage, and you shouldn't try to make it alone."

Jess didn't argue, but only because she wasn't up to the effort. She wasn't good for much of anything right then. Up in the facial reconstruction unit of the Whittington Hospital in Archway, surrounded by people who mostly maintained a professional deadpan, she felt like a prisoner in a tower made out of other people's words. Alex was dead. That little kid, who never caught a single piece of good luck in his life, was dead. And they were saying she did it.

She couldn't even protest her innocence. Saying you didn't do it and saying you didn't remember doing it were two different things. She was sure in her own mind that something else had happened. Any one out of a million something elses. Alex had fallen down the stairs. His parents had killed him and then gone looking for a scapegoat. He'd killed himself. She wandered in her mind through the maze of these possibilities—and believed in none of them, because in her mind, Alex Beech was still alive. Still keeping up his endless vigil on the stairs. Nothing else made sense to her.

She had an unreliable temper (when was there ever an addict who didn't?) but almost always when she got angry it was with herself. For cowardice, passivity, lack of backbone. For being so woefully short on what her Aunt Brenda (*oh Brenda, I need you now!*) used to call stick-to-it-iveness. True, she had hated John in recent times, and often wished him dead. But wishing without doing was exactly her speed. Surely you couldn't become a murderer without knowing it. Maybe you could forget the act because of trauma or madness, but you couldn't forget the intent. If it had ever been there, it would still be inside you, in your head or your heart, and a thorough search of the premises would find it.

Jess carried out a lot of searches, came up empty and went into the trial still believing in herself.

Over the space of two weeks, that belief was inexorably demolished.

introducing

If you enjoyed
THE LAST DAYS OF JACK SPARKS,
look out for

FEEDBACK

by Mira Grant

There are two sides to every story....

We had cured cancer. We had beaten the common cold. But in doing so we unleashed something horrifying and unstoppable. The infection spread leaving those afflicted with a single uncontrollable impulse: FEED.

Now, twenty years after the Rising, a team of scrappy underdog reporters relentlessly pursue the facts while competing against the brother and sister blog superstars, the Masons.

Surrounded by the infected, and facing more insidious forces working in the shadows, they must hit the presidential campaign trail and uncover dangerous truths. Or die trying.

The world isn't so good with funerals anymore.

Deaths, sure; we have plenty of those. We can give you death in any shape or size you want. Good death, bad death, slow death, fast death—the modern world is the fucking Amazon. com of dying. Maybe it wasn't like that before the Rising hit and the dead started to walk, but hey, guess what: All that shit happened, and now we're the rats in the wreckage, living and dying in the aftermath of our parents' mistakes.

2014. That was the year when everything changed, when a bunch of bored jerks broke into a lab and let a nifty synthetic virus out into the world to have a party in the stratosphere. Only the virus didn't stay up there, where it wasn't hurting anybody. It dropped back down to Earth and got to work infecting people. Maybe that would have been cool—I've never had a head cold or a stuffy nose, and I understand that those were right annoying—but it met up with another nifty synthetic virus, and the two of them hit it off right away. They got right to the business of having babies, and like all babies, these ones took after both sides of the family. They got their airborne daddy's communicability. They got their slower, stealthier mama's adaptability. And then they got the world as a birthday present. Where Kellis-Amberlee walked, the dead got up and joined in the fun.

So yeah, we're real good at dying. Every human on this planet has been in a full-time immersion course on the subject since the summer of 2014. What we're not good at is burying our dead without putting a bullet between their eyes first.

I'd been waiting across the street from the funeral home for the better part of an hour, fussing with the hem of my floral sundress and wishing for an excuse to go do something else. Anything else. Taxes? I'm there. Trip to the licensing board to explain why my tracker sometimes went offline for no apparent reason? Okay, I'm your girl. Cleaning out my in-boxes on the various social media sites that I was supposedly curating for the team? All right, let's not push it. Although it still might have been easier on my nerves.

Loitering has been illegal essentially forever, even before the Rising, although it used to be more erratically prosecuted. People got more nervous about it once we started coexisting with zombies, since now the weird guy who's been standing on the corner for the last hour watching the traffic lights change is potentially getting ready to eat you and your entire family. The patrol cars had been circling the block with increasing frequency, and I was pretty sure all the local CCTV cameras were focused on me, waiting for the moment when I did something actionable. Again, technically, loitering was actionable: I was breaking the law by staying exactly where I was. But the local cops would have needed to get out of their vehicles to mess with me, and that would have put them out in the open. Nobody likes being out in the open.

Well. Most people don't like being out in the open. The majority of the human population would be perfectly happy living and dying in hermetically sealed little rooms, never seeing the outside world again. Most people are pretty terrible, really.

A patrol car appeared around the corner, slowing until it was creeping along at maybe three miles per hour, the officers inside watching me suspiciously through the closed window.

They were getting bolder, which meant they were getting ready to ask why I was mooching around the streets alone, with no visible weaponry. I stayed where I was, crouched gargoyle-style atop a weird modern art piece that had been installed to commemorate local victims of the Rising, and dipped a hand into my purse.

Before the dead walked, that sort of thing could have gotten me killed. Reaching into a bag while under police surveillance was likely to be interpreted as reaching for a gun—and back then, just *having* a firearm in the presence of the cops was considered a totally valid reason for them to start shooting. If the Rising hadn't happened when it did, the police would probably have triggered a civil war. That would have been even nastier than the zombies, if you ask me. At least zombies were acting on hunger and instinct and blind need, not racism and paranoia and carefully nurtured power trips.

The patrol car slowed to a stop as I pulled out my license and held it out for both them and the nearest cameras to see. The thumbnail photo of me had been taken right after a bad haircut and a worse bar fight, which was why I kept it: Given my line of work, if someone was ever trying to identify my body it was a pretty sure thing that I'd be covered in bruises and rocking some seriously hideous hair.

"Aislinn North, journalist, license number IQL-33972." The "I" identified me as a journalist of foreign origin, granted permission to work on American soil. "I'm waiting for my colleague, Benjamin Ross, who is currently engaged in a legal visit to the Oumet Brothers Funeral Home." I nodded meaningfully toward the building on the other side of the street. "This is a public street. I don't have to file any paperwork to be here, and as a licensed journalist, I'm exempt from local vagrancy and loitering restrictions. Now shoo. I'm working."

I grinned, revealing the gap where my left incisor had been prior to a nasty encounter with a man who thought that running a zombie dog-fighting ring would be a great way to spend his twilight years. Ben always says I'd be more photogenic and pull better ratings if I got it fixed, but Ben can stuff it. I don't have the time or patience to mess around with dentures and bridges, and given the odds and how I tend to do my job, I'll probably be a zombie someday. Being a zombie with unbreakable titanium implants in my mouth seems like an asshole thing to do. Besides, I hate dentists. They act like everyone is a walking biohazard zone, like it's somehow our fault that they decided to go into a profession that involves blood.

The policemen stared at me, mouths open and eyes wide, before hitting the gas and roaring down the road, probably breaking several municipal speed laws in the process. I didn't know for sure. Northern California's weird local regulations were a little outside of my comfort zone. Give me a small town in the Irish countryside, surrounded by rolling hills and burial mounds, and I'm your girl. Give me a city that should have been abandoned during the Rising, where the skyscrapers are just one more excuse for people to lock themselves away from the natural world, and I can rock it. But the suburbs of California? Nah. Unsafe, uncool, and not my favorite place to kill an afternoon.

The doors of the funeral home opened as the mourners began emerging. There was no reception line for people to tell the family how sorry they were: That had been handled inside, followed by the line for the blood tests that would clear them to go back out into the world. No one looked around or even hesitated as they beelined for their respective cars, unlocking the doors, sliding inside, and shutting themselves in the latest in the series of boxes that defined their lives. I would have been impressed by how efficient they were, if I hadn't been so busy shaking my head at their cowardice.

"World didn't end when the virus hit, you assholes," I muttered, shifting positions atop the statue. The bronze was warm where it touched my skin. I could have stayed where I was all day long, bored but comfortable.

Fortunately, I didn't have to. The crowd finished flooding into the parking lot, and there was a moment of chaos while they all tried to leave at the same time, cramming their cars into the exit without stopping to think about the fact that this was going to slow *everybody* down. I tapped the camera attached to my dress strap, zooming in on gridlock. The footage might be useful for something later, if I could go for a tight enough focus to keep people from realizing that it had been shot at a funeral home. No one likes to be reminded of the finality of death, and footage that forces that reminder never plays well. Kinda ironic, given how well the finality of death plays for an audience when it's up and walking around, taking bites out of the neighbors. A good zombie video is still money in the bank, even all these years after the end of the old world and the beginning of the new.

The last car pulled away. The funeral home was still, save for a few crows that had landed on the lawn and were now pecking at the grass. They took wing, cawing frantically, as the door swung open one last time and a tall, angular black man in an even blacker suit stepped out, his hand up to shield his eyes from the sun.

I didn't wave. I didn't move. Ben was always trying to take in as much of his environment as he could. His defense against the so-called glare was just as likely to be his attempt to steal a moment to get the lay of the land. That was my cue to blend in as much as I could, settling into the deep, utterly practiced stillness that had seen me through my childhood.

Ben scanned the street for a few seconds before his eyes focused on me. Raising one hand, he signed "okay" in my direction, signaling that I had been well and truly spotted. I nodded, coming out of my crouch and sliding down from the statue.

The soft thump when I hit the sidewalk was almost obscured by the sound of wind rustling through the eucalyptus trees. I reached up and patted my former perch fondly. Much as I'd hated being here, the statue had been a good place to kill the afternoon, and I was going to miss it, at least until I found something else to sit on, some new high ground to claim. There was always new high ground. It was all a matter of knowing how to look for it.

"Ash," said Ben, once he was close enough to speak without shouting. He never did enjoy raising his voice, not even in an emergency. "Any trouble?"

"Some local cops got a trifle too interested in me when I didn't move for an hour, but I showed them my license and they moved on," I said. "I'm guessing I'll have a ping from the licensing board by the weekend, reminding me that the police are not here for my amusement and should be treated with respect. Aside from that, there was nothing. No shamblers, no ramblers, no major local alerts. We missed a few little stories. Someone broke into a mini-mart near Mount Diablo—they named the mountain after the devil, Ben, this is where you've brought me—and someone else started a fire when they tried to cremate their dead parakeet. Nothing worth chasing. Hell, I wouldn't even have turned my camera on if we'd been there."

Now Ben looked amused, despite the pain lurking in his dark eyes. He was asking about the news because that was who he was: That was how he coped. I was less clear on why I was going along with it. Ben might be all about repression, but I've never seen the point of it.

Maybe that's why we're still married, apart from all the nonsense with immigration and then his mum getting sick and everything. I'm afraid that if I divorced him without someone else standing ready to take my place as terrible influence, he'd crawl into his own head and never come out again.

"You know," he said, "I don't think I've ever seen you turn your cameras off."

"True," I said, blithely. "Did you know that border guards have scramblers in their collars to keep their faces from showing up on video? It's like they think people would illegally film the customs process."

Ben raised an eyebrow.

"This is where you point out that one, I *do* illegally film the customs process, and two, Mat unscrambles that sort of shit in their sleep, and so what's the big deal? I'll tell you what the big deal is, Ben. The big deal is how it shows an essential lack of faith in the population." I crossed my arms and pouted as exaggeratedly as I could. "Am I not an American citizen now? Do I not deserve the benefit of the doubt?"

"You've been an American citizen for less than two years," said Ben. "Talk to me again once you've been tapped for jury duty and lost a week to sitting in a little box, staring at a bunch of grandstanding attorneys who see you as their ticket to a top-rated Internet talk show."

I snorted, but I didn't argue. The fondness of attorneys for shoving journalists in their jury box was well documented, even if being a journalist had been a get-out-of-jury-free card before the Rising. Making us serve was a way to punish us for our tendency to film whatever the hell we wanted—which had led to a whole lot of convictions over the years, including a few murder cases, which had become notoriously hard to prosecute since Johnston's Law made manslaughter impossible in high-hazard zones and Willis's Law made "he was a zombie when I shot him" a valid defense. Kellis-Amberlee activated in the blood almost instantly upon disruption of the body's electrical systems, no matter what caused the disruption. Shoot somebody in the forehead and they'd die without reanimating, but any blood tests you cared to do would still show that boy howdy, they'd sure been a zombie when you took them out. Naughty, naughty zombies, always trying to eat the living.

Journalists screwed that up. Journalists did weird shit like strapping cameras to crows in order to get overhead shots of the city, and sometimes that meant we turned a misdemeanor "you shouldn't discharge an unlicensed firearm after nine o'clock in a school zone" into a rare felony "you shouldn't kill people, it's rude." So the attorneys made us suffer for our sins whenever they could, knowing we'd chase the story as soon as the verdict was in and we were legally allowed to get into the meat of it. Sometimes that made the attorneys look like heroes, because it was a better story that way. Sometimes it got them out of their crappy public service jobs and into something cushy and media-related, where they never had to be in an open courtroom again. Either way, it wasted a lot of our time, and that was what they lived for.

Ben rubbed his face. "No word from Mat?"

"Mat's busy," I said. Mat was always busy. A planet-buster comet could be falling from the sky and the people of Earth could be scrambling for their shelters, and Mat would hold up a hand and say "Sorry, come back later, this hard drive isn't going to reformat itself." If I hadn't been so fond of them, I would probably have started keeping water balloons in my purse. "But I did hear from Audrey. She says, and I quote, 'Tell Ben we got this. He can take all the time he needs.'" I smiled serenely. "You see? They got this. This has been gotten. We do not need to rush back. Want to go for a milkshake? I could commit crimes that would get me deported for a milkshake. Twice if the shop had violet on tap."

"You shouldn't drink violet milkshakes," said Ben. "Nothing consumable should be that shade of purple."

"And yet I drink them anyway. Come on, Ben. Let's go to Berkeley and have something nice before we head home. You can have boring vanilla and pretend it makes you morally superior. Maybe we'll get lucky and a bunch of zombies will attack the soda fountain while we're there, and then we can be Johnny on the spot for a story right in the middle of the Masons' home territory. Can you imagine the looks on their faces?" I was laying it on a little thick, but that didn't matter as much as getting Ben to agree to do something—anything—apart from heading home and wallowing in his sorrow.

Wallowing is dangerous. Wallow too much and you can forget what it means to do anything else. Maybe that's not so bad for some people, the ones who live in gated subdivisions with guards at the gate and snipers standing at the ready, but for people like us? People who go out into the world and bring back the facts of the matter, whatever those facts happen to be? Wallowing gets us killed. There's no room for grief in this post-Rising world, where bodies are cremated as soon as they hit the ground to keep them from getting up and going for the people they used to love. There's only room for moving on, putting the sadness behind us, and letting the world back in. It sucks, sure, but it's the kind of suck that keeps people alive.

"Heh," said Ben, a smile tugging at the corners of his mouth. I beamed at him. His smile died instantly, replaced by something far more familiar: regret. "You know, my mama would have been happy to have you at the funeral."

I stopped beaming. "Ben, don't."

416

"She liked you. I know she always said she didn't, but she didn't mean it. She didn't like what you represented, that was all. She knew you didn't mean me any harm. Sometimes she even said you were a gift from God, since you gave me an excuse for good Christian charity."

"I don't want to have this conversation." Not in public: not where some asshole with a camera could come along and turn *us* into the news. Everyone in the business knew what our deal was. I'd talked about it on my blog more than once. That didn't mean that some people wouldn't be happy to come along and start muckraking, trying to prove that we had never even been friends; that everything about our relationship was a business arrangement, and not true, if platonic, love.

Ben's face fell. "Ash..."

"Milkshakes. Come on. Milkshakes, and distance, and time. I'm sorry about your mother, we all are. We want you to take the time you need to get all the way better. We can cover for you for at least a week before anyone notices, if that's what it takes. Mat says they can spoof your email address and handle all of the merch orders, if you want them to. We're just waiting on your word. I'll even talk about your mother with you, if that's what you want me to do, but please, not here. Not on the street, not where we don't know who's listening. Please." I gave him my best pleading look.